MACUNAÍ

Mário de Andrade in São Paulo, 1929

MÁRIO DE ANDRADE

Macunaíma

The Hero with No Character

translated from the Portuguese
by Katrina Dodson

*with an introduction
by John Keene*

A NEW DIRECTIONS
PAPERBOOK ORIGINAL

MINISTÉRIO DA CIDADANIA   MINISTÉRIO DA   MINISTÉRIO DAS
Fundação BIBLIOTECA NACIONAL   CIDADANIA   RELAÇÕES EXTERIORES

Obra publicada com o apoio do Ministério da Cidadania do Brasil | Fundação
Biblioteca Nacional em cooperação com o Ministério das Relações Exteriores
Published with the support of the Brazilian Ministry of Citizenship | National
Library Foundation in cooperation with the Ministry of Foreign Affairs

First published as New Directions Paperbook 1560 in 2023
Manufactured in the United States of America
Design by Erik Rieselbach

Library of Congress Cataloging-in-Publication Data
Names: Andrade, Mário de, 1893–1945, author. | Dodson, Katrina, translator.
Title: Macunaíma : the hero with no character / Mário de Andrade ;
translated from the Portuguese by Katrina Dodson.
Other titles: Macunaíma. English
Description: New York, NY : New Directions Publishing Corporation, 2023.
Identifiers: LCCN 2022057388 | ISBN 9780811227025 (paperback ; acid-free paper)
| ISBN 9780811227032 (ebook)
Subjects: LCGFT: Magic realist fiction. | Novels.
Classification: LCC PQ9697.A72 M313 2023 | DDC 869.3/41—dc23/eng/20221202
LC record available at https://lccn.loc.gov/2022057388

2 4 6 8 10 9 7 5 3 1

New Directions Books are published for James Laughlin
by New Directions Publishing Corporation
80 Eighth Avenue, New York 10011

For Paulo Prado

CONTENTS

INTRODUCTION

Macunaíma: The Hero with No Character, Mário de Andrade's fictional masterpiece published in 1928, may be one of the greatest twentieth-century epics, and major works of Brazilian and modernist literature that many Anglophone readers have neither read nor heard of. Initially composed in six days by Andrade, with a little less than a year and a half of revision to follow, this novel is as startling, mystifying, and enchanting today as when it initially appeared nearly a century ago, baffling and mesmerizing Brazilian critics and readers in equal measure. *Macunaíma*'s apparent obscurity in English mirrors that of its polymathic author, Andrade (1893–1945), who by the time of his death had become one of the central and most generative figures in Brazilian modernism, with an oeuvre spanning poetry, fiction, and travelogues, as well as photography, musicology, art criticism, folkloric, mythological, and cultural studies, filmmaking, and more. With this new edition of *Macunaíma*, superlatively translated by Katrina Dodson, I for one hope that English-language critics' and readers' interest in *Macunaíma* and Andrade will increase significantly.

Provoking astonishment and criticism were hardly novel for Andrade, a mixed-race São Paulo native whose queerness was as veiled, if nevertheless evident to those in his circle, as his racial background. A product of the country's burgeoning, turn-of-the-century middle class, Andrade, tall, prematurely bald, a dandy in his dress and self-presentation, publicly telegraphed his aesthetic interests. In February 1922, six years prior to *Macunaíma*'s publication, he had sparked a public furor among São Paulo's cultural leaders and bourgeoisie, and lit the modernist fuse for the country as a whole, as one of the chief organizers, along with painter Emiliano Di Cavalcanti, of São Paulo's germinal and now legendary Modern Art Week (*Semana de Arte Moderna*). He was soon to become a member of the avant-garde Group of Five (*Grupo dos Cinco*), comprising the poets Oswald de Andrade, similarly named but not a relative, and a sometime antagonist, and Menotti Del Picchia; and visual artists Anita Malfatti and Tarsila do Amaral; Andrade had collaborated with most of this group and fellow vanguardists to present the weeklong exhibition in São Paulo's Municipal Theater, featuring visual art, theoretical lectures, musical concerts, and readings that would herald and mark a giant shift in Brazilian art and culture. The Modern Art Week showcased new and at times shocking aesthetic works and modernist trends akin to those unfolding in a variety of movements (such as cubism, primitivism, futurism, etc.) across the continent and globe. At the end of the week, on the Municipal Theater's stage, Andrade provided the gathering's pièce de résistance, declaiming selections from his experimental, impressionistic poetry collection, *Pauliceia desvairada* (*Hallucinated São Paulo*), which melded European and Brazilian influences, to boos and catcalls from the audience.

Andrade's stylistic leaps in *Pauliceia desvairada* and subsequent poetic works pointed the way to some of the linguistic and textual innovations of *Macunaíma*, as did Andrade's novel *Amar, verbo intransitivo* (*To Love, Intransitive Verb*, titled *Fräulein* in its original 1933 English translation), published shortly before *Macunaíma*, in 1927. In both texts Andrade sampled and followed the organizational and semantic principles of everyday Brazilian speech, utilizing and juxtaposing colloquialisms, slang, neologisms, syntactic abruptions, and apparent solecisms; he was creating a new style and texture, in lyric and narrative form, that departed from the mainstream or canonical Brazilian and Lusophone literature of the time. Additionally, Andrade's theoretical "Extremely Interesting Preface" to *Pauliceia* notes the relationship between his unique syntactic arrangement of poetic language and "oral harmony," to produce a jarringly exquisite "genuine dissonance." *Macunaíma* employs a version of this fruitful dissonance in numerous ways, as well as other linguistic experiments, on a grander scale, which is to say over the scope of an extended narrative; he produces a text of striking capaciousness despite its actual brevity, with leaps in logic and time, radical juxtapositions of style, character, and incident, and an insistent playfulness and ribald humor.

While *Amar* is a novel that portrays and sends up the domestic, bourgeois world of Andrade's youth, in *Macunaíma* Andrade takes up the challenge of reflecting in novelistic form Brazil's geographical vastness, its cultural diversity and complexity, and its distinctive capacity for change and reinvention. We see fewer of the European, fin-de-siècle figures and tropes, such as the repeatedly invoked "harlequin," of his *Pauliceia*. Instead, Andrade centers *Macunaíma* within the originary sphere of Indigenous cultures, while also incorporating aspects of the country's long history as a European colony, its later status as a New World empire, and finally, shortly before his birth, its development into a republic. The novel, which he considered a "rhapsody" in keeping with his poetic and musical interests, also incorporates the profound imprint left by centuries of chattel slavery and the African presence that has continued to powerfully shape Brazil. In true modernist fashion, however, *Macunaíma* does not depict this plenitude through the lens of realism, but instead refracts it, to produce a text that proceeds like a mosaic dizzyingly pieced together, bursting with story. Reading the novel, it can feel as if multiple storytellers are simultaneously telling parallel tales in different genres (satire, allegory, fable, etc.), as the plot figuratively races wildly forward, though Andrade never loses his central thread, which follows his "hero with no character."

The eponymous Macunaíma, as the reader quickly learns, possesses a surfeit of character, much like the text itself, such that the epithet ironically comes to mean almost the opposite of what it suggests: Macunaíma, as a novel, a character, and a metonym for Brazil, has *so much character*, perhaps too much at times. Macunaíma is a character of such abundance, he contains so many multitudes, many of them seemingly in opposition, that he is a figure of supreme negative capability, and one of the thrills of the plot—which unreels as a fantastical tragicomic epic, often in picaresque fashion, as antic at times as a children's TV cartoon—is to experience how Andrade manages or fails—if momentarily, which may be the point—to hold the narrative together. Even in physical terms Macunaíma is a contradiction; a fully grown human, he possesses a child's head; born "jet black" in skin tone to an Afro-Indigenous mother, he turns fully white after bathing in an enchanted pool; he possesses magical powers and deploys them regularly throughout the novel, yet he is also as vulnerable as any human, especially after losing his special talisman, his "muiraquitã," which is sold to his archenemy. As with Macunaíma, I might analogize the numerous oppositions so inherent in this novel—the belonging and alienation, the constant transformations, the mixing of myths and fantasies, the intermingling of registers, the unstable narrative ontology, which combined produce a text of surpassing queerness and beauty—to the writer himself, in whose very person these oppositions were playing out, as well as to the country and society in which he lived and wrote.

Andrade's white-heat compositional method was actually the result of a longer latent period of composition, in his head and notebooks. During the period between São Paulo's Modern Art Week and *Macunaíma*'s publication, he had traveled throughout large swaths of Brazil's interior, as well as along its coasts, documenting various aspects of local folk cultures, noting the music and tales, and also all manner of imagery and idioms, particularly the Indigenous and Afro-Brazilian influences. All of this research would provide a rich cache of material for *Macunaíma*. Another crucial source for *Macunaíma*—including the novel's title and the protagonist's name and exploits—was the second volume in German ethnologist Theodor Koch-Grünberg's five-part study *Vom*

Roroima zum Orinoco (*From Roraima to the Orinoco*, published from 1917 to 1928), which focused heavily on Indigenous myths, providing an invaluable foundation for Andrade's novel. This borrowing would prove controversial to some critics, but Andrade later publicly acknowledged his debt. Additionally, the canon of earlier Brazilian, Lusophone, and European literature, which Andrade was very familiar with and drew upon, and against which he was writing, provided yet another foundation. Nevertheless, *Macunaíma*, with its collage-like melding and layering, is very much Andrade's own, distinctive literary gem. Readers of this edition are fortunate to have the exceptional notes translator Katrina Dodson has compiled, illuminating many of the references, along with her insightful, contextualizing afterword, which delves more deeply into all of the points I touch upon here.

One motif that runs throughout *Macunaíma* is that of the cannibal, and it is linked directly and indirectly to the "*Manifesto Antropófago*" ("Cannibalist Manifesto") and the corresponding Cannibalist Movement, published by the aforementioned Group of Five member Oswald de Andrade and inspired by the work of another member, his wife Tarsila do Amaral. Her painting *Abaporu* appeared in the movement's journal, which also published an early snippet of *Macunaíma*. Oswald de Andrade's and the Cannibalist Movement's chief idea, distilled, was that Brazilian art could and should take whatever it wanted and needed from European sources, or in other words, "cannibalize" them, but also tap into the incalculably rich intellectual and cultural trove Brazil and the New World—beginning with Indigenous antecedents— provided, as a counterweight to European cultural and aesthetic hegemony. (I should note here the movement's very problematic fascination with "cannibalism" and its connection to ideas of dehistoricized and racialized social and cultural "primitivism.") Certainly *Macunaíma*, as a novel, and Macunaíma the protagonist, are desiring and devouring machines, and in most ways appear to manifest many of the manifesto's chief tenets; the novel gathers up innumerable, sometimes incommensurate strands, from all the sources Andrade recorded or consulted, as well as from his fecund imagination, in its quest to create a coherent whole. Yet for Andrade the novel was not so much an exemplar of the movement's ideas—however much it confirmed some of its key propositions—but rather it was sui generis, and any reading of *Macunaíma* will substantiate that it is anything but a programmatic text. Instead, from the opening page, one launches into a work that appears to defy any plan or program at all.

In addition to the cannibal motif and actual cannibalism in the text, contemporary readers may be taken aback by other elements and moments in the novel that are misogynistic and sexist, racist, and appropriative (truly, the novel itself represents on one level the epitome of cultural appropriation and remixing). Rather than dismiss these critiques outright, or argue that the novel's comic through line leavens or excuses them, or turn to the fact of Andrade's queerness and African ancestry, I will note that *Macunaíma* is, alongside its inventiveness, still very much a text in and of its era, with all the limitations that entails. I would also note that in some ways, *Macunaíma*'s transgressions represent—and here this word is key—Andrade's attempt to embody in thematic, psychic, and synecdochic ways Brazilian culture in much of its fractious complexity, indexing aspects of the country's ongoing social, political, and economic relations, in all their ugliness and brutality, through means other than realism (social, materialist, or otherwise). It is up to readers today, in Brazil and elsewhere, to decide how adroitly this approach succeeds or falters, without losing sight of or dismissing the work out of hand.

I will conclude by saying that English-language readers have a rare gift in Katrina Dodson's translation. Again and again she has found a way to render this text—a marvel and puzzle in the original Portuguese—into an English that sparkles with the sense and spirit of its source. She thankfully has not prettified Andrade's text for the Anglophone eye or ear, but she has captured its essential music and rhythms, its brio, in a way that brings it alive anew. Moreover, a crucial component of her translation involves her painstaking archival research into every aspect of the text, particularly those grounded in Andrade's studies of Afro-Brazilian culture, uncovering information that has revealed greater insight into some of his experimentation and play, which had eluded or confounded some prior critics and readers. We thus have the best translation of one of the greatest novels, by one of the greatest figures in Brazilian, Latin American, and global literature.

Once we have concluded our reading of the novel and marveled at the work the translator and Andrade have undertaken for us, we will surely be able to recall without hesitation our hero Macunaíma's mythic roller coaster of a life, his epic journey which was and is Brazil's, so *full of character*, and conclude by recalling the novel's simple and perfect ending, recounted, like the entire text, by Macunaíma's parrot: "And that's all."

JOHN KEENE

MACUNAÍMA

Chapter 1. *Macunaíma*

In the depths of the virgin-forest was born Macunaíma, hero of our people. He was jet black and son to fear of the night. There came a moment when the silence grew so great listening to the murmuring Rio Uraricoera, that the native Tapanhumas woman birthed an ugly child. That child is the one they called Macunaíma.

Even as a boy he did bewildering things. First off he went more than six years without talking. If they coaxed him to talk he'd holler:

"Ah! just so lazy! . . ."

and not a word more. He kept to a corner of the family maloca, perched on a platform of paxiúba palm, watching the others work, specially his two brothers, Maanape the geezer and Jiguê in the prime of manhood. For fun he'd pick the heads off saúva ants. All he did was lie around but if ever he set eyes on money, Macunaíma would toddle for a penny. And he'd perk up whenever the family went to bathe in the river, all naked together. He'd spend the whole time diving underwater, and the women would squeal in delight on account of those guaiamum crabs said to inhabit the freshwater there. Back at the family mocambo if a girl came up to cuddle, Macunaíma would stick his hand on her charms, the girl would jump back. As for the males he'd spit in their faces. Nevertheless, he respected the elders and wholeheartedly joined

Notes for each chapter can be found beginning on p. 219. –Tr.

in the murua the poracê the torê the bacororô the cucuicogue, all the religious dances of the tribe.

When it was time for bed he'd climb into his little macuru, always forgetting to pee. Seeing as his mother's hammock was right under his hanging cradle, the hero's steaming piss would splash onto the old woman, shooing the mosquitoes real good. Then he'd drift off dreaming of bad-words and outrageously immoral acts, kicking at the air.

At the peak of day the women's chatter always came round to the hero's naughty pranks. They'd laugh knowingly, remarking, "Though you may be expectin' a little tickle, even a pipsqueak thorn packs a prickle," and during a Pajelança ceremony King Nagô gave a speech and revealed that indeed the hero was intelligent.

Soon as he turned six they gave him water out of a rattle and Macunaíma started talking just like everybody else. And he asked his mother to put down the manioc she was grating and take him for a walk in the woods. His mother didn't want to cause she couldn't just put down the manioc, nossir. Macunaíma sat whining all day long. At-night he kept wailing. The next day he waited with his left eye a-snoozing for his mother to start her work. Then he asked her to put down the basket she was weaving from guarumá-membeca grasses and take him for a walk in the woods. His mother didn't want to cause she couldn't just put down the basket, nossir. So she asked her daughter-in-law, Jiguê's gal, to take the boy. Jiguê's gal was very young and her name was Sofará. She came up hesitating but this time Macunaíma stayed stock-still without sticking his hand on anybody's charms. The girl put the kid on her back and went out to where the aninga lily grew along the banks of the river. The water had lingered there to plunk out a whimsical tune on the fronds of the javari palm. Off in the distance it was a pretty sight to see, with lotsa biguá and biguatinga birds darting round where the river branched off. The girl put Macunaíma down on the shore but he started whining, there were too many ants! . . . and he asked Sofará to bring him up to the ridge deeper in the forest. The girl did. But no sooner did she lay the tot down among the tiriricas, tajás and trapoerabas on the forest floor, than he grew manly in a flash and became a handsome prince. They were out there walking a good long time.

When they got home to the maloca the girl seemed mighty worn out from carrying the kid on her back all day. It was because the hero had played around with her a whole lot . . . No sooner did she lay Macunaíma in his hammock than Jiguê came back from net fishing and his gal hadn't done a lick of work. Jiguê flew off the handle and after picking for ticks really laid into her. Sofará weathered the blows without a peep.

Jiguê didn't suspect a thing and started braiding a rope from curauá fiber. He'd just spotted some fresh tapir tracks and was fixing to make a trap to catch the critter. Macunaíma asked his brother for a bit of curauá but Jiguê said it weren't no kiddie toy. Macunaíma started wailing again and it was one helluva night for them all.

Next day Jiguê got up bright and early to set the trap and seeing the kid pouting he said:

"Good morning, everybody's lil sweetheart."

But Macunaíma sulked silently.

"Don't wanna talk to me, huh?"

"I'm mad."

"What for?"

Then Macunaíma asked for some curauá fiber. Jiguê glared at him and told his gal to get some twine for the boy. The girl did. Macunaíma thanked her and went to ask the pai-de-terreiro to braid him a rope and blow some petum smoke over it.

When everything was good and ready Macunaíma asked his mother to leave her caxiri brew fermenting and take him for a walk in the woods. The old woman couldn't on account of her work but Jiguê's sly sweetie told her mother-in-law that she was "at your command." And she went into the woods with the kid on her back.

When she put him down among the carurus and sororocas on the forest floor, the little one started growing started growing and turned into a handsome prince. He told Sofará to hold on a sec he'd be right back so they could play around and went to lay a snare at the tapir's watering hole. No sooner did they get home from their walk, mighty late, than Jiguê also came back from setting his trap on the tapir's tracks. His gal hadn't done a lick of work. Jiguê was mad as heck and before picking for ticks really let her have it. But Sofará weathered the beating with patience.

Next day as the dawn rays were just clearing the treetops, Macunaíma woke everybody up, bawling frightfully, to hurry! hurry over to the watering hole and fetch the critter he'd caught! . . . However, nobody believed him and they started in on the day's work.

Macunaíma was very upset and asked Sofará to hop over to the watering hole real quick just to see. The girl did and came back telling everybody that in-fact there was a very big very dead tapir in the snare. The whole tribe went to fetch the critter, ruminating on the tot's intelligence. When Jiguê came home with his curauá rope empty, he found everybody dressing the kill. He lent a hand. And while divvying it up, he didn't give Macunaíma a single piece of meat, just the tripe. The hero swore vengeance.

Next day he asked Sofará to take him for a walk and they stayed in the woods till night-fall. No sooner did the boy touch the leafy forest floor than he turned into an ardent prince. They played around. After three go-rounds they ran through the forest cuddling each other. After the poking cuddles, they did the tickling cuddles, then buried each other in the sand, then burned each other with flaming straw, it was plenty of cuddling. Macunaíma grabbed the trunk of a copaíba and hid behind a piranhea. When Sofará came running, he whacked her in the head with the timber. It made such a gash that the girl fell writhing in laughter at his feet. She pulled him by a leg. Macunaíma moaned with pleasure clutching the gigantic trunk. Then the girl bit off his big toe and swallowed it. Wailing with glee Macunaíma tattooed her body with the blood from his foot. Then he flexed his muscles, lifting himself onto a vine trapeze, and leaped in a flash onto the piranhea's highest branch. Sofará clambered up after him. The tender limb bowed swaying under the prince's weight. When the girl made it up top they played around again swinging in the sky. After playing Macunaíma wanted to cuddle Sofará. He coiled his body ready to pounce in a frenzy but got no farther, the bough broke and down they went crashing all the way splat to the ground. When the hero came to, he looked round for the girl, she wasn't there. He was getting up to find her but piercing the silence from a low branch overhead came the fearsome yowling of a suçuarana cougar. The hero keeled over in fright and shut his eyes so he'd be eaten without seeing. Then he heard a giggle and Macunaíma got smacked in the chest with a gob of spit, it was the girl. Macunaíma started chucking rocks at her and whenever she got hit, Sofará would shriek with excitement tattooing his body below with the blood she spat. Finally a rock clipped the girl right in the kisser and busted three teeth. She leaped off the branch and thwap! landed straddling the hero's belly as he wrapped his whole body round her, howling with pleasure. And they played around some more.

Papaceia the star was twinkling in the sky by the time the girl got home looking mighty worn out from carrying the kid on her back for so long. But Jiguê, getting suspicious, had followed the pair into the woods witnessing the transformation and all the rest. Jiguê was a big dummy. He got real angry. Grabbed an armadillo-tail whip and whacked the hero's rump with all his might. The bellowing was so tremendous that it cut short the immensity of the night and lotsa birds fell to the ground in fright and were transformed into stone.

When Jiguê could spank him no more, Macunaíma ran out to the new growth in the clearing, chewed some cardeiro root and came back healed. Jiguê took Sofará back to her father and slept easy in his hammock.

Chapter 2. *Coming of Age*

Jiguê was a big dummy and the next day he showed up pulling a young woman by the hand. She was his new gal and her name was Iriqui. She kept a live rat hidden in her mass of hair and was always getting dolled up. She painted her face with araraúba and jenipapo and each morning she'd rub açaí berry on her lips making them all purple. Next she'd dab some bilimbi fruit over it and her lips would turn all scarlet. Then Iriqui would wrap herself in a striped cotton shawl dyed black with acariúba and green with tatajuba and scent her hair with essence of umiri, she was lovely.

Well now, after everyone had eaten Macunaíma's tapir, famine struck the mocambo. As for hunting, nobody caught any more game, not even a single armadillo turned up! and seeing as Maanape had killed a river dolphin for them to eat, the cunauaru toad called Maraguigana, Father of the Dolphin, was angered. He sent a flood and the cornfield rotted. They ate up everything, even the stale rinds ran out and the bonfire that burned night and day didn't roast a thing, nossir, all it did was ease the chill that had fallen. There wasn't even a scrap of jerky for folks to grill.

So then Macunaíma wanted to have some fun. He told his brothers there was still lotsa piaba lotsa jeju lotsa matrinxão and jatuaranas, all them river fish, just hit em with some poison timbó! Maanape said:

"We can't find any more timbó."

Macunaíma gave a make-believe answer:

"Right by that grotto where there's buried money I saw a whole motherload of timbó growing."

"Alright then come show us where it's at."

They went. The bank was treacherous and you couldn't tell what was land and what was river among the mamorana groves. Maanape and Jiguê went searching searching in the mud up to their teeth, slipping and sliding thwap! in bogs covered by the floodwaters. And they went jumpingjumping out those holes, hooting and hollering, hands over their behinds on account of them dirty rotten candiru fish trying to get inside. Macunaíma was laughing on the inside watching his brothers monkey around hunting for timbó. He acted like he was looking too but didn't dip a toe in, nossir, staying high and dry on solid ground. Whenever his brothers passed close by, he'd squat and groan wearily.

"Quit busting your tail like that, kiddo!"

So Macunaíma plunked down on a riverbank and kicked his feet in the water shooing away the mosquitoes. And it was lotsa mosquitoes black flies no-see-ums gallinippers katynippers sandflies skeeters mitsies maringouins midges gadflies, that whole mess of bloodsuckers.

When late-afternoon rolled around the brothers came to fetch Macunaíma, all in a tizzy cause they hadn't come across a single patch of timbó. The hero got scared and played dumb:

"Find any?"

"We found squat!"

"Well I spotted timbó right here. Timbó used to be folk just like us once ... He caught wind they were hunting for him and split. Timbó used to be folk just like us once ..."

His brothers marveled at the boy's intelligence and the three went back to their maloca.

Macunaíma was very upset on account of being so hungry. The next day he said to his old lady:

"Mama, who's gonna take our house to the other side of the

river up on that rise, huh, who's gonna? Shut your eyes for a sec, old lady, and ask it like that."

The old lady did. Macunaíma asked her to keep her eyes shut some more and carried their tejupar platforms arrows baskets barrels sacks sieves hammocks, all them bits and bobs, over to a clearing in the woods up on that rise on the other side of the river. When the old woman opened her eyes it was all there along with fish game ripe banana trees, way too much food. So she went to hack down a buncha bananas.

"Pardon my asking, Mama, why're you pulling down so many naners like that!"

"To take back to your brother Jiguê with his lovely Iriqui and for your brother Maanape who're all starving hungry."

Macunaíma was very upset. He stood pondering pondering and said to the old woman:

"Mama, who's gonna take our house to the other side of the river down where it's flooded, huh, who's gonna? Ask it like that!"

The old woman did. Macunaíma asked her to keep her eyes shut and took the entire load, the whole shebang, to the place from just-today over in the flooded swamplands. When the old woman opened her eyes everything was back where it was before, right next to the tejupars of brother Maanape and brother Jiguê with his lovely Iriqui. And they all rumbled with hunger once more.

So then the old woman flew into a devilish rage. She put the hero on her hip and took off. She marched through the woods and made it way out to that great big clearing known as No Man's Land. She walked a league and a half in, you couldn't even see the woods anymore, it was a grassy plain whose only movement was the gentle swaying of the cashew trees. Not even a guaxe bird livened up the solitude. The old woman put the tot down in the field where he couldn't grow up no more, nossir, and said:

"Now your mama's going away. You'll be lost out here in this field where you can't grow up no more, nossir."

And she disappeared. Macunaíma took a good look round that

desert and felt like he was gonna cry. But wasn't nobody around, he didn't shed a tear, nossir. He plucked up his courage and hit the road, a-trembling on his little bowlegs. He wandered from hill to dale a whole week, till he happened upon the Currupira roasting some meat beside his trusty hound Papamel. And the Currupira lives in a tucunzeiro sapling and asks folks for tobacco. Macunaíma said:

"Hey Grampa, gimme some meat to eat, wontcha?"

"Sure thing," went the Currupira.

He cut a chunk from his leg roasted it and gave it to the boy, asking:

"Whatcha doing out in this here field, junior!"

"Taking a stroll."

"You don't say!"

"Yessir, just taking a stroll . . ."

Then he told all about his mother's punishment on account of him being so darn mean to his brothers. And as he was telling about moving the house back to where there wasn't any game to hunt he howled with laughter. The Currupira looked at him and muttered:

"You ain't a kid no more, junior, you ain't a kid no more, nossirree . . . That there's what grownups do . . ."

Macunaíma thanked him and asked the Currupira to show him the way back to the Tapanhumas mocambo. But what the Currupira wanted was to eat the hero, he showed him a fake way:

"You go this-a-way, child-man, go that-a-way, cut in front of that tree, hang a left, turn around and head right back under my uaiariquinizês."

Macunaíma started down that route but when he got in front of the tree, he scratched his little leg and murmured:

"Ah! just so lazy! . . ."

and went straight.

The Currupira waited a good long time but the tot wasn't turning up . . . So then the monster mounted a stag, which is his horse, dug his round foot into the sprinter's groin and took off shouting:

"Flesh of my leg! flesh of my leg!"

From inside the hero's belly the flesh answered:

"What's up?"

Macunaíma sped up and dashed into the caatinga scrubland but the Currupira outran the boy, coming up hot on his heels and gaining fast.

"Flesh of my leg! flesh of my leg!"

The flesh replied:

"What's up?"

The kid was desperate. It was the fox's wedding and that old lady Vei, the Sun, was flashing in droplets of rain threshing the light just like corn. Macunaíma went up to a puddle, drank some muddy water, and upchucked the flesh.

"Flesh of my leg! flesh of my leg!" the Currupira came shouting.

"What's up?" the flesh replied from the puddle.

Macunaíma stole into the thickets on the other side and got away.

A league and a half farther he heard a voice from behind an anthill singing like this:

"Acuti pita canhém . . . ," very slowly.

He went over there and happened upon the agouti making manioc flour in a tipiti woven from jacitara palm.

"Hey Granny, gimme me some yuca to eat, wontcha?"

"Why sure," went the agouti. She gave the boy some yuca, asking:

"Whatcha doing out in this here caatinga, sonny?"

"Taking a stroll."

"Good gracious me!"

"Taking a stroll, uh huh!"

He told all about how he'd tricked the Currupira and howled with laughter. The agouti eyed him and muttered:

"Chilren don't do that, sonny, chilren don't do that, nossiree . . . I'm gonna fix your body to match that big ol' noggin."

Then she picked up a wooden dish full of poison yuca water and hurled the runoff at the tyke. Macunaíma jumped back thunderstruck but only managed to save his head, the whole rest of his body got wet. The hero sneezed and grew manly. He started straightening out growing up getting stronger and reached the size of a strapping man. But his head which didn't get wet was blunted forevermore and stuck with that sickening little kid face.

Macunaíma thanked her for doing that and took off singing toward his native mocambo. The beetle-swarmed night came on, tucking the ants into the earth and luring the mosquitoes out the water. The air was stifling hot like a nest. The old Tapanhumas woman heard the voice of her son in the dusky distance and was flabbergasted. Macunaíma showed up scowling and said to her:

"Mama, I had a dream my tooth fell out."

"That means a death in the family," the old woman remarked.

"Don't I know it. You'll live just one more Sun. All because you birthed me."

Next day the brothers went off fishing and hunting, the old woman went out to the crops and Macunaíma stayed home alone with Jiguê's gal. Then he turned into the quenquém ant and bit Iriqui to cuddle with her. But the girl hurled the quenquém far away. So then Macunaíma turned into an urucum tree. The lovely Iriqui laughed, gathered its seeds and dolled herself up painting her face and distinctive parts. She was ever so lovely. And Macunaíma was so delighted he turned back into a person and shacked up with Jiguê's gal.

When the brothers came home from hunting Jiguê noticed the swap right away, but Maanape told him that Macunaíma was a man for good now, not to mention big and brawny. Maanape was a shaman. Jiguê saw that the maloca was full of food, there was bananas there was corn there was cassava, there was aluá and caxiri brew, there was mapará and camorim fish, maracujá-michira ata abiu sapota sapodilla fruit, there was deer jerky and roast agouti, all them good things to eat and drink . . . Jiguê figured it wasn't worth the trouble to go fighting his brother and let him have the lovely Iriqui. He sighed picked his ticks and slept easy in his hammock.

Next day after playing around with the lovely Iriqui first thing, Macunaíma went for a little walk. He crossed the enchanted kingdom of Pedra Bonita in Pernambuco and nearing the city of Santarém happened upon a doe that had just birthed.

"I'm gonna catch her!" said he. And chased after the doe. She slipped away easily but the hero managed to nab her little baby that could hardly even walk yet, hiding behind a carapanaúba tree and poking the fawn to make it bleat. The doe went wild, her eyes bugged out she froze got discombobulated and came closer came closer froze right in front of them wailing with love. Then the hero shot his arrow at the doe that had just birthed. She collapsed flailed her legs and went rigid sprawled on the ground. The hero crowed in victory. He went up to the doe peered close peered closer still and let out a shriek, fainting. It had been a trick of the Anhanga spirit . . . It wasn't a doe at all, but his very own Tapanhumas mother that Macunaíma had shot with an arrow and who was lying there dead, all scratched up from the spiky titara palms and mandacaru cacti in those woods.

When the hero came to, he went and called his brothers and the three kept vigil all night long sobbing profusely drinking oloniti brew and eating fish with carimã. At sun-up they laid the old woman's body in a hammock and went to bury her beneath a stone in a place called Father of the Tocandeira. Maanape, who was a Catimbó shaman of the highest order, was the one to inscribe the epitaph. And it looked like this:

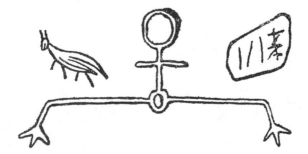

They fasted for as long as custom demanded and Macunaíma spent the whole time wailing heroically. The deceased woman's belly started swelling started swelling and when the rains came to an end she'd turned into a soft mound. Then Macunaíma took Iriqui by the hand, Iriqui took Maanape by the hand, Maanape took Jiguê by the hand, and the four of them set out for this wide world.

Chapter 3. *Ci, Mother of the Forest*

One time the four were heading down a path in the woods mighty parched with thirst, far from the flooded forests and lakes. There weren't even any juicy umbu plums in the neighborhood and Vei, the Sun, was slashing through the foliage, constantly whipping at the backs of the wayfarers. Sweating just like in a Pajelança ceremony where everyone slathers their bodies with pequi oil, onward they marched. Suddenly Macunaíma stopped short, scratching that night of silence with a sweeping gesture of alarm. The others froze in their tracks. Not a thing could be heard but Macunaíma whispered:

"Something's there."

They left the lovely Iriqui making herself pretty seated on the sprawling roots of a samaúma tree and proceeded cautiously. Vei had got her fill of whipping at the backs of the three brothers when a league and a half farther Macunaíma the scout happened upon a sleeping woman. It was Ci, Mother of the Forest. He knew right away, from her withered right breast, that the maiden was part of that tribe of lone women dwelling on the beaches of Moon Mirror Lagoon, fed by the Rio Nhamundá. The woman was beautiful, her body ravaged by vice and painted with jenipapo.

The hero flung himself on top of her to play around. Ci didn't want to. She wielded a three-pronged arrow like a spear while Macunaíma drew his bowie knife. It was a tremendous rumble and the roaring of the fierce combatants resounded beneath the forest canopy, making the bodies of the little birds dwindle with fright. The hero was getting clobbered. He'd taken a punch that bloodied his nose and had a deep gouge in his rear from her txara trident. The Icamiaba woman didn't have the slightest scratch and her every move drew more blood from the body of the hero whose formidable roars made the bodies of the little birds dwindle with fright. Finally realizing he was on the ropes cause he just couldn't keep up with the Icamiaba woman, the hero made a break for it shouting to his brothers:

"Help or else I'll kill her! come help or else I'll kill her!"

The brothers came and grabbed hold of Ci. Maanape tied her arms behind her while Jiguê knocked her coconut around with his murucu spear. And the Icamiaba woman collapsed helplessly among the samambaias on the forest floor. When she lay stock-still, Macunaíma came up and played around with the Mother of the Forest. Then there came flocks of jandayas, flocks of scarlet macaws blue-winged parrotlets conures parakeets, flock after flock of parrots to salute Macunaíma, the new Emperor of the Virgin-Forest.

And the three brothers went on their way with this new gal. They traversed the City of Flowers skirted the River of Affliction passed under Happiness Falls, traipsed down the Highway of Delights and made it to My True Love's Thicket in the hills of Venezuela. It was from there that Macunaíma reigned over those mysterious forests, while Ci led her women on raids wielding three-pronged txaras.

The hero lived peacefully. He spent his lucky-duck days in his hammock killing taioca ants, slurping on pajuari wine and whenever he'd burst into song accompanied by the twangly strums of his cocho guitar, the forests resounded with sweetness lulling to sleep the snakes the ticks the mosquitoes the ants and the bad gods.

At night Ci would come home wafting with the scent of tree resin, bloodied from battle, and climb into the hammock she'd woven from her very own strands of hair. The two would play around and lie there afterward laughing with each other.

There they'd lie laughing a long while, all cozy together. Ci smelled so good that Macunaíma felt heady with languor.

"Holy smokes! you smell good, honey!"
he'd murmur in ecstasy. And flare his nostrils even more. Such a potent headiness would wash over him that sleep would start dripping from his eyelids. But the Mother of the Forest wouldn't even be close to satisfied yet, nossir, and with a flick of the hammock entwining them both she'd beckon her guy for another go-round. Near dead asleep, pestered all to hell, Macunaíma would play around just to keep up his reputation, but when Ci wanted to laugh with him in satisfaction:

"Ah! just so lazy! . . ."
the hero would sigh in exasperation. And turning his back to her he'd fall fast asleep. But Ci wanted to play some more . . . She'd ask and ask . . . The hero sleeping like a log. Then the Mother of the Forest would grab her txara and start poking her guy. Macunaíma would bolt awake howling with laughter writhing from all that tickling.

"C'mon don't do that, you minx!"
"I will too!"
"Let's go to sleep, yer darling . . ."
"Let's play."
"Ah! just so lazy! . . ."
And they'd play around some more.

However on days when much pajuari wine had been imbibed, Ci would find the Emperor of the Virgin-Forest sprawled out three sheets to the wind. They'd start playing around and the hero would trail off in the middle.

"Well, hero!"
"Well what!"
"You're not gonna keep going?"
"Keep going where!"

"Well, my naughty little pet, here we are playing around and you just up and stop in the middle!"

"Ah! just so lazy . . ."

Macunaíma would be so far gone he could hardly go through the motions. And seeking someplace soft in his lover's tresses he'd nod off happy as can be.

So then Ci would resort to a sublime strategy to get him going. She'd search the woods for stinging nettles and thrash em around tickle-tickling the hero's chuí and her own nalachítchi. This would rile-rile Macunaíma into a lion who wanted it bad. The same for Ci. And the two of them would play and play much as can be in a most prodigiously ardent bout of debauchery.

But it was on sleepless nights that their ecstasy was more inventive still. When all the bright burning stars poured down onto Earth a scorching oil so hot that nobody nohow could stand it, a fiery presence shot through the forest. Not even the little birds in their nests could bear it. They'd twist and turn their necks restlessly, flit to the next branch and in the greatest miracle this world has ever seen invent a sudden dark dawn, singsonging on and on without end. The clamor was tremendous the scent overpowering and the heat even stronger.

Macunaíma would shove the hammock so hard that Ci would go flying. She'd wake in a fury and pounce on him. That's how they'd play. And now wide awake with ecstasy they'd invent new arts of playing around.

No sooner had six months passed than the Mother of the Forest gave birth to a scarlet son. Upon which there came the famous mulattas from Bahia, Recife, Rio Grande do Norte and Paraíba, and they gave the Mother of the Forest a ruby-red bow the color of evil, since now she'd be mistress of the scarlet group in all the Christmas pageants. After that they took their leave with pleasure and good cheer, dancing round and round, followed by the soccer pros big shots small fry sweethearts serenaders, that whole pack of golden boys. Macunaíma rested for the customary month but refused to fast. The little squirt had a flat head and Macunaíma flattened it even more by patting it every day and telling the tyke:

"Now grow up fast, junior, so you can go off to São Paulo and make lotsa money."

All the Icamiabas cherished the little scarlet boy and at his first bath they placed all the tribe's jewels on him so the little one would be rich forevermore. They sent someone off to Bolivia for a pair of scissors and left em open under his pillow or else Tutu Marambá would come and suck at the tot's belly button and Ci's big toe. Tutu Marambá came, saw the scissors and got fooled: he sucked at its rings and went off satisfied. All anybody ever did now was think about the little squirt. They sent someone off to São Paulo for those famous woolen booties knit by Dona Ana Francisca de Almeida Leite Morais and to Pernambuco for that special lace in the "Rose of the Alps," "Guabiroba Flower" and "Pining for You" patterns handmade by Dona Joaquina Leitão, better known by the name of Quinquina Cacunda. They strained the best tamarind from the Louro Vieira sisters of Óbidos, so the boy could gulp down the juice mixed with a little remedy for roundworm. O happy days, life was good! ... Another time a jucurutu owl landed on the Emperor's maloca and hooted ill tidings. Macunaíma trembled with fear shooed away the mosquitoes and fell upon his pajuari wine to see if he might shoo away his fear as well. He drank and slept the whole night through. Then the Black Snake came and sucked so much at Ci's only working breast there wasn't a single drop left. And since Jiguê hadn't managed to deflower any of the Icamiabas, the tiny tot had no wet nurse and sucked at his mother's breast the next day, sucked some more, let out a poisoned sigh and died.

They put the little angel in an igaçaba burial urn carved with the form of a jabuti tortoise and so the boitatá fire snakes wouldn't devour the eyes of the deceased they buried him right in the center of their taba with lotsa singing lotsa dancing and lotsa pajuari wine.

Now that her purpose had ended, Macunaíma's gal, all done up still, took from her necklace a famous muiraquitã amulet, gave it to her guy and climbed a vine up to the sky. That's where Ci lives now roaming around in high style, free from the ants, all done up still, all done up with light, turned into a star. She's Beta Centauri.

The next day when Macunaíma went to visit his son's grave he saw that a little plant had sprouted from his body. They tended it with utmost care and it was guaraná. Using the pounded seeds of this plant folks can cure many diseases and cool off during heat waves from Vei, the Sun.

Chapter 4. *Boiuna Moon*

Next day bright and early the hero, aching with longing for Ci, his lover who was unforgettable forevermore, pierced his lower lip and made the muiraquitā into a tembetá. He felt like he was gonna cry. He quickly called for his brothers, bid the Icamiabas farewell and took off.

They went roaming and ranging through all the forests over which Macunaíma now reigned. Everywhere they went he received tributes and was accompanied all the while by a retinue of red macaws and jandaya parakeets. On bitter nights he'd climb atop an açaí palm ripe with fruit as purple as his soul and contemplate the fetching figure of Ci up in the heavens. "My she-devil!" he'd moan ... And oh how he suffered, oh! and he'd invoke the benevolent gods, while chanting canticles that went on and on ...

> *Rudá, Rudá! ...*
> *Thou who makest the rains run dry,*
> *Send the ocean winds so wild*
> *A-whipping across my land so that*
> *The clouds will rush away and so*
> *My she-devil may shine so bright*
> *Clear and steady in the sky! ...*
> *Hush all the waters that run throughout*
> *The rivers in this land o' mine*
> *So that I may splash around*

Playing with my she-devil
In the mirror reflection of the waters! . . .

Like that. Then he'd climb down and cry his eyes out on Maanape's shoulder. Sobbing in sympathy, Jiguê would light the bonfire
so the hero wouldn't feel cold. Maanape would choke back his
own tears, invoking the Acutipuru the Murucututu the Ducucu,
all those lords of sleep in lullabies like this:

> *Acutipuru,*
> *O lend thy sound sleep*
> *To Macunaíma*
> *Who does nothing but weep! . . .*

He'd pick the hero's ticks and soothe him rocking gently back and
forth. The hero would quiet down quiet down and fall fast asleep.
    The next day the three ramblers set off once more through
those mysterious forests. And Macunaíma was followed all the
while by that retinue of red macaws and jandaya parakeets.
    Wandering wandering on, one time as the dawn rays were just
scattering the dark of night, they heard in the distance the sorrowful lament of a maiden. They went to have a look-see. Walking
a league and a half they came upon a waterfall sobbing endlessly.
Macunaíma asked the waterfall:
    "What's up?"
    "The sky."
    "C'mon, tell me."
    So the waterfall recounted what had befallen her.
    "Can't you see that my name is Naipi and I am the daugh-
ter of the tuxaua named Mexô-Mexoitiqui which in my language
means Big-Cat-Crouching. I was the prettiest of maidens and all
the neighboring tuxauas wished to sleep in my hammock and
taste of my body, more languid than the flowering embiroçu. Yet
whenever one came, I'd bite and kick, eager to test his strength.

24

And none could withstand it and they'd go away so mournful.

"My tribe was enslaved to Capei, the boiuna water snake who lived deep in a cavern in the company of saúva ants. During the season when the ipê trees along the river bloomed yellow with flowers the boiuna would come to our taba and choose a virgin girl to sleep with in her underground cave full of skeletons.

"When my body began weeping blood pleading for a man's strength to serve, the suinara owl sang at first light in the jarina palms of my tejupar, Capei came and chose me. The ipês along the riverbank were glimmering with yellow and all their flowers fell upon the sobbing shoulders of the young Titçatê, one of my father's warriors. A great sadness had come marching into our taba like a line of sacassaia ants and devoured even the silence.

"When the wise old pajé pulled the night back out from its hole, Titçatê gathered all the little flowers nearby and brought them to the hammock on my last night of freedom. And then I bit Titçatê.

"Blood gushed from the young man's wounded wrist but he made no fuss at all, furiously moaning, making love, filling my mouth with flowers so I couldn't bite anymore. Titçatê leaped into the hammock and Naipi served Titçatê.

"After we played like crazy mingling streaming blood with the little ipê flowers, my champion carried me on his shoulders, tossed me into his ipeigara moored in a place hidden among the aturiás and sped like an arrow out to the waters of the Raging River, fleeing the boiuna snake.

"The next day when the wise old pajé tucked the night back into its hole, Capei went to fetch me and found the bloody hammock empty. She roared and dashed off to find us. She was coming closer coming closer, we could hear her roaring close by, closer still right up close till finally the waters of the Raging River reared up churning from the boiuna's body.

"Titçatê was so dead tired he could paddle no more, bleeding all the while from the bite on his wrist. That's why we couldn't escape. Capei caught me, spun me round, put me to the egg test, it worked and the boiuna saw that I had already served Titçatê.

"She was so full of wrath that she wished to put an end to this world, I don't know . . . she turned me into this rock and hurled Titçatê onto the river's shore, transformed into a plant. It's that one over there, down there, right there! He's that ever so lovely floating mururé you can see, waving in the water at me. His purple flowers are the drops of blood from the bite, frozen solid by my cold cold waterfall.

"Capei dwells down below, always checking to see whether that boy really did play around with me. Indeed he did and I'll go on weeping over this rock till the end of what has no end, aching so from never again serving my warrior T'çatê . . ."

She stopped. Her tears splashed onto Macunaíma's knees and he shook with sobs.

"If . . . if . . . if that bo-boiuna ever showed up I . . . why I'd kill her!"

Right then a colossal roar was heard and Capei came surging out the water. And Capei was the boiuna snake. Macunaíma thrust out his torso a-glinting with heroism and charged at the monster. Capei swung her maw wide open and out came a swarm of apiacás. Macunaíma beat them back beat them back defeating those marimbondo wasps. The monster lashed out with her tintinnabulating tail, but right then a tracuá ant bit the hero's heel. Distracted by the pain he dropped to a crouch and the tail flew past him hitting Capei smack in the face. Then she roared even more and struck at Macunaíma's thigh. He simply dodged, grabbed a big sharp rock and thwap! knocked that varmint's head clean off.

Her body went writhing away on the current while the head with those big doe eyes came to kiss the feet of its vanquisher in submission. The hero got scared and hightailed it into the woods with his brothers.

"C'mere, siriri, c'mere!" the head shouted.

The three shot away even faster. They ran for a league and a half and looked back. Capei's head kept rolling closer ever on the lookout for them. Onward they ran and when they were too worn out to go on they climbed a bacupari tree by the river to see if the head might keep going. But the head stopped under the tree and asked for some bacupari. Macunaíma shook the branches. The head gathered the fruits off the ground, ate them and asked for more. Jiguê shook some bacupari into the river but the head declared no way was she going in. Then Maanape hurled a fruit with all his might far as could be and when the head went to fetch it the brothers scrambled down and snuck away. Running running onward, a league and a half farther they came upon the house where the Bachelor of Cananéia lived. The old coot was sitting by the front door reading profound manuscripts. Macunaíma asked him:

"How goes it, Bachelor?"

"Can't complain, unknown voyager."

"Getting some fresh air, huh?"

"C'est vrai, as the French say."

"Well, so long, Bachelor, I'm kinda in a hurry . . ."

And they shot off like blazes again. They traversed the prehistoric sambaqui shell mounds of Caputera and Morrete in a single breath. Just up ahead was an abandoned shanty. They went in and shut the door tight. And then Macunaíma noticed that he'd lost the tembetá. He was distraught because it was the only memento of Ci that he'd kept. He made to leave in search of the stone but his brothers wouldn't let him. Wasn't long before the head showed up. Thwap! it knocked.

"What d'ya want?"

"Open the door and let me in!"

But did the alligator open up? neither did they! so the head couldn't come in. Macunaíma didn't know that the head had become his slave and didn't mean them no harm. The head waited a long time but seeing how they really weren't gonna open up, she mulled over what she wanted to be. If she became water, others would drink her, if she became an ant they'd squish her, if she became a mosquito they'd zap her, if she became a train she'd get derailed, if she became a river they'd put her on the map . . . She made up her mind: "I'll go be the Moon." Then hollered:

"Open up, folks, I want a couple things!"

Macunaíma peered through the crack in the door and warned Jiguê as he was opening it:

"She's on the loose!"

Jiguê shut the door again. That's why there's that expression "On the loose!" for when someone doesn't act how we want.

When Capei saw that they weren't opening the door she started feeling awful sorry for herself and asked the birdeater tarantula to help her get up to the sky.

"The Sun melts my thread," the great big spider replied.

So the head asked the xexéu birds to flock together and dark night fell.

"Nobody can see my thread at night," the great big spider said.

The head went off to get a calabash bowl of ice-cold from the Andes and said:

"Pour out a drop every league and a half, the thread will turn white with frost. Now we can go."

"Alright then let's go."

The iandu began spinning her web on the ground. At the first breeze the filmy thread rose into the sky. Then the great big spider went up and at the very top poured out a bit of frost. And as the iandu tarantula spun more thread from up top, down below it was turning all white. The head shouted:

"Farewell, my people, I'm off to the sky!"

And there she went eating the thread all the way up to the vast field of the heavens. The brothers opened the door and peered out. Up and away went Capei.

"Are you really going up to the sky, head?"

"Mm-hmm," she went, not able to open her mouth anymore.

In the wee hours before dawn Capei the boiuna made it to the sky. She was chubby from eating all that spider web and ghostly pale with exertion. All her sweat was falling to the Earth in droplets of fresh dew. That frosty thread is the reason why Capei's so cold. In olden times Capei used to be the boiuna snake but now she's that Moon head up there in the vast field of the heavens. And ever since that time tarantulas prefer to spin their webs at-night.

The next day the brothers went searching all the way to the banks of the river but they went searching searching in vain, not a trace of the muiraquitã. They asked all the creatures, the aperemas saguis mulita-armadillas tejus muçuã mud turtles of the land and trees, the tapiucabas chabós matintapereras peckerwooders and aracuans of the air, they asked the japiim bird and its compadre the marimbondo wasp, the little cockroach looking to get hitched, the bird that cries "Yark!" and its mate that replies "Yeek!," the gecko who plays hide-and-seek with the rat, the tambaqui tucunaré pirarucu curimatá fish of the river, the pecaí tapicuru and iererê waders of the shore, all those living beings, but nobody had seen a thing, nobody knew a thing. So the brothers hit the road again, roving across the imperial domains. The silence was foul and so was the despair. Once in a while Macunaíma would pause lost in thought over his she-devil . . . Oh the desire throbbing in him! He'd stop for a spell. And weep for ages. The tears streaming down the hero's childlike cheeks baptized his hairy chest. Then he sighed shaking his little head:

"Well, brothers! With love number one, you're forever undone! . . ."

Onward he wandered. And everywhere he went he received tributes and was followed all the while by that bright-dappled retinue of jandaya parakeets and red macaws.

One time after he lay down in a shady spot waiting for his brothers to get done fishing, the Little Black Herder Boy to whom Macunaíma prayed every single day took pity on the cursed wretch and decided to help him. He sent the little uirapuru bird. All of a sudden the hero heard some frantic flapping and the little uirapuru bird landed on his knee. Macunaíma flailed in annoyance and shooed the little uirapuru. Not a minute passed before he heard the clamor again and the little bird landed on his belly. Macunaíma didn't make a fuss this time. Then the little uirapuru bird burst into sweet song and the hero understood everything he was singing. And it was that Macunaíma was most unfortunate cause he'd lost the muiraquitã on the river beach back when he was climbing the bacupari tree. But now, went the uirapuru's lament, Macunaíma would never be a lucky-duck ever again, cause a tracajá had swallowed the muiraquitã and the fisherman who'd caught that turtle had sold the magic green stone to a Peruvian riverboat peddler who went by the name of Venceslau Pietro Pietra. The talisman's owner had struck it rich and was living it up as a moneybags rancher in São Paulo, that mighty city lapped by the waters of the Igarapé Tietê.

Having thus spoken, the little uirapuru bird made a flourish in the air and vanished. When his brothers got back from fishing Macunaíma said to them:

"I was heading down this trail tryna lure a caatinga deer and lo and behold, I felt a chill down my spine. Stuck my hand back there and out came a tame centipede that told me the whole truth."

Then Macunaíma told them of the muiraquitã's whereabouts and declared to his brothers that he had a mind to go to São Paulo and track down this Venceslau Pietro Pietra and take back the stolen tembetá.

". . . and may the rattlesnake build a nest if I don't lay my hands on the muiraquitã! If y'all come with me that's fine and dandy, but if you don't, well sir, better to go it alone than in poor company! But I'm stubborn as a toad and when I fix on something I hold tight. Go I shall, if only to show up that little uirapuru bird, just kidding! I meant the centipede."

After his speech Macunaíma howled with laughter imagining what a trick he'd played on that little bird. Maanape and Jiguê decided to go with him, since the hero needed protecting after all.

Chapter 5. *Piaimã*

Early the next day Macunaíma hopped in his ubá and paddled over to the mouth of the Rio Negro so he could leave his conscience on the Isle of Marapatá. He left it on the tippity top of a thirty-foot mandacaru cactus, so it wouldn't get eaten by saúva ants. He went back to where his brothers were waiting and at the day's peak the three made their way along the left bank of the Sun.

Untold adventures transpired on that journey through caatinga scrublands riverruns uplands, creek after creek, tabatinga clay corridors virgin-forests and miracles of the sertão. Macunaíma and his brothers were coming to São Paulo. The Rio Araguaia eased their travels. In the course of so many conquests and so many feats, the hero hadn't saved a cent but all that treasure inherited from the Icamiaba star was hidden deep in mining caverns way up in Roraima. For the journey Macunaíma set aside from this loot no less than forty times forty million cacao beans, the traditional currency. He figured they needed a whole flood of vessels to bring it all. And it was ever so lovely that massive fleet of igaras making its way up the Araguaia, two hundred lashed together one by one like an arrow skimming the river's surface. At the head stood Macunaíma glowering, scanning the horizon for the city. He was ruminating ruminating gnawing at his fingers now covered in warts from always pointing at Ci the star. His brothers went on paddling shooing the mosquitoes and each jerk of the paddles went reverberating down the two hundred tethered igaras, spilling boatloads of beans along the river's surface, leaving a wake of chocolate where all the camuatá pirapitinga dourado piracanjuba uarú-uará and bacu fish feasted to their delight.

One time the Sun covered the three brothers in a slick layer of sweat and Macunaíma remembered to bathe. However this was impossible in that river on account of the exceedingly voracious piranhas that every now and then would leap in clusters more'n three feet out the water while fighting to snatch a morsel of a dismembered sibling. Then Macunaíma spotted a hollow full of water in a big rock slab smack dab in the middle of the river. And the hollow looked just like a giant's footprint. They landed. After hooting and hollering on account of the cold water the hero got in and washed himself all over. But the water was enchanted cause that hole in the rock was the humongous footprint of Sumé, from way back when he went around preaching the gospel of Jesus to the Brazilian Indians. When the hero got out he was white, blond with the bluest eyes, the water had washed away all his blackness. And not a soul would recognize him anymore as a son of the jet-black tribe of the Tapanhumas.

No sooner did Jiguê witness the miracle than he threw himself into Sumé's humongous footprint. However the water was already so dirty from the hero's darkness that much as Jiguê rubbed himself like a madman splashing water everywhere he only managed to turn the color of new bronze. Macunaíma felt sorry and consoled him:

"Look here, brother Jiguê, you didn't turn white, but the black went away so look on the bright side: better to have a nasal voice than no nose at all."

Then Maanape went to wash himself off, but Jiguê had sloshed all the enchanted water out the hollow. There was only a splish left at the very bottom and Maanape managed to wet just his soles and palms. That's why he remained a black son of the Tapanhumas tribe through and through. Except his palms and soles got ruddy from being scrubbed with that holy water. Macunaíma felt sorry and consoled him:

"Now don't be peeved, brother Maanape, don't be peeved, nossir, our Uncle Judas had it a whole lot worse!"

And it was the loveliest sight under the Sun on that rock the three brothers one blond one red another black, standing up tall and naked. All the creatures of the forest gaped in awe. The black alligator the little white-bellied alligator the great big alligator the ururau alligator with the big yellow snout, all them gators poked their craggy eyes out the water. In the branches of the ingas the aningas the mamoranas the embaúbas the catauaris growing along the riverbank the capuchin monkey the squirrel monkey the guariba howler the bugio howler the spider monkey the woolly monkey the bearded saki the tufted cairara, all the forty monkeys of Brazil, all of em, gaped drooling with envy. And the sabiá song thrushes, the sabiacica the sabiapoca the sabiaúna the sabiá-piranga the sabia-gongá that never shares its food, the ravine-sabiá the miner-sabiá the orangetree-sabiá the gumtree-sabiá, all were wonderstruck and forgot to finish their warbling, eloquently clamoring clamoring on. Macunaíma was furious. He put his hands on his hips and hollered at nature:

"Ain't nothing to see here!"

And so the natural creatures scattered back to living and the three brothers went on their way once more.

However they were entering the lands of the Igarapé Tietê where bourbon coffee reigned and the traditional currency was no longer cacao, but instead was called coin contos clackers bits tokens shillings two-pence ten-cents, fifty bucks, ninety clams, and cash coppers pennies loot greenbacks gravy marbles moolah dough vouchers peanuts frogs smackeroos, and the like, where you couldn't even get a pair of sock garters for two thousand cacao beans. Macunaíma was very upset. He'd have to bust his tail, him, the hero! . . . He murmured despondently:

"Ah! just so lazy! . . ."

He decided to abandon the whole enterprise, heading back to his native lands where he was Emperor. But Maanape piped up:

"Quit being a dope, brother! The whole swamp doesn't go into mourning just cause one crab kicks the bucket, dammit! don't lose heart, I'll handle it!"

When they got to São Paulo, they bagged up some of their treasure to eat and after trading the rest on the Exchange made out with nearly eighty contos de réis. Maanape was a sorcerer. Eighty contos wasn't all that much but the hero thought on it and told his brothers:

"Chin up. We'll get by on this. He who holds out for a flawless horse ends up walking . . ."

On this pocket change Macunaíma survived.

And one cool evening at sun-down the brothers came upon the mighty city of São Paulo sprawling along the riverbanks of the Igarapé Tietê. First came the shrieks of the imperial parrots bidding the hero farewell. Then off flew the bright-dappled flock back up to the forests of the North.

The brothers entered a savanna full of palm trees, inajás ouricuris ubuçus bacabas mucajás miritis tucumãs, sprouting smoke plumes instead of coconuts and fronds. All the stars had come down from the mist-drenched white sky and drifted brooding through the city. Macunaíma remembered to look for Ci. Ah! never ever could he forget that one, since the bewitched hammock she'd strung up for playing around had been woven from her very own hair and this made the weaver unforgettable. Macunaíma searched and searched but the roads and yards were jampacked with women so white so very pale, oh! . . . Macunaíma moaned. He rubbed up against the women, murmuring sweetly, "Mani! Mani! little daughters of manioc . . . ," lost in pleasure amid so much beauty. Finally he chose three. He played around with em in a strange hammock planted in the ground, in a maloca taller than Paranaguara Peak. Afterward, on account of how hard that hammock was, he slept across the women's bodies. And the night set him back four hunnerd smackeroos.

The hero's intellect was downright confounded. He awoke to the roaring of beasts in the streets below, zooming between the formidable malocas. And that great big devil of a sagui-açu that had carried him to the top of the towering tapiri in which he'd slept ... What a world of beasts! what a mess of grunting ogres, demonic mauaris blaring juruparis hopping sacis and fiery boitatás snaking through alleyways down subterranean pits on cables up hillsides gouged by huge grottoes outta which poured crowds cheek by jowl of the whitest of white people, most certainly the sons and daughters of manioc! ... The hero's intellect was downright confounded. The women had chuckled as they taught him how that great big sagui-açu wasn't a monkey at all, it was called an elevator and it was a machine. At day-break they taught him how that whole gaggle of peeps howls war-whoops blasts grunts thundering roars wasn't any of those at all, but was actually klaxons bells whistles horns and they were all machines. The pumas weren't pumas, they were called Fords Hupmobiles Chevrolets Dodges Marmons and they were machines. The tamanduás the boitatás the inajás all abloom with smoke plumes were actually trucks trolleys streetcars clocks traffic-lights neon-signs radios motorcycles telephones chisels lampposts chimneys ... They were machines and the whole city was made of machines! The hero took it in silently. Once in a while he trembled. Then he'd go still again listening conjecturing machinating in an awestruck reverie. He was seized with an envious respect for this truly powerful goddess, the renowned Tupã whom the children of manioc called Machine, who liked to sing even more than the Mother-of-Water, in a bewildering clamor.

So then he figured he'd go play around with the Machine so he'd be emperor of the children of manioc too. But the three women laughed themselves silly declaring all that stuff about gods to be a fat old lie, there wasn't any god at all and no one can play around with the machine cause it's deadly. The machine wasn't a god at all, it didn't even possess those distinctive feminine parts the hero liked so much. It was made by men. And set in motion by electricity by fire by water by wind by smoke, men taking advantage of the forces of nature. But did the alligator believe it? neither did the hero! He leaped out of bed and in one fell swoop, yessir! all puffed up with disdain, hmmph! thrust his left forearm into the crook of his other arm, jerked his right fist vigorously at the three women and took off. Right then, so they say, he invented that notoriously offensive gesture: the banana.

And off he went to live in a boarding house with his brothers. He got thrush in his mouth from that first night of Paulistano love. He moaned with pain and wasn't getting any better till Maanape nicked the key to a tabernacle for Macunaíma to suck on. The hero sucked and sucked and got better again. Maanape was a sorcerer.

Macunaíma then went a week without eating or playing just machinating on the no-win battles between the sons of manioc and the Machine. The Machine killed men but it was men who commanded the Machine . . . It dawned on him in amazement that the sons of manioc were masters with no mystery and no power of the machine with no mystery no desire no satiety, incapable of explaining any misfortunes. It made him nostalgic. Till one night, perched on the terrace of a skyscraper with his brothers, Macunaíma concluded:

"The sons of manioc can't beat the machine nor can the machine beat them in this battle. It's a draw."

He didn't come to any other conclusions seeing as he still wasn't used to speeches but throbbing inside him was the foggy notion, foggy indeed! that the machine must be a god that men could never truly master simply because they hadn't made her into an explicable Iara but rather a mere reality of the world. Out of all this brewing confusion his mind hailed a shining light: the men were machines and the machines were men. Macunaíma howled with laughter. He realized that he was free once more and felt an enormous satisfaction. He turned Jiguê into a telephone machine and called some cabarets, ordering up fresh lobsters and French girls.

Next day he was so spent from the bender that homesickness hit. He rcmembered the muiraquitã. And decided to act fast, for it's the first strike that kills the snake.

Venceslau Pietro Pietra lived in a magnificent tejupar surrounded by woods at the end of Rua Maranhão overlooking the shady slopes of neighboring Pacaembu. Macunaíma told Maanape he was gonna hop over there cause he was hankering to meet Venceslau Pietro Pietra. Maanape gave a speech enumerating the inconveniences of going over there cause that river peddler walked with his heels in front and if God had put the mark on him, it sure as heck wasn't on a whim. He was most indubitably a malevolent mauari demon . . . Who knew if he wasn't Piaimã the Giant, eater of men! . . . Macunaíma didn't wanna hear it.

"Well I'm going anyhow. They gimme respect wherever I'm known, and wherever I ain't, they will or they won't!"

So Maanape went along with his brother.

Behind the riverboat peddler's tejupar there lived the Dzalaúra-Iegue tree, which bears every kind of fruit, cashew cajá cajá-mango mango-mango pineapple avocado jaboticaba graviola sapodilla pupunha pitanga guajiru that smells like a black woman's armpit, ripe with all that fruit and tall as can be. The two brothers were hungry. They made a zaiacúti blind out of leafy branches gnawed by saúva ants, a hideout on the tree's lowest branch from where they could shoot arrows at all the game eating up the fruit. Maanape told Macunaíma:

"Look here, if a bird calls don't answer, brother, or else you can kiss it all goodbye!"

The hero nodded. Maanape started shooting his blowgun and Macunaíma scooped up the game raining down behind the zaiacúti. The game came crashing down with a ruckus as Macunaíma caught the monkeys marmosets monk-sakis muriquis mutum birds jacus jaós toucans tinamous, all that game. But the ruckus roused Venceslau Pietro Pietra from his leisurely snooze and he went to see what it was. And Venceslau Pietro Pietra was Piaimã the Giant, eater of men. He came to his front door and sang like a bird:

"Ogoró! ogoró! ogoró!"
as if a ways off. Macunaíma answered immediately:

"Ogoró! ogoró! ogoró!"
Maanape recognized the danger and murmured:

"Better hide, brother!"
The hero hid behind the zaiacúti among the dead game and ants. Then out came the giant.

"Who answered?"
Maanape replied:

"Dunno."

"Who answered?"

"Dunno."
Thirteen times. Then said the giant:

"It was a person. Show me who."
Maanape chucked down a dead tinamou. Piaimã gobbled up the tinamou and said:

"It was a person! Show me who!"
Maanape chucked down a dead monkey. Piaimã gobbled it up and went on:

"It was a person! Show me who!"
Then he spotted the hidden hero's pinky and aimed a baníni at it. There was a long moaning cry, yaaawp! and Macunaíma dropped to a crouch with the arrow buried in his heart. The giant said to Maanape:

"Toss down the person I just caught!"

Maanape tossed down guaribas jaós mutum birds, shore-mutum fava-mutum mutumporanga urus urumutum piaçocas, all that game but Piaimã kept gobbling em up then asking for the person he'd shot with his arrow. Maanape didn't want to give up the hero and chucked down more game. They went on like that for a long time and by then Macunaíma had died. Finally Piaimã let out a fearsome bellow:

"Maanape, sonny, cut the crap! Toss down the person I caught or else I'll kill you, you ol' rascal!"

Maanape really didn't want to chuck down his brother, so he desperately scooped up six animals all in one go, a monkey a tinamou a jacu a jacutinga a picota and a piaçoca, and tossed em to the ground shouting:

"Get a load of this six!"

Piaimã flew into a rage. He wrangled four timbers from the woods, an acapurana an angelim an apió and a carauá, and came bearing down on Maanape:

"Outta the way, you filthy pig! a gator ain't got no neck, an ant ain't got no pecs! can't trump my four clubs comin' atcha fast, you double-dealer of trick game!"

Then Maanape was scared outta his wits and flung, slap! the hero to the ground. And that's how Maanape and Piaimã invented the sublime card game known as truco.

Piaimã was appeased.

"That's the one."

He grabbed the deceased by a leg and dragged him along. He went inside the house. Maanape climbed down from the tree in despair. Heading after his deceased brother he ran into the little sarará ant named Cambgique. The sarará asked:

"Whatcha doing round here, pardner!"

"I'm going after the giant that killed my brother."

"I'm coming too."

Then Cambgique sucked up the hero's blood that was splattered on the ground and in the branches and showed Maanape the trail as he went along sucking up the drops.

They went in the house through the front hall and dining room, past the pantry out to the side porch and stopped at the basement. Maanape lit a jutaí torch so they could make their way down the pitch-dark stairs. They tracked the last drop of blood right to the door of the wine cellar. The door was shut. Maanape scratched his nose and asked Cambgique:

"Now what?!"

Then out from under the door came Zlezlegue the tick who asked Maanape:

"What now, pardner?"

"I'm going after the giant that killed my brother."

Zlezlegue said:

"Alright. Then shut your eyes, pardner." Maanape shut em.

"Open your eyes, pardner."

Maanape opened em and Zlezlegue the tick had turned into a Yale key, Maanape grabbed the key off the ground and opened the door. Zlezlegue turned back into a tick and gave these instructions:

"Get those bottles way up top and you'll win over Piaimã."

Then he vanished. Maanape grabbed ten bottles, opened em up and out came the most impeccable aroma. It was that famous cauim called Chianti. Then Maanape entered another room in the wine cellar. The giant was in there with his wife, an old caapora crone called Ceiuci who always smoked a pipe and was a big ol' glutton. Maanape gave the bottles to Venceslau Pietro Pietra, a chunk of Acará tobacco to the caapora, and the couple left the world behind.

The hero who'd been diced into twenty times thirty bits of crackling was bubbling in the boiling polenta. Maanape picked out the bits and bones and laid em on the concrete to air out. After they'd cooled, Cambgique the sarará ant poured the blood he'd slurped over em. Then Maanape wrapped all the bloody morsels in banana leaves, threw the bundle in a saddlebag and doubled back to the boarding house.

When he got there he set the basket at his feet blew smoke over it and out from the leaves came Macunaíma, still more corn mush than not, weak as can be. Maanape gave his brother some guaraná and he was fit as a fiddle once more. He shooed the mosquitoes and asked:

"What the heck happened to me?"

"Well, dearie, didn't I tell you not to go answering any bird calls?! indeed I did, so there you go! . . ."

The next day Macunaíma woke up with scarlet fever and spent the course of it thinking on how he needed a pistol machine to kill Venceslau Pietro Pietra. No sooner did he recover than he headed over to the English traders to ask for a Smith & Wesson. The Englishmen said:

"The pistols are still quite green but let's have a look in case there's a ripe one."

So they went to stand under the pistol tree. The Englishmen said:

"Now wait here. If a pistol drops, grab hold of it. But don't let it hit the ground!"

"Done."

The Englishmen went a-shaking a-shaking the tree and out fell a ripe pistol. The Englishmen said:

"That's a jolly good one."

Macunaíma thanked em and took off. He wanted the others to think he spoke English but couldn't even say "sweetheart," it was his brothers who knew how. Maanape wanted pistols bullets and whiskey too. Macunaíma advised him:

"Your English ain't so good, brother Maanape, you could go and come back awful sorry. Say you ask for a pistol and they give you preserves. Better let me go."

And he went to talk to the English again. Under the pistol tree the Englishmen went a-rustling a-rustling the branches but not a single pistol fell. So they went under the bullet tree, the Englishmen shook it and a whopping load of bullets rained down. Macunaíma let em hit the ground and scooped em up.

"Now for the whiskey," he said.

They went under the whiskey tree, the Englishmen shook it and out dropped two cases that Macunaíma caught in mid-air. He thanked the Englishmen and headed back to the boarding house. Once he got there he hid the two cases under the bed and went to have a word with his brother:

"I spoke English with em, brother, but there wasn't any pistols or whiskey on account of a whole line of jaguar ants came marching up and ate it all gone. Here's the bullets I brought. Now I'll give you my pistol and if anyone messes with me, ya shoot."

Then he turned Jiguê into a telephone machine, called up the giant and cursed his mother.

Chapter 6. *The French Lady and the Giant*

Maanape really liked coffee and Jiguê really liked sleeping. Macunaíma wanted to pitch a papiri for the three to live in but the papiri never got done. Their group effort always petered out cause Jiguê slept all day and Maanape sat around drinking coffee. The hero got mad. He grabbed a spoon, turned it into a little critter and said:

"Now go hide in the ground coffee. When brother Maanape comes to drink some, bite his tongue!"

Then picking up a cotton pillow, he turned it into a fuzzy white caterpillar and said:

"Now go hide in the hammock. When brother Jiguê comes to sleep, suck his blood!"

Maanape was already heading into the boarding house for more coffee. The critter pricked his tongue.

"Ouch!" went Maanape.

Macunaíma played dumb saying:

"Does it hurt, brother? When a critter pricks me, doesn't hurt a bit."

Maanape got mad. He sent the critter flying as he said:

"Scram, you pest!"

Then Jiguê went into the boarding house to catch some shuteye. The furry white grub sucked so much of his blood it turned pink.

"Ouch!" cried Jiguê.

And Macunaíma:

"Does it hurt, brother? Well I'll be darned! When a caterpillar bites me it actually feels good."

Jiguê got mad and sent the caterpillar flying as he said:

"Scram, you pest!"

And the three brothers went back to building the papiri. Maanape and Jiguê stood on one side and Macunaíma caught the bricks his brothers tossed over. Maanape and Jiguê were in a tizzy and wanted to get square with their brother. The hero didn't suspect a thing. Well now, Jiguê grabbed a brick but turned it into a hard leather ball so it wouldn't hurt as bad. He passed the ball to Maanape farther up and Maanape kicked it hard at Macunaíma. It flew smack into the hero's nose.

"Ow!" went the hero.

The brothers played dumb shouting:

"Aww! does it hurt, brother! Cause when we get hit by a ball, doesn't hurt one bit!"

Macunaíma got mad and sent the ball flying with a kick saying:

"Scram, you pain!"

He came over to where his brothers were standing:

"That's it, I'm done with this here papiri!"

And he turned bricks stones tiles hardware into a swarm of içá ants that descended on São Paulo for three days.

The critter landed in Campinas. The caterpillar landed over yonder. The ball landed in a field. And that's how Maanape invented the coffee leaf critter, Jiguê invented the pink bollworm and Macunaíma invented soccer, those three plagues.

Next day, with his thoughts ever fixed on that She-devil, the hero realized that he'd blown it once and for all and couldn't ever show his face again on Rua Maranhão cause now Venceslau Pietro Pietra knew exactly who he was. He let his imagination go roaming roaming and come 3 p.m. had an idea. He decided to fool the giant. He stuck a membi flute down his gullet, turned Jiguê into a telephone machine and phoned up Venceslau Pietro Pietra saying a French lady would like to speak with him in regards to a matter of a business machine. The giant answered why yes of course and that she could come over right this minute seeing as the old Ceiuci was out with their two daughters and that way they could talk business at their leisure.

So then Macunaíma borrowed from the boarding house madam some pairs of froufrou things, a rouge machine, a silk-stockings machine, a slip machine scented with sacaca bark, a girdle machine fragrant with lemongrass, a décolleté machine spritzed with patchouli, lacy fingerless glove machines, all them froufrou things, then he dangled two pointy banana flowers from his chest and got dressed up like that. To complete the look he smeared some blue dye from the campeche tree over his little kid eyelids which grew languid. All that stuff sure was heavy but he'd turned into the most beautiful French lady perfumed with jurema and a sprig of Paraguayan pine pinned onto her heaving patriotism to ward off the evil eye. And she set out for the palazzo of Venceslau Pietro Pietra. And Venceslau Pietro Pietra was Piaimã the Giant, eater of men.

On his way out the boarding house Macunaíma ran into a scissor-tailed hummingbird. He didn't like that bad omen one bit and considered ditching the rondayvoo but since a promise made is a debt unpaid, he did an incantation and kept going.

He got there to find the giant at the front gate, waiting. After several deep bows Piaimã picked the French lady's ticks and led her to the loveliest alcove with beams and rafters made from acaricoara and itaúba wood. The checkerboard parquet was made of dark muirapiranga and blond satinwood. The alcove was furnished with those famous crocheted white hammocks from Maranhão. Right in the center was a carved jacaranda table set with red-and-white porcelain dishes from Breves and ceramics from Belém, arranged on a lace tablecloth woven from banana fiber. Steaming in enormous clay vessels originally found in the caves along the Rio Cunani was tacacá with tucupi, soup made from a Paulista man out of the industrial freezers at the Continental meat-packing plant, alligator stew and polenta. The wines were a superior Ica varietal procured from Iquitos, an imitation port from Minas Gerais, an eighty-year-old caiçuma liqueur, ice-cold champagne from São Paulo and a genipap fruit cordial of great renown and foul as three days of rain. Adding the most charming decorative touch were those exquisite Falchi bonbons with colorful paper cutouts and cookies from Rio Grande piled high in shiny black bowls lacquered with cumaté sap and engraved with a pocketknife, sourced from Monte Alegre.

The French lady seated herself in a hammock and made dainty gestures as she began chewing. She was awfully hungry and dug in. Afterward she washed it all down with a glass of the premium vintage Ica and made up her mind to just waltz right in to the matter at hand. She asked straight out whether it was indeed true that the giant possessed a muiraquitã in the shape of an alligator. The giant left the room and came back holding a snail. And he pulled from it a green stone. It was the muiraquitã! Macunaíma felt a chill pass through him from so much emotion and realized he was gonna cry. But he covered it up, asking whether the giant might care to sell the stone. But Venceslau Pietro Pietra winked suggestively saying the stone wasn't for sale. So then the French lady begged him to let her take the stone home on loan. Venceslau Pietro Pietra winked suggestively again saying the stone couldn't go out on loan neither.

"You really think I'll give in after a coupla giggles, Mademoiselle? Come now!"

"But I want that stone ever so much! . . ."

"Well you can go on wanting it!"

"Why then I couldn't care less, Mr. River Peddler sir!"

"River peddler my foot, Mademoiselle! Bite your tongue! A collector is what I am!"

He left the room and came back carrying a humongous grajau woven from embira fiber and brimming with stones. There was turquoise emeralds beryl polished pebbles, rutile nuggets in needle formation, chrysolite teardrops ringing rocks emery stone pegmatites dove-egg quartz cat's-eye kyanite hatchets machetes chiseled arrowheads, gris-gris amulets jagged crags petrified elephants, Greek columns, Egyptian gods, Javanese Buddhas, obelisks Mexican tables, Guyanese gold, ornithomorphic stones from Iguape, opals from the Igarapé Alegre, rubies and garnets from the Rio Curupi, itamotingas from the Rio das Garças, itacolumite, tourmaline from Vupabuçu, hunks of titanium from the Rio Piriá, bauxite from the Riberão do Macaco, limestone fossils from Pirabas, pearls from Cametá, the humongous boulder that Oaque, Father of the Toucan, shot out his blowgun from that mountain on high, a lithoglyph from Calamare, all those stones were in that basket.

Then Piaimã told the French lady that he was a celebrated collector, he collected stones. And the French lady was Macunaíma, the hero. Piaimã confided that the jewel of his collection was precisely the muiraquitã in the shape of an alligator purchased for a thousand contos from the Empress of the Icamiabas on the faraway beaches of Lake Jaciuruá. And it was a whole pack of lies made up by the giant. Now then, he sidled up to the French lady in the hammock, right up close! and murmured that with him it was all or nothing, he wouldn't let the stone go up for sale or out on loan but he just might be liable to give it away . . . "So long as . . ." What the giant really wanted was to play around with the French lady. When the hero understood from Piaimã's manner what this "so long as" meant, he got real nervous. He wondered, "Does the giant actually think I'm a French lady?! . . . Get away, you shameless Peruvian!" And dashed out into the garden. The giant chased after him. The French lady dove into a bush to hide but there was a little black girl there. Macunaíma whispered to her:

"Caterina, get outta there wontcha?"

Caterina wouldn't budge. Macunaíma, getting cross with her, whispered:

"Caterina, get outta there or I'll hit you!"

The little mulatta just stood there. Then Macunaíma gave the brat a hearty slap and his hand stuck fast.

"Caterina, let go my hand and get outta here or I'll slap you silly, Caterina!"

But Caterina was a doll made of carnaúba palm wax that the giant had put there. She stood stock-still. Macunaíma slapped her again with his free hand and got stuck even worse.

"Caterina, Caterina! let go my hands and get outta here you nappyhead! or else I'll kick you!"

He kicked her and got stuck even worse. Eventually the hero got all tangled up in the little Catita. Then Piaimã showed up with a basket. He plucked the French lady from the trap and bellowed to the basket:

"Open your mouth, basket, open your big mouth!"

The basket opened its mouth and the giant dumped Macunaíma inside. The basket shut its mouth again, Piaimã brought it back home. Instead of a purse the French lady had been carrying a mênie quiver for blowgun darts. The giant set the basket down by the front door and went in the house to stash the mênie with his stone collection. But the mênie was made from cloth that reeked of game. This made the giant suspicious and he asked:

"Is your mama as plump and sweet-smelling as you, my pet?"

And rolled his eyes in delight. He reckoned that the mênie was the French lady's little tot. And the French lady was the hero Macunaíma. From inside the basket he heard the question and started getting exceedingly nervous. "So does this Venceslau guy really think I went under nature's rainbow and came out the other way? Get thee back, for crissake!" Then he blew on some cumacá root powder that frays rope, frayed the basket, and hopped out. While getting away he ran into the giant's mangy mutt Xaréu, named after a fish so he wouldn't catch hydrophobia. The hero was scared outta his wits and sped off like a shot into the park. The hound chased after him. They ran and ran. They passed right by Calabouço Point, headed for Guajará Mirim then veered east again.

Macunaíma made it to Itamaracá with just enough time to eat a dozen jasmine-mangos said to have sprung from the body of Dona Sancha. The two headed southwest and in the highlands of Barbacena the fugitive spotted a cow at the top of a steep lane paved with pointy cobblestones. He remembered to drink some milk. He was wise to stride up the middle of the flagstone path so he wouldn't get worn out but the cow was that feisty Guzerat breed. She hid her meager milk. But Macunaíma said a prayer that went like this:

> *Our Lady, give me strength,*
> *Oh Saint Anthony of Nazareth,*
> *Meek cows give their milk with ease,*
> *Feisty ones, only if they please!*

The cow was tickled, gave him some milk, and the hero shot off toward the south. Crossing Paraná already on his way back from the Pampas, he was itching to climb one of those trees but there came that yipping hot on his tail and gaining fast and the hero just couldn't shake that mangy mutt. He yelled:

"Outta my way, tree!"

And dodged every nut tree, every pau-d'arco, every cumaru good for climbing. Just past the city of Serra in Espírito Santo he nearly busted his head on a rock carved with lotsa paintings he couldn't understand. It had to be buried money ... But Macunaíma was in a hurry and darted off to the sandy riverbanks of the Isle of Bananal. Finally he spotted an anthill a hunnerd feet tall with an opening on the ground floor. He barged his way in wriggling up the hole and hid at the top. The mangy mutt sat back on its haunches ready to pounce.

Then the giant came and found his mutt cornering the anthill. The French lady had accidentally dropped a silver chain right at the entrance. "My precious treasure is here," the giant murmured. And then the mutt vanished. Piaimã yanked up an inajá palm roots and all, not a trace in the ground. He chopped the root bulb off the tree and stuck it in the hole to make the French lady come out. But did the alligator come out? neither did she! She opened her legs and the hero got impaled on the inajá, so they say. Seeing that the French lady really wasn't coming out, Piaimã went to get some pepper. He brought back a whole swarm of anaquilā ants, which is pepper for giants, stuck them in the hole, they stung the hero. But that didn't even make the French lady come out. Piaimā swore vengeance. He chucked the ants away and yelled at Macunaíma:

"Now I'm really gonna get you cause I'm gonna find Elitê the jararaca viper!"

This made the hero freeze. Ain't nothing you can do against the jararaca viper. He hollered at the giant:

"Hold on a sec, giant, I'm coming out."

However to buy some time he pulled the pointy banana flowers from his chest and put them at the mouth of the hole saying:

"But first take this out, pretty please."

Piaimā was so steaming mad that he hurled the banana flowers into the distance. Macunaíma kept a close eye on the giant's temper.

He took off the décolleté machine, placed it at the mouth of the hole, saying once more:

"Take this out, pretty please."

Piaimā flung the dress even farther. Then Macunaíma put the girdle machine out, then the shoes machine and so on with the rest of the clothes. At this point the giant was seething with rage. He tossed everything into the distance without even looking at what it was. Then ever so gently the hero put his yessiree-bob at the mouth of the hole and said:

"Now just take this last stinky gourd out for me."

Blind with rage Piaimā grabbed the yessiree-bob without seeing what it was and hurled the yessiree-bob, hero and all, a league and a half away. And he stood there waiting endlessly while the hero was already gaining the mororó trees in the distance.

He made it back to the boarding house in a doozy, asking the dog's blessing and calling the cat uncle, you had to see it! sweating buckets all banged up with fire in his eyes, huffing and puffing his lungs out. He took a breather and seeing as he was hungry enough to eat a horse, slapped together some baked mussels from Maceió, dried duck from Marajó and washed it all down with mocororó. He rested a spell.

Macunaíma was very upset. Venceslau Pietro Pietra was a celebrated collector and he wasn't. He was sweating with envy and finally made up his mind to do like the giant. But he didn't see any fun in collecting stones cause his land already had a whole crapload of em scattered throughout the towering peaks, in mountain springs rushing rapids rugged passes and alpine deposits. And all those stones had once been wasps ants mosquitoes ticks animals birdies folks ladies and girlies and even the charms of the ladies and girlies . . . What good is more stones when all they do is weigh you down! . . . He stretched his arms languidly and murmured:

"Ah! just so lazy! . . ."

He mulled it over mulled it over and made up his mind. He'd make a collection of bad-words which he liked so much.

He got right down to business. In a split-second he gathered zillions of em in all the living tongues and even in the Greek and Latin languages that he'd been studying a bit. His Italian collection was complete, with words for every time of day, every day of the year, every single life circumstance and human sentiment. Every foul mouthful! But the jewel of his collection was a phrase from India that you can't even say.

Chapter 7. *Macumba*

Macunaíma was very upset. He hadn't managed to recover the muiraquitã and this made him furious. Best thing to do was go kill Piaimã . . . So he left the city and went out to the So-and-So Forest to test his strength. He searched for a league and a half and finally spotted a peroba tree that went on and on. He stuck his arm into the massive tangle of roots and heaved with all his might to see if he could yank out the tree but only the wind rustled the leaves at the tippy top. "Nope, ain't strong enough yet," Macunaíma reckoned. Seizing a tooth from a little rat called crô, he made a big gash in his leg, as prescribed for weaklings, and headed back to the boarding house bleeding. He was feeling downhearted cause he wasn't strong yet and went along so awful distracted that he stubbed his toe. It hurt so bad that the hero saw the stars up above and in their midst he saw the crescent Capei cloaked in fog. "When the Moon's a-waning, you're best off refraining," he sighed. And it cheered him on his way.

Next day it was freezing cold and the hero decided to get revenge on Venceslau Pietro Pietra by giving him a good walloping to heat things up. But seeing as he wasn't strong he was scared as heck of the giant. So he decided to hop a train to Rio de Janeiro to get some help from Exu the devil in whose honor they were holding a Macumba ceremony the next day.

It was June and the weather was freezing cold. The Macumba was being held out in the Mangue area in that big ol' rowdy house run by Tia Ciata, a sorceress like no other, a renowned mãe-de-santo and guitar-picking songstress. Macunaíma got to that hole in the wall at eight o'clock in the evening with the requisite bottle of booze under his arm. There were lotsa folks there, upstanding folk, poor folk, lawyers garçons bricklayers apprentices congressmen crooks, all them folks, and the main event was just getting started. Macunaíma took off his socks and shoes like everyone else and slipped around his neck a milonga amulet made of tatucaba wasp wax and dried açacu root. He went into the crowded room and shooing away the mosquitoes dropped to all fours to pay his respects to the Candomblé priestess sitting motionless on a three-legged stool, not uttering a sound. Tia Ciata was an old black woman with a century of suffering, exceedingly tall and thin as a rail with white hair fanning out like rays round her petite head. Nobody could see her eyes anymore, she was just a buncha bones all hangingdangling drowsily to the ground.

Now then, a young son of Oxum, so they said, son of Our Lady of the Immaculate Conception whose Macumba celebration was held in December, went round passing out a lit candle to each and every one of the sailors joiners journalists fat-cats jerry-riggers hussies civil-servants, lotsa civil-servants! all them folks and he turned off the gas lamp lighting the room.

Then the Macumba ceremony really got going with everyone joining a sairê to hail the saints. And it went like this: At the head came the ogã playing the atabaque, a towering black son of Ogum, a pockmarked fado musician by profession, who went by the name of Olelê Rui Barbosa. The drum went poundingpounding a steady rhythm that guided the whole procession. And the candles cast slow wavering shadows like ghosts onto the floral wallpaper. Behind the ogã came Tia Ciata barely moving, just her lips chanting the prayer in monotone. Following her came lawyers deckhands healers poets the hero crooks senators Portagees, all them folks dancing and singing in response to the prayer. And it went like this:

"Let's-go sa-ra-vá! . . ."

Tia Ciata sang the name of the saint they were hailing:

"Oh Olorung!"

And the folks replying:

"Let's-go sa-ra-vá! . . ."

Tia Ciata kept going:

"Oh Dolphin-Tucuxi!"

And the folks replying:

"Let's-go sa-ra-vá! . . ."

Softly chanting in steady monotone.

"Oh Iemanjá! Anamburucu! and Oxum! three Mothers-of-Water!"

"Let's-go sa-ra-vá! . . ."

Like that. And when Tia Ciata came to a halt shouting with a sweeping gesture:

"Come out Exu!"

for Exu was the limping devil, a malevolent bealseybub, but good nevertheless for playing dirty tricks, a tumult afflicted the room howling:

"Oohwoo! . . . oohwoo! . . . Exu! Our father Exu! . . ." And the name of the devil resounded with a thundering boom, dwindling the immense night out there. The sairê went on:

"Oh King Nagô!"

"Let's-go sa-ra-vá! . . ."

Chanting softly in that monotone.

"Oh Baru!"

"Let's-go sa-ra-vá! . . ."

When all of a sudden Tia Ciata came to a halt shouting with a sweeping gesture:

"Come out Exu!"

for Exu was ol' splitfoot, a malevolent jananaíra. And once more came that tumult afflicting the room howling:

"Oohwoo! . . . Exu! Our father Exu! . . ."

And the name of the devil resounded with a thundering boom cutting short the night.

"Oh Oxalá!"

"Let's-go sa-ra-vá! . . ."

So it went. They hailed all the saints of the Pajelança ceremony, the White River Dolphin who brings love, Xangô, Omulu, Iroco, Oxosse, the fierce Mother Boiuna, Obatalá who gives strength for lotsa playing around, all them saints, and the sairê was done. Tia Ciata sat on her three-legged stool in a corner and all them sweaty folks, doctors bakers engineers shysters cops maids hack reporters hit men Macunaíma, they all came over to set their candles round the stool. The candles cast the shadow of the motionless mãe-de-santo onto the ceiling. Most everybody had already peeled off some clothes and was wheezing on account of the smell mingling animal musk Coty perfume fishy fumes together with all their sweat. Then it came time to drink. And that's when Macunaíma had his very first taste of that formidable caxiri that goes by the name of cachaça. He tasted it smacking his lips with glee and burst into laughter.

After that drink, in between drinks, came the chanting invocations. Everybody was restless, ardently yearning for a saint to show up to that evening's Macumba. It had been a while since any had come no matter how much the others prayed. Because Tia Ciata's Macumba wasn't one of them fake Macumbas, nossir, where the pai-de-terreiro was always pretending that any ol' Xangô or Oxosse whoever had shown, just to satisfy the Macumbeiros. Hers was a serious Macumba and when saints appeared, they appeared for real without no hocus-pocus. Tia Ciata wouldn't let anyone tarnish the reputation of her house like that and it had been twelve months and counting since either Ogum or Exu had appeared out there in the Mangue. Everyone was a-yearning for Ogum to show. Macunaíma wanted Exu just so he could get revenge on Venceslau Pietro Pietra.

Between sips of the first round, some kneeling, others on all fours, all them half-naked folks chanted in a circle round the sorceress praying for a saint to appear. At midnight they went inside to eat the goat whose head and hooves were already in the peji shrine room, in front of the effigy of Exu that was an ant nest with three shells for his eyes and mouth. The goat had been killed in the devil's honor and seasoned with powdered horn and the spurs of a fighting cock. The mãe-de-santo kicked off the feasting, respectfully making the sign of the cross three times. All them folks vendors bibliophiles bums academics bankers, all them folks dancing round the table were singing:

> *Bamba querê*
> *Come out Aruê*
> *Mongi gongô*
> *Come out Orobô*
>   *Hey!* . . .

> *Oh mungunzá*
> *Good acaçá*
> *C'mon Nhamanja*
> *From Pai Guenguê,*
>   *Hey!* . . .

And while chatting carousing they devoured the consecrated goat and every one of em was looking round for his own bottle of booze cause nobody was s'posed to go drinking from nobody else's, they were all drinking lotsa rum, a whole lot! Macunaíma was howling with laughter and suddenly spilled wine on the table. It was a sign of boundless joy for him and everyone thought the hero was the chosen one on that holy night. Nope, wasn't him.

No sooner had the chanting started back up than they saw a hussy leap into the middle of the room hushing them all with her wailing moan and starting up a new song. A tremor went through everyone and the candles cast the young woman's shadow into a corner of the ceiling looking just like a writhing monster, it was Exu! The ogã struggled to catch the crazy rhythms of this new song with the beat of his tabaque drum, a free melody, full of breathless notes arduously jumping octaves, a raving mad low-pitched ecstasy a-trembling furiously. And the Polack tart with the painted face, her slip straps torn off, was shuddering in the middle of the room, her fat rolls almost entirely bared. Her breasts went swingalinging slapping her shoulders her face then her belly, thwap! with a thundering boom. And that redhead there just singing and singing. Finally as foam flecked from her smeared lips, she let out a shriek that dwindled the immense night even more, swooned onto the saint and lay rigid.

A span of sacred silence passed. Then Tia Ciata rose from her stool so a little mazomba girl could swap it out quick for a fresh seat never been used, now it was auntie's. The mãe-de-ter-reiro came closer came closer. The ogã came with her. Everyone else was leaning up against the wall. Only Tia Ciata came closer came closer and got up real close to the Polack tart's body lying rigid right smack in the middle of the room. The sorceress took off all her clothes, stark naked, with nothing but her necklaces bracelets silver-beaded earrings dripping over her bones. From the gourd bowl that the ogã brought over she started spooning the curdled blood from the devoured goat and rubbing the paste on the head of the babalaô. But when she poured the greenish efém from above, the stiff lady started writhing and moaning and the air went heady with an iodine stench. Then the mãe-de-santo intoned Exu's sacred prayer, a monotone melopoeia.

When it was all over, the hussy opened her eyes, started moving a whole lot different than just-today and wasn't a hussy no more, she was the saint's horse, it was Exu. It was Exu, the impish trickster who'd come to join them for some Macumba.

The pair of naked women improvised a festive jongo, keeping time to the popping of the old auntie's bones, the thwapping of the fat lady's breasts and the ogã slapping on the drums. Everyone else was naked too and waiting for the Son of Exu to be chosen by the great Hellhound in their presence. That fearsome jongo . . . Macunaíma quivered in anticipation hoping for the Cariapemba spirit so he could request a good licking for Venceslau Pietro Pietra. Nobody knows what got into him all of a sudden, he started dodging and weaving into the middle of the room knocked Exu over and fell on top of him playing around in triumph. And the consecration of this new Son of Exu was celebrated with everybody's approval and they all anointed themselves with urari powder in honor of the Icá devil's new son.

Once the ceremony ended the devil was brought over to the stool, inaugurating the adoration. The thieves the senators the bumpkins the blacks the old ladies the soccer pros, all of em, went dragging themselves around under the powdery dust turning the room orange, and after pounding the left side of their heads on the ground, they kissed the knees kissed the uamoti demon's whole body. The rigid red Polack a-trembling foam flecking her mouth in which they all were wetting their flea-squishers to bless themselves with the sign of the cross, went moaning out guttural grunts half sobbing half squealing in ecstasy and she wasn't a Polack tart no more, it was Exu, the almightiest Jurupari of that religion.

After everybody kissed worshipped and blessed themselves a bunch, it was time for pleas and promises. A butcher asked for everyone to buy his spoiled meat and Exu granted it. A farmer asked for no more ants or malaria on his land and Exu laughed saying no way would he grant that. A loverboy asked for his girl to get a job as a schoolteacher so they could get married and Exu granted it. A doctor gave a whole spiel asking to write spoken Portuguese with the utmost elegance and Exu did not grant that. And so on. Finally it came turn for Macunaíma, the fiend's new son. And Macunaíma said:

"I came to ask my father for something on account of I'm very upset."

"What's your name," asked Exu.

"Macunaíma, the hero."

"Hmm ...," muttered the big boss, "names that begin with Ma are a malediction ..."

But he took a shine to the hero and promised to grant all that he asked seeing as Macunaíma was his son. And the hero asked for Exu to bring suffering upon Venceslau Pietro Pietra who was Piaimã the Giant, eater of men.

And what happened next was horrible. Exu grabbed three sprigs of lemon balm blessed by an apostasized priest, tossed them in the air, made a cross, sending Venceslau Pietro Pietra's I into Exu himself to get beat up. He waited a moment, the giant's I came, entered the hussy and Exu ordered his son to beat up the I incarnated in that Polack body. The hero grabbed a crossbar and swung at Exu with all his might. The blows rained down. Exu cried:

> Go slow when you whack me!
> Cause it hurts ow ow ow!
> I've got a family, you see
> And it hurts ow ow ow!

Finally, all black and blue from the pummeling bleeding from the nose the mouth the ears he fell to the ground unconscious. And it was horrible ... Macunaíma ordered the giant's I to take a bath in boiling saltwater and Exu's body started steaming getting the ground all wet. And Macunaíma ordered the giant's I to go walking on broken glass through a bramblewood of nettles and cats-claw vines to the high passes of the Andes in midwinter and Exu's body bled from where the shards had slashed the thorns had scratched and the nettles had pricked, panting with exhaustion and shivering from the freezing cold. It was horrible. Then Macunaíma ordered Venceslau Pietro Pietra's I to get butted by a charging bull, kicked by a bucking bronco, bit by a gator and stung by forty times forty thousand fire ants and Exu's body writhed bleeding blistering on the ground, with a row of teeth in one leg, ant stings covering his now-invisible skin, his forehead split open from a bronco's hoof and a gash in his belly from a sharp horn. The room filled with an intolerable stench. And Exu moaned:

> *Go slow when you gore me*
> *Cause it hurts ow ow ow!*
> *I've got a family, you see*
> *And it hurts ow ow ow!*

Macunaíma gave a whole lotta orders like that for a whole lotta time and Venceslau Pietro Pietra's I bore the brunt of it through Exu's body. Finally the hero's vengeance couldn't come up with anything else and he stopped. The hussy was breathing faintly sprawled on the dirt floor. There was an exhausted silence. And it was horrible.

Over at the palazzo on Rua Maranhão in São Paulo there was a constant flurry hither and thither. Doctors came the ambulance came everybody was beside themselves frantic. Venceslau Pietro Pietra was roaring bleeding all over. His belly was showing a gouge from a horn, his forehead was split from what looked like a colt's hoof, he was burned frozen bitten and all covered in welts and bruises from getting the living daylights beat out of him with a stick.

At the Macumba ceremony the horrified silence went on. Tia Ciata proceeded gracefully and started reciting the supreme devil's prayer. It was the most sacrilegious prayer of them all, one word out of place was deadly, the prayer of Our Father Exu, and it went like this:

"Father Exu of our very own, who art in the thirteenth hell on the left down below, we shall adore thee greatly, each and every one of us!"

"We shall adore thee! we shall adore thee!"

". . . Give us this day our daily Father Exu, thy will be done, as it is on the grounds of the sanzala that belongs to our Father Exu, for ever and ever, amen! . . . Glory be to the Jeje fatherland of Exu!"

"Glory be to the son of Exu!"

Macunaíma said thank you. The old auntie ended with:

"Chico-t was a Jeje prince who became our Father Exu and ever shall be, world without end, amen."

"For ever and ever, amen!"

Exu started healing healing, all that stuff vanished magically as the rum went round and the Polack tart's body became hale and hearty once more. A big hullabaloo was heard and the scent of burning pitch seized the space as the hussy expelled a jet ring from her mouth. Then she came to, all ruddy and fat but clear worn out and now it was just the Polack tart there, Exu had gone.

And to bring it all to a close everyone made merry together feasting on excellent ham and dancing a spirited samba in which all them folks reveled whooping it up lustily. Then it all ended up becoming real life. And the Macumbeiros, Macunaíma, Jayme Ovalle, Dodô, Manu Bandeira, Blaise Cendrars, Ascenso Ferreira, Raul Bopp, Antônio Bento, all them Macumbeiros set out into the dawn.

Chapter 8. *Vei, the Sun*

Macunaíma was walking along and came upon the very tall tree Volomã. On a branch was a pitiguari bird who, soon as he spotted the hero, opened his gullet singing: "Look who's a-coming down the road! Look who's a-coming down the road!" Macunaíma looked up intending to say thank you but there was Volomã bursting with fruit. The hero had been starving for hours and his belly balked at the sight of those sapotas sapodillas sapotis bacuris apricots mucajás miritis guabijus melons ariticums, all that fruit.

"Volomã, gimme some fruit," Macunaíma asked.

The tree didn't want to. So the hero shouted twice:

"Boiôiô, boiôiô! quizama quizu!"

All the fruit fell and he ate his fill. Volomã was furious. He grabbed the hero by the feet and hurled him past Guanabara Bay onto a deserted little island, inhabited in times of yore by Alamoa the nymph who came over with the Dutch. Macunaíma was positively drooping with exhaustion and nodded off in mid-air. He landed fast asleep under a very fragrant guairô palm atop which a vulture was perched.

Now the bird had to do its business, went, and the hero was left dripping in the vulture's muck. It was already near-dawn and freezing cold. Macunaíma woke up shivering, completely soiled. All the same he took a good look around that peewee rock of an islet to see if there might be any caves with buried money. Nope there weren't.

Not even that enchanted silver chain that leads the finder to Dutch treasure. Nothing but little red jaquitagua fire ants.

Then Caiuanogue, the morning star, passed by. Macunaíma was sorta fed up by now from so much living and asked if she'd carry him up to the sky. Caiuanogue approached but the hero stank to high heaven.

"Go take a bath!" she said. And took off.

And that's how the expression "Go take a bath!" came to be, which Brazilians use when referring to certain European immigrants.

Capei the Moon was passing by. Macunaíma shouted at her:

"Bless me, Nanny Moon!"

"Mm-hmm . . ." she replied.

So then he asked the Moon to carry him to the Isle of Marajó. Capei started approaching but the hero really stank like the dickens.

"Go take a bath!" she said. And took off.

And the expression stuck definitively.

Macunaíma shouted at Capei to at least give him a little fire to keep warm.

"Ask the neighbor!" she said pointing to the Sun who was already approaching from a distance rowing across the vast sea. And took off.

Macunaíma was shivering and shivering and the vulture kept doing its business right on top of him. It was on account of that rock being so teeny-tiny. Vei came closer all red and slick with sweat. And Vei was the Sun. That was just fine and dandy for Macunaíma since back home he always used to make little cassava cake offerings for the Sun to lick dry.

Vei brought Macunaíma onto her raft which had a rust-colored sail dyed with muruci berries and made her three daughters get the hero washed up, pick his ticks and check that his nails were clean. And Macunaíma was nice and neat once more. However on account of her being an old lady all red and sweating buckets

Macunaíma didn't suspect that the old bag was actually the Sun, good ol' Sun, the poor man's poncho. That's how come he asked her to call Vei over with her heat cause he was squeaky clean but shivering cold. Vei was really the Sun and scheming to make Macunaíma her son-in-law. Thing was, she couldn't warm anyone up just yet, cause it was too early, she didn't have the strength. To stall for time she whistled a special way and her three daughters fell to petting and tickling the hero all over.

He squealed with laughter, squirming under their stroking and enjoying himself mightily. Whenever they stopped he'd beg for more, writhing on the verge of ecstasy. Vei caught sight of the hero's shamelessness, lost her temper. She didn't much feel like pulling fire from her body and heating anyone up. Then the girls grabbed their mother, tied her up tight and Macunaíma socked the old hag's belly a buncha times as a little flame came puff-puffing out from behind and everybody got warm.

A sweltering heat started up that seized the raft, spread out over the waters and gilded the air's clear cheek. Macunaíma lay on the raft lizarding there in a blue languor. And the silence expanding everything . . .

"Ah . . . just so lazy . . ."

the hero sighed. You could hear the murmuring waves, that's it. A contented torpor flowed through Macunaíma's body, so good . . . The youngest girl played the urucungo her mother had brought from Africa. The sea was vast and there wasn't a cloud in the glittering mineral sky. Macunaíma crossed his wrists behind his head with his hands for a pillow and, as the eldest daughter of light shooed the swarming mosquitoes, the third little China girl used the pointy ends of her braids to make the hero's belly quiver with pleasure. And laughing with utmost joy, then bursting into bliss from verse to verse, he sang:

> *When I'm dead and buried, don't you cry for me,*
> *I'll leave this life with nary a sigh;*

—Mandu sarará . . .
My only pa was exile,
My ma was misery,
—Mandu sarará . . .

Oh Papa came and told me:
"You'll never find true love!"
—Mandu sarará . . .
Then Mama came and gave me
A necklace made of woe,
—Mandu sarará . . .

May the armadillo dig a grave
With his lil toothless teeth,
—Mandu sarará . . .
For the sorriest wretch
That you ever did see,
—Mandu sarará . . .

Life was good . . . His body gleamed with gold glinting in the crystalline specks of salt, and on account of the sea air, on account of Vei's sluggish paddling and with his belly getting rile-riled from a woman's tickling touch, ah! . . . Macunaíma burst into our ecstasy of ecstasies, ah! . . . "Holy hot damn! . . . what a daughter of . . . of scrumptious delights, hoo boy!" he shouted. And shutting his roguish eyes, grinning the grin of a naughty ragamuffin living it up, the hero went on basking basking in it and fell fast asleep.

When Vei's jacumã paddle stopped rocking his slumber to and fro, Macunaíma woke up. What stood out most in the distance was a rosy pink skyscraper. The raft was moored at the fishing docks of the sublime maloca of Rio de Janeiro.

Right there on the waterfront was a long expanse of savanna densely lined with Brazilwood trees and colorful palazzos on both sides. And that savanna was Avenida Rio Branco. That's where Vei the Sun lived with her three daughters of light. Vei wanted Macunaíma to be her son-in-law since he was a hero after all and had offered her so many cassava cakes to lick dry, so she said:

"My dear son-in-law: you must marry one of my daughters. For a dowry I'll give you Yerup France 'n Bahia. But you gotta be faithful, don't go playing around with other girls all over town."

Macunaíma thanked her and promised he'd be true, swearing on the memory of his mother. Then Vei set off with her three daughters to make the day out on the savanna, ordering Macunaíma one more time not to leave the raft so he wouldn't go playing around with other girls all over town. Macunaíma promised again, swearing on his mother once more.

No sooner did Vei and her three daughters reach the savanna than Macunaíma was filled with the desire to go play around with a girl. He lit a cigarette and desire rose up. Out there flocks of purty chick chick chickadees were strolling beneath the trees shimmyshimmying with such beauty and verve.

"Burn it all down!" Macunaíma shouted. "I ain't a sissy man now who lets a woman do me wrong!"

And a vast light shone in his brain. He stood on the raft and with his arms waving over this country solemnly declared:

"ANTS APLENTY AND NOBODY'S HEALTHY, SO GO THE ILLS OF BRAZIL!"

He leaped from the raft in a flash, went off to salute the statue of Saint Anthony, who was captain of the regiment, then started coming on to girls all over town. Soon enough he met a broad who'd been a fishwife back in the land of that ol' ditty "Compadre Chegadinho" and what's more, still smelled like it too! boy did she reek of fish. Macunaíma winked at her and the two came back to the raft to play around. So they did. It was plenty of playing around. Now there they are laughing with each other.

When Vei and her three daughters came home from the day

and it was night-fall, the young ladies got there first and found Macunaíma and the Portuguese girl playing some more. Then the three daughters of light flew into a rage:

"So that's how you do it, hero! Why, didn't our mama Vei tell you not to leave the raft and go playing around with other girls all over town?!"

"I was so awfully blue!" went the hero.

"Don't gimme that boo hoo, I was so blue, hero! Now you're gonna get a tongue lashing from our mama Vei!"

And they turned fuming to the old lady:

"Look, Mama Vei, lookit what your son-in-law did! Soon as we went off to the savanna he snuck out, started coming on to some dish, brought her back to our raft and they played around till they couldn't no more! Now there they are laughing with each other!"

So then the Sun flared up and laid into him:

"Well well well, dearie! Now didn't I tell you not to go coming on to any girls?! . . . Indeed I did! And on top of that you go and play around with her right here on my raft and now there you are laughing with each other!"

"I was so awfully blue!" Macunaíma repeated.

"Why, if you'd listened to me you'd have married one of my daughters and you'd be young and handsome forever and ever. Now you won't be young for long, just like all the other fellas and soon enough you'll be old and ugly as sin."

Macunaíma felt like he was gonna cry. He sighed:

"If only I'd known . . ."

"Your 'if only I'd known' is the saint that never did nothing for nobody, dearie! You've been real naughty, yessir! I'm not giving you any of my three daughters no more!"

So then Macunaíma fanned the flames higher:

"You know, I didn't want any of them three anyway! The devil comes in threes!"

Then Vei and her three daughters went to go find a hotel and left Macunaíma to sleep with the Portagee on the raft.

When it was just about time for dawn, the Sun and her girls came for a stroll round the bay and found Macunaíma and the Portuguese girl still sound asleep. Vei woke the pair and presented Macunaíma with the Vató stone. And the Vató stone makes fire whenever folks want. And off went the Sun with her three daughters of light.

Macunaíma spent the day playing around with the fishwife all over town. When night-time came they were sleeping on a bench in the Flamengo district when a terrifying phantom appeared. It was Mianiquê-Teibê come to swallow up the hero. He breathed through his fingers, listened through his belly button and had eyes where his nipples ought to be. His mouth was two mouths, hidden in the folds between his toes. The phantom's stench woke Macunaíma and he hightailed it outta Flamengo. So Mianiquê-Teibê ate the fishwife and took off.

The next day Macunaíma no longer took a shine to the capital of the Republic. He traded his Vató stone for a picture in the paper and went back to the taba on the Igarapé Tietê.

Chapter 9. *Letter to the Icamiabas*

To our most cherished subjects, Mesdames Amazons.
The Thirtieth of May, One Thousand Nine Hundred and Twenty-Six,
São Paulo.

Mesdames:

It shall cause you no small astonishment, to be sure, to note the address and contents of this missive. It is incumbent upon us, notwithstanding, to commence these lines of longing and utmost affection, with unpleasant tidings. 'Tis indeed true that in the good city of São Paulo—the greatest in the universe, as its prolix inhabitants are wont to declare—ye are not known as "Icamiabas," a spurious locution, but rather by the appellation of Amazons; and in regards to you, 'tis averred, that ye mount bellicose stallions and hail from classical Hellas; and thus are ye called. Such absurdities of erudition have weighed heavily upon us, your Imperator, yet nonetheless shall ye herewith be in agreement with us that, thusly, do ye become all the more heroic and prominent, burnished with that respectable platina of tradition and ancient purity.

Yet we ought not to while away your ferocious time, much less conturbate your comprehension, with reports of poor calibre; let us proceed, thus, immediately, to the relating of our exploits down here.

Not five suns had come and gone since we took leave of you,

when the most dreadful misfortune befell Us. One fair evening on the ides of May in the year set down, we lost the muiraquitã; which others have spelled as *muraquitã*, and, certain learned gentlemen, ever vigilant of extravagant etymologies, orthographize as *muyrakitan* and even *muraqué-itã*, laugh not! Ye shall know that said vocable, so familiar to your Eustachian tubes, is virtually unheard of here. Throughout these highly civilized parts, the warriors are called policemen, traffic cops, civic-guards, boxers, legalists, rabblerousers, etc.; a portion of these terms being preposterous neologisms—nefarious rubbish by which derelicts and dandies do besmirch good Lusitanian speech. Yet we have not the leisure to go rambling on for the purposes of discoursing "sub tegmine fagi," upon the Portuguese language, also known as Lusitanian. It shall be of surpassing interest to you, most assuredly, to discover that the warriors from here do not seek out warlike damsels in epithalamic union; rather they do prefer those who are docile and easily won in exchange for volatile little pieces of paper that would in vulgar parlance be called money—the "curriculum vitae" of Civilization, to which we presently make it a point of honor to belong. Therefore, the word *muiraquitã*, which presently wounds the Latinate ears of your Emperor, remains unknown to these warriors, and to all who generally respire hereabouts. Only a select few "individuals of importance in virtue and letters," as that fine old classical Friar Luís de Sousa hath declared, as cited by Dr. Rui Barbosa, persist in casting their light upon these muiraquitãs, so as, in turn, to appraise them to be of but middling value, deriving from Asia, and not from your fingers, that do give them a rough polish.

We were still grievous stricken of heart from having lost our muiraquitã, saurian in form, when perchance due to some metapsychic confluence, or, qui lo sá, provoked by some manner of nostalgic libido, as expounded by the Teutonic sage, Dr. Sigmund Freud (pronounced Froyd), there appeared to us in a dream a wondrous archangel. It was through him that we thereupon discovered that the lost talisman, lay in the esteemed hands of Sir Venceslau Pietro Pietra, subject of the Viceroyalty of Peru, and of frankly Florentine descent, like to the Cavalcantis of Pernambuco. And given that this gentleman did reside in the illustrious city of Father Anchieta, we departed hither posthaste, in pursuit of the stolen fleece. Our present relations with Sir Venceslau remain as favorable as possible; and undoubtedly shall ye in brief time receive the felicitous tidings that we shall have recovered the talisman; *whereupon we shall claim our reward of you.*

Because, esteemed subjects, it stands without contest that We, your Imperator, should find ourselves in a most precarious condition. As regards the treasure that we brought from there, it became imperative upon us to convert it into the prevailing currency of this country; and such conversion hath rendered our livelihood most difficult to maintain, owing to fluctuations of the Exchange Rate and cacao beans going bust.

Ye shall know further that the ladies hereabouts do not get clubbed head over heels into submission nor do they play around merely for the sake of playing, gratuitously, but rather when plied with outpourings of base metal, *champagne* gushing from emblazoned fountains, and comestible monsters, vulgarly bestowed with the name of lobster. And what enchanting monsters, Mesdames Amazons!!! From a polished and rubescent carapace, formed in the style of a ship's hull, there emerge arms, tentacles, and oarlike tail, of diverse aspect; so that the ponderous contraption, when placed on a dish of Sèvres porcelain, doth conjure before our very eyes some such trireme galley gliding wanton down the waters of the Nile, bearing in its protruding belly the inestimable body of Cleópatra.

Pay close heed to the accentuation of this vocable, Mesdames Amazons, for heavy should it weigh upon us were ye not to share our preference, for this pronunciation, in accordance with the lessons of the classics, contrariwise to the pronunciation as Cleopátra, in more modern diction; and to which certain vocabulists frivolously subscribe, failing to perceive that 'tis but contemptible residua, brought over, in that torrent from France, by those Gallicists of ill repute.

Hence it is by means of this delicate monster, vanquisher of the most delicate palatines, that the ladies here do tumble into the nuptial bed. *It thus behooves you to comprehend what manner of reward whereof we speak*; for these lobsters are marvelous dear, dearest subjects, and we have acquired a portion at the cost of over sixty contos; which, converted into our traditional currency, is tantamount to the voluminous sum of eighty million cacao beans ... Ye may well conceive, then, how much we have already spent; and that we are forthwith in dire need of that base metal, so as to play around with such difficult damsels. Verily did we wish to impose an abstinence upon our ardent flame, no matter the suffering, so as to spare you the expense; yet what stalwart will hath not yielded before the enchantments and coquetries of such pleasing shepherdesses!

They go about clothed in scintillating jewels and the finest of fabrics, which accentuate their graceful bearing, and barely cover their charms, which, yield to no other in shapely splendour and hue. They are always exceedingly pale, the ladies here; and such is the great variety and nature of talents that they exhibit when it comes to playing around, that to enumerate them, herewith, would mayhap be tedious; and would, most certainly, violate the dictates of discretion, as is requisite in the relation of an Imperator unto his subjects. What beauties! What elegance! What *cachet*! What flammiferous, ignivomous, devouring *dégagé*!! Our thoughts are ever fixed on them, even as our attention never lapses, , unmindful, from our muiraquitã.

For our own part, it appeareth, illustrious Amazons, that ye would profit much in learning from them, the acquiescence, games, and wiles of Love. Thereupon would ye abandon your proud and solitary Law, in favor of more amorous occupations, in which the Kiss sublimates, Voluptuosities incandesce, and the subtle force of the *Odor di Fêmia*, as the Italians write it, is made manifest in all its glory, "urbi et orbe."

And insomuch as we have lingered thus upon this delicate subject, we shall not abandon it anon without some further observations, which may indeed prove useful to you. The ladies of São Paulo, in addition to being most comely and wise, content themselves not with the gifts and excellence that Nature hath bestowed upon them; they are greatly preoccupied with their selves; and should not have been able to accomplish their finishing touches, had they not procured from all four corners of the globe, all that which is most sublime and genteel after having been purified in the crucible of the fescennine, that is, the feminine science of ancestral civilizations. Thus do they summon mistresses from old Europe, especially from France, and do learn from them how to pass the time in a manner quite contrary to yours. At times they cleanse themselves, devoting hours to this delicate occupation, at times they dazzle the convivial society at theatre gatherings, at times they do nothing at all; and spend their days so industriously entwined in these labours that, when night descends, they possess hardly the leisure to play around, and hastily deliver themselves unto the arms of Orpheus, as they say. But ye shall know, my dear mesdames, that hereabouts, day and night diverge most singularly from the bellicose hours that ye keep; the day commences at a time that for you would be its peak, and the night, when ye are in your fourth slumber, which, being the final one, is the most restorative.

In all this have the Paulistano ladies been instructed by the mistresses from France; and in the polishing and lengthening of their nails withal, as well as, "horresco referens," the further lengthening of certain horned parts of their lawful companions. Pray avert your eyes from this most florid of ironies!

Much more is there still to relate to you on the manner whereby they shear their locks, in a style so charming and virile, that they more resemble ephebes and Antinous, perversely recalled, than matrons of such direct Latin lineage. Notwithstanding, you shall be in agreement with us, as concerns the unsuitability of long plaits here, should you heed the aforementioned; given that the gentlemen of São Paulo do not fell their objects of courtship by force, but rather in exchange for gold and locustas, said locks are but trifling; besides which, moreover, this style doth quell certain ills, as such locks do harbour, in providing habitation and routine pasture for insects most ruinous, as doth occur amongst yourselves.

Thus not being satisfied by what they have learned from France, of subtleties and artful gallantry à la Louis XV, the Paulistano ladies import from the more inhospitable regions whatsoever may further enhance their savour, such as little Nippon slippers, rubies from India, North American brazenness; as well as various other international teachings and treasures.

Now shall we speak to you at greater length, albeit superficially, of a resplendent herd of gentlewomen, originating from Poland, who dwell hereabouts and reign with generosity. They are quite robust in build and more numerous than sands in the oceanic sea. Like unto you, Mesdames Amazons, these damsels form a gynaeceum; the men who inhabit these houses being therein reduced to slaves, and condemned to the ignoble function of serving them. By reason whereof they are not called men, responding only to the spurious locution of *garçons*; and they are passing polite and silent, always dressed in the same solemn attire.

These damsels live ensconced in a single locale, known hereabouts as the quarter, also called boarding houses or the "redlight district"; duly noting that the latter expression would not be appropriate, owing to its coarseness, in this report on matters in São Paulo, were it not for our eagerness to be precise and knowledgeable. Howsoever if, like you, these dear ladies form a clan of women, indeed do they diverge greatly from you in physique, way of life, and ideals. Thus shall we inform you that they live by night, and neither give themselves over to the errands of Mars nor burn their left breast, but rather pay court to Mercury alone; and as for their breasts, they let them evolve, akin to gigantic and flaccid pomes, which, if adding not to their graceful bearing, do indeed serve in numerous and arduous labours of excellent virtue and prodigious excitation.

Further still is their physique distinguished, monstrous as it may be, albeit a lovable monstrosity, in that their brains are located in their pudendal parts, and they have, as is so well put in madrigalesque language, their heart in their hands.

They speak numerous languages most swift of tongue; they are well-travelled and exceedingly refined; and they remain uniformly obedient, though richly disparate amongst themselves, some fair, some dark, some are *maigres*, some rotund; and so abundant are they in number and diversity, that verily doth it trouble our reason, that all this great many, should derive originally from a single country. Moreover, all are bestowed with the titillating, though unjust, epithet of "French ladies." We harbour the suspicion that not all these damsels originate from Poland, but that they lack veracity, and indeed are Iberian, Italianate, Germanic, Turkish, Argentine, Peruvian, and hail from every other fertile part of one or another hemisphere.

Gladly would we rejoice should ye share in our suspicions, Mesdames Amazons; and should ye invite withal some of these damsels to dwell awhile in your lands and our Empire, so that ye may learn from them a modern and more lucrative way of life, which shall greatly augment your Emperor's treasures. And even so, should ye wish not to give up your solitary Law, in any case the existence of a few hundred of these damsels among you, would greatly facilitate a certain "modus in rebus," between us, upon our return to the Empire of the Virgin Forest, which name, by the by, we would propose changing to Empire of the Virgin Woodland, more in keeping with the lessons of the classics.

Nevertheless, so as to conclude this business of paramount importance, we had best caution you against a danger that this importation may bring about, should ye fail to permit a number of powerful gentlemen to breach the outer limits of the State, while we are as yet away. These women be quite fiery and free; they might very well grow unduly burdened by the aberrant sequestered state in which ye live, and, so as not to lose the sciences and secrets by which they earn their daily bread, may very well go to the extreme of utilizing the wild-beasts, bogio howlers, tapirs, and those cunning candiru fish. And it would weigh heavier still on our conscience and noble sense of duty, should ye, our subjects, learn from them certain grave abuses, such as did occur with the female companions of that genteel versifier Sappho on the rosy Isle of Lesbos—vices which cannot withstand censure in the light of human potentialities, much less under the scalpel of strict and sound morality.

As you can see, we have taken utmost advantage of this stay in the illustrious land of the bandeirante frontiersmen, and while we have not lost sight of our talisman, indeed we most certainly have spared neither effort nor base coin, so as to learn the things most principal to this everlasting Latin civilization, so that we might initiate, upon our return to the Virgin Forest, a series of improvements, which, shall greatly facilitate our existence, and further extend our proud lineage as a cultured nation amongst the most cultured in the Universe. And therefore shall we now tell you some things about this noble city, for we intend to build its like in your domains and our Empire.

São Paulo is built upon seven hills, in the traditional style of Rome, the Caesarian city, "capita" of the Latinity whence we derive; and its feet are kissed by the most lissome and restless lymph of the Tietê River. Its aqueous bodies are magnificent, its air as agreeable as that of Aquisgrana or Anvers, and its area so like to them in salubriousness and abundance, that one could very well aver, in the fine manner of the early chroniclers, that 'twas these three A's that did spontaneously engender the urban fauna.

The city is breathtaking, and its convivial life most delightful. 'Tis intersected in its entirety by skillfully narrowed streets and overtaken by ever so charming and finely wrought statues and street lamps; all of it diminishing the space so astutely, such that these thoroughfares cannot contain the population. This obtains the effect of a great accumulation of peoples, whose estimated number can be inflated at will, this being propitious to the elections which are the invention of the inimitable denizens of Minas Gerais; while at the same time the aediles do propound a broad range of issues in bursts of eloquence, immaculate in style and most sublimely embellished, whence they gain honorary days and widespread admiration.

The aforementioned thoroughfares are thickly layered in ricocheting bits of paper and sailing fruit peels; and principally with an ultrafine dust that dances about, and daily disseminates a thousand and one specimens of voracious macrobes, which decimate the population. In this manner hence, have they resolved, our elders, the issue of traffic congestion; since these insects devour the meager lives of the riffraff and impede the accumulation of industrial labourers and the unemployed; hence the number of people always remains the same. And not satisfied at this dust being kicked up by strolling pedestrians and roaring machines which they dub "automobiles" and "trams" (some employ the word *Bond*, a spurious locution, undoubtedly derived from English), the industrious aediles have hired assorted anthropoids, monstrous blue roan and pure-color hippocentaurs, conglob'd under the title of Public Sanitation; so that "per amica silentia lunae," when all the bustle ceases and the dust settles innocuously, they emerge from their mansions, and, tails spinning like cylindrical brooms, pulled by mules, they go stirring up the dust from the asphalt and rousing the insects from their slumber, inciting them to activity with broad strokes and a terrible cry. These nocturnal tasks are discreetly carried out beneath diminutive lights, set at such lengthy intervals, so that near total darkness persists, leaving the work of malefactors and thieves undisturbed.

The copiousness of the latter strikes us as truly excessive; and we are of the opinion that 'tis but the sole custom that does not agree with our temperament, being orderly and pacific by nature. Nonetheless, far be it for us to reproach the administrators of São Paulo in any way, since we are well aware that the valorous Paulistas find these malefactors and their arts pleasing. The Paulistas are a hotblooded and belligerent people, well accustomed to the hardships of war. They are perpetually engaged in singular and collective combat, all armed to the teeth; hence the disturbances are surpassing numerous in these parts, in which, not infrequently, do hundreds of thousands of heroes, called *bandeirantes*, go down fighting in the arena of battle.

For the selfsame reason, São Paulo is endowed with an exceedingly warlike and voluminous Police Force, which resides in white palaces engineered at great cost. This Police Force is further tasked with balancing out the excesses of public wealth, so as not to devalue the Nation's innumerable stores of gold; and it employs such diligence in this undertaking, to such an extent that it doth devour the national money supply in every which way, be it in parades and gleaming apparel, or in physical fitness regimens from the highly commendable Eugenia, whose acquaintance we have not yet had the pleasure of making; or finally in attacking the heedless bourgeoisie returning home from their theatre, their cinema, or taking their automobiles for a spin through the pleasant orchards that encircle the capital. This Police Force is tasked, moreover, with entertaining the Paulistano class of housemaids; and to their credit 'tis said that they do so with daily expediency, in parks, which are constructed "ad hoc," such as Parque Dom Pedro II and the Jardim da Luz. And whenever the expenditures for this Police Force do increase, their men are dispatched to the country's distant and less fertile plateaus, so that they may be devoured by rogue bands of cannibal giants, which infest our geography, engaged in the inglorious task of toppling honest Governments to the ground, and to the utter delight and general consent of the population, as absolved at the ballot box and in government banquets. These rabblerousers grab the policemen, roast them, and eat them in the German style; and the piles of bones strewn across the barren land serve as excellent fertilizer for future coffee plantations.

Thus do the well-organized Paulistas live and prosper in the most perfect order and progress; and scarce do they lack the time to build generous hospitals, thus attracting lepers hither from all over South America, from Minas Gerais, Paraíba, Peru, Bolivia, Chile, Paraguay, who, prior to venturing off to live in those ever so lovely leper colonies, and being served by damsels of dubious and decadent beauty—damsels, always!—do enliven the highways of the State and the streets of the capital, in jovial caravans on horseback or in superb marathons that are the pride of our sporting race, in whose aspect pulses the blood of the heroic bigae and quadrigae Latin chariots!

Nevertheless, my dear mesdames! There remain still, throughout this grandiose country, diseases and insects to which we must attend! . . . Everything rushes headlong into ruin, we are eaten away by morbidity and myriapods! In brief time shall we again become a colony of England or North America! . . . Whereupon and on behalf of the eternal memory of these Paulistas, who are the only useful people in this country, and hence known as locomotives, we have devoted ourselves to the task of composing a dictum, which doth encompass the secrets of so much misfortune:

ANTS APLENTY AND NOBODY'S HEALTHY,
SO GO THE ILLS OF BRAZIL.

This dictum is what we deemed best to set down in the register of Illustrious Visitors to the Butantan Institute, on the occasion of our visit to that establishment, renowned in Europe.

The Paulistanos live in imposing palaces of fifty, one hundred storeys or more, which, during the mating season, are invaded by clouds of mosquitoes, multifarious in specie, greatly to the liking of the natives, which bite the men and ladies with such propriety in their distinctive parts, that they have no need of stinging nettles to give titillating massages, as is the practice amongst the inhabitants of the jungle. The mosquitoes take up this task; and do perform such miracles that, in the most wretched neighborhoods, innumerable masses of rambunctious lads and lasses, whom we call "wee Italians," surge forth annually; destined are they to feed the factories of the gilded potentates, and to serve, as slaves, at the perfumed leisure of every Croesus.

These and other multimillionaires are the ones who have erected the twelve thousand silk factories that environ the *urbs*, as well as the famous Cafés in every secluded corner, the greatest in the world, replete with ornately carved rosewood adorned in gold leaf, and inlaid with seabrined tortoiseshell.

And the Government Palace is made entirely of gold, in the style of the Queen of the Adriatic; and, at the close of each day, the President, who maintains several spouses, goes riding about in silver carriages lined with the finest of furs, smiling in repose.

Of still further and manifold grandiosities might we elaborate, Mesdames Amazons, were it not to prolongate this epistle in excess; however, in affirming this to be, beyond the shadow of a doubt, the most beauteous of terrestrial cities, much have we accomplished on behalf of these most distinguished men. But we should hang our head in shame were we to occlude in silence, a singular curiosity of this people. Now ye shall know that their wealth of intellectual expression is so prodigious, that they speak in one language and write in another. Having thus arrived in these hospital provinces, we fell to the task of immersing ourselves in the ethnology of the region, and amidst the great many surprises and wonders that we encountered, this linguistic originality was not the least of them, to be sure. In conversation, the Paulistanos employ a barbarous and multifarious dialect, crass in feature and impure in its vernacularity, yet not wanting, nevertheless, in a particular force and flavour inherent to its interjections, as well as in its utterances for playing around. Of this and more have we gained intimate acquaintance, with utmost solicitude; and it shall be a most pleasing enterprise to instruct you upon our arrival thither. If the natural born inhabitants of this land employ such deplorable language in their conversation, no sooner do they take up the quill, than they do strip themselves of so much coarseness, and thus emerges Homo Latinus, derived from Linnaeus, expressing himself in an entirely separate language, approaching that of Virgil, in the words of one panegyrist, a tender idiom, which, with imperishable gallantry, is granted this title: the language of Camões! Of such originality and richness ye cannot but feel gratified to possess cognizance, and ye shall be further struck with wonder to discover, that for the vast and near total majority, these two languages do not yet suffice, but rather are enriched by the most authentic Italian, being more musical and charming, and which is fluently spoken throughout every corner of the *urbs*. Of all this have we become most satisfactorily acquainted, thanks be to the gods; and many an hour have we spent profitably, discoursing upon the *z* in the term "Brazil" and the matter of the personal pronoun "se." Likewise have we acquired various bilingual books, known as "ponies," as well as the Petit Larousse dictionary; and we are now possessed of the circumstances in which to cite, in the original Latin, various celebrated phrases from the philosophers and texticles of the Bible.

At long last, Mesdames Amazons, ye must perforce know further that this great city hath been elevated to these heights of progress and shining civilization, by dint of its elders, also known as politicians. This appellation designates a most refined race of learned gentlemen, so unfamiliar to you, that ye would deem them monsters. Monsters they are, in sooth, but for the incomparable grandiosity of their audacity, sapience, honesty, and morality; and though they may resemble something akin to men, they are descended from the regal uirauaçu harpy eagles and have passing little to do with humans. They all obey an emperor, known

83

as Big Daddy in the common parlance, and who resides in the oceanic city of Rio de Janeiro—the most beautiful in the world in the opinion of all the foreign poets, and verified with mine own eyes.

Finally, Mesdames Amazons and most beloved subjects, a great deal have we suffered and borne of arduous and constant travails, after the duties of our position caused us to part from the Empire of the Virgin Forest. Hereabouts 'tis but delight and fortuitous ventures, yet we shall have neither enjoyment nor rest, so long as we have yet to recover our lost talisman. We deem it best to repeat notwithstanding that our relations with Sir Venceslau are as excellent as possible; that negotiations are under way and moving along swimmingly; and ye may very well dispatch the aforementioned reward in advance. Your abstemious Emperor shall be content with a pittance; should ye be unable to dispatch two hundred igaras laden with cacao beans, then do send one hundred, or even fifty!

Receive herewith the blessing of your Emperor, along with good health and fraternal affection. Heed these poorly scrawled lines with respect and obedience; and, most importantly, forget not the reward and the Polish girls, of which we have utmost necessity.

May Ci protect Your Excellencies.

Macunaíma,
Imperator

Chapter 10. *Pauí-Pódole*

Venceslau Pietro Pietra had been beat to a pulp and was swathed head to toe in bunches of cotton. He was laid up in his hammock for months. Macunaíma couldn't even make a move to take back the muiraquitã that was now tucked away in that snail under the giant's body. He thought about sticking termite ants in the giant's sandals cause it's deadly they say, but Piaimã's feet faced backwards and he didn't wear sandals. Macunaíma was very upset at this fish-or-cut-bait situation and lay in his hammock all day munching on tapioca pancakes in between long swigs of hooch. Right about then Antônio the Indian, the famous saint, came round looking for lodging at the boarding house with his lady friend, Mother of God. He paid Macunaíma a visit, gave a speech and baptized the hero in front of the god to come who took the form of neither fish nor tapir. That's how Macunaíma joined the Caraimonhaga faith that was all the rage in the backlands of Bahia.

Macunaíma made the most of waiting around by honing his proficiency in the two languages of the land, spoken Brazilian and written Portuguese. By now he knew the names of everything. One time it was Flower Day, a celebration invented so Brazilians would be charitable, and there were so many mosquitoes that Macunaíma quit studying and went downtown to give his ideas a breath of fresh air. Off he went and saw a whole mess of things. He stopped in front of every shop window and examined heap after heap of monsters in each one, so many that it looked like the Ererê

85

Mountains where everything took refuge back when the great flood inundated the world. Macunaíma went strolling strolling along and came upon a girl with an urupema basket overflowing with roses. The little missy made him stop and stuck a flower in his lapel, saying:

"That'll cost a buck."

Macunaíma was very upset cause he didn't know the name of that little hole in the clothes machine where the girl had inserted the flower. And the hole was called a buttonhole. He racked his brain, rummaging around in his memory, but he'd never nohow heard the name of that hole before. He wanted to call it a hole but saw immediately how it would be confused with the other holes in this world and felt ashamed in front of the girl. "Orifice" was the word that folks wrote but nobody nohow never said "orifice." After he stood thinking and thinking on it awhile there really wasn't any way to figure out the name of that thing and suddenly he realized that he'd walked from Rua Direita where he'd met that girl all the way out to São Bernardo, past Master Cosme's place. So he went back, paid the young lady and declared with his nostrils flaring:

"Ma'am, you've given me a real doozy of a day. Don't go sticking any more flowers in this here . . . in this here puíto, lady!"

Macunaíma was a big potty mouth right then. He'd uttered an awfully dirty word, indeed! The girl didn't have a clue that puíto was a bad-word and as the hero marched back to the boarding house with his head spinning from the episode, she chuckled to herself, charmed by that funny word. "Puíto . . ." she kept saying. And repeating in delight, "Puíto . . . Puíto . . ." She figured it was the latest thing. So then she started asking everybody if they wanted her to stick a rose in their puíto. Some did others didn't, the other girls heard the word, started using it and "puíto" caught on. Nobody mentioned a boutonnière ever again for example; just puíto, puíto was all you ever heard.

Macunaíma sat stewing for a week, not eating not playing not sleeping all because he wanted to learn the languages of the land. He remembered to ask other folks what the name of that hole was but he was ashamed on account of them thinking he was ignorant and tongue-tied. Finally Sunday Funday rolled around and it was Cruzeiro Day, a new holiday invented so Brazilians could rest some more. In the morning there was a parade in the Mooca neighborhood, at noon an open-air mass at the Coração de Jesus parish church, at 4 p.m. a motorcade with confetti along Avenida Rangel Pestana and in the evening, after elected officials and the unemployed had marched down Rua Quinze, they'd have a fireworks display in Ipiranga. So to take his mind off things Macunaíma went to see the fireworks in the park.

No sooner did he leave the boarding house than he happened upon a fair maiden, blonde as can be, a little daughter of manioc through and through, dressed all in white with a red tucumã straw hat covered in little daisies. Her name was Fräulein and she was ever in need of protection. They went off together and made it to the park. It was a sight to behold. There were so many fountain machines mingling with the electric lamp machine that folks were leaning on each other in the dark clutching hands just to take in all that wonder. That's what the lady did and Macunaíma whispered sweetly:

"Mani . . . little daughter of manioc! . . ."

Well then, the little German lass, a-weeping with emotion, turned round and asked whether he'd let her slip that daisy in his puíto. At first the hero was absolutely taken aback, indeed! and he was fixing to give her a piece of his mind but then he put two and two together and realized that he'd been quite intelligent indeed. Macunaíma burst into laughter.

Turns out that "puíto" had already made it into the journals dedicated to the highly scientific study of written and spoken languages and was now well beyond firmly established via the laws of catalepsis ellipsis syncope metonymy metaphony metathesis proclisis prosthesis aphaeresis apocope haplology popular etymology, all those laws, and the word "buttonhole" had eventually led to "puíto," by means of an intermediary word, "rabanitius" in Latin parlance (buttonhole-rabanitius-puíto), given that rabanitius, though not to be found among medieval manuscripts, has nevertheless been affirmed by the experts to have most certainly existed and to have circulated in popular usage in the sermo vulgaris.

Right that moment a most mulatto of all mulattos climbed atop a statue and launched into a lively speech explaining to Macunaíma what Cruzeiro Day was all about. There wasn't a cloud in the wide open night sky not even Capei. People could make out those they knew, the fathers of trees fathers of birds fathers of beasts and their kin brothers fathers mothers aunties sisters-in-law ladies girlies, all those stars twinklingwinking happy as can be in that land without ills, where everybody was healthy and ants weren't so plenty, up there in the firmament. Macunaíma listened very appreciatively, agreeing with the long-winded lecture that the orator was giving him. It was only after the man started pointing a bunch and describing a bunch that Macunaíma noticed that this Cruzeiro was none other than those four stars that he darn well knew were the Father of the Mutum living up in the field of the heavens. He was angry at the mulatto's lies and yelled:

"No it ain't!"

". . . My dear gentlemen," the fellow was holding forth, "those four stars scintillating like ardent tears, in the words of the sublime poet, are the sacrosanct and traditional Southern Cross, which . . ."

"No it ain't!"

"Shh!"

". . . the most sublime . . ."

"No it ain't!"

"Hear, hear!"

"Beat it!"

"Shh! . . . Shh! . . ."

". . . and ma-marvelous symbol of our be-be-loved fatherland is that mysterious, shimmering Southern Cross that . . ."

"No it ain't!"

". . . y-you can see with . . ."

"Quit mucking it up!"

". . . its . . . four . . . bright spangles all silv . . ."

"No it ain't!"

"No it ain't!" cried the others too.

All that hullabaloo finally flummoxed the mulatto and everyone there got riled up by the hero's "No it ain't!" itching to raise a ruckus. But Macunaíma was trembling in such a tizzy that he didn't even notice. He hopped up on the statue and started telling the story of the Father of the Mutum. And it went like this:

"No it ain't! My dear ladies and gentlemen! Those four stars up there are the Father of the Mutum! I swear it's the Father of the Mutum, my fine folks, floating up there in the vast field of the heavens! . . . This was back in the time when animals were no longer men and it took place in the great So-and-So Forest. Once upon a time there were two brothers-in-law who lived very far away from each other. One was called Camã-Pabinque and he was a Catimbó shaman. One time Camã-Pabinque's brother-in-law went into the woods cause he felt like hunting a bit. That's what he was doing when he ran into Pauí-Pódole and his lil compadre Camaiuá the firefly. And Pauí-Pódole was the Father of the Mutum. That great bird was sitting pretty up on the top branch of the acapu tree, taking it easy. Well now, the shaman's brother-in-law went back to the maloca and told his gal that he'd run into Pauí-Pódole and his compadre Camaiuá. And way back in olden times, both the Father of the Mutum and his lil compadre used to be folks just like us. The man also said he'd wanted so bad to kill Pauí-Pódole with his blowgun but couldn't reach the Father of the Mutum's perch high up in that acapu. So he grabbed his pracuuba spear with a taboca tip and went off fishing for carataís.

Soon enough Camã-Pabinque showed up at his brother-in-law's maloca and said:

"'Hey sister, what exactly did your husband tell you?'

"Well the sister told the shaman everything and said that Pauí-Pódole was perched high up in an acapu with his compadre Camaiuá the firefly. First thing the next morning Camã-Pabinque left his papiri and found Pauí-Pódole chirping away in the acapu tree. So then the Catimbó shaman turned into Ilague the tocandeira ant and started climbing up the tree but the Father of the Mutum spotted that big ol' ant and screeched, blowing hard as he could. An enormous wind kicked up, so mighty that the shaman plummeted from the tree, landing in the capituvas on the forest floor. Then he turned into Opalá the much tinier tacuri and started climbing back up but Pauí-Pódole spotted the ant again. He huffed and puffed and there came a breezy gust that whooshed Opalá down onto the trapoerabas on the forest floor. Then Camã-Pabinque turned into the foot-washer called Megue, that itty bitty fire ant, climbed the acapu, stung the Father of the Mutum right in his little nose hole, curled up her teensy body and bringing her you-know-what between her pincers, thwap! squirted formic acid up there. Jccz! my fine folks! After that, Pauí-Pódole took wing all discombobulated from the pain and sneezed out Megue far far away! The shaman couldn't even leave Megue's body anymore, he'd had such a fright. And so we got stuck with yet another plague, the itty bitty foot-washer fire ant ... Folks!

> *Ants aplenty and nobody's healthy,*
> *So go the ills of Brazil!*

like I said ... Next day Pauí-Pódole wanted to go live up in the sky so he wouldn't suffer anymore from the ants of our land, so he did. He asked his lil compadre the firefly to light the way with his tiny green lantern shining bright. Cunavá the firefly, the compadre's nephew, went ahead lighting the way for Camaiuá then asked his brother to go ahead lighting the way for him too. The brother asked his father, the father asked the mother, the mother asked her whole generation, the chief of police, the local sheriff and many many more, a whole cloud of fireflies went lighting the way for each other. Up they went, took a liking to it there, and going up and away one by one never did come back down from the vast field of the heavens. It's that trail of light you can see from here shooting across space. Then Pauí-Pódole flew up to the sky and stayed there. My fine folks! those four stars ain't the Cruzeiro—Southern Cross no way no how! It's the Father of the Mutum! The Father of the Mutum! my fine folks! That's the Father of the Mutum, Pauí-Pódole floating up there in the vast field of the Heavens! . . . And that's all."

Macunaíma stopped, clean worn out. Then there rose from the masses a lengthy murmur of joy making the folks twinkle even more, the fathers of birds fathers of fishes fathers of insects fathers of trees, all the folks they knew floating up there in the field of the heavens. And the contentment in that crowd of Paulistanos was immense as they cast wonderstruck eyes up at those folks, at all those fathers of the living, shining at home up there in the sky. And all those wonders were people at-first then afterward became the mysterious wonders who brought all the living beings into existence. And now they're the little stars in the sky.

The people went away deeply moved, glad in their hearts full of explanations and full of the living stars. No one made a fuss anymore about Cruzeiro Day or the fountain machines mingling with the electric lamp machine. They went home to tuck sheepskins under the sheets since on account of playing with fire that night, they'd be sure to wet the bed. Everyone went to sleep. And darkness fell.

Macunaíma had stayed out there alone stock-still atop the statue. He too was feeling moved. He peered high up above. Southern Cross no way no how! That was Pauí-Pódole it was clear to see from here . . . And Pauí-Pódole was laughing at him, thanking him. Suddenly Pauí-Pódole let out a long screech sounding like a steam engine. It wasn't a train but a screech and that breath blew out all the lights in the park. Then the Father of the Mutum waved a wing gently bidding the hero farewell. Macunaíma was about to thank him, but the bird took flight in a cloud of dust leaving a long streak spilling across the vast field of the heavens.

Chapter 11. *Old Ceiuci*

The next day the hero woke up very constipated. It was because in spite of the sweltering night he'd slept with his clothes on for fear of the Fogmull that comes to get anyone who sleeps naked. But he was all puffed up with pride from the success of his speech the day before. He waited impatiently for the fifteen days the ailment lasted eager to tell more stories to the people. However by the time he was feeling better it was early morning and he who tells tales by the light of day, grows a guinea pig tail straight away. That's why he asked his brothers to come hunting, so they did.

When they got to the Bosque da Saúde the hero murmured: "This'll do."

He left his brothers lying in wait, set a fire in the grove and hid with them in the bushes waiting for a deer to come out so he could catch it. But there weren't any deer in there and when the flames died down, did the alligator come out? well, neither did any forest deer or caatinga deer, just two scorched rats. So the hero caught the two scorched rats, ate em and went back to the boarding house without calling his brothers.

When he got there he rounded up all the neighbors, servants the landlady womenfolk typists students civil-servants, lotsa civil-servants! all them neighbors and told em he'd gone hunting at the market on Arouche Square and killed two . . .

". . . deer, no wait not forest deer, no it was two caatinga deer that me and my brothers ate. I even brought back a piece for you guys but see, I tripped on the corner, took a tumble dropped the bundle and a dog ate it up."

Everybody was dumbfounded by what had happened and didn't believe the hero one bit. When Maanape and Jiguê came home, the neighbors went to ask em if it was true that Macunaíma had caught two caatinga deer at the market on Arouche Square. The brothers got all bent out of shape cause they didn't know how to lie and yelled in exasperation:

"Hold on what kinda deer was it! The hero ain't never killed no deer! Weren't no deer out there to hunt! He's all bark and no bite, folks! Matter of fact it was two scorched rats that Macunaíma caught and ate."

That's when the neighbors realized it was all a pack of lies, got mad as heck and burst into the hero's room demanding satisfaction. Macunaíma was tootling away on a little flute made from a papaya stem. He paused between breaths and whittled the flute's mouth hole, looking mildly bemused:

"What's this ragtag bunch doing in my room now! . . . It's bad for your health, folks!"

They asked him:

"So what pray tell did you catch, hero?"

"Two forest deer."

Then the servants womenfolk students civil-servants, all them neighbors started laughing at him. Macunaíma sat whittling away at the little flute's mouth hole all the while. The landlady crossed her arms and scolded him:

"Come now, dearie, why on earth did you say it was two deer when it was really just two scorched rats?!"

Macunaíma fixed his eyes on her and answered:

"I lied."

All the neighbors got sheepish and everyone went home feeling even-stevens. And Steven was a neighbor who always got a fair deal. Maanape and Jiguê exchanged looks, jealous of how intelligent their brother was. Maanape started in again:

"But why on earth did you lie, hero!"

"It wasn't on purpose . . . I just wanted to tell em what happened to us and next thing you know I was lying . . ."

He tossed the flute aside, grabbed a ganzá shaker cleared his throat and sang to the beat. All the livelong afternoon he sang a ballad so mournful, oh so mournful, that his eyes streamed with tears at every verse. He stopped cause his sobs wouldn't let him go on. He put down the ganzá. The view outside was the most sorrowful gloaming drenched in mist. Macunaíma felt most forlorn and his heart longed for the unforgettable Ci. He called his brothers over so they could take comfort together. Maanape and Jiguê sat next to him on the bed and the three talked a good while about the Mother of the Forest. And chasing away the blues they talked about the forests and plains rolling mists gods and treacherous banks of the Uraricoera. Up where they'd been born and had laughed together for the first time in their little macurus . . . Nestled in the maquiras past the clearing near the mocambo the guirá cuckoos would go on singing more than the day is long and they numbered over five hundred, the families of guirá . . . Near fifteen times a thousand animal species darkened the forest made of so many millions of trees well past counting . . . One time a white man had brought down from the land of the English, in a gothic saddlebag, the constipation that was now making Macunaíma cry his eyes out with longin' . . . And the constipation had gone to live inside the lair of the dark black mumbuca ants. In the gloom the heat would ease up like getting out of water; to work you had to sing; our mother was laid facedown in a grassy knoll in a place called Father of the Tocandeira . . . Ah, just so lazy . . . And the three brothers could hear the murmuring Uraricoera so very close! Oh! life was good up there . . . The hero flung himself back on the bed sobbing.

When he didn't feel like crying anymore, Macunaíma shooed the mosquitoes and wanted to take his mind off things. He remembered to insult the giant's mother with a brand new swear word from Australia. He turned Jiguê into a telephone machine but his brother was still out of sorts from that whole rigamarole with the hero's lies and there was no way to call. The apparatus was on the fritz. So Macunaíma smoked some paricá beans to have delectable dreams and slept soundly.

Next day he remembered he needed to get revenge on his brothers and decided to pull a fast one on them. He got up at the crack of dawn and went to go hide in the landlady's bedroom. He played around to pass the time. Afterward he came back breathlessly telling his brothers:

"Hey brothers, I found some fresh tapir tracks right in front of the Commodities Exchange!"

"Say what, chicken butt!"

"Well I'll be. Who'd a thunk it!"

Nobody had ever killed a tapir in the city before. The brothers were dumbfounded and went with Macunaíma to hunt the animal. They got there, started looking round for tracks and that wide world of folks wholesalers resellers shortsellers Matarazzos, seeing the three brothers hunched over the asphalt looking around, started searching too, that whole wide world of folks. They kept looking around looking around, didya find anything? neither did they! So they asked Macunaíma:

"So where exactly did you find those tapir tracks? Sure aren't any round here!"

Macunaíma never stopped searching repeating all the while:

"Tetápe dzónanei pemonéite hêhê zeténe netaíte."

And the brothers traders hawkers peddlers Magdalenes and Hunkies went back to looking around for tracks. When they got tired and stopped to ask questions, Macunaíma searching all the while would answer:

"Tetápe dzónanei pemonéite hêhê zeténe netaíte."

And that whole wide world of folks kept looking. Night was fast approaching when they got discouraged and gave up. Then Macunaíma begged their pardon:

"Tetápe dzónanei pemo ..."

They wouldn't even let him finish, everybody asking what the heck that phrase was s'posed to mean. Macunaíma replied:

"Beats me. I learned those words at home when I was little."

And everybody got all fired up. Macunaíma backed away playing dumb:

"Take it easy, folks! Tetápe hêhê! I didn't say there are tapir tracks, nossir, I said there were! Now there's not anymore."

That was worse. One of the merchants really blew his lid and the reporter right next to him seeing the other guy in conniptions went positively apoplectic.

"This will not stand, nossir! Here we are busting our tails day in and day out just to put food on the table and along comes this wise guy bamboozling us out of a day's work just to go chasing after some lousy tapir tracks!"

"But I didn't ask anybody to go looking for tracks, young man, beg your pardon! It was my brothers Maanape and Jiguê who went around asking, not me! It's their fault!"

Then the people who were already seething with rage turned on Maanape and Jiguê. It was everybody now, lotsa folks! all itching for a fight. Then a student jumped on the hood of a car and gave a speech denouncing Maanape and Jiguê. The people were in an uproar.

"My dear gentlemen, life in a great urban center such as São Paulo presently requires such relentless hard work that it can no longer permit even the most fleeting passage of innocuous beings amidst the magnificent intermeshing gears of its progress. We must rise up una voce against deleterious miasmas that sully our social organism and since the Government turns a blind eye and depletes the coffers of the Nation, we ourselves must become the enforcers of justice ..."

"Lynch em! Lynch em!" the people started shouting.

"Lynching no way no how!" yelled Macunaíma, sticking up for his brothers.

97

And everybody turned on him again. Now they were in a downright uproar. The student went on to himself:

"... and when the honest work of the people is disrupted by a stranger ..."

"What! who're you calling a stranger!" hollered Macunaíma, offended to his depths.

"You!"

"Am not, so there!"

"Are too!"

"Hey mind your own beeswax, junior! Your dear old mother's a goddamn stranger, ya hear!" then turning toward the people: "What's got into your heads, huh? I ain't scared, nossir! not of a single one a yous not of two not of ten thousand and right about now I'm gonna smash the whole lot to smithereens!"

One of the Magdalenes, who was standing right in front of the hero, turned to the merchant behind her and snapped:

"Get your paws off me, you shameless pig!"

The hero, blind with rage, thought she was talking to him and:

"Now it's 'get your paws off'! I ain't tryna cop a feel on no one, you skinny ol' busybody!"

"Lynch the creep! Stick it to him!"

"Come and get me, bastards!"

And he lunged into the mob. The lawyer tried to get away but Macunaíma shoved a foot in his back and charged into the crowd tripping and headbutting folks left and right. Suddenly he came face to face with a very good-looking tall blond man. And the man was a traffic cop. Macunaíma was furious at all that handsomeness and landed a savage blow square on the cop's mug. The cop bellowed, saying something in a foreign language as he seized the hero by the scruff of the neck.

"You're under arrrrest!"

The hero froze.

"Under arrest for what?"

The policeman replied with a buncha stuff in a foreign language and held on tight.

"I'm not doing anything!" the hero muttered fearfully.

But the cop didn't wanna hear it and marched down the steep lane with all the people close behind. Another traffic cop showed up and the two of them said lotsa stuff, a whole lot! in a foreign language and kept shoving the hero down the hill. Someone who'd witnessed the whole thing recounted what happened to an old man standing in the doorway of a greengrocer and the old man was so indignant that he cut through the crowd and made the officers stop. They were already at Rua Líbero. Then the old man gave the coppers a whole speech, about how they shouldn't throw Macunaíma in jail cause the hero hadn't done a thing. A whole buncha traffic cops had gathered but none of em understood the speech cause none of em spoke a word of Brazilian. The women were all a-wailing feeling awful sorry for the hero. The cops were talking up a storm in a foreign language and a voice shouted:

"Oh no ya don't!"

And once again the people were really spoiling for a brawl and from all sides now they started shouting: "Let him go!," "Don't take him away!," "Oh no ya don't!," "Oh no ya don't!," a complete ruckus, "Let him go!" A farmer had a mind to give a speech insulting the Police. The traffic cops didn't understand a word and kept gesticulating, confounded as all get out, yammering away in a foreign language. A fearsome riot broke out. Then Macunaíma took advantage of the mayhem and let his legs carry him willy-nilly! A trolley was coming round the bend bells a-clanging. Macunaíma hopped the moving trolley and went to see how the giant was doing.

Venceslau Pietro Pietra was now on the mend from the beating he'd taken during the Macumba ceremony. The house was sweltering cause it was time to cook polenta and it was nice and cool outside on account of the southern breeze. That's why the giant with his old Ceiuci their two daughters and all the help brought some chairs out so they could sit by the front door and enjoy the fresh air. The giant was still swaddled up and looked just like a walking bale of cotton. They took a seat.

That kid Drizzle was going around misting up the neighborhood and ran into Macunaíma lurking on the corner. He stopped short gawking at the hero. Macunaíma turned around:

"Ain't nothing to see here!"

"What the heck're you doing there, buddy!"

"I'm scaring Piaimã the Giant and his family."

Drizzle ribbed him:

"Come on! I'd like to see him get spooked by the likes of you!"

Macunaíma glared at the dropsied kid and got mad. He wanted to hit him but remembered by heart: "Any time you start losing your head, just count up your buttons three times instead," so he counted and calmed back down. Then answered:

"Wanna bet? Just wait and see, I guarantee you Piaimã's gonna run back inside scared as heck of me. Hide right over there so you can hear what they say."

Drizzle warned:

"Hey, buddy, watch out for that giant! You know all too well what he's capable of. Piaimã may be weak as weak can be right now, but it's better to let sleeping dogs lie . . . If you're really not scared, then it's a bet."

He turned into a droplet and dripped right past Venceslau Pietro Pietra along with his wife their daughters and all the servants. Then Macunaíma grabbed the first bad-word from his collection and threw it in Piaimã's face. The cuss word slammed into him but Venceslau Pietro Pietra didn't even bat an eye, just like an elephant. Macunaíma launched an even filthier profanity at the caapora crone. The insult slammed into her but didn't bother nobody in the least. So then Macunaíma hurled his entire collection of dirty words and it was ten thousand times ten thousand dirty words. Venceslau Pietro Pietra said to his old Ceiuci, very softly:

"There's some we ain't never heard before, better save em for the girls."

Then Drizzle went back to the corner. The hero was ready to brag:

"Were they scared or what!"

"Not one bit, buddy! the giant even told his wife to save the new dirty words for their daughters to play with. I'm the one they're scared of, wanna bet? Get up real close and just you listen."

Macunaíma turned into a caxipara which is the male saúva ant and went winding his way up and around the bunches of cotton padding the giant. Drizzle gathered himself into a thick fog and as he was passing right over the family tinkled a little in the air. He started sprinkling a light shower. When the rain began to fall the giant peered at a droplet clinging to his hand and was petrified of all that water.

"Let's get outta here!"

And everyone ran inside scared outta their wits. Then Drizzle came back down and said to Macunaíma:

"See?"

And that's how it is to this day. The giant's family is scared of a little Drizzle but not of any bad-words whatsoever.

Macunaíma was feeling downright sore about it and asked his rival:

"Tell me something: do you speak Igpay Latin?"

"Never heard of it!"

"Well then, my foe: Ogay eatay itshay!"

And he slinked back to the boarding house.

But he was very upset at having lost the bet and remembered to go out fishing. However he couldn't catch a thing, not with arrows or poisonous plants, not timbó not jotica not cunambi not tingui, not in macerá or pari traps, not with line or harpoon or juquiaí or sararaca or bobber or sinker or caçuá or itapuá or jiqui or trotline or jererê, guê, trammel trawl weir lure snagger snood fyke gillnet scoopnet dropshot fishpot hook-n-rod, all them implements traps and poisons, seeing as he didn't have a single one. He made a hook out of mandaguari beeswax but a catfish chomped it, making off with hook line and sinker. However there was an Englishman close by catching aimarás with a real hook. Macunaíma went home and said to Maanape:

"What do we do! We've gotta nab an Englishman's hook. I'm gonna turn into a fake aimará and swipe the bait. When he catches me and bops me on the head I'll go 'yawp!' and play dead. He'll toss me in his samburá basket, you come round asking for the biggest fish to eat and that'll be me."

So he did. He turned into an aimará jumped in the lake, the Englishman caught him and bopped him on the head. The hero cried, "Yawp!" But the Englishman pulled the hook out the fish's jaw all the same. Maanape came round and laid it on thick, asking the Englishman:

"Gimme a fish, wontcha, Mr. Yes?"

"Alright." And he gave him a little red-fin lambari.

"I'm starving hungry, Mr. Englishman! Gimme a whopper, come on! hows about that fatty in your samburá!"

Macunaíma had his left eye a-snoozing but Maanape recognized him straight away. Maanape was a sorcerer. The Englishman gave the aimará to Maanape who thanked him and took off. When they were a league and a half away the aimará turned back into Macunaíma again. That's how it went three times over, the Englishman always pulling the hook out the hero's jaw. Macunaíma whispered to his brother:

"What do we do! We've gotta nab that hook from the Englishman. I'm gonna turn into a fake piranha and yank the hook off his pole."

He turned into a ferocious piranha and jumped into the lake yanked off the hook and turning back around went a league and a half downriver to a place called Umbu Springs where there were stones covered in the scarlet inscriptions of Phoenician folk, pulled the hook out his jaw quite pleased since now he'd be able to catch corimã piraíba aruana pirara piaba, all those fish. The two brothers were just leaving when they overheard the Englishman telling an Uruguayan:

"What shall I do now! I haven't any more hooks since that piranha swallowed it. Guess I'll head over to your country, mate."

Then Macunaíma flailed his arms wildly and shouted:

"Hold on a sec, tapuitinga!"

The Englishman spun around and Macunaíma turned him into the Bank of London machine just for laughs.

The next day he told his brothers he was heading out to catch some big fish on the Igarapé Tietê. Maanape warned him:

"Don't go, hero, or else you'll run into old Ceiuci, the giant's wife. She'll gobble you up, ya hear!"

"Hell hath no terror for he who has braved the Falls!" Macunaíma shouted. And set off.

No sooner did he cast his line from atop a platform in the trees than old Ceiuci came along for some net fishing. The caapora crone spotted Macunaíma's shadow reflected in the water and quickly cast her big round net catching nothing but shadow. The hero didn't even think it was funny seeing as he was a-trembling with fear, and well, to thank her said:

"Good morning, granny."

The old lady swung her head up and spied Macunaíma perched on the platform.

"C'mere, sonny boy."

"No way no how."

"Well then I'll send some marimbondos up there."

So she did. The hero grabbed a bunch of fragrant pataqueira leaves and killed the wasps.

"Get down here, sonny boy, or else I'll send some twig ants up there!"

So she did. The twig ants stung Macunaíma and he fell in the water. Then the old lady cast her net, snared the hero and went on home. When she got there she set the bundle down in the living room which had a scarlet lamp and went to call her older daughter, who was very handy, so the two of em could eat the sitting duck she'd caught. And that duck was Macunaíma the hero. However, the big daughter was kept busy seeing as she was quite handy indeed and the old lady had gone to build the fire to move things along. The caapora crone had two daughters and the younger one, who wasn't handy at all and couldn't do anything but sigh, noticed the old lady building a fire and wondered, "Mother whenever you get back from fishing you always say what you caught right away, but not today. I'll go have a look-see." She unwound the netting and out popped a young man very much to her taste. The hero said:

"Hide me!"

So the girl, being very kindhearted since she'd had nothing to do in so long, took Macunaíma back to her room where they played around. Now there they are laughing with each other.

When the fire was piping hot, old Ceiuci came over with her handy big daughter so they could pluck the ducky but all they found was the fishing net. The caapora crone went berserk:

"Must have been that little baby daughter of mine who's so kindhearted . . ."

She pounded on the girl's door, shouting:

"Oh little baby daughter of mine, hand over my ducky right this instant or else I'll throw you outta my house for good!"

The girl got scared and told Macunaíma to toss twenty bucks under the door to see if it might satisfy the greedy grubber. In a panic Macunaíma quickly tossed a hunnerd that turned into piles of partridges lobsters sea bass perfume bottles and caviar. The greedy old glutton swallowed the lot of it and asked for more. So then Macunaíma tossed a whole conto de réis under the door. The conto turned into more lobsters rabbits pacas champagne doilies mushrooms frogs, and the old lady kept gobbling it up and asking for more. So then the kindhearted girl opened the window overlooking the deserted Pacaembu neighborhood and said:

"I'll tell you three riddles, and if you get them right, I'll let you go. Riddle me this: What's long and rounded with a hole in it, goes in hard and comes out soft, satisfies our craving and isn't a naughty word?"

"Aha! that one sure is naughty!"

"Silly billy! it's pasta!"

"Ahh . . . so it is! . . . Funny, huh?"

"Now riddle me this: In what place do women have the kinkiest hair?"

"Oh ho, very nice! I know this one! right down there!"

"You dirty dog! In Africa, of course!"

"Show me, pretty please!"

"Okay this is your last chance. Tell me what this is:

> *Dear brother, now let us do*
> *As God intends:*
> *Bring hair to hair,*
> *And leave the bald one in there.*"

And Macunaíma:

"Sheesh! Everybody knows that one too! But listen close, between you and me, missy, you sure are one shameless hussy!"

"You figured it out. Aren't you thinking about how we sleep with our eyelashes touching and leave the naked eye on the inside? Well if you hadn't got at least one riddle right, I'd've turned you over to that greedy mother of mine. Now scat without raising a stink, I'm getting thrown out, I'll fly up to the sky. On the corner you'll find some horses. Take the dark chestnut trotter, he'll clip-clop through rocks and muddy water. That one's a beaut. If you hear a birdie shrieking 'Awooga! Awooga!,' then it's old Ceiuci swooping in. Now scat without raising a stink, I'm getting thrown out, I'll fly up to the sky!"

Macunaíma thanked her and jumped out the window. On the corner were two horses, a dark chestnut and a dapple gray. "God created the dapple gray to win the race day after day," Macunaíma murmured. He hopped on that one and galloped away. Roaming roaming roaming he rode and just as he was nearing Manaus at full tilt the horse stumbled so hard it split the earth wide open. At the bottom of the hole Macunaíma caught sight of something gleaming. He dug quickly and found the remains of the god Mars, a Greek sculpture that had been discovered thereabouts back during the Monarchy and also last April First, in Araripe de Alencar's column in a newspaper called *Comércio do Amazonas*. He was contemplating that almighty torso when he heard "Awooga! Awooga!" It was old Ceiuci swooping in. Macunaíma dug his spurs into the dapple gray and after riding past Mendoza in Argentina and almost crashing into a galley slave from French Guiana who was also on the run, he made it to a place where some priests were making honey. He cried:

"Hide me, Fathers!"

No sooner did the priests hide Macunaíma in an empty jug than the caapora crone came riding up on a tapir.

"Did you happen to see my grandson pass by grazing his horsie?"

"He already came through."

Then the old lady got down from the tapir and climbed onto another horse, a green-eyed cremello, who always ends up a worthless fellow, and kept going. When she rounded the Paranacoara Range the priests pulled the hero out the jug, gave him a handsome honey bay, a horse as fine as its neigh, and sent him on his way. Macunaíma thanked em and went galloping off. Soon enough he came upon some wire fencing but he was a true horseman: he jerked on the reins, pulled his steed up sharp and gathering the downed animal's limbs in one fell swoop, spun the horse round and slid him under the wire. Then the hero hopped the fence and got back in the saddle again. Galloping galloping galloping he went. Passing through Ceará, he deciphered the indigenous inscriptions at Aratanha; weaving his way along the coastal ridge known as Baldy Hill in Rio Grande do Norte he deciphered some more. In Paraíba, riding from Manguape to Bacamarte, he passed by Pedra Lavrada, site of so many stone engravings they amounted to a novel. He didn't read them seeing as he was hot to trot, nor did he read the Barra do Poti ones in Piauí, nor the Pajeú ones in Pernambuco, nor the ones in the Inhamum Narrows which was already on day four and in the air was heard close as can be: "Awooga! Awooga!" It was old Ceiuci swooping in. Macunaíma dashed willy-nilly into a eucalyptus grove. But the birdie was hot on his heels and gaining fast and Macunaíma just couldn't shake that old crone. Finally he came upon the ramshackle den of a deadly surucucu viper who was in cahoots with Old Scratch.

"Hide me, surucucu!"

No sooner did the surucucu hide the hero in his latrine pit than old Ceiuci showed up.

"Did you happen to see my grandson pass by grazing his horsie?"

"He already came through."

The greedy grubber got down from the green-eyed cremello, who always ends up a worthless fellow, and mounted a blaze-face horse, which is a lame horse of course of course, and took off.

Then Macunaíma overheard the surucucu viper conspiring with his gal to roast the hero on a spit. He leaped out that hidey hole of a room and hurled a flashy diamond ring to the ground, the one he'd got as a present for his little finger Pinky. The diamond turned into four contos' worth of cartful after cartful of corn, some Polisu fertilizer and a secondhand Tin Lizzie. As the surucucu surveyed it all with satisfaction, Macunaíma, to give the honey bay a rest, mounted a spirited silver pinto colt, the kind that's always rarin' to bolt, and went galloping over plains wide and narrow. In a flash he crossed that desert sea stretching across the vast Parecis Plateau, up and over steep ridges and sheer bluffs into the caatinga scrublands and spooked the chickens with their golden chicks in Camutengo coming up on Natal. A league and a half farther, parting ways with the banks of the Rio São Francisco all mucked up from the Easter floods, he entered a breach high in the mountains. He was riding along when he heard a woman go "Psst." Scared stiff he stopped dead in his tracks. Then out from a poinciana stepped a tall homely lady with a long braid down to her ankles. And the lady asked the hero in a whisper:

"Have they gone yet?"

"Who's gone!"

"The Dutch!"

"You've gone batty, what Dutch're you talking about! Ain't no Dutch round here, lady!"

It was Maria Pereira, the Portagee shut-in who lived tucked away in that mountain gap ever since the war with the Dutch. Macunaíma couldn't tell what part of Brazil he was in anymore and remembered to ask.

"Say, tell me something, if the son of a possum's a fox, what do they call this pile of rocks?"

The woman answered haughtily:

"'Tis the Hole of Maria Pereira."

Macunaíma let out a huge guffaw and split, while the woman went back into hiding. The hero kept on and crossed to the far bank of the Rio Chuí. That's where he happened upon the tuiuiú stork doing some fishing.

"Cousin Tuiuiú, wontcha take me home?"

"Sure thing!"

Right on the spot the tuiuiú transformed into an aeroplane machine, Macunaíma straddled an empty aturiá basket and they took off. They flew over the Urucuia tablelands in Minas Gerais, did a lap around Itapecerica and made off for the Northeast. Passing over the dunes of Mossoró, Macunaíma looked down and spotted Bartolomeu Lourenço de Gusmão, his cassock hiked up, struggling to cross that vast expanse of sand. The hero shouted at him:

"Come fly with us, illustrious sir!"

But the priest shouted with a sweeping gesture:

"Enough already!"

After skirting the Tombador Range in Mato Grosso and passing the rolling prairies of Sant'Ana do Livramento on their left, Macunaíma and the tuiuiú-aeroplane shot all the way up to the Roof of the World, quenched their thirst at the headwaters of the Rio Vilcanota and flying the last leg over Amargosa in Bahia, over Gurupá then over the Gurupi, with its enchanted city, finally landed back in that illustrious mocambo on the banks of the Igarapé Tietê. Before long they were at the front door to the boarding house. Macunaíma thanked him very much and wanted to pay for the lift but remembered he was hard up. He turned to the tuiuiú and said:

"Look here, cousin, I'm too broke to pay you but here's some words of wisdom: In this world, there are three bars that'll bring a man down: sand bars, gold bars, and bars full of women, watch out!"

However, he was so used to being a big spender that he forgot all about pinching pennies. He gave the tuiuiú ten contos, went up to his room feeling quite pleased and recounted everything to his brothers who were put out by the delay. The whole escapade had ended up costing a bundle. Maanape then turned Jiguê into a telephone and lodged a complaint with the Police who deported the greedy old glutton. However, Piaimã pulled some strings and his wife came back with the opera company.

The daughter who got thrown out goes shooting across the night sky, kicking around the heavens on high. She's a comet.

Chapter 12. *The Perky Peddler, Shiny Cowbird, and the Injustice of Men*

The next day Macunaíma woke up feverish. Turns out he'd been delirious all night long and dreamed about a ship.

"That means travel by sea," the boarding house madam said.

Macunaíma thanked her and was so pleased that he immediately turned Jiguê into a telephone machine just so he could insult Venceslau Pietro Pietra's mother. But the telephone operator shadow informed him that nobody was picking up. Macunaíma found it peculiar and had a mind to get up and go see what was going on. But he felt a terrible itchy heat coursing through his body along with a liquid languor. He murmured:

"Ah . . . just so lazy . . ."

He turned to face the corner and started uttering profanities. When his brothers came over to see what was going on, turned out to be a bad case of the measles. Maanape ran off to fetch Bento the famous healer from Beberibe who cured people with his Indian soul and water from a jug. Bento gave him a splash of water and chanted a prayer. In a week's time the hero was already scabbing off. Then he got up and went to see what had happened to the giant.

There was nobody home at the palazzo and the neighbor's scullery maid told him that Piaimã and the whole family had gone off to Europe to take it easy after the beating. Macunaíma lost all his swagger and got very upset. His head was spinning as he played around with the maid then trudged morosely back to the boarding house. Maanape and Jiguê met the hero at the front door and asked him:

"Aw, who killed your puppy dog, lil dearie?"

Then Macunaíma told what had happened and started bawling. His brothers felt awful blue seeing the hero like that so they took him for a visit to the leper colony in Guapira, but Macunaíma was very upset and the excursion was no fun at all. When they got back to the boarding house it was getting dark and everybody was feeling down in the dumps. They took a huge pinch of snuff from a powder horn imitating a toucan's head and had a good sneeze. After that they were able to mull things over.

"That's how it goes, lil dearie, you kept dillydallying, twiddling your thumbs, twiddling your thumbs, and the giant wasn't just gonna wait around, so he took off. You made your bed, now lie in it!"

Which made Jiguê smack his head and shout:

"I got it!"

The brothers jumped in alarm. Then Jiguê reminded them they could go to Europe too, on the trail of the muiraquitã. As for money, they still had forty contos left from selling the cacao beans. Macunaíma was all for it from the get-go but Maanape who was a sorcerer sat pondering pondering and concluded:

"There's a better way."

"Well spit it out then!"

"Macunaíma pretends he's a pianist, scores a Government grant and goes on his own."

"But why's it gotta be so complicated if we're rolling in dough and you brothers can gimme a hand in Europe?!"

"You say the darndest things! We very well could indeed, but brother, ain't it better to go on the government's dime? Sure is. So there you have it!"

Macunaíma reflected awhile and suddenly smacked his forehead:

"I got it!"

The brothers jumped in alarm.

"What's up!"

"Alright, but I'll pretend I'm a painter, that's got more pizzazz!"

He went off to get a tortoiseshell spectacles machine a little gramophone some golf-socks gloves and looked every bit the painter.

Next day while waiting to be awarded the grant he killed time by making some paintings. Like this: he grabbed an Eça de Queirós novel and went for a stroll in the Cantareira Mountains. Then right past him came a traveling salesman who was a real lucky-duck on account of having a magic little woodpecker leaf. Macunaíma was sprawled on his belly amusing himself by squishing tapipitinga anthills. The perky peddler said hello:

"Greetings, friend, howdy do, just dandy, much obliged. Workin' hard, eh?"

"Gotta bring home the bacon."

"Yes, indeedy. Okie dokie, see ya later."

And he went on his way. A league and a half farther he came upon a micura and remembered that he had to bust his tail a bit too. He scooped up the little possum, dropped ten silver pieces worth two bucks down its gullet and came back with the critter under his arm. Sidling up to Macunaíma he started hawking his wares:

"Greetings, friend, howdy do, just dandy, much obliged. I'll sell you my micura if you like."

"What the heck am I s'posed to do with a smelly ol' critter like that!" answered Macunaíma, putting his hand over his nose.

"He sure does stink but this one's a keeper! When he does his business only money comes out! I'll cut you a deal!"

"Quit blowing smoke, you flimflammer! Who ever saw a micura like that!"

Then the perky peddler squeezed the possum's belly and the critter gave up the ten silver coins.

"Looky here! He does his business and it's nothin' but money! Save it up and you'll be filthy rich! I'll cut you a deal!"

"What's it cost?"

"Four hunnerd contos."

"No can do, alls I got is thirty."

"Alrighty then seeing as you're a first-time customer, I'll make it thirty contos just for you!"

Macunaíma unbuttoned his pants and pulled out the money belt from under his shirt. But all he had was a banknote worth forty contos and six casino chips from the Copacabana Palace Hotel. He handed over the banknote and was too embarrassed to take the change. He even tossed in the tokens as a tip and thanked the perky peddler for his kindness.

No sooner did the huckster slip into the woods among the sapupira guaruba and parinari trees than the micura had to do its business again. The hero opened his pocket wide to catch it and the whole load of crap plopped in. Then it dawned on Macunaíma that he'd been had and he let loose the most wretched hollering, all the way back to the boarding house. Turning a corner he ran into José Prequeté and hollered at him:

"Hey Zé Prequeté, pick those jiggers out your feet, now there's something good to eat!"

José Prequeté was furious and insulted the hero's mother but that didn't bother him one bit, he howled with laughter and went on his way. After a while he remembered he'd been storming home in a huff and started hollering again.

His brothers hadn't got back yet from the Government maloca and the landlady went into Macunaíma's room to comfort him, they played around. After playing the hero started bawling again. When his brothers came home everybody was flabbergasted cause their faces had grown over a dozen feet long. Wouldn't you know, the Government already had a thousand times a thousand painters being sent off to Europe on that grant and Macunaíma would get one too but not till Hell froze over. It was a long ways off. Their ruse had gone bust and the brothers were long in the face with disappointment. When they saw their brother bawling, they got alarmed and wanted to know what was the matter. And as they forgot all about their disappointment their faces went back to normal, Maanape the geezer and Jiguê in the prime of manhood. The hero was going:

"Waahwaahwaah! that peddler bamboozled me! Waahwaah-waah! I bought his possum and it set me back forty contos!"

This had the brothers pulling their hair out. Now they sure as heck weren't going to Europe, nossir, cause all they had left to their name were night and day. They started a-wailing mournfully while the hero rubbed andiroba oil over his body so the mosquitoes wouldn't pester him and slept like a log.

The next day dawned in a godawful heat and Macunaíma was sweating buckets left and right fuming at the injustice of the Government. He wanted to go out to take his mind off things but all them clothes were making it hotter . . . He got even more worked up. He was ranting and raving so much he had a bad feeling he was coming down with a case of butecaiana which is rabies. Then he shouted:

"Heck! Just lemme get hot under the collar, so what if folks hoot 'n holler!"

He took off his pants to air out and stomped on em. His anger cooled down lickety-split and feeling pleased as punch, Macunaíma said to his brothers:

"Chin up, brothers! Nope! No way am I going to Europe. I'm an American and America's where I belong. European civilization most indubitably mucks up the integrity of our character."

For a whole week the trio roamed far and wide all over Brazil along sandy seashore shoals and sparsely wooded shoals, steep banks flanking channels, vast clearings, riverruns scrublands shrublands and bushlands, tidal islands gullies waterspouts and deep hollows full of frost, mudflats flumes rockbeds sinkholes ravines chasms and shallows, all those places, scouring convent ruins and peeking under crosses just in case they found any buried pots of money. They didn't find squat.

"Chin up, brothers!" Macunaíma repeated morosely. "Let's go play the lottery!"

And he went to Praça Antônio Prado to meditate on the injustice of men. There he stood leaning against a mighty fine sycamore. All the merchants and that whole mess of machines passed right by the hero wrapping his head around the injustice of men. Macunaíma was on the verge of changing his dictum to: "Painters aplenty and nobody's healthy, so go the ills of Brazil," when he heard a "Waahwaahwaah!" crying behind him. Turning round he spied a sparrow and a shiny cowbird on the ground.

The sparrow was itty bitty bitty and the cowbird was a whopper. The little sparrow was flitting to and fro with that big ol' cowbird following him around the whole time crying for the other bird to give him something to eat. It was maddening. The little sparrow thought that big ol' cowbird was his baby chick but no way no how. So he'd fly off, rustling up sumpin ta eat over yonder that he'd stick in that great big cowbird's beak. The big ol' cowbird would gulp it down and start whining again: "Waahwaahwaah! Mama ... gimme sumpin ta eat! ... gimme sumpin ta eat! ..." in his language. The little sparrow was dizzy with hunger and that exasperating yadda-yadda-yadda yadda-yadda-yadda at his back, whining "Gimme sumpin ta eat! ..., gimme sumpin ta eat! ..." was just too much for his poor suffering heart. Neglecting himself, he'd fly off to find a little bug, a bit of cracked corn, all them sumpins ta eat, then stick it in the big ol' cowbird's beak and that great big shiny cowbird would gulp it down and go after the little sparrow again. Macunaíma was meditating on the injustice of men and felt an immense rancor at the injustice of that big ol' cowbird. It was because Macunaíma knew that back in the beginning, birdies used to be folks just like us ... So the hero grabbed a club and killed the little sparrow.

Off he went. After walking a league and a half he got hot and

116

remembered to cool off with a splash of moonshine. In his coat pocket he always kept a flask of moonshine attached to his puíto by a silver chain. He uncorked it and took a little tipple. That's when all of a sudden he heard a "Waahwaahwaah!" blubbering from behind. Dumbstruck he turned round. It was that big ol' shiny cowbird.

"Waahwaahwaah! Papa . . . gimme sumpin ta eat! . . . gimme sumpin ta eat! . . ." he went in his language.

Macunaíma was furious. He opened the pocket full of the possum's stuff and said:

"Then eat up!"

The great big cowbird hopped onto the edge of his pocket and ate it all up, none the wiser. He got fatter and fatter, turned into a humongous black bird and flew off into the woods shrieking, "Nyah nyah nyah nyah nyah nyah!" Now he's the Father of the Cowbird.

Macunaíma went on his way. A league and a half farther there was a woolly spider monkey munching on some baguaçu nuts. He'd grab a little palm nut, put it together with a rock in the gap between his legs, squeeze, and thwap! the fruit would crack open. Macunaíma came up and stared, eyes wide mouth watering. He said:

"Greetings, uncle, howdy do?"

"So-so, nephew."

"And the family?"

"Same ol'."

And kept on chewing. Macunaíma stood there, eyeballing him. The monkey's temper flared:

"You got a staring problem? Keep looking and I'll charge admission!"

"What the heck're you doing there, uncle!"

The big monkey hid the palm nut in his fist and replied:

"I'm busting my toaliquiçus to eat."

"Go pull someone else's leg!"

"Shoot, nephew, if you don't believe me, then why'd you ask!"
Macunaíma really wanted to believe him and ventured:

"So they're tasty, huh?"

The monkey smacked his lips:

"Hoo wee! just try it!"

He cracked another little coconut on the sly, pretending it was one of his toaliquiçus, and gave it to Macunaíma to eat. Macunaíma liked it a whole lot.

"That sure is tasty, uncle! Got any more?"

"They're all gone now but if mine were so good hows about yours! Eat em up, nephew!"

The hero was scared:

"Doesn't it hurt?"

"Gee whiz, it even feels good! . . ."

The hero grabbed a cobblestone. Laughing on the inside, the muriqui monkey added:

"You got the balls to do it, nephew?"

"Heel toe do-si-do, c'mon now, ready set go!" the hero shouted brashly. He tightened his grip on the cobblestone and thwap! right in the toaliquiçus. He dropped dead. The monkey taunted him:

"Well, lil dearie, didn't I say you were gonna die?! Sure did! But you don't listen! See what happens to those who misbehave? And now: sic transit!"

Then he donned his balata gloves and took off. Before long there came a downpour that freshened up the hero's greening flesh, putting a stop to the putrefaction. Soon enough, swarms of guaju-guaju and murupeteca ants came marching up to the dead body. The line of ants piqued the interest of that lawyer Mr. So-and-So leading him right smack up to the deceased. He crouched, fished out the corpse's wallet but the only thing in it was a visiting card. So he decided to bring the deceased back to the boarding house, and he did. He hiked Macunaíma onto his back and started walking. However the deceased was too heavy and the lawyer realized he couldn't handle all that weight. So then he set the corpse down and clobbered it with a stick. The deceased got lighter and lighter and that lawyer Mr. So-and-So was able to bring it back to the boarding house.

Maanape sobbed and sobbed flinging himself onto his brother's body. Then he realized what had been crushed. Maanape was a sorcerer. Straight away he asked to borrow two Bahian-coconuts from the landlady, tied em in a double constrictor knot to where the crushed toaliquiçus had been and puffed smoke from a pipe over the deceased hero. Macunaíma started sitting up weak as can be. They gave him some guaraná and soon enough he was single-handedly killing the ants still chomping at him. He couldn't stop shivering on account of the downpour bringing on a sudden cold snap. Macunaíma pulled the flask from his pocket and drank the rest of the moonshine to warm up. Then he asked Maanape for a lucky number in the hundreds and went off to find a gambling den to play the animal lotto. Mid-afternoon when they checked, turns out the lucky number had paid off. And that's how they lived off the hunches of their eldest brother. Maanape was a sorcerer.

Chapter 13. *Jiguê's Lousy Lady*

The next day on account of the bruising Macunaíma woke up with an angry rash all over his body. They went to check it out and it was St. Anthony's fire, a lingering ailment. The brothers took real good care of him and each day they'd bring home all the erysipelas remedies recommended by their neighbors and acquaintances, all those Brazilians. The hero was laid up in bed for a week. At-night he kept dreaming of boats and come-morning when the boarding house madam stopped in eager to see how the hero was doing she'd always declare that boats most indubitably meant travel by sea. Afterward she'd go, leaving the *Estado de São Paulo* on the sickbed. And the *Estado de São Paulo* was a newspaper. Then Macunaíma would spend the day reading all those ads for erysipelas remedies. It was a whole lotta ads!

By the weekend the hero was already scabbing off nicely and he went downtown itching for trouble. He drifted around brooding brooding, and clean worn out on account of his weak condition he stopped at Anhangabaú Park. He'd walked right up to the foot of a monument honoring Carlos Gomes who'd been a widely celebrated musician and was now a little star in the sky. The sound of the fountain murmuring in the late-afternoon conjured for the hero a vision of the waters of the deep blue sea. Macunaíma sat on the edge of the fountain and contemplated the bucking bronze sea colts weeping water. And there in the gloom of that grotto behind the drove of horses he witnessed a light. He squinted harder and could make out the most beautiful boat floating across the waters. "It's a sailing skiff," he murmured. However the vessel kept getting bigger the closer it came. "It's a riverboat," he murmured. But the riverboat was getting huge as it came closer, so huge! that the hero jumped high in surprise and hollered into the echoing dusk, "It's a sternwheeler!" The ship was now clear as day behind the bronze colts. Its silver hull was cut for speed and its raked masts were a-flutter with flags pressed flat between blades of air whipping in its swift wake. The hollering had brought all the chauffeurs over from the esplanade and they watched the hero's frozen expression curiously, following his line of sight right smack into the shadowy fountain.

"What's up, hero?"

"Look over there! . . . Lookit that whopping sternwheeler coming this way across the high seas!"

"Where's it at!"

"Right behind that horse on the starboard side!"

Then everyone saw the ship approaching just behind the starboard horse. It was getting close and passing between the horse and the stone wall, now reaching the mouth of the grotto. And it was a colossal ship.

"Why that's no sternwheeler, nossir! that's a transatlantic liner crossing the sea!" cried a Japanese chauffeur who'd traveled by sea many a time. And it was an enormous ocean liner. It was fast approaching, lights all a-twinkle glittering gold and silver so merrily festooned. The cabin portholes were necklaces strung along the hull and music wafted over the decks stacked five high, full of crowds dancing a raucous cururu. The gang of chauffeurs remarked:

"She's from the Lloyd fleet!"

"Naw, she's from the Hamburg line!"

"Get outta town! I can see it now! uh-huh! That's il piróscafo Conte Verde!"

And indeed it was the SS Conte Verde. And it was the Mother-of-Water passing herself off as an Italian steamship to get a rise out of the hero.

"Well folks! adieu, folks! I'm off to Europe where it's better! I'm off to find Venceslau Pietro Pietra, who's Piaimã the Giant, eater of men!" the hero declared.

And the whole gang of chauffeurs hugged Macunaíma as he said goodbye. The steamer was there and Macunaíma had already hopped onto the fountain pier to climb aboard the piróscafo Conte Verde. The whole crew was lined up in front of the music beckoning and calling to Macunaíma and there were strapping sailors, there were high-class Argentines and loads of the most ravishing ladies for folks to play around with till they got sick from the rollicking waves.

"Lower the gangway, captain!" shouted the hero.

Then the captain doffed his feathered headdress and made a flourish in the air. And everyone, the sailors the classy Argentines and the ravishing ladies for Macunaíma to play around with, the whole crew started booing and jeering uproariously at the hero as the ship kept maneuvering without stopping turned its poop landward and shot back toward the depths of the grotto. And the whole crew caught erysipelas as they went on jeering at the hero. And as the steamship navigated the strait between the grotto wall and the portside colt its great big smokestack spit up a whole cloud of mosquitoes, of midges gnats horseflies spiderwasps hornets rove-beetles botflies, all them bloodsuckers chasing away the drivers.

The hero sat suffering on the rim of the fountain all covered in bites and even worse erysipelas, all covered in St. Anthony's fire. He felt a chill and fever set in. Then he swatted at the mosquitoes and walked back to the boarding house.

Next day Jiguê brought a girl home, made her swallow three lead pellets so she wouldn't have a baby and the pair went to sleep in his hammock. Jiguê had shacked up with a woman. He was a fightin' man. He spent all day cleaning his shotgun and sharpening his blade. Every morning Jiguê's gal would go out to buy cassava for the four of em to eat and her name was Suzi. However, Macunaíma, who was Jiguê's gal's lover, would buy her a lobster every day, put it in the bottom of her jamaxi basket and scatter cassava on top so nobody'd raise an eyebrow. Suzi was quite a sorceress. Whenever she got home she'd leave the basket in the sitting room and go to sleep to dream. While dreaming she'd say to Jiguê:

"Jiguê, oh Jiguê my darling, I'm dreaming there's lobster under the cassava."

Jiguê would go look and there it was. Day in and day out that's how it went and Jiguê who kept waking up with jealous pangs got suspicious. Macunaíma noticed his brother's pangs and cast a mandinga spell to see if they might go away. He took a carved gourd bowl and left it on the terrace at-night, chanting softly:

> *O water from the heavens*
> *Enter this gourd,*
> *Paticl enter this water,*
> *Moposêru enter this water,*
> *Sivuoímo enter this water,*
> *Omaispopo enter this water,*
> *O Lords of Water chase away all cuckold pangs!*
> *Aracu, Mecumecuri, Paí may you enter this water,*
> *And chase away all cuckold pangs of he who drinks this water,*
> *Enchanted with the Lords of Water!*

He gave it to Jiguê to drink the next day but it didn't produce the desired effect and his brother kept on feeling mighty suspicious.

Whenever Suzi got dressed to go to market, she'd whistle a popular foxtrot tune for her lover to come along. Her lover was Macunaíma, he'd come. Jiguê's gal would leave and Macunaíma would follow. They went around playing and when it was time to go home there wouldn't be any cassava left at the market. So then Suzi would sneak behind the house, sit on the jamaxi and pull some cassava out her maissó. Everyone ate heartily, except for Maanape who'd mutter:

"Half-breed Indian from Taubaté, horses not worth their goddamn hay, women who stand up to pee, libera nos Domine!" and push the food away.

Maanape was a sorcerer. He didn't want anything to do with that cassava, nossiree, and seeing as he was starving hungry he sat chewing ipadu leaves to fool his belly. At-night when Jiguê wanted to hop in the hammock, his gal would start moaning, saying she was stuffed from swallowing so many pitomba pits. It was just so Jiguê wouldn't play around with her. Jiguê was mad as heck.

Next day she went to the market and whistled the popular foxtrot tune. Macunaíma followed after. Jiguê was a fightin' man. He grabbed a humongous mirassanga club and snuck after them very slowly. He went looking looking and found Suzi and Macunaíma holding hands in the Jardim da Luz. There they were already laughing with each other. Jiguê swung the mirassanga down on the two of em, brought his gal back to the boarding house and left his brother clear worn out by the lakeshore among the swans.

From the next day on Jiguê did the shopping, leaving his gal locked in the bedroom. Suzi had nuthin' ta do and passed the time flouting morality but one time Saint Anchieta came passing through this world, went by her house and was moved by compassion to teach her how to pick nits. Suzi had red hair that she wore à la garçonne and it was home to lotsa lice, a whole lot! Now she no longer dreamed there was lobster under the cassava nor did she commit immoral acts. Whenever Jiguê left she'd remove her tresses and setting em on her guy's club, start picking nits. But she had lotsa lice, a whole lot! And so on account of being scared that her guy would catch her red-handed, she said:

"Jiguê, oh Jiguê my darling, knock on the door first thing when you get back from the market, wontcha, knock awhile every day so I'll be tickled pink and go cook the cassava."

Jiguê said sure thing. Every day he'd go to the market and buy cassava and when he got back he'd knock on the door a spell. Then the girl would put her tresses back on her head and sit waiting for Jiguê.

"Suzi, oh Suzi my darling, I've been knocking awhile, have you cheered up yet?"

"Oh yes!" she'd say. And go cook the cassava.

And that's how it went day in and day out. But she had lotsa lice, a whole lot! It was cause she'd count up the nits she picked one by one and that's why the lice kept multiplying. One time Jiguê sat ruminating on whatever it was his gal was getting up to whenever he went to the market and he wanted to catch her by surprise, so he did. He kicked his legs in the air and came up walking on his hands. He opened the door and caught Suzi by surprise. She shrieked and stuck her mane back on her head all flustered. And the front of her hair sat on the back of her head and the back of her hair flowed down the front. Jiguê cussed her out calling Suzi a filthy pig and smacked her around till he heard someone coming. It was the cows come home. So Jiguê gave it a rest and went to go sharpen his blade.

Next day Macunaíma had another hankering to go play with Jiguê's gal. He told his brothers he was heading out to hunt a long ways off but he didn't go, nossir. He bought two bottles of butiá palm wine from Santa Catarina a dozen sandwiches two pineapples from Pernambuco and holed up in his little room. After a while he popped out and said to Jiguê, showing him the bundle:

"Brother Jiguê, at the end of many many roads, keep walking, there's this fruit tree where all the animals go. I saw a whopping load of game round there, go see for yourself!"

His brother eyed him suspiciously but Macunaíma put on a good act:

"Look, there's pacas, armadillas, and agoutis galore! . . . Just kidding, I didn't see no agoutis. Pacas and armadillas, but no agouti, nossir."

Jiguê fell for it completely and ran to fetch his shotgun, saying:

"Alrighty, brother, I'll go but first you gotta swear you won't play around with my steady."

Macunaíma swore on the memory of their mother that he wouldn't so much as look at Suzi. Then Jiguê got his bang-bang shoot-em-up and his rusty-trusty knife and hit the road. No sooner did Jiguê turn the corner than Macunaíma gave Suzi a hand opening the bundles and laying out a tablecloth made from that famous "Honeycomb Lace" whose pattern had been stolen on Muriú Beach in Ceará-Mirim by that doggone Geracina from Ponta do Mangue. When everything was ready the two of em hopped in the hammock and played around. Now there they are laughing with each other. After a hearty round of laughter, Macunaíma said:

"Pop open a bottle and let's have a drink."

"Sure thing," said she. And they drank the first bottle of butiá which was downright tasty. The two of em smacked their lips and hopped in the hammock again. They played around to their hearts' content. Now there they are laughing with each other.

Jiguê walked for a league and a half, all the way to the very end of those roads, looked round for that fruit tree a couple times, for ages, but did the alligator find it? neither did he! There weren't any fruit trees whatsoever and Jiguê went home searching down each and every road the whole way. Finally he got back and went up to the bedroom and found his brother Macunaíma already laughing with Suzi. Jiguê was mad as heck and knocked his gal around. Now she's crying. Jiguê grabbed the hero and clubbed him with all his might. The blows rained down till he cried, "Uncle!" And Uncle was the name of the boarding house manservant, an islander. Now the hero's clean worn out. And Jiguê who got back so hungry he could eat a horse, proceeded to gobble up the sandwiches the pineapples and guzzle all the butiá wine.

The pair who got beat up spent the night moaning and groaning. The next day Jiguê got fed up, grabbed his blowgun and went to see if he could track down that ol' fruit tree. Jiguê was a big dummy. Suzi saw him leave, dried her eyes and said to her lover:

"Let's don't cry."

Then Macunaíma turned his frown upside down and pulled himself together to go talk to his brother Maanape. Jiguê got back to the boarding house and asked Suzi:

"Where's the hero?"

However she was real teed off and started whistling a tune. So then Jiguê grabbed his club, went up to his gal and said real hangdog like:

"Get lost, you infernal temptress!"

At that she grinned with glee. She picked the rest of her lice without counting em up and it was lotsa lice, she fastened em all to a rocking chair, sat in it, the lice went a-leaping and Suzi went up to the sky changed into a leaping meteor. She's a shooting star.

No sooner did the hero spot Maanape in the distance than he took to moaning and groaning. He flung himself into his brother's arms and told a long-winded tale of woe proving how Jiguê had no reason whatsoever to beat him up so bad. Maanape was furious and went to give Jiguê a talking to. But Jiguê was also coming to talk to Maanape. They bumped into each other in the hallway. Maanape told Jiguê everything and Jiguê told Maanape everything. And so they confirmed that Macunaíma was a lowdown dirty sneak with no character. They went back to Maanape's room and found the hero moaning and groaning. To cheer him up they took him for a spin in an automobile machine.

Chapter 14. *Muiraquitã*

The next morning no sooner did Macunaíma open the window than he spotted a little green birdie. The hero was exceedingly pleased and was still feeling pleased when Maanape burst into his room declaring that the newspaper machines were announcing the return of Venceslau Pietro Pietra. So Macunaíma decided to quit ruminating on the giant and go kill him. He left the city and went out to the So-and-So Forest to test his strength. He searched for a league and a half and finally came upon a peroba tree with sprawling buttress roots big as a trolley. "This'll do," he said. He stuck his arm into the massive tangle of roots, yanked with all his might and the tree came right out, not a trace in the ground. "Yep, sure am strong now!" Macunaíma shouted. He felt pleased again and headed back to the city. However he could hardly walk on account of being so full of ticks. Slow as molasses, Macunaíma said to em:

"Dammit, ticks! get lost, people! I don't owe you diddly squat!"

So then that whole gang of ticks dropped to the ground under the spell and skedaddled. Ticks used to be folks just like us . . . One time a tick set up shop on the side of the road and did lotsa business cause he didn't mind selling on credit. He sold so much on credit so much on credit, and so many Brazilians never paid that finally the tick went broke and got kicked out on the street. He clings to folks so much cause he's reclaiming his debts.

By the time Macunaíma got back to the city it was the deep

of night and he headed right over to ambush the giant's house. A thick fog lay over the world and it was so pitch dark there was nobody home. Macunaíma remembered to find a maid to play around with but on the corner was a stand of taxi machines and the girls were already playing around over there. Macunaíma remembered to set up his arapuca to catch finches but there wasn't any bait. There was nothing to do and he got sleepy. But he sure didn't want to fall asleep seeing as he was waiting for Venceslau Pietro Pietra. He thought, "Now I'm gonna keep watch and when Sleep comes I'll throttle him." Soon enough he saw a figure approaching. It was Emoron-Pódole, Father of Sleep. Macunaíma stayed very still among the termite nests so he wouldn't scare off the Father of Sleep and that way he could kill him. Emoron-Pódole came closer came closer and just when he was right there, the hero nodded off, hit his chin on his chest, bit his tongue and cried out:

"Yikes!"

Sleep got away fast. Macunaíma trudged on disappointed. "Well, look here! I didn't catch him but it was close . . . I'm gonna wait some more and let monkeys lick me if I don't catch the Father of Sleep this time around and throttle him!" That's what the hero thought to himself. There was a creek nearby with a fallen tree for a footbridge. Farther off, a lagoon shimmered white in the pale moonlight now that the fog had lifted. The view was tranquil and very soothing on account of the brook crooning the poor man's lullaby. The Father of Sleep had to be hiding round there. Macunaíma crossed his arms and stayed stock-still among the termite nests with his left eye a-snoozing. Before long he spied Emoron-Pódole approaching. The Father of Sleep came closer came closer and stopped all of a sudden. Macunaíma heard him saying:

"Uh-uh that guy ain't dead. Who ever saw a dead guy not burp!"

Then the hero burped "yawp!"

"Who ever saw a dead guy burp, folks!" Sleep scoffed and got away fast.

That's why the Father of Sleep's still around and as punishment mankind can't sleep standing up anymore.

Macunaíma was just about feeling disappointed with how things had turned out when he heard a clamor and spotted a chauffeur on the other side of the creek gesticulating like he was trying to get his attention. Macunaíma was thrown for a loop and shouted in a tizzy:

"You talking to me, pal! I ain't no French lady!"

"Scram, you're bad luck!" went the young man.

Then Macunaíma set eyes on a little housemaid in a linen dress dyed yellow with extract of tatajuba. She was crossing the creek over the fallen tree. After she went by, the hero hollered at the footbridge:

"See anything, tree?"

"Saw her charms!"

"Haw! haw! haw haw haw! . . ."

Macunaíma howled with laughter. Then he followed the pair. They'd already played around and were relaxing on the shores of the lagoon. The girl was sitting on the edge of a beached igarité. Stark naked after swimming she was eating live tambiú fish, laughing with the young man. He'd sprawled facedown in the water by the girl's feet and was plucking little lambari fishies from the lagoon for her to eat. Frolicking little waves crested over his back and cascaded down his wet naked body back into the lagoon in peals of laughing droplets. The girl was slapping her feet in the water and it was just like a fountain spirited away from Luna, the majestic spray blinding the young man. Then he began dunking his head in the lagoon and coming up with his mouth full of water. The girl squeezed his cheeks with her feet making the water spout onto her belly. The breeze tousled the girl's hair, blowing the silken strands straight across her face one by one. The boy noticed. Resting his chin on his gal's knee he lifted his torso out of the water, reached his arm up and started pulling the girl's hair out of her face so she could eat her tambiús in peace.

Then to thank him she stuck three little fishies in his mouth and bursting with laughter slipped her knee away fast. The boy's torso had nothing to lean on now and his mug went splat in the water hitting rock bottom, the girl's feet still gripping his neck. She went sliding without even noticing, just having the time of her life. She kept sliding till finally the canoe flipped over. Go on, let it flip! Merrily, merrily, merrily, merrily . . . The girl went tumbling hilariously on top of the boy and he wrapped himself round her like an affectionate strangler fig. All the tambiús swam away as the two played around in the water again.

Macunaíma showed up. He sat on the end of the overturned igarité, waiting. When he saw they were done playing around, he said to the chauffeur:

> *Been three days since I ate,*
> *A whole week since I spit,*
> *Adam was made of dirt, ya dig,*
> *C'mon nephew, gimme a cig.*

The chauffeur replied:

> *Awful sorry, kin o' mine,*
> *But I can't spare a smoke;*
> *Paper match and all the fillings*
> *Fell in the water, done got soaked.*

"Don't worry I got one," Macunaíma answered. He pulled out a tortoiseshell cigarette case made by Antônio do Rosário in Pará, offered some hand-rolled tauari cigarettes to the boy and the maid, struck one match for them and a separate one for himself. Afterward he shooed the mosquitoes and started spinning a yarn. The evening went by quickly that way and folks didn't mind the call of the sururina keeping time through the dark of night. And it went like this:

"Long long ago, youngsters, the automobile wasn't a machine the way it is now, it was a puma. Her name was Palauá and she dwelled in the great So-and-So Forest. Well now, Palauá told her eyes:

"'Go out to the seashore, green eyes o' mine, fast as fast can be!'

"Off went her eyes and the puma was blind. But she lifted her muzzle, made it sniff the wind and catching a whiff of Aimalá-Pódole, Father of the Traíra, swimming out there in the sea, she cried:

"'Come back from the seashore, green eyes o' mine, fast as fast can be!'

"Her eyes came back and Palauá could see again. The black tiger who was mighty ferocious was passing by and said to Palauá:

"'Whatcha doing, sister!'

"'I'm sending my eyes out to see the sea.'

"'Is it nice?'

"'It's the cat's pajamas!'

"'Well then send mine too, sister!'

"'No can do cause Aimalá-Pódole's out there by the seashore.'

"'You better send em or else I'll swallow you whole, sister!'

"So then Palauá said:

"'Go out to the seashore, yellow eyes o' my sister the tiger, fast as fast can be!'

"Off went her eyes and the black tiger was blind. Aimalá-Pódole was out there and thwap! swallowed up the tiger's eyes. Palauá had a bad feeling that was gonna happen cause the Father of the Traíra was giving off a mighty strong smell. She was fixing to bolt. However the black tiger who was mighty ferocious had a notion she was about to split and said to the puma:

"'Hold on a sec, sister!'

"'Dontcha know I gotta go rustle up dinner for my cubs, co-madre. Alright, till next time.'

"'First make my eyes come back, sister, I've had my fill of the dark.'

"Palauá cried:

"'Come back from the seashore, yellow eyes o' my sister the tiger, fast as fast can be!'

"But the eyes didn't come back, nossir, and the black tiger was fury itself.

"'Now I'm gonna swallow you whole, sister!'

"And she chased after the puma. They streaked through the woods in such a mad dash that eeek! the little birds went itty bitty teeny tiny with fright and the night had such a bad scare that she got paralyzed. That's why whenever it's day-time up in the tree-tops, down in the woods it's always night. The poor thing can't move anymore . . .

"After Palauá ran a league and a half she looked back clear worn out. The black tiger was getting close. Well now, Palauá made it to a mountain called Ibiraçoiaba and happened upon a giant anvil, the very one that belonged to the foundry of Afonso Sardinha back in the beginnings of Brazilian life. Next to the anvil were four abandoned wheels. So then Palauá strapped em to her paws so she could glide without too much effort and, so they say: she gave the slip again, off like a shot! The puma covered a league and a half in the blink of an eye but the tiger was hot on her heels and gaining fast. They kicked up such a ruckus that the little birds got itty bitty teeny tiny with fright and the night grew even heavier on account of she couldn't move. And the clamor got even spookier with the nightjar a-moaning . . . The nightjar is the Father of the Night, youngsters, and he was wailing over his daughter's misery.

"Hunger gnawed at Palauá. That tiger right on her tail. But Palauá just couldn't go on running like that with her stomach all tied up in knots, now then, a ways up ahead just as she was speeding past the sandbar off Boipeba Island where the Wicked One dwells, she saw a motor close by and swallowed it whole. No sooner did the motor plop into the puma's belly than the poor thing got a second wind and shot off like blazes. She made it a

134

league and a half and looked back. Just like that the black tiger was practically pouncing on her. The darkness was so thick on account of the night's melancholy, you had to see it, that right before the edge of a ravine the puma ran smack into a hillside, and by the skin of her teeth, that was nearly the last of Palauá! Well now, she scooped up two great big fireflies in her mouth and held em in her jaws to light the way ahead. No sooner had she gone another league and a half than she looked back. That there tiger breathing down her neck. It was on account of the puma was giving off a mighty strong smell and that blind varmint had the nose of a bloodhound. Well now, Palauá guzzled some castor oil laxative, got a can of that substance known as gasoline, dumped it in her X and off she went vroomvroom! vroom! just like one a them pooting donkeys. The racket was so loud you couldn't even hear the ghostly tinkling of plates breaking over on Whistler Mountain. The black tiger was completely discombobulated on account of she was blind and couldn't pick up her comadre's stink anymore. Palauá ran a ton more and looked back. She didn't see the tiger. And she couldn't run no more neither with all that heat steaming out her nostrils. Close by was a whopping banana grove on a swampy spit of land, cause by then Palauá had made it all the way to the port of Santos. Well now, the creature poured some sluggish water into her muzzle and cooled down. Then she hacked off a humongous banana leaf and hid underneath, draping the leaf over her like a great big cape. She fell asleep like that. The black tiger who was mighty ferocious even passed right by, not a peep from the puma. And the other feline passed awful close without even sensing her comadre's presence. Then the puma was so afraid that she never did let go of all the things that helped her escape. She roams all around with wheels on her paws, a motor in her belly, castor oil in her gullet, water in her nostrils, gasoline in her derriere, those two great big fireflies in her mouth, with that banana leaf cape on top, holy moly! ready to take off like a shot. Specially if she steps on a line of what they call taxi ants and a little guy marches up her shiny fur and bites her ear, whoa! she'll shoot off faster'n God Almighty! . . . And she even took up a funny name to disguise herself even more. It's the automobile machine.

"But on account of drinking that sluggish water Palauá got all foggy-headed. Owning an automobile makes you foggy in the head, youngsters.

"They say later on the puma gave birth to an enormous litter. She had sons and daughters. Some boy cubs some girl cubs. That's why we call a Ford a 'he' and a Chevy a 'she' . . .

"And that's all."

Macunaíma stopped. Gut emotion wailed from the mouths of the youngsters. The cool air floated belly-up over the water. The young man dunked his head to hide his tears and brought back a tambiú in his teeth, its tail flapping like crazy. He shared the snack with the girl. Then over by the front door a Fiat puma opened its maw and roared at the moon:

"Awooga! Awooga!"

A formidable din was heard and the air seized up with the overpowering stench of fish. It was Venceslau Pietro Pietra arriving. The driver sprang up and so did the maid. They held out their hands to Macunaíma, inviting him along:

"Mr. Giant's back home from his trip, shall we all go see how he is?"

So they did. They came upon Venceslau Pietro Pietra at the front gate chatting with a reporter. The giant chuckled at the three of em and said to the driver:

"Shall we go in?"

"Sure thing!"

Piaimã had pierced ears on account of his earrings. He stuck one of the young man's legs in his right ear, the other in his left and carried the boy on his back. They crossed the park and went in the house. Right smack in the middle of the entry hall paneled in acapu and furnished with couches woven out of titica vines by a German Jew from Manaus, you could see an enormous hole with a japecanga vine swing over it. Piaimã sat the boy on the vine and asked if he wanted to swing for a bit. The boy nodded. Piaimã sent him swingalinging, then yanked all of a sudden. Japecangas have thorns . . . The thorns dug into the chauffeur's flesh and blood started flowing into the hole.

"Okay! that's enough for me!" cried the chauffeur.

"Swing, I say!" answered Piaimã.

The blood was flowing. The giant's ol' caapora crone was standing under the hole and the blood was dripping into a vat of pasta that she was making for her sweetie. The young man moaned on the swing:

"If only Mama and Papa were here godwillin', I wouldn't be stuck in the hands of this villain! . . ."

Then Piaimã gave the vine a mighty yank and the boy fell into the pasta sauce.

Venceslau Pietro Pietra went to fetch Macunaíma. The hero was already laughing with the little maid. The giant said to him:

"Shall we go in?"

Macunaíma stretched his arms whispering:

"Ah! . . . just so lazy! . . ."

"C'mon let's go! . . . Shall we?"

"Sure alright . . ."

Then Piaimã did the same to him as he did to the chauffeur, carrying the hero upside down on his back with his feet stuck through the holes in his ears. Macunaíma aimed his blowgun and riding upside how he was, it was like watching a sharpshooter at the circus, hitting his target right in the peanuts. The giant got real irritated turned round and saw what was going on.

"Cut that out, my noble countryman!" he said.

He took the blowgun and hurled it away. Macunaíma grabbed all the branches that brushed past his hands.

"Hey what're you doing?" asked the giant suspiciously.

"Can't you see those branches are hitting me in the face!"

Piaimã turned the hero right side up. Then Macunaíma tickled the giant's ears with the branches. Piaimã howled with laughter and hopped in delight.

"Quit pestering me, my noble countryman!" he went.

They got to the entry hall. Under the stairs was a golden cage full of little songbirds. And the giant's songbirds were snakes and lizards. Macunaíma leaped into the cage and started eating snakes on the sly. Piaimã called him over to the swing but Macunaíma was swallowing snakes counting:

"Five to go . . ."

And he swallowed another varmint. Finally the snakes were all gone and the hero burst furiously out of the cage right foot first. Seething with rage he glared at the muiraquitã robber and growled:

"Grrr . . . just so lazy!"

But Piaimã insisted the hero have a go.

"I don't even really know how to swing . . . You better go first," Macunaíma growled.

"Fat chance, hero! It's easy as pie! Just giddyup on that jape-canga 'n go: I'm a-swinging!"

"Okay I'll go but you first, giant."

Piaimã insisted, but he kept telling the giant to go first. So then Venceslau Pietro Pietra got up on the vine and Macunaíma swung him harder and harder. He sang:

> *Rock-a-bye, captain,*
> *O captain, my captain,*
> *Sword at his waist and*
> *Steed in his hand!*

He yanked hard. The thorns pierced the giant's flesh and blood gushed out. The caapora crone down below didn't know all that blood was coming from her giant and she caught the downpour in the pasta. The sauce was getting thicker.

"Stop! Stop!" cried Piaimã.

"Swing, I say!" Macunaíma replied.

He swung till the giant was dizzy as can be then gave the jape-canga vine a tremendous yank. It was cause he'd eaten snakes and was a raging ball of fury. Venceslau Pietro Pietra fell into the hole bellowing in singsong:

"Ding dong ding . . . if I get outta this thing, I won't eat anyone ever again!"

He caught sight of the steaming pasta below and bellowed at it:

"Outta the way or else I'll swallow you whole!"

But did the alligator get outta the way? neither did that pot! The giant fell into the boiling pasta and such a powerful stench of cooked leather wafted into the air that every last sparrow in the city dropped dead and the hero keeled over. Piaimã put up a good fight and was now hanging on by a thread. With a gargantuan effort he lifted himself from the bottom of the vat. He swatted away the noodles streaming down his face, rolled his eyes upward, licked his bristling mustache:

"IT NEEDS CHEESE!" he shouted . . .

And breathed his last.

That was the end of Venceslau Pietro Pietra who was Piaimã the Giant, eater of men.

When Macunaíma came to, he went to fetch the muiraquitã and took the trolley machine back to the boarding house. And he sobbed a-wailing like this:

"Muiraquitã, muiraquitã of my lovely, you're all I see, but where oh where is she! . . ."

Chapter 15. *Oibê's Innards*

And so the three brothers returned to their native birthplace.

They were pleased as punch but the hero was happiest of all since he possessed those feelings that only a hero can: an immense satisfaction. They set off. While crossing Jaraguá Peak, Macunaíma turned round contemplating the mighty city of São Paulo. He ruminated mournfully a long while and in the end shook his head murmuring:

"Ants aplenty and nobody's healthy, so go the ills of Brazil . . ."

He dried his tears, steadied his quivering bottom lip. Then he cast a caborje spell: waving his arms in the air he turned that gigantic taba into a sloth made entirely of stone. They set off.

After much deliberation, Macunaíma had spent every last penny on what thrilled him most from the Paulista civilization. He took with him a Smith & Wesson revolver a Patek Philippe watch and a pair of leghorn chickens. Macunaíma had made the revolver and watch into earrings and carried a cage with the hen and rooster. Not one red cent was left from all his lottery winnings but there swingalinging from his pierced bottom lip was the muiraquitã.

And on account of it the going was easy. There they went rolling down the Rio Araguaia and when Jiguê paddled Maanape would steer with his little oar. They were feeling real lucky-duck again. Meanwhile Macunaíma sat ready for action in the bow, taking note of all the bridges that needed to be built or repaired in order to better the lives of the people of Goiás. After night-fall, catching sight of the flickering lights of drowned folk dancing a mellow samba across the flooded marshlands, Macunaíma sat gazing gazing and fell sound asleep. He sprang wide awake the next day and standing tall in the bow of the igarité with his left arm looped through the birdcage handle, he strummed his little guitar singing his cares to the world belting out his longing for his native land, like this:

> Antianti the tapejara guides us,
> —Pirá-fish hey hey,
> Ariramba the cook feeds us,
> —Pirá-fish hey hey,
> Taperá, where's our long-lost tapera
> Home on the banks of the Uraricoera?
> —Pirá-fish hey hey . . .

And his gaze went skimming skimming along the surface of the river seeking his childhood homeland. Down the river they went and every whiff of fish every cluster of craguatá every single everything sent a jolt of excitement through him and the hero sang his cares to the world like a madman improvising dueling ballads and nonsense medleys:

> Taperá tapejara,
> —Caboré,
> Arapaçu paçoca,
> —Caboré,
> C'mon brothers, let's light out for
> The banks of the Uraricoera!
> —Caboré!

The Araguaia's waters went murmuring along coaxing the igarité on course with its soft crooning and from a long ways off came the lyrical siren song of the uiaras. Vei, the Sun, lashed at the sweat-slicked backs of Maanape and Jiguê as they paddled and at the hero's hairy body as he stood there. The sweltering heat fanned the flames of delirium in the trio. Macunaíma remembered that he was Emperor of the Virgin-Forest. He gestured fiercely at the Sun, shouting:

"Eropita boiamorebo!"

All at once the sky went dark and a reddening cloud rose up from the horizon, dusking over the calm of day. The reddening came closer came closer and it was that flock of scarlet macaws and jandayas, all them chatterboxes, it was the trumpeter-parrot it was the yellow-faced parrot it was the bobtail parakeet it was the xarã the purple-breasted parrot the blue-fronted ajuru-curau the ajuru-curica arari ararica araraúna araraí araguaí arara-taua maracanã maitaca ararapiranga catorra teriba camiranga anaca anapura blue-and-gold macaws blue-winged parrotlets parakeets galore, all of em, that bright-dappled cortege of Macunaíma the emperor. And all them chatterboxes formed a canopy of squawking and wings shielding the hero from the Sun's vengeful spite. It was such a clamor of waters gods and birdies that nothing else whatsoever could be heard and the igarité came to a near standstill in bewilderment. But every so often Macunaíma would gesture fiercely at everything, spooking the leghorns as he hollered:

"There once was a brown cow that went moo, whoever talks first has to eat up its poo! Ring-a-ding stop!"

The world went mute not uttering a peep and the silence slackened the sultry air in the shade of the igarité. And far far away faintly faintly you could hear the babbling Uraricoera. And it got the hero all the more excited. The little guitar twanged on. Macunaíma would hock and spit in the river and as the sinking gobs transformed into sickening little matamatá turtles, the hero sang his cares to the world like a madman with no clue what the heck he was singing, like this:

Panapaná pá-panapaná,
Panapaná pá-panapanema:
Boop-oop-a-doop on the poop-oop-a-doop,
*   —Lil sister,*
On the banks of the Uraricoera!

Afterward the yawning-night swallowed up all the clamoring and the world went to sleep. The only one left was Capei, the Moon, big and fat, chubby-cheeked just like one of them Polack broads after one of them nights, hoo boy! all that gleeful getting up to no good all pretty girls and all that caxiri! . . . Then Macunaíma was struck with longing for all that had happened in that great big Paulistano taba. He saw all those ladies with skin so very pale who he'd played husband and wife with, what good times! . . . He whispered sweetly, "Mani! Mani! little daughters of manioc! . . ." His bottom lip started quivering from so much emotion that the muiraquitã just about fell in the river. Macunaíma stuck the tembetá back in his lip. Then he thought very solemnly about the muiraquitã's mistress, that vixen, that delectable hellcat who used to beat him up so bad, Ci. Ah! Ci, Mother of the Forest, that she-devil who'd become unforgettable on account of making him sleep in a hammock woven out of her hair! . . . "When far and away true loves must part, long is the labor for the suffering heart . . ." he cogitated. What a bewitching she-devil! . . . And she was drifting around brooding up there in the field of the heavens in high style all done up roaming around playing with who only knows . . . He got jealous. Flinging his arms in the air and spooking the leghorns he prayed to the Father of Love:

Rudá! Rudá!
Thou who art in the heavens above
And sendest forth the rains to us.
Rudá! make it so that my beloved,

For as many lovers as she may take,
Finds that they all wimp out!
Awaken in that she-devil
Longin' for her he-devil!
Make her remember me tomorrow
When the Sun goes down in the west! . . .

He gazed hard at the sky. There was no sign of Ci up above, just Capei, that fatty, hogging everything. The hero lay down in the igarité, used the cage for a pillow and fell asleep among the black flies no-see-ums skeeters.

The night was already turning golden when Macunaíma woke up to the cowbirds squawking in a bamboo grove. He contemplated the view and hopped down to the beach, telling Jiguê:

"Hold on a sec."

He went deep into the forest, a league and a half in. He went to find the beautiful Iriqui, his gal who used to be Jiguê's and who was waiting there making herself pretty and scratching at her mucuim bites, seated on the sprawling roots of a samaúma. The two cuddled up gleefully, played around a bunch and came back to the igarité.

When they got there toward noon the flock of parrots fanned out once more guarding Macunaíma. And so it went for days on end. One afternoon the hero was sick and tired of it and remembered to sleep on solid ground, so he did. No sooner did he set foot on the beach than a monster rose up before him. It was that beast Pondê, a jurucutu owl from the Rio Solimões that turned into a person at-night and gobbled up stragglers. However Macunaíma grabbed an arrow tipped with the flat head of the sacred ant known as curupê and without even aiming, bullseye! what a beaut. That beast Pondê burst back into an owl. Up ahead after crossing a plain and now climbing a jagged peak full of outcroppings he ran into that Mapinguari Monster monkey-man who roams the woods doing naughty things to young ladies. The monster grabbed Macunaíma but the hero pulled out his toaquiçu and showed it to the Mapinguari.

"Get it straight, pardner!"

The monster guffawed and let Macunaíma pass. The hero walked a league and a half searching for someplace to rest without any ants. He climbed to the tippy top of a cumaru tree well over a hunnerd feet tall and after squinting hard he finally spotted a faint glimmer in the distance. He moseyed out there and came upon a shanty. And the shanty belonged to Oibê. Macunaíma knocked and a sweet lil voice croaked from inside:

"Who goes there!"

"I come in peace!"

Then the door opened and there appeared a creature so humongous that the hero was thunderstruck. It was that monster Oibê, the great big terrible worm. The hero felt a chill down his spine but remembered his Smith & Wesson, plucked up his courage and asked for lodging.

"Come on in, make yourself at home."

Macunaíma went on in, took a seat in a wicker basket and stayed put. Finally he asked:

"Wanna talk?"

"Sure."

"Bout what?"

Oibê scratched his goatee mulling it over and on the spur of the moment thought up a good one:

"Wanna talk about dirty stuff?"

"Hoo wee! that's awful, I like it!" the hero cried.

And they talked a whole hour's worth of dirty stuff.

Oibê was cooking up his din-din. Macunaíma wasn't the least bit hungry but he put the cage down and rubbing his belly just for show went:

"Yawp!"

Oibê muttered:

"What's that all about, folks!"

"It's the hunger talking!"

Oibê picked up a big wooden dish, tossed in some beans and yams, filled a gourd bowl with manioc flour and gave it to the hero. But he didn't offer a single morsel of the innards grilling on a sassafras skewer and smelling so tasty. Macunaíma swallowed everything without chewing then wasn't hungry at all but his mouth started watering on account of them roasting innards. He rubbed his belly and went:

"Yawp!"

Oibê muttered:

"What's that all about, folks!"

"It's the thirst talking!"

Oibê got a pail and went to fetch water from the well. While he was gone, Macunaíma pulled the sassafras skewer from the coals swallowed the innards whole without chewing and sat waiting carefree as ever. When the great big worm brought back the pail, Macunaíma gulped down a whole coco full. Sprawling out afterward he sighed:

"Yawp!"

The monster was thunderstruck:

"What now, folks!"

"It's the sleep talking!"

So then Oibê took Macunaíma to the guest room said nighty-night and closed the door behind him. He went to have supper. Macunaíma put the cage in a corner, covering the pair of chickens with some patchwork quilts. He took a gander round the room. There was a low steady din coming from all over. Macunaíma struck his flint stone and saw that it was cockroaches. He climbed into his hammock all the same but not before peeking once more to see if there was anything else his leghorns needed. The pair were mighty content, indeed, eating their fill of roaches. Macunaíma chuckled to himself, burped and fell asleep. Soon enough he was covered in roaches licking at him.

When Oibê saw that Macunaíma had eaten up the innards, he was mad as heck. He snatched up a little bell, draped himself in a white sheet and went to go haunt his guest. But just as a joke. He knocked on the door and wiggled the bell, ding-ding!

"Hello?"

"I've come for my innards-nards-nards-nards-nards, ding-ding!"

Then Macunaíma realized that it wasn't a ghost after all, but that monster Oibê, the great big terrible worm. He plucked up his courage grabbed his left earring which was the revolver machine and shot at the ghost. But that didn't faze Oibê who kept coming closer. The hero got the heebie-jeebies again. He leaped out the hammock snatched up the cage and slipped out the window, chucking roaches as he went. Oibê chased after him. But it was just as a joke that he wanted to eat the hero. Macunaíma streaked across the arid backcountry but the great big worm was hot on his heels. Then he stuck his pointer finger down his pie-hole, tickled around and heaved up the manioc flour he'd swallowed. The flour turned into a colossal sand plain and as the monster struggled to cross that wide world of sand slipping and sliding all over, Macunaíma got away. He cut right, scrambled down Thunderclap Mountain which goes off every seven years, picked his way through some thickets and after fording some white-capped rapids made it clear across the state of Sergipe and stopped short panting for breath in a narrow pass. Before him loomed a huge rock formation cut through by a cavern with a little shrine inside. At the entrance to the cave stood a friar. Macunaíma asked the friar:

"What name do you go by?"

The friar fixed a pair of steely eyes on the hero and answered slow as molasses:

"I am the painter Mendonça Mar. Three centuries ago, disgusted by the injustice of men, I retreated from them, making a go of it out here in the sertão. I discovered this grotto built this shrine called Bom Jesus da Lapa with my own two hands and here I live pardoning folks, changed into the Friar Francisco da Soledade."

"That's nice," Macunaíma said. And shot off like blazes.

But that territory was full of caverns and not far ahead was another stranger making such silly movements that Macunaíma stopped in his tracks dumbfounded. It was Hércules Florence. He'd put a piece of glass over the opening of a peewee cave, and was covering and uncovering the glass with a big taioba leaf. Macunaíma asked:

"Well well well! Say, what're you doing there, mister!"

The stranger turned to him, eyes shining with joy, and said:

"Gardez cette date: 1927! Je viens d'inventer la photographie!"

Macunaíma burst into laughter.

"Hoo wee! They invented that years ago, mister!"

Then Hércules Florence fell upon his taioba leaf in a stupor and began setting down musical notation of a scientific memory in regards to birdsong. What a crackpot. Macunaíma sped off.

After running a league and a half he looked back and saw that Oibê was already catching up. He stuck his pointer finger down his pie-hole and splat on the ground went all the yam he'd swallowed which turned into a squirming mass of turtles. Oibê had a heck of a time gulping down that crapload of turtles and Macunaíma got away. A league and a half farther he looked back. Just like that Oibê was on his tail. Then he stuck his pointer finger down his pie-hole and heaved up nothing but beans 'n water. It all turned into a muddy bog brimming with bullfrogs and as Oibê wrangled his way across all that muck, the hero scooped up some worms for the chickens and blew outta there. He had a good head start so he stopped for a breather. Boy was he surprised cause he'd run so darn far he was right back at the front door to Oibê's shanty. He decided to go hide in the orchard. There was a starfruit tree and Macunaíma started yanking off its branches to hide underneath. The broken branches took to dripping tears and the starfruit tree's lament was heard:

My dear father's gardener,
No don't you cut my hair,
'Cause the wicked one did bury me
For the fruit of the old fig tree
That all the little birdies did eat . . .
    —Shoo, little birdie, shoo shoo!

All the little birdies sobbed a-wailing with pity in their nests and the hero froze in fright. He clutched the special pouch he wore around his neck with his other charms and cast a mandinga spell. The starfruit tree turned into a very chic princess. The hero had a burning desire to play around with the princess but Oibê was like to be crashing round those parts already. In-fact:

"I've come for my innards-nards-nards-nards-nards, ding-ding!"

Macunaíma took the princess by the hand and they made a break for it. Up ahead was a strangler fig with a massive tangle of roots hanging down. By now Oibê was nipping at their heels and Macunaíma didn't have time for anything. So he and the princess slipped into a gap between the roots. But that great big worm stuck his arm in and grabbed hold of the hero's leg. He was about to pull but Macunaíma burst into knowing laughter and said:

"Ha, you think you got my gam, but that ain't it! That's a root, you dimwit!"

The great big worm let go. Macunaíma hollered:

"Actually that really *was* my leg, you nincompoop!"

Oibê stuck his arm back in but the hero had already pulled his leg away and the great big worm found nothing but roots. There was a heron close by. Oibê said to her:

"Hey heron, keep an eye on the hero, wontcha sister? Don't let him get away cause I'm gonna get a hoe to dig him out."

The heron stood watch. When Oibê was far away Macunaíma said to her:

"Oh really, you ninny, that's how you keep an eye on a hero?! Come closer 'n keep your eyes peeled!"

So the heron did. Then Macunaíma hurled a fistful of fire ants in her eyes and while the blinded heron was shrieking he and the princess burst out the hole and slipped away again. Approaching Santo Antônio in Mato Grosso they came across a banana tree and were starving to death. Macunaíma said to the princess:

"Shimmy up there, eat the green ones those are good and toss me the yellow ones."

So she did. The hero stuffed himself silly while the princess danced with indigestion for his enjoyment. Oibê was already gaining on em and they gave him the slip again.

After running another league and a half, they finally reached a patch of high ground jutting out of the Araguaia. But the igarité was beached a good ways down on the far bank with Maanape Jiguê and the beautiful Iriqui, all those companions fast asleep. Macunaíma looked back. Oibê catching up. Then he stuck his pointer finger down his pie-hole for the last time, tickled around and plunked the innards in the water. The innards turned into a floating island lush with vegetation. Macunaíma set the cage gently on the soft grasses, tossed the princess over there and shoving off hard from the bank with his foot, got the island far enough from the shore for the current to take hold. Oibê showed up but the fugitives were already long gone. Then the great big worm who was a famous werewolf started shivering and yelping up a storm getting smaller getting smaller all shivering grew a tail and turned into a crab-eating fox. He opened his disenchanted jaw wide and out from his belly came a blue butterfly. It was the soul of a man who'd been trapped inside the wolf's body under the spell of the fearsome Carrapatu who dwells in the Iporanga Grotto.

Macunaíma and the princess went downriver playing around. Now there they are laughing with each other.

When they floated right past the igarité, Macunaíma's hollering woke his brothers who followed after. Iriqui got jealous straight away seeing as the hero didn't want nothing to do with her no more and only ever played around with the princess. And to see if she could win back the hero she launched into a stupendous fit of bawling. Jiguê felt sorry for her straight away and told Macunaíma to go play around with Iriqui for a spell. Jiguê was a big dummy. But the hero, who was already exasperated with Iriqui, replied:

"Iriqui's just ho-hum, brother, but the princess, wowza! Don't pay no mind to Iriqui! Listen, never trust a thief you'll be sorry if you do, never trust a woman she'll make a monkey out of you, boo hoo hoo . . . don't nobody fall for it!"

And he went off to play around with the princess. Iriqui felt sad as sad can be, woe is me, summoned six blue-and-gold macaws, went up with them to the sky, weeping light, and turned into a star. The bright yellow macaws turned into stars too. They're the Seven Sisters.

Chapter 16. *Uraricoera*

The next day Macunaíma woke up with a bad cough and a slight fever that wouldn't let up. Maanape had an inkling and went to boil avocado sprouts, supposing the hero had consumption. Actually it was impaludism, and the cough was just on account of the laryngitis that everyone gets in São Paulo. Now Macunaíma spent the whole time belly down in the bow of the igarité and wasn't ever getting better. When the princess couldn't stand it anymore and came over to play around, the hero actually refused for once sighing:

"Oof . . . just so lazy . . ."

The next day they reached the headwaters of a river and heard the babbling of the Uraricoera close by. There it was. A loud-mouth little birdie high up in a munguba tree caught sight of the merry band of travelers, crying out at once:

"Heigh ho, harbor missus, wontcha let me pass!"

Macunaíma thanked him gladly. Standing there he surveyed the passing landscape. They were coming up on Fort São Joaquim built by the great Marquis of Pombal's brother. Macunaíma said so-long to the corporal and the private whose sole possessions were some tattered breeches and the caps on their heads and who spent their days guarding the saúva ants from the cannons. At last, it was all familiar as ever. You could make out the gentle mound that had once been mother, in that place called Father of the Tocandeira, you could see that deceiving swamp strewn with

Victoria regia water lilies hiding the puraquês and pitiús and past the tapir's watering hole you could see the old field that now lay fallow and the old maloca that now lay in ruins, an abandoned tapera. Macunaíma wept.

They landed and went inside the tapera. Night-fall was coming on. Maanape and Jiguê had a mind to go torch fishing to catch whatever they could and the princess went to see if she could rustle up some arezi for them to eat. The hero stayed behind resting. That's what he was doing when he felt a hand weighing on his shoulder. He turned round and stared. Next to him was a bearded old man. Says the old codger:

"Who be ye, noble foreigner?"

"I'm no stranger, pal. I'm Macunaíma the hero and I've come back to settle once more in the land of my people. Who're you?"

The old man shooed the mosquitoes bitterly and replied:

"I am João Ramalho."

Then João Ramalho stuck two fingers in his mouth and whistled. Out came his wife and their fifteen kids lined up like steps one after another. And off they went in search of a new homeland with nobody else there.

Bright and early the next day everybody went off to bust their tails. The princess went out to the crops Maanape went into the woods and Jiguê went down to the river. Macunaíma excused himself, climbed into his dugout canoe and hopped over to the mouth of the Rio Negro to find the conscience he'd left on the Isle of Marapatá. Did the alligator find it? Neither did he. So the hero took the conscience of a Spanish-American man, stuck it in his head, and it worked out fine all the same.

He passed a piracema of jaraqui migrating upstream. Macunaíma fell to fishing and let his mind go wandering wandering till he realized he was at the town of Óbidos, his dugout chockfull of fresh fish. But the hero had to toss it overboard cause in Óbidos the saying goes, "Just one taste of jaraqui, and you'll never leave," and he had to get back to the Uraricoera. He got back and as it was still the peak of day he lay in the shade of an inga tree picked his ticks and fell asleep. As afternoon rolled around everyone came back to the tapera except not Macunaíma. The others went out to wait for him. Jiguê crouched putting his ear to the ground to see if he could hear the hero's footsteps, not a thing. Maanape climbed an inajá sapling to see if he could spot the glint of the hero's earrings, not a thing. So then they walked through the woods and the freshly cleared field shouting:

"Macunaíma, oh brother of ours! . . ."

Not a thing. Jiguê got to the foot of the inga tree and shouted:

"Oh brother of ours!"

"What's up!"

"There you are, bet you were sleeping!"

"Uh-uh, not a wink! I was luring a humongous tinamou. You made such a hullabaloo, the inambu got away!"

They headed home. And that's how it went day after day. The brothers were getting mighty suspicious. Macunaíma noticed and laid it on thick:

"I go out hunting but I don't find squat. Jiguê doesn't hunt doesn't fish, just sleeps all day."

Jiguê got mad cause the fish were getting scarce and the game even scarcer. He went down to the river beach to see if he could catch anything and ran into the shaman Tzaló, who's only got one leg that's all. The Catimbó shaman had a magic gourd bowl made from half a jerimum squash. He dipped the gourd in the river, filled it halfway with water and dumped it on the beach. A whole mess of fish spilled out. Jiguê paid close attention to what the shaman did. Tzaló tossed the gourd aside and started clubbing the fish dead. Then Jiguê stole the gourd from the shaman Tzaló, who's only got one leg that's all.

Later on he did just like he'd seen and out came loads of fish, out came pirandira out came pacu out came catfish out came mudcat jundía tucunaré, all them fishes, and Jiguê took as much as he could carry back to the tapera after hiding the gourd in some hanging vine roots. Everybody was thunderstruck by that whole world of fish and ate their fill. Macunaíma got suspicious.

Next day he waited with his left eye a-snoozing for Jiguê to go fishing, then followed. He figured everything out. After his brother took off, Macunaíma put the cage with the leghorns on the ground got the hidden gourd and did just like his brother. And out came loads of fish, out came acará out came piracanjuba out came aviú guarijuba, piramutaba mandi surubim, all them fishes. Macunaíma tossed the gourd aside in his hurry to kill all that fish, the gourd bowl fell on a rock and thwap! plunged in the river. The pirandira named Padzá was swimming by. The fish took it for a punkin and swallowed the gourd which turned into Padzá's bladder. Then Macunaíma slipped the cage on his arm went back to the tapera and told what had happened. Jiguê was mad as heck.

"Look here, princess sister-in-law, I'm the one fishing, your guy just sleeps under the inga tree and still manages to trip everyone up!"

"Liar!"

"Okay then what'd you do today?"

"I caught a deer."

"Where's it at!"

"Gee whiz, I ate it! There I was, heading down a trail, see, when I ran smack into the tracks of a . . . caatinga deer, no wait it was a forest deer. I got real low and followed its tracks. Eyes to the ground eyes to the ground, you know, bumped my head on something soft, what a hoot! guess what it was! why, the deer's butt, folks! (Macunaíma howled with laughter.) The deer asked me, 'Whatcha doing back there, kin o' mine!' 'Looking for you!' I replied. Now then, I killed that caatinga deer and ate him up, tripe and all. I was bringing back a piece for you guys, but well, I slipped crossing the bog, went a-tumbling, meat went flying and got swarmed by a buncha tanajura ants."

It was such a tall tale that Maanape got suspicious. Maanape was a sorcerer. He got right up in his brother's face and asked:

"Did you go hunting?"

"Well, I mean . . . yep."

"What'd you catch?"

"A deer."

"Malarkey!"

Maanape made a sweeping gesture. The hero blinked fearfully and confessed it was all a fib.

Next day Jiguê was out looking for the gourd when he ran into the giant-armadillo shaman known as Caicãe, who never had a mother don't know why. Sitting by the front door to his burrow Caicãe took up the little guitar he'd made from the other half of the magic punkin and fell to singing like this:

> *Whoa whoa porcupine!*
> *Whoa whoa coati!*
> *Whoa whoa tayassu!*
> *Whoa whoa peccary!*
> *Whoa whoa jaguar too!*
> > *Pee yew! . . .*

Just like that. A whole lotta game showed up. Jiguê kept watching. Caicãe tossed his magic guitar aside, grabbed a club and went to whack that whopping load of game all in a daze. Then Jiguê stole the guitar from the shaman Caicãe, who never had a mother don't know why.

Later on he sang just like he'd heard and a whole flood of game stopped right in front of him. Jiguê took as much as he could carry back to the tapera after hiding the guitar in some other vine roots. Everyone was astounded once again and ate their fill. Once again Macunaíma got suspicious.

Next day he waited with his left eye a-snoozing for Jiguê to leave, then followed. He figured it all out. After his brother went back to the tapera Macunaíma got the guitar, did just like he'd seen, and there came a crapload of game, deer agoutis anteaters capybaras armadillas aperemas pacas pampas-foxes otters muçuã-mud-turtles musk-hogs muriquis tegus collared peccaries white-lipped peccaries tapirs, the sabatira tapir, wild cats, the spotted jaguar the deer-eater the panther the margay ocelot oncilla, suçuarana cougar, it was a whole crapload of game! The hero got spooked by that tremendous bevy of beasts and streaked outta there sending the guitar hurtling. The cage swinging from his arm went banging into trees and the rooster and hen went buck buck bacaw in deafening squawks. The hero thought it was that whole bevy of beasts and sprinted even faster.

The guitar fell into the jaws of a white-lipped peccary who had a belly button on its back and broke all to smash into ten times ten shards that the wild beasts swallowed thinking it was jerimum squash. The shards turned into the animals' bladders.

The hero crashed into the tapera like a desperado huffing and puffing his lungs out. Soon as he caught his breath he told what had happened. Jiguê was furious and said:

"From now on, no more hunting and no more fishing neither!"

And he went to sleep. Everybody started getting awful hungry. Beg as they might Jiguê just hopped in his hammock and shut his eyes. The hero swore vengeance. He made a fake fishing hook out of a sucuri fang and told the magic charm:

"Listen fake hook, if brother Jiguê comes to try you out, prick his hand."

Jiguê couldn't sleep on account of being so hungry and catching sight of the fishing hook said to his brother:

"Say brother, that hook any good?"

"Expialidocious!" Macunaíma went and kept cleaning the birdcage.

Jiguê decided to go fishing since he was godawful hungry, and said:

"Lemme see if that hook's any good."

He grabbed the magic charm and tried it out on his palm. The sucuri fang pierced his skin and shot all its venom in there. Jiguê ran into the woods and for as much wild manioc as he chewed and swallowed, wasn't no use at all. So then he went looking for the head of an anhuma bird that folks used to put on snake bites. He laid it on his hand. Wasn't no use at all. The venom turned into a leprous sore and started eating away at Jiguê. First it ate an arm then half his body then his legs then the other half of his body then the other arm then his neck and his head. All that remained was Jiguê's shadow.

The princess was furious. It was cause lately she'd been playing around with Jiguê. Macunaíma knew all about it but figured, "You reap what you sow, that's how it goes, and opportunity makes a thief of us all, so be it! . . ." Then he shrugged his shoulders. The angry princess told the shadow:

"When the hero starts roaming around hungry turn yourself into a cashew tree a banana tree and some roast deer."

The shadow was poisonous on account of the leprosy and the princess wanted to kill Macunaíma.

Next day the hero woke up so hungry that he went roaming to take his mind off it. He came across a cashew tree bursting with fruit. He wanted to eat some but bore witness to the leprous shadow and kept going. A league and a half farther he came across some roast deer that was still smoking. By now he'd gone purple with hunger but saw that the roast meat was the leprous shadow and kept going. A league and a half farther he came across a banana tree heavy with ripe fruit. But now the hero was cross-eyed with hunger. His crossed eyes made him see his brother's shadow on one side and the banana tree on the other.

"Yee haw, now I can eat!" he went.

And gobbled up all the bananas. And the bananas were the leprous shadow of his brother Jiguê. Macunaíma was gonna die. Then he remembered to spread the disease to others so he wouldn't die all by his lonesome. He picked up a saúva ant and rubbed it all over the sore on his nose, ants used to be folks just like us, and the ant got leprosy. Then the hero grabbed a jaguataci ant and did the same thing. The jaguataci got leprosy too. Next in line was the aqueque ant, devourer of seeds, then the guiquém ant, then the tracuá ant, and the deep black mumbuca ant, they all got leprosy. There weren't any more ants near where the hero was sitting. He felt too lazy to reach his arm out on account of being at death's door. He waited for his dying rally to kick in, got a surge of strength, and caught the birigui biting his knee. He gave the disease to that little sandfly. That's why nowadays when that bloodsucker bites us, he gets under the skin, passes right through the body and out the other side, while the hole he went in turns into that horrible festering wound called a Bauru sore.

Macunaíma had spread leprosy to seven other folks and bounced back all of a sudden, heading back to the tapera. Jiguê's shadow conceded that indeed the hero was very intelligent and getting discouraged decided to go back to its family. It was already night-time and the shadow got all mixed up with the dark and couldn't find the nearest path anymore. It sat on a rock and bellowed:

"Bring some fire, princess sister-in-law!"

The princess came hobbling over with a glowing ember to light the way, hampered by a bad case of zamparina. The shadow swallowed up both fire and sister-in-law. It bellowed again:

"Bring some fire, brother Maanape!"

Maanape soon came with another glowing ember to light the way. And he shuffled along in a stupor since the kissing bug had sucked his blood and Maanape was suffering from hookworm. The shadow swallowed up both fire and brother Maanape. It bellowed:

"Bring some fire, brother Macunaíma!"

It was aiming to swallow up the hero too but upon realizing what had happened to his brother and his gal, Macunaíma shut the door and stayed very quiet in the tapera. The shadow kept asking for fire, kept asking but getting no reply, stayed put whimpering into the wee hours. Then Capei appeared, illuminating the land, and the leprous shadow managed to reach the tapera. It sat in the canjerana tree by the entryway and waited for dawn to get revenge on its brother.

Come-morning it was still crouched there. Macunaíma woke up and listened. Not a sound was heard so he concluded:

"Yee haw! It went away!"

And set out for a stroll. When he stepped out the door the shadow climbed up on his shoulder. The hero didn't suspect a thing. He was starving hungry but the shadow wouldn't let him eat. It swallowed up whatever Macunaíma could find, tamorita mangarito taro biribá cajuí guaimbé guacá uxi inga bacuri cupuaçu pupunha taperebá graviola grumixama, all them forest fruits and roots. Then Macunaíma went fishing since now there wasn't anybody left to fish for him anymore. But for every fish he'd pluck off the hook and toss in his basket, the shadow would hop off his shoulder, swallow up the fish and get back on its perch. The hero sat stewing on it: "Just you wait, I'll fix you good!" When he got a bite, Macunaíma mustered a heroic bout of strength, swung his fishing rod with such brute force that the momentum sent that fish flying all the way to Guiana. The shadow chased after the fish. Then Macunaíma winged it outta the woods in the opposite direction. When the shadow got back and didn't find its brother anymore, it sped off on his trail. After sprinting a spell, passing through the land of the White-Armadillo Indians and getting such a mighty fright from the shadows of Jorge Velho and Zumbi having it out that he scooted by without begging their pardon, the hero, clear outta steam, looked back and saw that the shadow was already closing in on him. He was in Paraíba and just didn't feel like speeding off so he stopped. It was because the hero had impaludism. Close by, some workers were destroying anthills so they could build a dam. Macunaíma asked for some water. They didn't have a single drop but they gave him some juicy umbu root. The hero quenched the leghorns' thirst, thanked the men and yelled:

"The devil take working folk!"

The workers sicced their hounds on the hero. That's exactly what he wanted cause it put him in a panic and he shot off like blazes. Before him stretched a long winding cattle trail. With the shadow hot on his heels and gaining fast, Macunaíma didn't think twice: he took the cattle route. Up ahead having a snooze was a Malabar bull named Espácio who'd come from Piauí. The hero was all riled up and gave him a furious shove. Which made the ox take off galloping wild with fright and charge blindly downhill past the herd. Then Macunaíma swerved haphazardly down a side trail and hid under a leafy mucumuco. The shadow heard all the racket from the galloping steer, thought it was Macunaíma and gave chase. It caught up to the ox and not wanting to have come all that way for nothing, perched on his back. And sang contentedly:

My ox so pretty,
Happy as can be,
Now bid farewell
To all the family!

Hey . . . ho boom-bah,
Rest easy my ox!
Hey . . . ho boom-bah,
Rest easy my ox!

Yet never again could the ox eat a bite, the shadow swallowed up everything before the poor beast could. Then the steer started getting so sad and blue so sad and blue, all skin and bones and moving painfully slow. When they passed by the grazing spot called Água Doce just outside Guararapes, the ox gaped in awe at the lovely sight right smack in the middle of that endless desert, a shady orange grove with chickens pecking in the dirt below. It was a harbinger of death . . . The hopeless shadow now sang:

My ox so pretty,
Hopeless ox o' mine,
Now bid farewell,
Until a year's time!

> *Hey . . . ho boom-bah,*
> *Rest easy my ox!*
> *Hey . . . ho boom-bah,*
> *Rest easy my ox!*

Next day the young steer was dead. It started turning green and
greener still . . . The grievous shadow consoled itself singing:

> *My ox is dead and gone,*
> *What shall become of me?*
> *Go send for a new one,*
> *   —Lil sister,*
> *Down in Bom Jardim . . .*

And Bom Jardim was a ranch down south in Rio Grande do Sul.
Then there came a giantess who liked to play around with the
steer. She saw the dead ox, cried her eyes out and wanted to take
the corpse away with her.

The shadow got angry and sang:

> *You'd best move along, miss giant,*
> *'Tis a treacherous affair!*
> *The one who leaves a lover*
> *Is kind beyond compare!*

The giantess said thank you and danced away. Then an individual
by the name of Manuel da Lapa passed by with bundles of cashew
leaves and cotton. The shadow greeted its pal:

> *Mister Manué who comes from Açu,*
> *Mister Manué who comes from Açu,*
> *Here he comes now with leaves of cashew!*
>
> *Mister Manué from the rocky sertão,*
> *Mister Manué from the rocky sertão,*
> *With bundles of cotton, here he comes now!*

Manuel da Lapa puffed up with pride at this greeting and did a little thank-you tap dance and covered the corpse in bundles of cashew leaves and cotton.

The old-timer was already pulling the night out from its hole and the shadow, getting all mixed up, couldn't see the ox anymore under the cotton tufts and foliage and started dancing around to find it. A firefly was mighty surprised at the sight and asked in song:

> *O lovely oxherd girl*
> *What brings you to these parts?*
>
> *I've come for my cattle,*
> > *—Lil sister,*
> *That hereabouts I lost.*

It was as if the shadow was singing the response. Then the dancing firefly zipped down the tree trunk and showed the ox to the shadow. It climbed onto the dead animal's green belly and stayed there weeping.

Next day the ox was rotten. Then a whole lotta vultures came flocking, there came the camiranga-vulture, there came the turkey vulture, there came the black vulture the red-faced buzzard the yellow-headed vultures, both lesser and greater, that eats just the tongue and eyes, all them baldies came and started dancing round with glee. The biggest one led the dance singing:

The vulture two-step gets things foul foul foul!
The vulture two-step cleans it up up up!

And he was the ruxama-vulture, the king-vulture, the Father of Vultures. Then he sent a little fledgling inside the bull to see if it was nice and rotten yet. So the little vulture did. It went in through one door and out another saying yes indeedy and they all made merry together dancing and singing:

> *My pretty ox,*
> *Zebedee was he called.*
> *Round the crows go circling,*
> *My ox who's dead and gone.*
>
> > *Hey . . . ho boom-bah,*
> > *Rest easy my ox!*
> > *Hey . . . ho boom-bah,*
> > *Rest easy my ox!*

And that's how they invented that famous ox festival called Bumba Meu Boi, also known as Boi-Bumbá.

The shadow got angry that they were eating up its ox and hopped onto the ruxama-vulture's shoulder. The Father of Vultures was quite pleased and shouted:

"Found some company for my head, folks!"

And he flew up high. Ever since that day the ruxama-vulture, who is the Father of Vultures, has got two heads. The leprous shadow is the head on the left. In the beginning the king-vulture used to have just one head.

Chapter 17. *Ursa Major*

Macunaíma dragged himself back to the now-deserted tapera. He was very upset cause he couldn't comprehend the silence. He was good as dead with no one to mourn him, utterly abandoned. His brothers had gone away transformed into the left head of the ruxama-vulture and there weren't even any girls around for folks to find. The silence started whispering along the riverbanks of the Uraricoera. Just so tedious! And most of all, oh! . . . just so lazy! . . .

Macunaíma was obliged to abandon the tapera whose last remaining wall, woven from catolé palm fronds, was falling down. But the impaludism didn't give him the gumption to build even a little papiri. He'd brought his hammock up to a rise near a rock that had money buried underneath. He strung the hammock between two leafy cashew trees and didn't leave it for days on end sleeping irritably and munching on the fruit. Just so lonesome! Even his bright-dappled retinue had dissolved. Quicker than the eye an ajuru-catinga parrot zipped past in a hurry. The other parrots asked their kin where he was headed.

"The corn's ripe up in the land of the English, that's where I'm going!"

So all the parrots flew off to eat corn up in the land of the English. But first they turned into parakeets so that way, they'd eat their fill and the parakeets would take the rap. The only parrot remaining was a chatterbox aruaí. Macunaíma consoled himself figuring, "The devil makes away with ill-gotten gains . . . so be it." He spent his days wallowing in tedium and amused himself by making the bird repeat in his tribe's language all the hero's adventures starting from childhood. Ahhh . . . Macunaíma would yawn letting cashew fruit dribble out, sprawling languid in his hammock, hands making a pillow behind his head, the pair of leghorns perched on his feet and the parrot on his belly. Evening would fall. Fragrant with cashew fruit the hero would drift into a deep sleep. When dawn's rays appeared the parrot would pull his beak from his wing and have breakfast gobbling up the spiders that would spin their night-time webs between the branches and the hero's body. Afterward he'd say:

"Macunaíma!"

The sleepyhead wouldn't move a muscle.

"Macunaíma! hey Macunaíma!"

"Lemme sleep, aruaí . . ."

"Wake up, hero! It's day-time!"

"Oh . . . just so lazy! . . ."

"Ants aplenty and nobody's healthy,

So go the ills of Brazil! . . ."

Macunaíma would burst into laughter and scratch his head full of red mites which are chicken-lice. Then the parrot would repeat the episode he'd learned the night before and Macunaíma would puff up with pride at all those past glories. He'd get real excited and start telling the aruaí an even more outlandish tale. And that's how it went day after day.

Whenever Papaceia, who is the Evening Star, appeared telling every thing to go to sleep, the parrot would get all worked up at having the story break off right in the middle. One time he insulted Papaceia the star. Then Macunaíma told him:

"Don't go insulting her, aruaí! Taína-Cã is good. Taína-Cã who is Papaceia the star takes pity on the Earth and orders Emoron-Pódole to grant the peace of sleep to all the things in this world that can have peace on account of not having thoughts the way we do. Taína-Cã is a person too . . . He used to twinkle up there in the vast field of the heavens and the oldest daughter of Zozoiaça, the morubixaba of the Carajá tribe, was an old maid named Imaerô who said:

"'Father, Taína-Cã twinkles so handsomely that I want to be his wife.'

"Zozoiaça laughed heartily on account of he couldn't possibly give Taína-Cã to his daughter in marriage. Well now, at night-time down the river came a piroga made of silver, a paddler got out, knocked on the bench by the doorway and said to Imaerô:

"'I am Taína-Cã. I heard your wish and came down in a piroga made of silver. Marry me please!'

"'Yes,' said she, overjoyed.

"She let her betrothed have her hammock and went to go sleep with her younger sister named Denaquê.

"The next day when Taína-Cã leaped out the hammock everyone was thunderstruck. He was an old geezer all wrinkly wrinkly, trembling just like the light from Papaceia the star. Well now, Imaerô said:

"'Get away, you geezer! You won't see me marrying some old fogey! For me it's gotta be a brave strong young man of the Carajá nation!'

"Taína-Cã felt so sad and blue so sad and blue and started pondering the injustice of men. However the youngest daughter of the morubixaba Zozoiaça took pity on the geezer and said:

"'I'll marry you.'

"Taína-Cã shimmered with pleasure. They were a match. Denaquê would sing night and day preparing her trousseau:

"'Tomorrow at this hour, bah-doom-boom-boom . . .'

"Zozoiaça would answer:

"'And me with your mother, bah-doom-boom-boom . . .'

"After all the fingers on your hands would be long gone, parrot, still waiting on a groom, they played around doing the dance of love in the hammock woven by Denaquê, bah-doom-boom-boom.

"No sooner was day breaking past the horizon, than Taína-Cã leaped from the hammock and told his gal:

"'I'm going off to clear a field in the woods. Now you stay in the mocambo and don't ever go spying on me out there.'

"'Yes,' said she.

"And she stayed in the hammock, ruminating pleasurably on that strange old-timer of hers who'd given her the most delightful night of love that folks can imagine.

"Taína-Cã cleared some trees, set fire to all the little ant macurus and tilled the land. Back then the Carajá nation still didn't know about the good plants. Fish and game were all that the Carajá ate.

"As the next night came to a close Taína-Cã told his gal that he was going out to find seeds to sow and repeated the warning. Denaquê lay in the hammock a little longer, ruminating on the fierce delights from those nights of love that her dear old geezer had given her. And she went off to weave.

"Taína-Cã hopped up to the sky, went over to Berô the creek, said a prayer and placing a leg on either bank, kept a lookout for water. Soon enough there came seeds of cururuca corn, tobacco, manioc, all those good plants streaming along the bristling water. Taína-Cã gathered everything that went past, came down from the sky and went to sow the field. He was busting his tail in the Sun when Denaquê showed up. It was cause she was pining for her man who gave her such fierce delights on their nights of love. Denaquê gave a cry of joy. Taína-Cã wasn't a geezer at all! Turns out Taína-Cã was a brave strong young man of the Carajá nation. They made a leafy mound of tobacco and manioc and played around romping under the Sun.

"When they got back to the mocambo laughing and laughing with each other, Imaerô flew into a tizzy. She screamed:

"'Taína-Cã is mine! He came down from the sky for me!'

"'Scram, you're bad luck!' said Taína-Cã. 'When I wanted it you didn't, so now go play with yourself!'

"And he climbed into the hammock with Denaquê. Most unhappy Imaerô sighed:

"'Just wait till later, alligator, cause the whole lake's gonna dry up!...'

"And she took off into the woods shrieking. She turned into the araponga bird that screams yellow with envy at the quiriri hush-hush of the diurnal forest.

"Ever since then, it's thanks to the goodness of Taína-Cã that the Carajá have manioc and corn to eat and tobacco to liven them up.

"And whatever the Carajá needed, Taína-Cã would go up to the sky and bring it back. Well of course Denaquê, who wanted it all, started making eyes at every star in the sky! Yes indeed, and Taína-Cã who is Papaceia saw everything. He even got dewy with such sorrow, rounded up his odds and ends and went up to the vast field of the heavens. There he remained, nothing more did he bring, nossir. If Papaceia had kept on bringing things from the far side of yonder, heaven would be right here, all ours. Now it belongs only to our desires.

"And that's all."

The parrot was sound asleep.

One time after January came round Macunaíma woke late to the foreboding cry of the tincuã bird. However, the day was well underway and the heavy mist had already gone back to its hole... The hero shivered and clutched the magic amulet dangling from his neck, a little bone from a dead pagan boy. He looked around for the aruaí, who'd disappeared. Just the rooster and hen fighting over one last spider. The sweltering heat was so still, so immense that you could hear the glassy chime of the locusts. Vei, the Sun, slid down Macunaíma's body, tickling him, now become a maiden's hand. It was the vengeful mother's wicked spite, all because the hero hadn't married one of the daughters of light. The maiden's hand came and slid oh so gently oh! down his body... Oh the desire that shot through his muscles perking up for the first time

171

in so long! Macunaíma remembered that he hadn't played around in ages. They say that cold water's good for splashing away desire . . . The hero slid out his hammock, tore at the feathery cobwebs cloaking his whole body and heading down into the Vale of Tears, went to bathe in a nearby pond that the rainy season floods had turned into a big lagoon.

Macunaíma set the leghorns gently on the beach and went up to the water. The lagoon was all covered in gold and silver, then showed its face, revealing what lay in its depths. And way down deep Macunaíma caught sight of the loveliest girl, so very pale, and his desire ached even worse. And this loveliest of girls was the Uiara.

She swam up acting like she couldn't care less, frolicking, winking at the hero, as if to say, "Get away, young master!" and backed away frolicking like she couldn't care less. It filled the hero with such immense desire that his whole body expanded and his mouth watered:

"Mani! . . ."

Macunaíma wanted the lady. He dipped his big toe in the water and in a flash the lagoon covered its face again in strands of gold and silver. Macunaíma felt the water's chill, pulled his toe out.

So it went over and over. The day was reaching its peak and Vei was seething with rage. She'd been hoping Macunaíma would fall into the treacherous arms of the lagoon maiden and there was the hero afraid of the cold. Vei knew that the maiden was no maiden at all, it was the Uiara. And the Uiara swam up frolicking again. What a beauty she was! . . . Dark-haired and rosy-cheeked just like the face of day and just like the day ever encircled by night, her face was swirled about by short hair as black black as the wings of the graúna. Her sharp profile possessed a nose so dainty it wasn't any good for breathing. Yet since she only showed her front and backed away without turning Macunaíma didn't see the hole in her nape through which the perfidious creature breathed. And the hero hesitating, do-I-or-don't-I. Sun lost her temper. She grabbed an armadillo-tail whip made of heat and slashed at the hero's back. The lady over there, so they say, started opening her arms wide revealing her charm closing her eyes languidly. Macunaíma felt flames down his spine, shuddered, took aim, flung himself right on top of her, thwap! Vei wept in triumph. Her tears fell into the lagoon in showers of gold upon gold. It was the peak of day.

When Macunaíma made it back ashore it was clear that he'd had quite a tussle down in those depths. He lay facedown for a spell, his life hanging on each ragged breath. He was bleeding and bitten all over, missing his right leg, missing his big toes and his Bahian-coconuts, missing his ears his nose all his treasures. Finally he managed to get up. When he took stock of all that he'd lost he was furious at Vei. The hen clucked as she laid an egg on the beach. Macunaíma grabbed it and hurled it into the Sun's smug fat face. The egg went splat across her cheeks staining them yellow forevermore. The afternoon waned.

Macunaíma sat on a rock slab that had once been a jabuti tortoise in olden times and went counting up all the treasures he'd lost underwater. And it was a whole lot, it was a leg his big toes, his Bahian-coconuts, his ears his two earrings made from the Patek Philippe machine and the Smith & Wesson machine, his nose, all those treasures . . . The hero jumped up with a cry that cut short the day. The piranhas had also eaten his lower lip and the muiraquitã! He went crazy.

He uprooted a mountain of timbó açacu tingui cunambi, all those plants, and poisoned the lagoon forevermore. All the fish died and went floating belly-up, blue bellies yellow bellies rosy bellies, all those bellies coloring the lagoon's cheek. It was late-afternoon.

Then Macunaíma gutted all those fish, all the piranhas and all the river dolphins, groping around for the muiraquitã in that mess of bellies. It was one helluva bloodbath flowing over the earth and everything was stained with blood. It was night-fall.

Macunaíma went searching searching. He found his two ear-rings found his toes found his ears his nuqiiris his nose, all those treasures, and stuck them all back in their places with sapé grass and fish glue. But neither his leg nor the muiraquitã turned up, nossir. They'd been swallowed by the Ururau Gator Monster that can't be killed by any club or timbó. The blood had congealed to black all over the beach and lagoon. And it was night-time.

Macunaíma went searching searching. He burst into such cries of lament the clamor cut down to size that whole bevy of beasts. Not a thing. The hero crossed the field, jumping on his one leg. He shouted:

"My memento! Lone memento of my she-devil true! Not a thing do I see, not her not you!"

And he hopped along. Tears dropped from his little blue eyes onto the little white flowers in the field. The little flowers were stained blue and became forget-me-nots. The hero couldn't go on, stopped short. He crossed his arms in such heroic despair that everything expanded in space to contain the silence of that suffering. Just one measly little mosquito bedeviled the hero's misery even more, buzzing ever so faintly: "I came from Minas . . . I came from Minas . . ."

And so Macunaíma no longer took a shine to this land. A brand new Capei was gleaming up there in the glittering mineral sky. Macunaíma deliberated, still a bit undecided, unsure whether to go live up in the sky or on the Isle of Marajó. For a moment he even considered living in the city of Pedra with the indefatigable Delmiro Gouveia, but couldn't muster the verve. To go live there, just the way he'd lived before was impossible. It was indeed for this very reason that he no longer took a shine to this Earth . . . All of his existence, in spite of so many adventures so much playing around so many illusions so much suffering so much heroism, in the end had amounted to no more than just drifting through life; and to settle down in Delmiro's city or on the Isle of Marajó which belong to this Earth, there had to be a purpose. And he didn't have the gumption to get things off the ground. He made up his mind:

"Nothing doing! . . . When the vulture's down on his luck, the one at rock bottom craps on the top, this world's lost its spark so I'm headed for the sky!"

He was headed up to the heavens to live with his she-devil. He was off to be the pretty but useless twinkle of yet another constellation. It wasn't so bad being a useless twinkle, not at all, at least it was the same as all that kin, as all the forefathers of all the living beings of his land, mothers fathers brothers sisters-in-law women girlies, all those familiar folks who now go on living in the useless twinkle of the stars.

He planted a seed of the matamatá vine, child-of-the-moon, and as the vine grew he grabbed a sharp itá and wrote on the slab that had once been a jabuti tortoise way back in olden times:

I DIDN'T COME INTO THIS WORLD TO BE A STONE

The plant had already grown tall and was clinging to a tip of Capei. The one-legged hero looped his arm through the leghorns' cage and went climbing up to the heavens. He sang mournfully:

> Let us say goodbye,
> 　　—Taperá,
> Like the swallow who knew best,
> 　　—Taperá,
> Took wing to the sky,
> 　　—Taperá,
> A lone feather in the nest.
> 　　—Taperá . . .

After making it up there he knocked at Capei's maloca. The Moon came down to the yard and asked:

"What d'ya want, saci?"

"Dear Godmother bless me please, wontcha gimme some bread and cheese?"

Then Capei saw that it wasn't the one-legged saci at all, it was Macunaíma the hero. But she didn't want to give him lodging, remembering the hero's former stench. Macunaíma blew his stack. He socked the Moon in her face a whole buncha times. That's why she's got those dark spots on her face.

Then Macunaíma went knocking at the home of Caiuanogue, the morning star. Caiuanogue came to the little window to see who it was and befuddled by the black of night and the hero's one-legged hopping, asked:

"What d'you want, saci?"

But she soon realized that it was Macunaíma the hero and didn't so much as wait for an answer remembering how much he really stank.

"Go take a bath!" she said shutting the window.

Macunaíma blew his stack again and shouted:

"Let's take it to the street, you lowlife scum!"

Caiuanogue was scared outta her wits, shaking as she peered through the keyhole. That's how come that pretty little star is such a pipsqueak and shivers so much.

Then Macunaíma went knocking at the home of Pauí-Pódole, Father of the Mutum. Pauí-Pódole was mighty fond of him since Macunaíma had defended him from that most mulatto of all mulattos during the Cruzeiro celebration. But he yelled:

"Aw, hero, you piped up too late! Would've been a great honor to welcome into my humble fly-trap a descendant of the jabuti tortoise, the first race of them all . . . In the beginning the Great Jabuti was all that existed in this life . . . It was he who in the silence of night plucked from his belly a man and his woman. They were the first living so-and-so's and the first folks of your tribe . . . After that came the others. You got here too late, hero! We already make twelve and with you it'd be thirteen at the table. Awful sorry, but there's no use crying over it!"

"Too bad, so sad, I'm glad!" the hero yelled.

Then Pauí-Pódole felt bad for Macunaíma. He cast a spell. He took three sticks and tossed em up high making a cross and turned Macunaíma and his whole kit and caboodle, rooster hen cage revolver watch and all, into a brand new constellation. That constellation is Ursa Major.

They say it was a German professor, naturally, who went around claiming that Ursa Major was the saci on account of having just one leg ... No way, no how! Saci's still hopping around this world setting fires and braiding together the manes of wild colts ... Ursa Major is Macunaíma. Yes indeed it's that one-legged hero who suffered so much in this land where ants come plenty and nobody's healthy, that he got fed up with it all, took off and goes drifting around brooding all by his lonesome up there in the vast field of the heavens.

Epilogue

Now ends the story and death comes for glory.

There was nobody left round there. The Tapanhumas tribe had got jinxed and its children dropped off one by one. There was nobody left round there. Those places those meadows waterways woodcutter trails tracks tricky ravines, those mysterious forests, all was desert solitude. An immense silence slumbered along the riverbanks of the Uraricoera.

There wasn't a single person left on Earth who knew how to speak the tribe's language or recount those outlandish tales. Who could possibly know about the hero? Now the brothers who'd turned into the leprous shadow were the second head of the Father of Vultures and Macunaíma was the constellation Ursa Major. Nevermore would anybody know all those wonderful stories or the language of the long-gone tribe. An immense silence slumbered along the riverbanks of the Uraricoera.

One time a man went there. It was the wee hours and Vei had sent her daughters to watch over the path of the stars. The sprawling desert was killing off all the fish and birdies with fright and even nature herself had swooned and collapsed, throwing up her hands. The muteness was so immense that it stretched the towering trees in space. Suddenly onto the man's aching chest fell a voice from the branches:

"Sqww-aawk, awk awk! sqww-aawk, awk awk!"

The man went cold with fright just like a child. Then a gua-numbi hummingbird came breezing up and burbled the man's lips:

"Coochy, coochy, coo . . . gotchyoo!"

And zipped up into the trees. The man followed the guanumbi's flight, looking up.

"Grab the branch by the horns, bull!" the hummingbird giggled. And slipped away.

Then up in the branches the man spotted a green parrot with a golden beak peering down at him. He said:

"Here, little parrot."

The parrot came and landed on the man's head and they became fast friends. Then the bird started talking softly in a new kind of speech, brand new! that was song and that was caxiri with wild honey, that was good and possessed the treachery of unfamiliar fruits of the forest.

The tribe was long gone, the family had become shadows, the maloca had fallen into ruin eaten away by saúva ants and Macunaíma had gone up to the heavens, but there remained the aruaí from the retinue in those times of yore when the hero had been the great emperor Macunaíma. And it was that lone parrot in the silence of the Uraricoera who saved those tales and that long-vanished language from oblivion. It was that lone parrot who preserved in the silence all the sayings and feats of the hero.

He recounted it all to the man then took wing for Lisbon. And that man is me, folks, and I've stayed behind to tell you this tale. That's why I came here. I crouched down on these leaves, picked my ticks, started strumming my guitar and in this ragged tune and impure speech, I've sung these cares to the world, telling all the sayings and doings of Macunaíma, hero of our people.

And that's all.

Mário de Andrade wrote two possible prefaces to *Macunaíma*. Though he never published them, they often appear in posthumous Brazilian editions of the novel. These prefaces are included here along with two other undated prefatory notes. The first preface is dated December 19, 1926, after Andrade wrote the initial draft of *Macunaíma* at the countryside home of his uncle Pio Lourenço Corrêa ("Tio Pio") in Araraquara, northwest of São Paulo. The second is dated March 27, 1928, just before he sent the final manuscript to the printer. The parentheses in these handwritten notes mark phrases that he considered deleting; in a few places where he deliberated over alternate wording that would translate similarly, I chose one solution. These prefaces are followed by two explanations that Andrade published in response to the book's reception: a 1931 open letter to Amazonian novelist Raimundo Moraes explaining to his friend why *Macunaíma* need not be defended from the charge of plagiarism, and an excerpt from a 1943 newspaper column reflecting on the book's ending, fifteen years after the novel's initial publication and nearly two years before Andrade's death.*

* The handwritten preface manuscripts are located at the Mário de Andrade archive at the Instituto de Estudos Brasileiros at the University of São Paulo. My translation of the letter and newspaper column are based on the versions in the Coleção Archivos critical edition of *Macunaíma* (1996), edited by Telê Ancona Lopez.

First preface (1926)

This book needs some explanation, so as neither to deceive nor disappoint people.

Macunaíma is not a symbol, nor should his adventures be taken as enigma or fable. It is a book written while on holiday in the midst of mangos pineapples and cicadas in Araraquara, a playful diversion. Amid allusions made with no ill intent or particular order, I unwearied my spirit in this big clearing freshly planted with reveries, out where folks can't hear the sounds of prohibitions or misgivings, the jolts of science or reality—police whistles, squealing brakes. Yet I imagine that as with all the rest, my diversion has been useful. I had a good time showing off treasures that perhaps no one thinks of anymore.

What got me interested in Macunaíma was undoubtedly my constant preoccupation with delving into and learning as much as I can about the national entity of the Brazilian people. Well, after an arduous struggle, I have confirmed one thing that seems certain: the Brazilian has no character. Someone may well have stated this before, yet my conclusion is novel to me since it arises from my personal experience. And with the word *character* I am determining not just a moral reality, but rather, what I understand to be a permanent psychic entity that manifests in everything, in customs in external action in feeling in language in History in a way of walking, for better and for worse.

(The Brazilian has no character because he possesses neither his own civilization nor a traditional consciousness. The French have a character, as do the Yoruba and Mexicans. Whether due to their own civilizations, the threat of imminent danger, or a consciousness formed over centuries, what's certain is that they all have a character.) (Not the) the Brazilian. He's just like a twenty-year-old kid: we might observe general tendencies more or less, but it's still not time to affirm anything whatsoever. I believe, optimistically, that it is from this lack of psychological character that we derive our lack of moral character. Hence our none-too-clever chicanery, (the elasticity of our honor), the lack of appreciation for true culture, our improvisation, the lack of an ethnic sensibility in families. And above all, an (improvised) existence living by our wits (?), while in the meantime a wildly imaginative delusion— following the lead of Columbus as its figurehead—searches this land with eloquent eyes for an El Dorado that can't possibly exist, amid cleaning rags and climates that are good and bad in equal measure, colossal hardships that can only be weathered with the frankness of accepting reality. It's ugly.

So there I was, ruminating on such things when I came across Macunaíma in Koch-Grünberg's German. And Macunaíma was a hero surprisingly lacking in character. (I was thrilled.) I lived his cycle of exploits up close. There were just a handful. The story with the girl could be grafted on this, thus singing to another, more sorrowful book, long ago and far away ... Then this idea came round, to make it all into a kind of troubadour ballad along with other legends tales diversions customs, either Brazilian or refashioned in Brazil. I hardly had to invent a thing in this poem that came so easily.

As for the style, I used this simple, very sonorous way of talking, music really, given its repetitions, which are customary to religious texts and the set storytelling repertoire of our traditional rhapsodes. I did it to clear the way of those folks who buy pornographic books for the pornography. Well, if it's true that my book possesses some whiff of pornography beyond sensuality, and even coprolalia, then at least no one will dispute the softening quality of this tempering style.

I could not excise the obscene documentation from these legends. One thing that fails to surprise me, but that, in fact, spurs my thoughts is that, by and large, this rhapsodic and religious literature is often pornographic and generally sensual. I need not cite examples. Now a certain disorganized pornography also belongs to our everyday national existence. Paulo Prado, the subtle spirit to whom I dedicate this book, will highlight this in a forthcoming work of which I've made advance use.*

And note the fact that I spoke of a "disorganized pornography." Because the scientific Germans, the socially minded French, the philosophical Greeks, the specialists of India, the poetic Turks etc., have existed and continue to exist, as we know. The pornography among them possesses an ethnic character. It's been said that if you get three Brazilians together, they'll start talking about dirty stuff . . . That's a fact. My interest in Macunaíma would have been much too hypocritically preconceived had I pruned the book of what occurs abundantly throughout our indigenous legends (Barbosa Rodrigues, Capistrano de Abreu, Koch-Grünberg) and had I given my hero Catholic loves and social discretions that no one would take to be his.**

Summing all this up with my profoundly pure Brazilian preoccupation, we get *Macunaíma*, this book of mine.

As for whatever possible scandal that this work may cause, without shaking off the dust from my sandals, since I don't wear those kind of sandals, I've always had a (very) pious patience for imbecility, so that my body's tempo never attains a steady cadence between my days of struggle and nights full of calm.

ARARAQUARA, DECEMBER 19, 1926

====

* Historian Paulo Prado's *Retrato do Brasil: ensaio sobre a tristeza brasileira (Portrait of Brazil: Essay on Brazilian Sorrow)* was published in November 1928, four months after *Macunaíma*, and criticizes the violent and voluptuous decadence of Brazil's colonial period and its lingering effects.

** Andrade refers to *Macunaíma*'s main sources of Indigenous myths: Brazilian folklorist João Barbosa Rodrigues's *Poranduba amazonense* (1890), Brazilian historian João Capistrano de Abreu's *A língua dos caxinauás* (1914), and German ethnologist Theodor Koch-Grünberg's *Vom Roroima zum Orinoco*, vol. 2: *Mythen und legenden Mythen und Legenden der Taulipang-und Arekuna-Indianer* (1924).

... so that there's never a steady cadence between my struggles and certain nights of sound sleep.

(In the end, this book is no more than an anthology of Brazilian folklore.)

(One of my aims was to disrespect geography and geographical flora and fauna in the manner of legends. In this way, I deregionalized creation as much as possible, while also achieving the merit of literarily conceiving Brazil as a homogeneous entity—an ethnic national and geographical conception.)

(This is also to say that I am not convinced that I have made a Brazilian work, simply from having made use of national elements. I don't know if I am Brazilian. It's an ongoing preoccupation of mine and something I keep delving into, yet I lack the conviction of having made any great stride forward.)

Undated prefatory note 1 (Dec. 1926 – Jan. 1927)

I am by no means so capricious as to go about afflicting or misleading anyone. To the contrary, I have already been feeling a certain precision in demonstrating that the changes my investigations have undergone from book to book are not drastic changes so much as a concatenated transformation, further honed and extended from the same initial investigations.

Those who are bound to imagine that with this book I have changed yet again strike me as completely mistaken. To the contrary: there was nothing more likely in my work after *Amar, verbo intransitivo* and *Clã do jabuti* than the present book.* All joking aside, I find a certain logic in laying out an equation like this:

---

* Andrade published the novel *Amar, verbo intransitivo* (translated as *Fräulein* in 1933; and as *To Love, Intransitive Verb* in 2018) and the poetry collection *Clã do jabuti* (*Clan of the Tortoise*) in 1927, one year before Macunaíma.

Discuss the deliberate geographical jumble of flora and fauna.

Undated prefatory note II (Dec. 1926 – Jan. 1927)

Clearly, I harbor no pretensions that my book will be of service to scientific studies of folklore. I let my imagination run wild when I wanted to and above all when I needed to, so that this invention would remain art, and not the dry documentation of scholarship. All it takes is seeing how deliberately the Rio de Janeiro Macumba ceremony has been deregionalized, combined with elements from Candomblé in Bahia and Pajelança in Pará. I constructed that chapter with elements from published studies, elements that I gathered from an ogã in Rio, "a pockmarked fado musician by profession," and from an expert on Pajelanças, to which I further added elements of pure fantasy.* My books may be the result of my scholarship, but don't anyone go studying my works of fiction, or you'll take a walloping.

Second preface (1928)

I finally decided to stop worrying and hand over this book of pure diversion whose first draft was written in six days straight in a hammock with cigarettes and cicadas at the home of Pio Lourenço in the countryside near that nest of light known as Araraquara. I was getting fed up with myself . . . Never have I faced such an impossibility of judging the potential value of my writing as with this work.

---

* Andrade quotes from the "Macumba" chapter, p. 54. See the endnotes for more on these Afro-Brazilian and Indigenous syncretic religions, especially p. 235.

I don't know how to assume false modesty, and if I publish a book, it's because I believe in its worth. I do recognize that I have often published something bad in itself, for the sake of other worthwhile things to which it may give rise. Such is the case with churning out essay after essay on Brazilian language, so disparate from one another, some truly awful. I don't get too upset at their being awful or even that my entire body of work might share the precarious transitory nature of my life. What I'm really after is to grant myself the destiny that my potential has granted me. And to have been useful: the preoccupations, attempts, friendships, and even (dynamic?) aversions that I've sparked have turned out well. The main result has been the ample pride that I possess, and which completely prevents me from any show of vanity. I did not content myself with yearning for happiness; I made myself happy.

Now this book, which was no more than a thoughtful and enjoyable way to spend one's holiday, shimmering with research and intentions, many of which only became conscious at the moment of writing, strikes me as worth a little something as a symptom of national culture.

I think the best elements of a national culture appear in it. It possesses its own psychology and its own manner of expression. It possesses an applied philosophy veering between excessive optimism and excessive pessimism, from a country where the average city dweller believes that Providence is Brazilian, and the rustic man puffs more on the concept of "why bother" in his pipe than tobacco. It possesses an acceptance of the national entity that's neither timorous nor bombastic and conceives it as so permanent and unified that the country appears to be deregionalized in its climate its flora its fauna its people, its legends, its historical tradition—to the extent that this can amuse or arrive at a given fact without being off-putting in its absurdity. To speak of "native homelands" and "birthplaces" in relation to the lands of the Uraricoera is good. Additionally, the work possesses foreign contributions and makes use of others, in an amenable way, without dread, and above all without exclusiveness, like all beings born for communist ideas. I got the book's hero himself from the German of Koch-Grünberg; you can't even say he's from Brazil. He's just as much Venezuelan as one of us, if not more, and he's not familiar with the stupidity of borders, so he can stay awhile in the "land of the English" as he calls British Guiana. This situation—that the book's hero isn't absolutely Brazilian—pleases me like no other. It makes my chest expand, something men used to express with, "It fills my eyes with tears."

Now, I don't want you all to imagine that I set out to make this book into an expression of Brazilian national culture. God forbid. It's only now, after having made it, that I seem to find in it a symptom of our culture. Legend, history, tradition, psychology, science, national objectivity, the participation of adapted foreign elements all pass through it. That's why I have my doubts about the complex phenomenon that renders it symptomatic.

As for what intentions embellished this scherzo, my intentions were all too many. The one thing I don't want is for Macunaíma and the other characters to be taken as symbols. I truly had no intention of synthesizing the Brazilian in Macunaíma or the foreigner in Piaimã the Giant. Despite all the figurative references that folks might observe between Macunaíma and the Brazilian man, Venceslau Pietro Pietra and the foreign man, there are two intentional omissions that remove any symbolic conception from the pair entirely: the symbolism is episodic, appearing sporadically when it happens to make for comic effect and with no antithesis. Venceslau Pietro Pietra and Macunaíma are neither antagonists, nor do they complement one another, and still less does the ongoing battle between the two have any sociological value. If Macunaíma manages to recover the muiraquitã, it's because I had to make him die in the North. And it's impossible to view anything resembling symbolism in the death of the giant. The allusions themselves, lacking any continuity with the foreign element that the giant introduces, contribute to my observation of the book's cultural symptom: lighthearted amenability, an adaptability so consciously accepted, that the giant's own wife is a caapora and his daughter becomes a star.* I would be utterly appalled if anyone saw in Macunaíma my intention to make him a national hero. He is the hero of this diversion, that's for sure, and the national values that animate him are merely his way of possessing Keyserling's "Sein," the indispensable meaning, as I see it, that awakens empathy. A meaning does not have to be total to be profound. It is by means of "Sein" (see the translator's preface to *Le monde qui naît*) that art can be accepted within life. It is what has made of art and life a system of communicating vessels, balancing out the liquid that presently it doesn't confound me to call tears.**

Another problem with the book that I need to explain is that of immorality. Upon my word, it would be a mistake to conclude from all the immorality and dirty stuff in here that I delight in it. If anything, I'll submit to the conclusion that I delight in ... the Brazilian. One thing that's easy to establish is the constant presence of dirty stuff and immorality generally found in primitive legends as well as in religious texts. Not only did I accept this, but I even accentuated it. No, I won't pardon myself by saying that the flowers of evil produce a horror of evil. In fact they spark quite a bit of curiosity ... My intention there was to confirm a certain Brazilian constancy that I am not the first to do, to poke fun at it with an amenable sort of mockery that satirizes it without

* Piaimã comes from the mythology of the northern Amazonian Pemon people, while the Caapora is a forest entity from Brazilian folklore, adapted from Tupi mythology. See the endnotes, pp. 231 and 246.
** Andrade cites the 1927 French translation of *The World in the Making* (*Die neuentstehende Welt*, 1926) by German philosopher Count Hermann von Keyserling (1880–1946). In his translator's preface, Christian Sénéchal asserts that Keyserling's philosophy is born of experience over theory and thus encompasses a more personal *Sein* (being) and adds that true philosophy is life itself, combining practice and theory, knowledge and being, wisdom and art.

making a big moral stink. Macunaíma ultimately loses his manly vigor and with the exertion of . . . a hero, he ends up taking the . . . bait. But I couldn't stomach handing out cheap thrills to kiddies and old-timers. I made use of every tempering effect possible: paraphrase, indigenous words, humor, and a poetic style directly inspired by religious texts. I believe that in this way I was able to reestablish peace among men of goodwill.

And there remains the situation of the hero's lack of character. Lack of character in the double sense of an individual with no moral character and with no set characteristics. That's right. Without this pessimism I would not be a sincere friend to my fellow countrymen. This is the book's harsh satire. It's easy to have bursts of heroism. However, as far as I know, the highest branch of a gigantic tree isn't the ideal perch from which folks can rest easy.

As you can see, it's neither prejudice against morals nor shame at coming off as a moralist in this still-decadent cycle that leads me to a certain permissiveness.

In eras of social transition like the present, it's tough to commit to what's to come, and hardly anyone knows. I don't know. I do not wish for a return to the past, and that's why I can't just pull out a standard fable from back then. On the other hand, Jeremiah's way strikes me as inefficient. The present is a vast fog. To hesitate is a sign of weakness, I know. But for me it's not a matter of hesitation. It has to do with a very real impossibility, the worst of all, of not even knowing what to call the unknowns. They'll say it's my fault, that I failed to regiment the spirit with legitimate culture. That's right. But this is what the arduous undertakings of Maritain say, what those raised on the word of Spengler say, as do those who think through Wells or Lenin, and long live Einstein!*

---

* Alongside well-known early-twentieth-century figures such as British science-fiction writer H. G. Wells (1866–1946), Russian communist revolutionary Vladimir Lenin (1870–1924), and German Jewish physicist

But the fact remains, for those like me who've made up their minds, that the fog of this era is killing the maternal comfort of museums. Between the decisive certainty that electrocutes and the candid faith that refuses to judge, I was born for the latter. Or the time was born for me . . . Others may well be more noble. Most certainly not calmer. But I am not afraid of being more tragic.

MARCH 27, 1928

Open letter to Raimundo Moraes in the Diário Nacional *newspaper (Sept. 20, 1931)*

My illustrious and always remembered writer,

You cannot imagine with what intense and moving surprise yesterday, while reading the entry on Theodor Kock Grunberg (of course you are referring to Koch-Grünberg, or in our spelling, Koch-Gruenberg) on page 146 of the second volume of your *Meu dicionário de cousas da Amazônia* (*My Dictionary of Amazon Things*), I came across the reference to my name and your defense of me. But since I have made this an open letter to demonstrate my elevated admiration for the author of *Na planície amazônica* (*On the Amazon Plain*), I think it best to cite the passage in your book so that readers may be acquainted with the matter:

> Naysayers claim that the book *Macunaíma* by the celebrated writer Mário de Andrade is wholly based on *Vom Roroima zum Orinoco*, written by the scholar (Koch-Gruenberg). Being unfamiliar with

---

Albert Einstein (1879–1955), Andrade cites French philosopher Jacques Maritain (1882–1973), an exponent of the doctrines of St. Thomas Aquinas; and German philosopher Oswald Spengler (1880–1936), who saw national culture as an evolving superorganism that peaks in civilization; he predicted the decline of Western civilization by the year 2000.

the German naturalist's book, I do not believe in these rumors, given that my fellow countryman and novelist, with whom I rubbed elbows in Manaus, possesses such talent and imagination that dispense with the need for outside inspiration.

Now all my stylized, external, and consciously cultivated humility aside, it is fair and just for me to imagine that, while you do not believe in the spite of these naysayers, their assertion has nevertheless dampened your spirit, hence you give credence to these rumors in order to credit my worth with indisputable exaggeration. I have long experienced your generosity, but it does not fail to cause me some degree of pain that your spirit, always soaring to the heights of your admiration for great men, and ever occupied with such formidable and absorbing anacondas as Hartt, Gonçalves Dias, Washington Luís, José Júlio de Andrade, presidents, interim governors, Ford and Fordlândia, should get upset on behalf of a puny little gnat like me.* Hence, to extinguish this concern from your spirit, I shall be so desperately bold as to confess to you what my *Macunaíma* is.

Sir, you know much better than I what the timeless rhapsodes are. You know that the northeastern troubadours, our present-day rhapsodes, make use of the same processes as the singing bards of most historical antiquity, from India, Egypt, Palestine, Greece, transporting everything they hear and read—wholesale and as

---

* The subjects of Raimundo Moraes's writing. Charles Frederick Hartt (1840–1878) was a Canadian-American naturalist who became a pioneer of Brazilian geology. Antônio Gonçalves Dias (1823–1864) was a Brazilian Romantic poet. Washington Luís Pereira de Sousa (1869–1957), the thirteenth president of Brazil (1926–1930), was overthrown in the coup known as the Revolution of 1930. José Júlio de Andrade (1862–1953) was one of the largest landholders in the Amazon. Fordlândia is a former company town in the Amazonian state of Pará founded by Henry Ford in 1928 for its proximity to the rubber industry.

primary material—into their poems; their constraints lie in selecting from what they have read and heard, and in fitting these selections into a rhythm to suit their songs. A northeastern Leandro or Ataíde will buy a grammar book or geography primer from the first used bookstore, or that day's newspaper, and use it to compose a dueling ballad full of learning, or a tragic love story, played out in Recife. That's what *Macunaíma* is, and these are what I am.

It was in fact while reading that brilliant German ethnographer that the idea came to me for turning Macunaíma into a hero, not of a "romance" in the novelistic sense, but a "romance" in the folkloric sense. As you can see, sir, I possess no particular merit in this, but for the circumstance that in a country where everyone dances and neither Spix and Martius, nor Schlichthorst, nor von den Steinen are translated, I happen to dance less often and instead nose around libraries with my ever-so-meager pocket change amount of German.* Yet Macunaíma was simply a being from the far North of the country, and it turned out that my rhapsodic preoccupation went somewhat beyond those boundaries. Now this preoccupation coincided with my gaining an intimate knowledge of a certain Teschauer, a Barbosa Rodrigues, a Hartt, a Roquette Pinto, and about three hundred other storytellers of Brazil—I went from one to the other, lifting whatever caught my

* Nineteenth-century German naturalists and travelers who wrote about Brazil. In 1817, Johann Baptist Ritter von Spix (1781–1826) and Carl Friedrich Phillipp von Martius (1794–1868) came to Brazil in the entourage of Maria Leopoldina of Austria on her voyage to marry Dom Pedro I, the first emperor of Brazil, and extensively documented the flora, fauna, geography, and Indigenous cultures. Carl Schlichthorst served as a mercenary lieutenant in Brazil from 1825 to 1826 and wrote a bitter memoir of the time, *Rio de Janeiro wie es ist* (*Rio de Janeiro As It Is*, 1859). Karl von den Steinen (1855–1929) laid the foundations for Brazilian ethnology with his expeditions studying Central Brazilian Indigenous cultures on the Xingu River between 1884 and 1888.

interest.* To the main action I further added typical incidents that I witnessed firsthand, popular sayings, turns of phrase, traditions yet to be recorded in books, syntactic formulations, processes of oral punctuation, etc. from native Indian speech or the ways Brazilians talk nowadays, elements dreaded and discarded by those dazzling Brazilian writers of the most exquisite Portuguese language.

Yes, I copied, my dear defender. What amazes me, and what I take to be a sublime kindness, is that the naysayers forgot everything they know, restricting what I copied to Koch-Gruenberg, when I copied everyone. Even you, sir, in the scene with the Boiuna. I confess that I copied, copying straight from the text at times. Do you really want to know? Not only did I copy the ethnographers and Amerindian texts, but further still, in the "Letter to the Icamiabas," I inserted entire sentences from Rui Barbosa, Mário Barreto, the colonial Portuguese chroniclers, and I ravaged the equal parts pretentious and solemn language of contributors to the *Revista de Língua Portuguesa (Journal of Portuguese Language)*.** This was inevitable since my ... that is, Koch-Gruenberg's hero, aspired to write in the most proper Portuguese. You may contradict me, sir, by asserting that in the German ethnographer's study, Macunaíma would never have aspired to write in proper Portuguese. I agree, but not even that is my own invention, given that it's an aspiration copied from ninety-nine percent of Brazilians! Of literate Brazilians.

---

* Alongside Charles Frederick Hartt, noted earlier, Andrade cites Brazilian scholars who extensively documented Indigenous stories and cultures: historian Carlos Teschauer (1851–1930), botanist João Barbosa Rodrigues (1842–1909), and anthropologist Edgar Roquette-Pinto (1884–1954).

** Andrade refers to Brazilian statesman Rui Barbosa (1849–1923), known for his erudition and belletristic Portuguese; Brazilian philologist Mário Barreto (1879–1931), author of various books on Portuguese language; and sixteenth-century Portuguese travelogues documenting Brazil's initial colonial period.

Finally, I must confess once and for all: I copied Brazil, at least that part by which I wished to satirize Brazil through its own self. But not even the idea of satirizing is mine, since it's been around ever since Gregório de Matos, for goodness sake! The only thing that I have left, then, is that due solely to the accident of all the Cabrals who, likely by accident, were likely the first to discover Brazil, Brazil belonged to Portugal.* My name is on the cover of *Macunaíma*, and no one can take it off. But that's the only reason that *Macunaíma* is mine. You can relax now. And rest assured that in me you have a daily admirer.

MÁRIO DE ANDRADE

Excerpt from "Daily Notes" feature in the Mensagem *literary magazine (July 20, 1943)*

[...] Sérgio Milliet's observation has obliged me to undertake this rereading of the last three chapters of *Macunaíma* ...

Frankly, even I get exasperated at times, frightened more often, by the variety of little intentions, innuendos, allusions, symbols that I scattered throughout the book. Perhaps I should write a book, or at least an essay, *In the Margins of Macunaíma*, providing commentary on everything that I put in it. Without even meaning to!

I hadn't recalled one of the allegories, which came back to me quite vividly upon reading it today. Perhaps the recollection returned so vividly now since I've been thinking about going back to working on my novel *Café*, and so have been preoccupied with the issue of our having formed, of our wanting to form, a culture

---

* Gregório de Matos (1636–1696) was a Brazilian poet from the colonial baroque era known for his satirical poems. The Pedro Álvares Cabral expedition is credited with Portugal's "discovery" of Brazil, on April 22, 1500.

and civilization based on a Christian-European foundation, which is basically the central argument of the novel.* I'd already forgotten about the allegory related to this that I'd put in *Macunaíma* ... But now it all came back to me vividly, upon reading the sentence: "It was the vengeful mother's wicked spite (Vei, the Sun), all because the hero hadn't married one of the daughters of light," that is, the great tropical civilizations, China, India, Peru, Mexico, Egypt, daughters of heat. The allegory gets developed in the chapter called "Vei, the Sun." Macunaíma agrees to marry one of the solar daughters, but as soon as his future mother-in-law goes off, he doesn't bother with the promise anymore, and ventures out looking for ladies. And he takes up with a Portuguese woman, the Portugal that has bequeathed us with Christian-European values. And that's why, here at the end of the book, in the final chapter, Vei takes revenge on the hero and wants to kill him. She's the one who conjures the Uiara who wreaks havoc on Macunaíma. It was the revenge of the hot solar region. Macunaíma doesn't fulfill his potential, doesn't manage to acquire a character. And he goes up to the sky, to live the "useless twinkle of the stars."

... to complete the note above: one of the cheerfully bitter elements of the allegory is the effort, Macunaíma's hesitation, when he wants to throw himself into the arms of the treacherous Uiara, through whom Vei, the Sun, plans to kill him. I'm referring to the image of the water being cold, artificially cold in that climate of the Uraricoera and at that peak hour of the day. The water unravels its ripples of "gold and silver" (an allusion to that Iberian nursery rhyme "Senhora Dona Sancha"), then the deceptive Uiara appears. Macunaíma feels an overwhelming desire to go play around with her, perhaps he might impregnate her, perhaps a new guaraná-son will be born, as from his lovemaking with Ci ... But he sticks his big toe in and gets scared of the cold—that is, he shrinks from civilization, a culture from a temperate Euro-

* Andrade's novel *Café* (*Coffee*) was published posthumously in 2015.

pean climate. And Macunaíma, as in a premonition, pulls back his toe, doesn't fling himself into the water. The hero saves himself that first time. And the water that the hero's big toe has disturbed weaves itself back into a gold and silver tapestry, hiding the apparition of the Uiara-Dona-Sancha—who's Dona Sancha because she's European, since Vei decides to Europeanize her instrument of vengeance instead of using one of her daughters. She realizes that, without the European style to which he's grown accustomed, Macunaíma won't be fooled. Vei doesn't give up and so as to prevail at last, she ends up relying on precisely a tropical proposition. She takes a whip made of heat and gives Macunaíma a licking. He no longer resists. And flings himself into the cold water, preferring the arms of the illusory Iara. And he'll be devoured by the creatures of the water, dolphins, piranhas.

He still manages to make it back to the beach, but he's a man in tatters. What now? missing a leg, missing this and that, and most of all missing the muiraquitã that gives him a reason for being, will he be able to pull himself together, to pull himself back together to get a legitimate, functional life off the ground? . . . Not a chance anymore. He gives up on going to live with Delmiro Gouveia, the great creator. He gives up on going to Marajó, the only place in Brazil that bears traces of a superior civilization. He's missing the national amulet; no longer will he triumph at anything. So he prefers to go up and twinkle the useless twinkle of the stars.

AFTERWORD
The Many Lives of Macunaíma

If you're not sure what to make of *Macunaíma: The Hero with No Character*, you're in good company. Even its own author couldn't decide whether this head-spinning tale was a masterpiece or a misfire, a whimsical diversion or bitter critique, and to what degree it represented Brazil and Brazilians. "I don't know, this book is truly becoming an obsession for me," he wrote to poet-critic Augusto Meyer in July 1928, just ahead of publishing it. "There are times when I think it's horrible. There are times when I think it's quite good. One thing's for certain: it's not the buffoonery it appears to be." Mário de Andrade was uneasy about what strange concoction he was unleashing into the world and how it would be received—a feeling I've shared while translating it for new readers in English, nearly a century later. "It's the most astonishing of all my work," he told another friend. "Frankly, it scares me."*

At the age of thirty-three, Andrade composed one of the most complex and original works of literature in a feverish burst of imagination that lasted six days, scribbling away and laughing to himself while chain-smoking in a hammock strung up under pineapple and mango trees as cicadas droned in the summer air. He was at his uncle's countryside home in Araraquara for the December holidays of 1926, a tranquil interlude from the noise and commotion of his life in the metropolis of São Paulo several hours southeast by train. At night he kept writing, even sneaking

* All translations are my own unless otherwise noted.

into the bathroom to maintain momentum after his worried aunt spotted the light on in his bedroom. This is the origin story of *Macunaíma*, as Andrade told it. But of course, the truth is more complicated.

Andrade later elaborated that he had written his most renowned work in a state of "prepared possession." Some months earlier, he had found inspiration in an obscure collection of myths and legends of the Taurepang and Arekuna people, who form part of the Indigenous Carib group known as the Pemon in the Amazonian region spanning Brazil, Venezuela, and Guyana. It was the 1924 second volume of a monumental study of Carib and Arawak peoples based on fieldwork in the northern Amazon from 1911 to 1913 by German ethnologist Theodor Koch-Grünberg, *Vom Roroima zum Orinoco* (*From Roraima to the Orinoco*, published in five volumes from 1917 to 1928; vol. 2 is subtitled *Myths and Legends of the Taulipang and Arekuna*). While sitting around campfires and floating down rivers, Koch-Grünberg transcribed what he called "a close-knit saga cycle," as told by two native informants: his guide, Mayuluaípu, the son of a renowned Taurepang storyteller, and Akuli, a shaman from the neighboring Arekuna. The fifty short "sagas" interweave origin myths full of fateful acts with the ribald, gross-out humor that marks drunken storytelling across cultures and eras. Andrade was particularly taken with stories featuring a trickster named Makunaíma, who was endowed with godlike powers of creation and transformation, but also foolish and spiteful; he played naughty pranks on his brothers and courageously battled Piai'mã, a cannibal shaman from the rival Ingarikó people.

Koch-Grünberg observed the confusion inherent in attempting to characterize this "supreme tribal hero," whose name he translated as "Big Evil." Conversely, British missionaries had substituted this powerful being for God in their Bible translations used to convert the Pemon. Reverend William Henry Brett described "Makonaima" as "the great Lord and Maker of all" in *The Indian Tribes of Guiana* (1868), the earliest mention of Makunaima in print.* Makunaíma struck Andrade as quintessentially Brazil-ian for having "no character"—meaning he lacked not only moral consistency but also coherent, fixed characteristics. He began jotting down scenes for a novel about a Brazilianized Macunaíma in the margins of the German book, which he brought to Arara-quara, along with dictionaries and annotations from his extensive readings in ethnography, history, linguistics, music, and folk tra-ditions related to Brazil.

He finished another draft back in São Paulo, where he lived in a comfortable but modest house with his widowed mother, sister, and aunt. His daily rhythms resumed in his work as a newspaper arts critic and music professor at the Conservatory of Dramatic Arts and Music, where he had studied to be a concert pianist. Over the next year and a half, Andrade would continue to embellish and revise the manuscript, grafting the Pemon stories onto other myths, folktales, songs, jokes, rhymes, sayings, and superstitions. These came mainly from within Brazil's borders, but were often Brazilian adaptations of elements from various origins, particu-larly the Tupi—the major Indigenous group comprising various nations, such as the Tupinambá and Tupiniquim, that dominated coastal Brazil in the sixteenth century when the Portuguese ar-rived and profoundly influenced Brazilian language and culture. A three-month voyage through the Amazon from May to August 1927 provided even more material, and led Andrade to change the name of the last chapter from "Eiffel Tower" to "Ursa Major," after being dazzled by the constellation on a clear Amazonian night.**

* This demigod's written name takes many forms, depending on pro-nunciation and language; Makunaima is the present standard, while Makunaíma with an accent refers to Koch-Grünberg's version.

** Andrade writes of seeing this constellation in his travelogue, *O tur-ista aprendiz* (*The Apprentice Tourist*), posthumously published in 1976. In 1923, historian Paulo Prado sent Andrade an Eiffel Tower postcard from Paris with the message, "This here's not worth it! Viva Brazil!"

Even after the novel debuted in 1928, he kept adding allusions and Indigenous or regional phrases and cutting sections—the version we read today is based on the 1937 second edition.

The final composition combines the trickster heroes, talking animals, metamorphoses, and magic that are common to fables and myths with an episodic quest that conjures classical epics and medieval chivalric romances, and drops it all into the fast-paced world of Brazil's capital cities. Macunaíma is a modernist reinvention of the capricious Pemon demigod, but his exploits are also based on Tupi tales about a clever tortoise, who could be a South American cousin of the coyote trickster from Navajo and Zuni traditions. When the hero participates in the Macumba ceremony, we learn that he is a "son" or devotee of Exu, a mischievous deity adapted into syncretic Brazilian spiritual practices from the West African Yoruba religion. He also belongs to a lineage of heroes (and antiheroes) who aren't bound by the typical noble principles. Like Odysseus, Macunaíma is capable of remarkable courage, ingenuity, and strength, but he's a liar and cheat when it suits him. And like Don Quixote and the Iberian folk hero Pedro Malasartes, he's a picaresque rogue, who lives by his wits and outsmarts his enemies, but just as often gets into ridiculous scrapes that require the help of his brothers.

As a result of Andrade's research-laced literary trance, *Macunaíma* has the feel of two books written by two authors: the madcap outpourings of a poet-musician's encyclopedic, free-associative brain gone wild, and also a densely layered compendium of language, culture, religion, geography, and history written by a self-taught scholar who was creating his own interdisciplinary field of Brazilian studies. In my translation, I have aimed to capture the vibrant energy of the first book, while the notes that follow this afterword invite a rereading of that initial flourish as grounded in a vast archive of Indigenous, Afrodiasporic, and Luso-Brazilian cultures, interwoven with natural history and colonial-era chronicles.

Self-published in an edition of eight hundred, the novel caused a sensation in the Brazilian literary community. Andrade already had a formidable reputation as a leading modernist writer, burnished by four books of poetry, a manifesto on modernist poetics, a short-story collection, and a novel of bourgeois São Paulo manners. But no one had ever written anything like this. Some praised *Macunaíma* as a work of poetic genius and a miracle of language, while others dismissed it as anti-literary, immoral, and incoherent, even as they recognized its author's undeniable talent—"a disaster, a respectable piece of nonsense," wrote one critic. More than one admirer predicted that this revolutionary work would not find its audience for some time. And indeed, it would take more than forty years for what Andrade called his "failed masterpiece" to be appreciated by the Brazilian public.

"Mário wrote our *Odyssey* and, with a swing of his native club, created our classical hero and the national poetic idiom for the next fifty years," declared the poet Oswald de Andrade shortly after *Macunaíma* was published. The two writers weren't kin but were avant-garde co-conspirators and sometime rivals; both had played a central role in the legendary 1922 Modern Art Week, a series of exhibitions and performances at São Paulo's Municipal Theater that heralded a new era of Brazilian modernism. Their generation wanted to "Brazilianize Brazil," as Andrade put it, instead of imitating European culture, and to do so with irreverence, breaking away from the earnest nation-founding epics of their Romantic predecessors.

Macunaíma is often understood in terms of the cultural cannibalism that Oswald de Andrade championed in his "Cannibalist Manifesto" (*"Manifesto Antropófago"*)—the rallying cry of the Cannibalist Movement, whose magazine, the *Revista de Antropofagia*, published the manifesto in its first issue, in May 1928, and *Macunaíma*'s opening chapter one month later. Inspired by ritual cannibalism among the Tupi, who ate their enemies to absorb their strength, Oswald's poem-manifesto proclaims a revolutionary Brazilian sensibility that would devour domestic and foreign cultures alike, digesting Freud, Montaigne, Shakespeare, and Hollywood, together with the Carib instinct, Tupi chants, and matriarchy of Pindorama (the Tupi name for Brazil). He opts for unabashed appropriation as an ironic solution to the impasse of the Brazilian subject, who can lay no claim to cultural or ethnic purity. The manifesto's most famous line—"Tupy or not Tupy, that is the question"—is in English, and turns Hamlet's existential crisis into a bilingual pun that winks at the absurdities of reclaiming Tupi as the Brazilian national language as an alternative to the colonizers' Portuguese. (Old Tupi, also known as Língua Brasílica, was the nation's lingua franca for the first two centuries of colonization, and is the source of thousands of words adapted into Brazilian Portuguese, especially names of flora, fauna, and places.)

Macunaíma is perhaps the fullest realization of the manifesto's proposition, but Mário didn't want to be labeled a Cannibalist because it detracted from *Macunaíma*'s singular complexity. Instead he saw his riffing and recycling as following Brazil's living tradition of rural bards: the improvising *repentista* folk singers and popular poets of *literatura de cordel* (called "string literature" for the way chapbooks are strung on a line at street fairs), whose repertoires stitch together ballads and story cycles often originating in Iberian versions of medieval Provençal love poems and chivalric romances. Andrade styled *Macunaíma* as "a kind of troubadour ballad," whose narrator and hero alike are singing storytellers. "Novel" is the catchall term that most people use for this unclassifiable work, but Andrade preferred "rhapsody," which refers to a musical composition of seemingly spontaneous medleys, as well as fragments of Homeric epic performed by classical rhapsodes, or "song-stitchers." He also called it a "folkloric romance" (*romance* in Portuguese means "novel" but also refers to medieval romances), an "anthology of folklore," and a "scherzo"—the quick-tempo movement of a symphony or sonata, from the Italian for "sportive jest."

A few years after *Macunaíma*'s publication, Andrade invoked "our present-day rhapsodes" in response to intimations that he had plagiarized Koch-Grünberg.* In a letter published in a São Paulo newspaper, the author acknowledged that he had indeed lifted from the Amerindian myths collected by the German ethnologist—and that he had done so in the tradition of Brazil's rural bards, who improvised from whatever was at hand. He then went on to list everyone else he'd copied: colonial Portuguese chroniclers, historians, naturalists, ethnographers, and folklorists, as well as pretentious scholars of the Portuguese language; but most of all, "I copied Brazil, at least that part by which I wished to satirize Brazil through its own self." He concluded, "My name is on the cover of *Macunaíma*, and no one can take it off. But that's the only reason that *Macunaíma* is mine."

In assembling this "copy" of Brazil, Andrade wanted to portray his country not as a poetic idealization of the nation, but as an unholy amalgam of sacred and profane influences from disparate traditions that coexist within the same territory. To register the chimerical nature of this national unity, he concocts a whirlwind tour of Brazil that crams four centuries and a continental expanse onto a single mythic plane, bending the rules of time and space. In chase scenes that evoke Wile E. Coyote and the Road Runner, the hero and his pursuers crisscross South America at impossible speeds, as when Macunaíma hops on a horse with old Ceiuci in hot pursuit, and they gallop from São Paulo to Manaus in the northwestern Amazon, then back down the continent to Mendoza, in Argentina. And the narrative enacts a mode of time travel through brief encounters with specters out of Brazil's colonial past—from legendary Portuguese castaways like João Ramalho to the Jesuit founding father of São Paulo, José de Anchieta, to Portuguese set-

* See "Open Letter to Raimundo Moraes" on p. 191.

tler Maria Pereira, said to have hid from the Dutch during their occupation of northeastern Brazil from 1630 to 1654.* Andrade also jumbles Brazil's flora and fauna across regions; for example, the mandacaru cactus, a signature feature of the arid Northeast, shows up in the Amazon rain forest. This "deregionalizing" method imagines Brazil "as a homogeneous entity—an ethnic national and geographical conception," as he explains in the first of two unpublished preface drafts.**

The novel's experimental idiom follows a similar approach to reflect a national language marked by multiplicity. The narrator's "impure speech" corrals regionalisms, slang, and archaic usages from all over the country, emphasizing the amount of non-Portuguese integrated into the Brazilian lexicon, especially in the long lists of flora and fauna from Tupi, and incantations that mix words of Bantu and Yoruba origin. Similar to how Walt Whitman and Mark Twain transformed American literary language, Andrade worked out a way to "write Brazilian" by creating a stylized pastiche of how Brazilians actually spoke, using phonetic spelling and syntax that went against the grain of European Portuguese conventions. The hero's overwrought style in the "Letter to the Icamiabas" satirizes the way Brazilian intellectuals affected this belletristic mode in their writing, perpetuating the divide between "the two languages of the land, spoken Brazilian and written Portuguese."

This patchwork portrait of Brazil turns out, paradoxically, to be somewhat indecipherable for most Brazilians—contemporary editions of the book often include glossaries and notes explaining its esoteric allusions. At the same time, the novel includes well-known sayings, rhymes, and songs; in fact, much of its language is still in colloquial use today. The resulting effect, which veers between alienation and recognition, conjures the sense of be-

---

* See the endnotes, pp. 243, 247, and 256.
** Both are included in this edition, beginning on p. 181.

ing "exiles in our own land," as the historian Sérgio Buarque de Holanda characterizes the national condition in *Raízes do Brasil* (*Roots of Brazil*, 1936).

Despite its challenges to comprehension, *Macunaíma* has become a touchstone of Brazilian culture, not only because it conjures the complexities of Brazilian identity, but also because it captures its author's conflicted feelings about a nation in transition. It expresses a sincere love of country that goes hand in hand with frustration and disappointment, alongside a suspicion of nationalist narratives and chest-thumping patriotism. Dwelling in the haunted legacy of colonization entangled with slavery and immigration, *Macunaíma* resonates with experiences across the Americas and in postcolonial nations elsewhere. It asks how a country can forge a coherent identity from a collision of histories and cultures that remain continually in flux.

"The Brazilian has no character because he possesses neither his own civilization nor a traditional consciousness," Andrade declared in his first preface draft, after that initial bout of writing. He contrasted Brazil's lack of an established national identity with the French, Yoruba, and Mexican cultures, which were rooted in ancient civilizations, and compared the young republic to a twenty-year-old kid still figuring out who he was. Though Prince Regent Pedro I had declared Brazil's independence from Portugal (and his father, King João VI) in 1822, it was a monarchy ruled by the Portuguese royal family until his son, Emperor Pedro II, was deposed in 1889, one year after slavery was abolished. Born in São Paulo in 1893, Andrade witnessed horse carts and gas lamps give way to electricity, trams, and cars, amid wave after wave of immigration, as the city's wealth and population exploded from the coffee industry boom. In just over two decades, his hometown transformed from a former colonial frontier outpost into the model city for a national project of industrialization. Brazilian modernism is marked by an apprehension of the incongruity of capital cities speeding toward the future even as the nation remained mired in colonial hierarchies and dependent on an agrarian economy.

At its most pessimistic, the novel presents a vision of Brazil as a country adrift, hindered by tropical malaise and a colonial inheritance of foundational violence that went hand in hand with a culture of extraction and exploitation driven by lust and greed.* Like the first colonizers to plunder Brazil, Macunaíma is money-hungry but work-averse; he'd rather search for buried treasure than toil away. The hero's sexual appetite is a primal instinct but also a means to power: he becomes emperor of the forest after raping Ci and believes he can do the same with the godlike "Machine" to conquer São Paulo. The notorious "Letter to the Icamiabas" takes aim at the city's capitalist excesses and political corruption, and recalls its belligerent founding heroes, the *bandeirantes*—adventurers who expanded Brazil's frontiers in their search for gold and Indians to enslave. The letter lampoons and inverts the founding document of Brazilian history: Pêro Vaz de Caminha's 1500 letter to the Portuguese King Manuel I, which details the first Portuguese encounter with this new world and lingers on descriptions of its native women. Macunaíma sums up his assessment of Brazil in the dictum "Ants aplenty and nobody's healthy, so go the ills of Brazil"—a pointed alternative to the nineteenth-century positivist motto emblazoned on the nation's flag: ORDER AND PROGRESS.**

In a second preface draft he wrote after completing the novel in 1928, Andrade expressed a more optimistic view, that *Macunaíma* had captured "the best elements of a national culture." In this colorful, frenetic universe, having "no character" isn't so

* *Macunaíma* is dedicated to Paulo Prado, a patron of the modernists, who expresses this melancholy view in *Retrato do Brasil: ensaio sobre a tristeza brasilieira* (*Portrait of Brazil: Essay on Brazilian Sorrow*, 1928).

** See the endnotes pp. 240–241 for more on this dictum

much a lack as a *multitude* of attitudes, cultures, and backgrounds that are constantly morphing and converging in ways that exceed definition. The strength of Brazilian traditions lies in their originality and ongoing inventiveness that freely adapts foreign elements in a "lighthearted amenability" to being infiltrated by otherness, "like all beings born for communist ideas" (and like Mário's rhapsode or Oswald's cannibal).

Andrade's magpie method of composition in *Macunaíma* reflects the formation of Brazilian culture as a mixed-race, multilingual, syncretic commons. The novel's allusions trace how various traditions became intertwined over centuries. The different iterations of the Boiuna across various chapters allude to its origins as an enchanted Tupi water snake and also register its metamorphosis in Brazilian folklore into the Mother-of-Water, a name for at least three different entities: 1) the treacherous magic water snake; 2) the Iara or Uiara female water sprite, also from Tupi myth, which Brazilians further conflated with European mermaids and sirens; and 3) the Afro-Brazilian water goddess Iemanjá. The "Macumba" chapter blends distinct but overlapping religious traditions that combine elements from Catholicism, African religions, and Indigenous shamanism. The novel also incorporates musical forms that Andrade discusses in *Ensaio sobre a música brasileira* (*Essay on Brazilian Music*), which he wrote concurrently with *Macunaíma* and published later that year, a book on Brazilian music in which he maps its Portuguese, African, and Amerindian roots and recognizes the influence of North American jazz and Argentine tango.

Underscoring this communal spirit that ignores boundary lines, Andrade notes in his 1928 preface that the book's hero is imported from Indigenous cultures by way of German and declares, "This situation—that the book's hero isn't absolutely Brazilian—pleases me like no other." Still, Andrade's Macunaíma remains a satirical take on a national hero, a shape-shifter who embodies "the three races" traditionally hailed as the foundation of the Brazilian people—Black, Indigenous, and white—as well as the pervasive stereotypes that target them.* The opening description of the hero's birth is a parodic tribute to a Romantic-era allegory of the founding of Brazil, José de Alencar's novel *Iracema* (1865): "In the depths of the virgin-forest was born Macunaíma, hero of our people," which echoes Alencar's description, "Far, far beyond those mountains, which yet do fade into the blue horizon, was born Iracema."** The titular heroine—whose name is an anagram for America—is a woman from a Tupi tribe who falls in love with a Portuguese colonizer, then dies after giving birth to their son, a symbol of the union of races that would people the new nation.

Whereas *Iracema* rewrites colonial history as a noble commingling of Europeans and Amerindians, *Macunaíma* shows the collision of races and cultures to be violent, hierarchical, and heterogeneous, though generative of a distinctly Brazilian hybridity that includes significant African heritage. Andrade turns to an Afro-Brazilian folktale, "The Three Races," to stage the symbolic scene of the three brothers' racial transformation before arriving in São Paulo; he embellishes the original story with "holy water" from a Catholic saint's footprint, which evokes Brazil's history of missionaries converting Native peoples. Macunaíma embodies multiple races but isn't an assimilated mestizo: he jumps between Indigenous and Afro-Brazilian contexts, both adopts and rejects European influences, and participates in syncretic blends of all three.

The book's moments of offhand racism and gender violence are largely taken from folktales, jokes, sayings, and songs, reflecting the commonplace beliefs—and prejudices—of the societies that produced them. In pulling at the threads of collective consciousness, *Macunaíma* challenges the fantasy of Brazil as a "racial democracy"—a term that took hold in the 1930s and echoes the

* See the endnotes pp. 220–222 for the ambiguity of "Tapanhumas" and the hero's other Afro-Indigenous associations.
** An early draft of *Macunaíma* included a dedication to Alencar.

nineteenth-century nationalist notion of Brazil as a land of harmony among races. While Andrade withholds moral judgment in *Macunaíma*, in later essays on folklore, he denounces prejudices against Black people that popular sayings and rhymes help to preserve, citing from some of the same sources he had used for the novel.*

To me, this book could only have been written by someone who, like his hero, inhabited an indeterminate identity that wasn't in step with the world around him. Andrade embraced the idea of a plural self in his poetry, calling himself a "mixed-race bard" (*bardo mestiço*) and taking on the persona of a costumed harlequin. He echoes Walt Whitman's claim to "contain multitudes" in one of his most famous verses: "I am three hundred, I'm three-hundred-and-fifty" (*Eu sou trezentos, sou trezentos-e-cinquenta*). In today's terms, Andrade would be a queer Black writer, yet both his race and sexuality have been sources of contention and suppression. His grandmothers on both sides were considered *mulatas*, but he didn't publicly claim his Black heritage, a reticence shared with other past Brazilian writers of both African and European descent, including Machado de Assis. Andrade's sexuality was an open secret, and he famously fell out with Oswald de Andrade due in part to Oswald's homophobic taunts. The topic was taboo until recently, after the 2015 publication of a previously censored letter in which he mentions "my much-discussed (by others) homosexuality." His love life remains an enigma, and some insist on his self-described "irreducible pansexuality," pointing to his declaration in another letter: "I've discovered I'm capable of having sexual relations with a tree!"

Mário de Andrade continues to be a figure of fascination and

---

* These essays written between 1938 and 1942 are collected in *Aspectos do folklore brasileiro* (*Aspects of Brazilian Folklore*, 2019), drawn from Andrade's preparations for a book on Black culture in Brazil, *Estudos sobre o negro*.

reverence nearly eighty years after his untimely death of a heart attack at fifty-one in 1945. Though best known as the "Pope of Brazilian modernism," he is also celebrated for his lasting impact on Brazilian cultural heritage through his pioneering studies in ethnomusicology and as founding director of São Paulo's Department of Culture and cofounder of Brazil's Society of Ethnography and Folklore with Dina Lévi-Strauss in the 1930s. *Macunaíma* is the book that most fully synthesizes the diverse range of his life's work—as the culmination of his modernist language experiments but also the crossroads that would lead him deeper into folkloric studies.

As with other works that are ahead of their time, broader recognition spread slowly but steadily, then like wildfire. It took nearly a decade for a second edition to come out, and another seven years for a third edition. Then in the late 1960s and '70s, the book connected with the zeitgeist, in a convergence of popular adaptations, influential scholarly studies, and a revival of interest in the 1920s avant-garde, led by the concrete poets and artists of the Tropicália movement. Published just two years before the 1930 revolution that installed eventual dictator Getúlio Vargas, *Macunaíma* emerged from a time of cultural reckoning and political instability, and this later generation turned to the novel amid the turbulence and repression of another dictatorship, which began with a 1964 military coup and lasted for twenty years. Concrete poet Haroldo de Campos found in Macunaíma "an anti-normative hero who points to a future, eventually more open, world." Cinema Novo director Joaquim Pedro de Andrade's 1969 film adaptation delivers a harsh critique of Brazil devouring itself, in the guise of a slapstick comedy. It was a box-office hit—and the main reason that *Macunaíma* became so well known. In 1974, a top Rio de Janeiro samba school, Portela, based their Carnival parade theme on the novel, among the highest honors in Brazilian popular culture. Four years later, Antunes Filho mounted a daring stage production that became one of Brazil's longest running theatrical performances. By the end of the decade, *Macunaíma* had become a true literary classic—that is, required reading in schools and hailed by people who had never read the book.

Even so, Andrade's novel is neither a relic nor confined to the classroom. Artists, filmmakers, musicians, writers, and scholars keep reanimating *Macunaíma* in ways that reflect their own time. The book's incorporation of Indigenous elements—from at least nineteen ethnic groups—had been long overlooked as raw material for modernist invention, but has gained unprecedented attention amid twenty-first-century reassessments of identity.[*] Indigenous artists have found in *Macunaíma* a generative antagonist and a vessel for examining their fraught relationships with Brazil. In 2018, a group of Indigenous performers, including Akuli's grandson, Avelino Taurepang, joined Brazilian writers and scholars to stage a play, *Makunaimã: o mito através do tempo* (*Makunaimã: The Myth Across Time*) at Andrade's house, now a museum in São Paulo. The play opens as they rouse the author from his eternal slumber with a clamor of "the Indigenous voices of the Pemon, Taurepang, Wapichana, and Macuxi, peoples who are the rightful heirs of Makunaimã," as Indigenous writer Cristino Wapichana describes the scene in his preface to the published script. These voices seek "to reclaim—right here in Mário de Andrade's home—his stereotypical Macunaíma, who mixes different Indigenous cultures and histories to comprehend the formation of the Brazilian people based on what's sacred to us."

Another participant in the performance, the late Macuxi artist Jaider Esbell—whose painting appears on the cover of this edition—expressed a similar critique, but also recognized in Andrade a fellow artist. Esbell called himself the grandson of Makunaima, Makunaimî, or Makunaimã, alternating between spellings that

---

[*] Several recent Brazilian editions foreground the Indigenous elements in essays and notes. Lúcia Sá's *Rain Forest Literatures* (2004) reads *Macunaíma* in the context of its Amerindian sources.

reflect different pronunciations of the creator-ancestor's name by various Amazonian Indigenous groups. He viewed Makunaima's transformation into a Brazilian icon as yet another deliberate metamorphosis of his mythical forebear, one that would bring his story and those of his people to the greater world. "I was the one who wanted to be on the cover of that book," Makunaima tells his grandson in Esbell's 2018 essay *"Makunaima, o meu avô em mim!"* ("Makunaima, My Grandfather in Me!"). "I was the one who wanted to make our history. There I saw every chance for our eternity."

On the translation

Every translation is a confrontation with the untranslatable. Yet some works bring this dynamic into starker focus, requiring the translator to reinvent her approach. My translation has, by necessity, been a "transcreation," to use the term coined by Haroldo de Campos: attuned to creatively rendering the work's musical momentum, orality, playfulness, and multilingualism, rather than misguidedly attempting word-for-word equivalence. Reproducing Andrade's linguistic exuberance was my primary aim, since the best way to first encounter *Macunaíma* is to surrender to the delight of its language without trying to understand every word. Sound often comes before sense in this composition by a poet and musicologist: this meant making many decisions by ear. I also wanted to re-create the feel of someone telling a story around a fire or in a rocking chair on a back porch; the language feels a bit breathless, with the kinds of run-ons, word pile-ups, and abbreviations that spill out when we're talking too fast to bother with grammar.

One major challenge was figuring out how to convey *Macunaíma*'s peculiar effect on Brazilian readers, for whom the novel feels alternately close to home and impenetrably foreign. My solution for approximating this correspondence was to make the translation seem irrevocably Brazilian *and* American at the same time. Just as Andrade "deregionalized" Brazil, I collapsed North and South America, displacing what we in the United States insist is *the* America. *Macunaíma* needs an American English translation because the novel is so deeply American. Andrade almost never left Brazil, and Macunaíma declares, "No way am I going to Europe. I'm an American and America's where I belong." When the hero returns to retrieve his conscience toward the end of the book and finds it missing, he takes one left by a Spanish-American man—that is, a subject of Spain's American colonies—"and it worked out fine all the same." After all, everyone is American in the New World.

To create a literary pastiche of an American vernacular that partakes of different regionalisms, I listened to the voices in works by Mark Twain, Zora Neale Hurston, and William Faulkner. I took further inspiration from the sounds of American folk in B. A. Botkin's *A Treasury of American Folklore: Stories, Ballads, and Traditions of the People* (1944), as well as in the Smithsonian Folkways music series and field recordings by ethnomusicologist Alan Lomax, Andrade's North American kindred spirit. I dipped into the online *Dictionary of American Regional English* to brainstorm lists that played on the profusion of names for similar things, like this swarm of biting insects: "black flies no-see-ums gallinippers katynippers sandflies skeeters mitsies maringouins midges gadflies, that whole mess of bloodsuckers." For the fast-talking, wisecracking lingo of the city scenes, I lifted phrases from noir and gangster films, screwball comedies, and Coen Brothers movies, as well as early Warner Brothers and Mickey Mouse cartoons. I also found an infectious, frenetic rhythm akin to *Macunaíma*'s in Ishmael Reed's *Mumbo Jumbo* (1972). For "Letter to the Icamiabas," which combines a send-up of the colonizers' archaic, convoluted language with a satire on the pedantic, Europeanized flourishes of erudite Brazilian writing in later centuries, I did my best mock-Elizabethan accent and cribbed from Sir Walter Raleigh's chronicle *The Discovery of Guiana* (1596), while also looking to Samuel Johnson and the "Oxen of the Sun" episode of *Ulysses* (1920), in which James Joyce performs a condensed history of the English language.

In 1930, when the American translator Margaret Richardson Hollingsworth approached Andrade about translating *Macunaíma*, he was excited by the prospect. The author believed that his hero with no character could speak to a more universal condition of modern times, an itinerant aimlessness and lack of moral resolve that led to an improvisatory approach to life. Hollingsworth never finished that translation, but did bring Andrade's earlier novel, *Amor, verbo intransitivo* (1927), into English as *Fräulein* in 1933. In notes to his translator that informed my approach, Andrade told her to "transport" *Macunaíma* into "the indolence of the American language," but instructed her to keep the music of the Indigenous names for flora and fauna. These dizzying catalogs work as lexical poems and evoke the outrageous lists in Rabelais's sixteenth-century chronicles of the father-and-son giants Gargantua and Pantagruel, as well as the proliferation of plants and animals that appear in the Pemon tales and in glossaries and dictionaries compiled by naturalists, such as the Bavarian duo Johann Baptist von Spix and Carl Friedrich Philipp von Martius, who traversed Brazil collecting specimens and language from 1817 to 1820.

I wanted to stay true to Andrade's use of native systems of naming flora and fauna instead of replacing them with foreign classifications that alienated them from their home forests (for example, keeping *pitanga* over "Suriname cherry" and *sororoca* over "South American traveler's palm"). However, I often had to make linguistic compromises, rearranging words for a better sound or translating certain Tupi-derived terms so that readers could get the joke or image when most Brazilians would. I broke rules of scientific classification when I translated *jacaré*, a well-known Tupian word for caiman, as "alligator," to keep the storybook feel. For the list that introduces São Paulo's coffee-based economy, I came up with a Luso-Brazilian-Anglo-American poetics of currency to convey the mix of familiar, obscure, and possibly made-up words for money, juxtaposing *contos* with bits, shillings, coppers, and pennies, and tossing in "greenbacks gravy marbles moolah dough vouchers peanuts frogs smackeroos, and the like."

Researching *Macunaíma*'s sources made me realize that the narrative's frequent eruption into non-Portuguese isn't just a product of Andrade's inventiveness, but also a demonstration of how the transmission of history and culture enacts an incredibly tangled game of telephone. *Macunaíma* is built on multiple iterations of translation. The Pemon tales were recounted to Koch-Grünberg in Portuguese by his Taurepang guide, Mayuluaípu, who also translated for Akuli. The ethnologist then translated his transcriptions into German, and Andrade translated the stories into his idiosyncratic Brazilian. In the "Piaimã" chapter, when the giant mimics a birdcall to lure the hero, "Ogoró! ogoró! ogoró!," I had assumed the phrase was a Brazilian onomatopoeia, but after seeing Andrade's edition of Koch-Grünberg's book, I learned that it was a transcription of a Pemon word (*okoro* is defined as "the call of the *piaimã* and other animals" in a Pemon-Spanish dictionary compiled by Venezuelan missionaries).

Many of the other colonial-era and nineteenth-century ethnographic and naturalist studies that the book draws on contain some element of multilingualism and untranslatable words in their combination of transcriptions of Indigenous languages, accompanied by translation into a European language. While looking at the text of Tupi lullabies that Andrade adapts from the collection *Poranduba amazonense* (1890), I saw that his versions would sometimes interweave bits of folklorist João Barbosa Rodrigues's transcriptions of Nheengatu (the modern form of Tupi spoken in the Amazon) with their translations into Portuguese—but also that some of the Amazonian songs had originally mixed Tupi and Portuguese lyrics, reflecting their singers' bilingual contexts. These discoveries led me to preserve more of the original language, especially when it was also confounding to most Brazilians.

When I started this project, I believed I already possessed a decent understanding of Mário de Andrade's Brazilian classic, a favorite of mine for nearly two decades. After more than five years of going down the rabbit hole of research and chasing after its mysteries, I feel that there is still so much I haven't yet grasped. To translate *Macunaíma* is to add another layer to a centuries-old palimpsest, leaving traces of the countless translations that came before. Makunaima leapt from Pemon into Portuguese into German into Brazilian, and into eleven other languages. Now he is leaping into U.S. American, and the myth will continue its metamorphosis in the mouths of whoever passes it on. Pass it on.

KATRINA DODSON

ENDNOTES

The theme of buried treasure recurs throughout *Macunaíma*, which serves as a map to an incredible wealth of cultural heritage. The notes that follow offer a window onto Mário de Andrade's extraordinary process of composition and illustrate specific ways in which his rhapsody weaves together various strands that make up Brazilian culture and history. Because *Macunaíma*'s references are so numerous and entangled, I wrote the endnotes as chapter summaries with key terms in bold. This format allows for the heady pleasure of reading the novel straight through, letting the music of unfamiliar words disorient you as Andrade intended, without the constant interruption of numbered footnotes droning like a swarm of mosquitoes. In this way, the notes are an invitation to reread and reflect after you've reached the end of the story, and not an "answer key" to be consulted at every puzzling turn.

These notes focus mainly on allusions that have a broader cultural or historical significance; many proverbs, superstitions, popular songs, and rhymes go unnoted. Much of the flora and fauna with Tupi-derived names can be found on the internet, though I include explanations for those that are more important to the narrative or difficult to find online. I paid particular attention to elements that are indebted to Indigenous and Afro-Brazilian cultures—in part because access to reliable information in these areas remains limited in English (and sometimes in Portuguese), but also as a way to bring much-deserved credit and visibility to these traditions that have historically been overlooked or misrepresented, including in past scholarship on *Macunaíma*. For the origins of Indigenous stories, I named specific ethnic groups if my sources identified them, but some folklore compendiums merely point to a generalized Indigenous provenance—often for Amazonian stories long-adapted into Brazilian culture.

This translation and the endnotes build on the decades-long work of other scholars and translators. An indispensable resource was the *Roteiro de Macunaíma* (*Guide to Macunaíma*, 1954), by Manuel Cavalcanti Proença, an exhaustive study of the novel's language and sources, which includes a detailed glossary and bibliography. I also relied on the 1996 Coleção Archivos critical edition of *Macunaíma* organized by Telê Ancona Lopez, including its glossary by Diléa Zanotto Manfio. I further referenced Noemi Jaffe's notes in a 2016 edition of *Macunaíma* (Editora FTD), as well as the notes by Andrade's cousin, literary critic Gilda de Mello e Souza, that accompany Hector Olea's Spanish translation in Andrade's selected works (*Obra Escogida*, Biblioteca Ayacucho, 1979). I updated and supplemented this information based on other scholarship, as well as my own research into Andrade's manucripts and original sources at the Mário de Andrade archive at the University of São Paulo's Instituto de Estudos Brasileiros. I plan to make available an expanded version of these notes with full citations, either a digital guide or a print companion to this book. Readers can also find a list of my main sources on the *Macunaíma* page of the publisher's website. All translations in the notes are mine unless noted.

Andrade's rhapsody revels in a confusion of tongues and deliberately emphasizes the instability and error that plague any attempt to codify systems of knowledge—including annotations! Most of the "Tupi," or Tupian, words noted here are forms that have been integrated into Brazilian Portuguese, through languages in the Tupi family known as Língua Geral and Nheengatu (modern Tupi); the latter is still spoken in the Amazon. The novel often plays with the variability of the written forms of these and other oral languages, and likewise, my endnotes contain variations in spelling and capitalization that may reflect these shifting forms within the narrative, point to other sources, or follow Brazilian conventions. For example, Andrade refers to the same water creature as both the Iara and Uiara. He also sometimes uses lowercase forms for these entities, as well as for the one-legged Saci and Boiuna water snake, which I capitalize in the notes according to standard practice in Brazil. And when citing from Theodor Köch-Grunberg's German translation of Pemon myths in *Vom Roroima zum Orinoco*, vol. 2, I follow his spelling, i.e., Makunaíma, Zigué, Ma'nápe, and Piai'mã; the numbered "sagas" and their titles refer to this collection.

Given the inevitable limitations of my attempts to synthesize scholarship in ethnography, comparative religion, botany, zoology, and other fields across several languages and centuries, please take these notes as a starting point for further investigation.

Notes to chapter 1. Macunaíma (pp. 3–7)

Andrade explains **Tapanhumas** as a "legendary tribe of Amerindians in Brazil with black skin," in a note to his American translator, Margaret Richardson Hollingsworth. The name is a plural variant of *tapanhuna*, the Tupi word for people of African descent. The Tapanhuna are also included in an 1848 registry of Indigenous groups in Mato Grosso state that German ethnologist Karl von den Steinen includes in *Among the Primitive People of Central Brazil* (*Unter den Naturvölkern Zentral Brasiliens*, 1894), though he never encountered them and doesn't offer any physical description.

The author emphasizes this ambiguous provenance by intermingling African and Indigenous elements. The Tapanhumas home is both a **maloca**—a Tupi word for a village or communal dwelling with a thatched roof (a longhouse or roundhouse)— and a **mocambo**, from the Angolan Kimbundu word *mú kambu* (hideaway), which in Brazil refers to a farmhand's shack or the settlements that made up quilombos, resistance communities of formerly enslaved Africans.

The **hero's catchphrase, Ah! just so lazy!** (*Ai! que preguiça!*), contains a bilingual pun linking Portuguese and Tupi. A sloth is called a *preguiça* in Portuguese, and in Tupi it is called *aig* (also transliterated as *ai* and *aígue*). Andrade underlined a passage in his copy of the sixteenth-century Spanish Jesuit José de Anchieta's letters to the Portuguese court in which Anchieta remarks, "There is another animal, which the Indians call Aig and we call Preguiça due to its excessive, ever so meandering slowness . . ."

The Tapanhumas participate in a **Pajelança** ceremony, an Amazonian healing ritual in which a **pajé** (shaman) or *curador* (healer) channels both Indigenous spirits and Afro-Brazilian entities. **King Nagô** is another name for **Xangô**, an Afro-Brazilian deity adopted from the Yoruba religion. Macunaíma requests a rope blessed with **petum** (tobacco) smoke from a **pai-de-terreiro**, a priest in Candomblé and other Afro-Brazilian religions; the name means "father of the temple," or area (*terreiro*) where ceremonies are held (see chapter 7 notes).

The hero participates in ritual dances from various Indigenous peoples: the **murua** and **cucuicogue** from the Pemon; the **poracê** (or *porakei*) from the coastal Tupi; the **torê**, practiced in various Indigenous and Afro-Brazilian religious ceremonies; and the **bacororô** from the Bororo in central-western Brazil.

Macunaíma sleeps in a **macuru**, a Tupi hanging crib; lullabies called *cantigas do makuru* (macuru songs) appear in chapters 4 and 16.

Much of the action in this chapter is based on the Pemon tale "Makunaíma's Exploits" (saga 6), in which the boy-hero **transforms into a man** to sleep with the wife of his brother, who discovers them and **beats him**, and gives Makunaíma the intestines after the boy **catches a tapir**.

Jiguê's wife, **Sofará**, comes from an Amazonian Indigenous myth about a woman who repopulates the world with her husband in the wake of a great flood, similar to the tale of Noah's Ark. The **playful yet bloody sexual encounter** between the hero and Sofará echoes various ethnographic accounts of Indigenous practices, including a study on the Kaingang people in southern Brazil highlighted in Andrade's research notes.

Papaceia is the northeastern Brazilian nickname for Venus as the "suppertime star."

SELECTED FLORA, FAUNA, AND FOOD
The **saúva** leafcutter ant (*Atta* genus) is a notorious destroyer of crops, whose colonial epithet was "the true King of Brazil." Macunaíma's mother weaves a basket from **guarumá-membeca** (*guarumá* is a calathea; *membeca* means "tender" and also refers to a grass, *Paspalum repens*) in order to drain grated manioc, which she ferments into **caxiri**, a beer-like Amerindian drink often made by women. The **javari** (or *jauari*) is the most common palm tree in the Amazon. The forest floor plants include **caruru** (redroot amaranth) and **sororoca** (South American traveler's palm). The hero heals his wounds by chewing the root of the **cardeiro**: either a poppy with narcotic properties or a regional name for a large cactus (*Cereus jamacaru*) found in Brazil's semiarid Northeast, better known as **mandacaru** (see chapters 2 and 5).

Notes to chapter 2. Coming of Age (pp. 9–16)

The **cunauaru toad called Maraguigana, Father of the Dolphin** combines three separate entities from Amazonian Indigenous traditions. The **cunauaru toad** is a poisonous tree frog associated with good fortune. The **Maraguigana** (also Marajigoana or Marajiguana) is a person's ghostly double that rises from the body at the moment of death. **Father of the Dolphin** is the protector ancestor of the Amazonian river dolphin, associated with an enchanted spirit (*encantado*). The belief in a "father" or "mother" ancestor or protector spirit that watches over each being connects Tupi and other Brazilian Indigenous traditions and recurs throughout the novel.

The scene in which **Macunaíma pretends to find timbó**—which designates various plants used to poison fish in a traditional fishing method—is based on the Pemon story cycle, "Kaláwunség the Liar" (saga 50).

The rest of the chapter adapts the same Pemon tale as in chapter 1, "Makunaíma's Exploits" (saga 6). After getting beaten by his brother, the hero **magically transports his mother** to a mountaintop with all their food, **lets his brothers go hungry**, and **seduces his brother's wife** again. Their **mother dies** suddenly in a place called Mura'zapómbo, which Koch-Grünberg translates as **Father of the Tocandíra** (Andrade spells it **Tocandeira**); *tocandíra* is the Tupi name for the bullet ant, known for its venomous sting.

Jiguê's new woman **Iriqui** comes from the Kaxinawa tale "One Brother Killed by the Other," in which she fools around with her husband's brother. All references to the Native Kaxinawa people of western Brazil and Peru (who call themselves Huni Kuin) come from Brazilian historian João Capistrano de Abreu's collection, *Rã-txa hu-ni-ku-ĩ: a lingua dos caxinauás do Rio Ibuaçu*, or *A língua dos caxinauás* (*The Language of the Kaxinawa*, 1914).

Andrade calls the Tapanhumas home a **tejupar** (or *tijupá*), a thatched hut with a peaked roof, much smaller than a **maloca**.

The **Currupira** (or Curupira) is a forest protector from Tupi-Guarani mythology, who became popularized throughout Brazil as a hairy, man-eating ogre and who sometimes has a **dog named Papamel** ("honey-eater")—a Brazilian nickname for the weasel-like tayra. Andrade borrows heavily from the Amazonian folktale "The Curupira and the Two Lost Boys," including the ogre's **talking leg flesh** and the **agouti who sings "Acuti pita canhém . . ."** Folklorist João Barbosa Rodrigues leaves the line untranslated in his collection of Amazonian legends and songs, *Poranduba ama-*

zonense (1890), with the note: "Words in a dialect that I don't recognize"; *acuti* is the Tupi word for agouti, but the rest is a mystery.

Uaiariquinizês means "testicles" in the language of the Nambikwara people from the Amazon and central-western Brazil.

The **caatinga** is an arid scrubland in Brazil's Northeast whose Tupi name means "white forest."

Pedra Bonita (Pretty Stone) is the site of a bloody days-long standoff in 1838 in the mountains of Pernambuco state in northeastern Brazil. Police forces intervened to stop members of a messianic cult, the Sebastianistas, from performing human sacrifices meant to bring the return of Portugal's King Sebastião I, whose 1578 death while crusading in Morocco led to the downfall of the Portuguese Empire.

The **Anhanga** is a Tupi-Guarani forest spirit who takes the form of a deer and punishes those who hunt animals still nursing their young.

Andrade's **drawing of the mother's epitaph** resembles an Amazonian petroglyph (Indigenous rock engraving) depicted in Jean-Baptiste Debret's lithograph "Sculpture en creux," in *Voyage pittoresque et historique au Brésil* (Plate 30, 1839).

SELECTED FLORA, FAUNA, AND FOOD

Andrade highlights natural dyes used by various Indigenous groups: red from **araraúba** tree bark (*Simira rubescens*) and **urucum** seeds (achiote or annatto dye); black from **jenipapo** fruit (genipap) and the **acariúba** tree (*Minquartia guianensis*); and yellow-green from the **tatajuba** tree (*Bagassa guianensis*). The **quenquém** leafcutter ant (*Acromyrmex* genus) is smaller and less voracious than the **saúva**. Most of **the fish** are freshwater characins, which include tetras and piranhas. Amazonians warn that the small, parasitic **candiru** catfish (*Vandellia cirrhosa*) can swim up human orifices. **Aluá**, from the Kimbundu *ualuá*, is a beer-like drink fermented from pineapple rinds, rice, or corn, and used in Afro-Brazilian religious ceremonies. **Oloniti** is an Indigenous alcoholic drink made from fermented buriti palm sap or wild manioc. **Carimã** is manioc cake or porridge. Andrade depicts **mandacaru cacti** in the rain forest with **titara palms** (short for *jacitara*), though the former grows in Brazil's semiarid Northeast.

Notes to chapter 3. Ci, Mother of the Forest (pp. 17–22)

The hero's love interest, **Ci**, whose name means "mother" in Tupi, is based on the character of Coia, the queen of the **Amazons**, a tribe of women who live on the Jamundá River (see below), in the 1925 Brazilian science fiction novel *A amazônia misteriosa* (*The Mysterious Amazon*), by Gastão Cruls. Here, she fights with a **txara**, a Kaxinawa trident. Macunaíma wields a frontier knife, while Jiguê uses a **murucu**, a redwood spear decorated with feathers, from the Amazonian Mura people.

Ci is queen of the **Icamiabas**, the Tupi name for the legendary tribe of warrior women that Spanish conquistador Francisco de Orellana claimed to have encountered in 1541 on the **Jamundá River** (also spelled **Nhamundá**) during his expedition through what is now called the **Amazon**—named for these warlike women that he associated with those from Greek mythology. Their Tupi name comes from the Itacamiaba mountains where they lived, near Lake Jaciuára (**Moon Mirror Lagoon**). Pemon lore also includes a similar tale of matriarchal warrior women, the Ulidján, living along the Uraricoera River, who Koch-Grünberg referred to as Amazons (saga 40).

Macunaíma plays the **cocho guitar** (*viola de cocho*), a lute-like instrument used by Brazil's rural bards and in religious folk dances, often accompanied by the **ganzá** shaker, which he plays in chapter 11.

Andrade adapts the words for the hero's **chuí** from the Maxuruna (Matses) people's word for penis and for Ci's **nalachítchi** from the Canamari people's word for vagina—as they appear in German botanist Carl Friedrich Phillipp von Martius's glossary of Brazilian Indigenous languages translated into Latin, *Glossaria Linguarum Brasiliensium* (1863).

Ci gives birth to a **scarlet son**, red like the sons of lightning in a Kaxinawa tale. This section incorporates customs and superstitions from all over Brazil, particularly the rural Northeast, such as **Christmas pageants** in which women sing and dance in two groups divided into blue or red costumes. **Tutu Marambá**, likely of Bantu origin, is a bogeyman used to scare children. The **jucurutu** is a horned owl associated with bad omens. A Luso-Brazilian superstition holds that snakes can suck a nursing mother's milk dry; Andrade combines this with the mythical Amazonian **Black Snake** (*Cobra Preta*), a river snake also called the **Boiuna** (see chapter 4 notes). The **boitatá** is a mythical Tupi-Guarani fire snake associated with blue-green phosphorescence in swamps and fields (will-o'-the-wisp in Anglo-American folklore).

Ci gives the hero her **muiraquitã before becoming a star**. The theme of a person transforming into a star or constellation to join their ancestors occurs throughout Brazilian Indigenous mythology. Muiraquitãs are Tupi artifacts found in the Upper Amazon region, talismans made of green jade or nephrite that are carved into the form of a frog, tortoise, or other totem animal; its name means "knot of wood" or "tree knot" in Tupi. The Icamiabas were said to retrieve the stones from their lake and present them as mementos to men with whom they had their annual tryst.

Their son is buried in an **igaçaba**—a burial urn from the pre-Columbian Marajoara civilization in the eastern Amazon. **Taba** is Tupi for "village." The origin story of **guaraná**, which sprouts from a young boy's corpse, comes from the Amazonian Mawé people, recognized as the first to domesticate and cultivate this stimulant with medicinal properties.

The **umbu** (or *imbu*) tree's roots and fruit, "Brazilian plums," provide an important water source in the drought-stricken northeastern **caatinga** region and **sertão** backlands. **Taioca ants** are army ants (*Eciton* genus), which can swarm in the thousands. **Pajuari**, from the Carib word *paiuá*, is a northern Amazonian Indigenous wine made from fermented manioc cakes.

Notes to chapter 4. Boiuna Moon (pp. 23–30)

Macunaíma's song to **Rudá**, the Tupi god of love, is based on a transcription in General José Vieira Couto de Magalhães's influential survey of Tupi religion, legends, songs, *O selvagem* (*The Savage*, 1876); Andrade suspected that it actually came from a Portuguese love prayer to God.

Maanape's songs are based on Tupi lullabies (*cantigas do makuru*) transcribed by Barbosa Rodrigues. The **Acutipuru** is an enchanted squirrel, the **Murucututu** is a horned owl (the same as the **jucurutu** in chapter 3), and the **Ducucu** is another nocturnal bird.

Naipi is a chieftain's daughter in an origin myth about Iguaçu Falls from the Kaingang people in southern Brazil, a subgroup of the Guarani. She angers the Guarani snake god Mboi after running off with a handsome warrior; the snake's thrashing body creates the cataracts, and he transforms Naipi into a rock formation and her lover into a palm tree.

Andrade takes the names of Naipi's lover, **Titçatê**, and father, **Mexô-Mexoitiqui**, from Kaxinawa tales. The lovers flee in an **ipeigara** (a Tupi canoe) out to the **Raging River**, a literal translation of the Kaxinawa name for the ocean.

The author also replaces the southern snake god, Mboi, with the northern Amazonian **Boiuna**, a mythical water snake also known as the **Mother of Water** (*Mãe d'água*). He further conflates the generally female Boiuna with the moon, feminine in Portuguese (*a lua*). **Capei** is the male Pemon moon—originally a wicked shaman who was banished from his village. In a Kaxinawa origin myth, the moon also starts out as a shaman who gets beheaded; his **decapitated head** chases after people, who flee up a **bacupari fruit tree**, but eventually gives up and becomes the moon.

The **Bachelor of Cananéia** was an early sixteenth-century *degregado* (criminals and political or religious prisoners who were abandoned in the Portuguese colony), cast away in what is now Cananéia in southern São Paulo state. He lived among the native Carijó, trafficked Indigenous slaves as part of his lucrative trade with Europeans, and founded a village on São Vicente Island that became the first Portuguese settlement in the Americas. He re-appears in chapter 10 as **Master Cosme**.

The **Little Black Herder Boy** (*Negrinho do Pastoreio*) is a ghostly youth from southern Brazilian folklore who rides with a herd of horses. Resurrected by the Virgin Mary after a violent death at the hands of a rancher (his enslaver in early versions), he helps find lost objects. Barbosa Rodrigues linked this figure to the **Saci**, a Tupi forest sprite who in some accounts is the youngest child of the **Curupira** and **Caapora**, but who is best known in the form adapted into Brazilian folklore: an impish one-legged Black boy who wears a red cap. Macunaíma gets mistaken for the Saci by Capei, who calls him **siriri**, one of the Saci's nicknames. The Saci is said to transform into several birds, including the good-luck **uirapuru** (organ wren), whose Tupi name means "bird that is not a bird," as well as the **matintaperera** and **suinara** owls, considered bad omens.

Andrade playfully calls the **Tietê River**, which traverses São Paulo city and state, an **igarapé**, Tupi for a small tributary.

SELECTED FLORA, FAUNA, AND FOOD

The **yellow ipê** (golden trumpet tree) has dramatic yellow blooms—the national flower of Brazil since 1961. The **aturiás** that hide the lovers' canoe are likely shrubs (*Machaerium lunatum*), though the Tupi word also refers to a hoatzin (skunk bird). Titçatê turns into a **mururé** (*Eichhornia azurea*), a water hyacinth that forms a floating mass. **Sacassaia** ants are the same army ants as **taioca** (chapter 3). The **tracuá** is a leafcutter ant. **Iandu** comes from Tupi for "spider." The black **xexéu birds** (yellow-rumped caciques) who make night fall are also called **japiim**, among the most common birds in the Amazon. The **pecaí** is a waterfowl in the grebe family, a **tapicuru** is a bare-faced ibis, and the **iererê** is in the same family as ducks and geese.

Notes to chapter 5. Piaimã (pp. 31–42)

The **ubá** and **igara** are Tupi canoes.

The **Isle of Marapatá** (*Ilha de Marapatá*), on the Rio Negro southwest of Manaus, is where newcomers looking to make their fortune in the Amazonian rubber trade were said to **leave their consciences behind**.

Sumé is short for São Tomé (St. Thomas the Apostle), based on a Tupi-Guarani legend about an old white man who taught them farming and fishing long before the Portuguese arrived and that Jesuits interpreted to be the saint. Andrade merges this legend with an Afro-Brazilian folktale, "The Three Races," about God's transformation of three Black brothers into the **"three races of Brazil"** by means of an enchanted spring; the story resembles racial origin stories from Afro-Cuban and African American folklore.

Mani, daughters of manioc refers to a Tupi origin story of manioc, in which a chieftain's virgin daughter gives birth to a fairskinned baby named Mani; the child dies, and manioc grows from her grave.

A **tapiri** is a thatched hut used as a rain shelter.

Mythological entities that the hero imagines in São Paulo include: Pemon **mauaris**, demons who haunt mountains, rivers, and lakes; **juruparis**, long, wooden trumpets played by men in ceremonies for the Tupi demigod Jurupari; as well as **sacis** (impish sprites; see chapter 4 notes) and **boitatás** (fire snakes; see chapter 3 notes).

Macunaíma elevates the individual machines (lowercase) into an amalgamated **Machine god**, which he identifies as **Tupã**, the Tupi concept of divine thunder, which missionaries interpreted as God. Yet the hero also **calls the Machine a goddess**—*máquina* ("machine") is feminine in Portuguese—and compares her to the **Mother-of-Water** (Andrade hyphenates the word), synonymous with the **Boiuna** snake but also another name for the **Iara** or **Uiara** (see chapter 15), a mythical Amerindian female that inhabits rivers and lakes and became conflated with mermaids and sirens in Brazilian folklore.

Piaimã is the ancestral shaman of the Ingarikó people, neighboring rivals of the Taurepang and Arekuna; he appears as a foreign cannibal giant and Makunaíma's enemy in the Pemon stories. **Ogoró** (or okoró) is the Piaimã's call in the Pemon language. Andrade's Piaimã has a dual identity as an Italian-Peruvian river peddler named **Venceslau Pietro Pietra**, who strikes it rich after finding the muiraquitã and moves from the Amazon to the wealthy São Paulo district of Higienópolis. Andrade's Piaimã also shares certain qualities with the **Curupira** Tupi forest-dweller adapted into Brazilian folklore (see chapter 2 notes), such as feet turned backwards.

The **giant's wife** combines two different Tupi entities adapted into Brazilian folklore: the **Caapora** (or Caipora) forest spirit, who loves tobacco and is the Curupira's wife in some stories; and **Ceiuci**, the virgin mother of Jurupari, who appears in Brazilian folklore as a greedy old woman (see chapter 11 notes).

Much of the **hero's encounter with Piaimã** comes from the Pemon myth "Death and Resurrection of Makunaíma" (saga 11), including the **Dzalaúra-Iegue**, a sacred tree of life. A **zaiacúti** is a leafy shield used for hunting by the Ariti people, part of the Paresi group in southern Brazil. A **banini** is a Kaxinawa arrow.

The final episode, in which the **hero gets pistols, bullets, and whiskey from trees** in colonial British Guiana is based on Pemon story cycles about two tricksters, named Kone'wó and Kaláwunség (sagas 49 and 50).

SELECTED FLORA, FAUNA, AND FOOD

The **ururau** is a broad-snouted caiman. Maanape tosses Piaimã a mix of monkeys and birds, incuding a **jaó** (**tinamou**), **picota** (guinea fowl), and various kinds of quail, guan, and curassow. **Sarará** is a Tupi word for a red ant. **Jaguar ants** (*formiga oncinha*), or velvet ants, are actually wingless female wasps. **Cauim** is an Indigenous alcoholic drink made from fermented manioc or corn mixed with fruit juice.

Notes to chapter 6. The French Lady and the Giant (pp. 43–51)

The opening episode on the **"three plagues"** of Brazil rewrites a Pemon origin myth (saga 7) in which Makunaíma transforms a big pointed arum leaf into a sting ray to attack his brother Zigué, who then turns a vine into a snake to bite Makunaíma while they build a house; here, they try to erect a thatched rain shelter called a **papiri** (the same as **tapiri** in chapter 5).

The hero's falsies allude to another Pemon origin myth, in which Makunaíma ties cone-shaped **banana flowers** to a woman's flat chest in retaliation for refusing his advances, fatefully changing the female form (saga 8).

The American-owned **Continental Products Company** built Brazil's second meatpacking plant in 1915 on the outskirts of São Paulo. **Falchi** was a São Paulo candy company.

Piaimã's **grajau** (an elongated woven basket) amasses mineral and archeological treasures, including a **gris-gris**, a West African amulet made of paper, wood, or shell inscribed with a spell and kept in a pouch. **Itamotinga** (Tupi for "white stone") is a sparkling river stone. None of my sources identify **Oaque, Father of the Toucan**.

The doll that traps Macunaíma is made of **wax from the carnaúba palm** (*Copernicia prunifera*), known as the "tree of life" in Brazil's Northeast. The episode is based on an Afro-Brazilian folktale, "The Monkey and the Granny," in which an old woman makes a wax girl darkened with charcoal to get revenge on a sneaky monkey; it recalls the tar baby stories attributed to African-American traditions. Both the monkey and Macunaíma address the doll as **Caterina**, the name of a Black woman in the **Bumba Meu Boi** pageant, a distinctive Brazilian folkloric tradition (see chapter 16 notes). This character is sometimes called **Catita** (from Kimbundu for "small"), which is also a doll made of dark wood or painted black that plays a central role in Maracatu, an Afro-Brazilian Carnival procession from the Northeast.

Andrade also incorporates the Pemon tale, "Makunaíma in Piai'mã's Snare" (saga 9), in which **the hero's hands and feet get stuck one by one in the giant's snare**. The hero's **mênie** is an animal hide quiver, but the word's provenance is unclear (it appears in Spix and Martius's 1817 *Travels in Brazil*, according to Cavalcanti Proença).

A Brazilian folk belief claims that whoever **passes under a rainbow changes sex**.

The **chase scene** covers all four corners of Brazil and highlights historical sites such as Rio de Janeiro's **Calabouço Point**, named for the Calabouço ("Dungeon") slave prison built in 1693. The Brazilian popular ballad of **Dona Sancha** is set during the 1630–1654 Dutch invasion of northeastern Brazil; the girl's parents refuse to let her marry her true love, who goes off to fight the Dutch, then becomes a priest. When they meet years later, the shock kills her, and the legendary **jasmine-mangos** (*mangajasmim*) grow from a tree planted on her grave. Macunaíma's "prayer" for cow's milk comes from a popular rhyme in historic gold-rush towns like Barbacena, in Minas Gerais state.

The final standoff follows the Pemon tale "Makunaíma and Piai'mã" (saga 10), in which Piai'mã's dog chases Makunaíma into a tree hollow. The giant gets some anaquilã ants (a Pemon word), then leaves to find Elitê, a pit viper (jararaca in Tupi).

The hero's escape is based on a Brazilian folktale in which a rabbit tricks an angry jaguar into tossing her out of a burrow by her ears.

In Pemon mythology, many rock formations used to be living creatures that Makunaíma transformed into stone (sagas 4 and 5).

SELECTED FLORA, FAUNA, AND FOOD
The içá is the female saúva leafcutter ant. The hero makes use of plants used in Afro-Indigenous healing rituals: sacaca (*Croton cajuçara*), a leafy shrub; jurema, a hallucinogenic from a rain tree (*Pithecellobium tortum*); Paraguayan pine (*Jatropha curcas*), a purgative used to expel evil spirits; and cumacá vine root (*Marsdenia amylacea*). Cumaté is a flowering tree (*Macairea glabrescens*) that produces a black lacquer. Caiçuma is an Indigenous beer-like drink made from corn or fruit. Mocororó is an Indigenous drink made from fermented cashew juice.

Notes to chapter 7. Macumba (pp. 53–62)

Macunaíma's strength test is based on an Amazonian folktale in which a hawk tries to uproot a tree ahead of seeking revenge on an old turtle who killed his father. The teeth of a rodent called "crô" are used in a male coming-of-age rite among the Apinajé people in central Brazil (the word appears in a 1930 account by Brazilian ethnographer Carlos Estevão de Oliveira).

The "Macumba" ceremony merges elements from regional

syncretic religions that are interrelated in their blend of African, Indigenous, and Catholic spiritual practices. **Macumba** from Rio de Janeiro and **Candomblé** from Bahia are Afro-Brazilian traditions based on the worship of **orixás** (Yoruba deities adapted in Brazil, where they often correspond to Catholic saints, similar to Cuban Santería). Macumba now has a pejorative connotation, but in Andrade's time, it was a branch of Candomblé that incorporated Bantu religions, Indigenous entities, and Spiritism (or Kardecism), the latter founded by Frenchman Allan Kardec. Macumba is similar to Umbanda, which developed in the 1920s among white middle-class worshippers in southeastern Brazil and is still popular today. **Pajelança**, the Amazonian shamanistic healing ritual that appears in chapter 1, conjures Indigenous *encantados* (enchanted beings) and other spirits, including Afro-Brazilian entities. This chapter's notes are largely based on the *Handbook of Contemporary Religions in Brazil* (2017), edited by Bettina E. Schmidt and Steven Engler, and *Candomblé e Umbanda: caminhos da devoção brasileira* (1994), by Vagner Gonçalves da Silva.

Macunaíma seeks help from **Exu**, an orixá based on the Yoruba deity Eshu-Elegba, keeper of gateways and crossroads, who grants favors (for a price) and delivers messages to the other orixás. Though a mischievous trickster, like the Pemon Makunaima, Exu is often identified with Satan in Brazil, which Andrade emphasizes by associating Exu with other devilish figures: the **jananaíra**, a malevolent Amazonian *encantado* who runs with wild dogs and eats people; the **Cariapemba**, a supernatural force of protection and destruction in Bantu cultures; **Icá**, a Kaxinawa devil; **Jurupari**, a sacred Tupi ancestral patriarch whom Catholic missionaries interpreted as the Devil; and the **uamoti**, an obscure word, from Tupi, meaning demon or evil spirit.

Tia Ciata (Hilária Batista de Almeida,1854–1924) was a Candomblé priestess and one of several "aunties," leaders in a community of Black migrants from Bahia state who went south to Rio de Janeiro after the 1888 abolition of slavery. They settled in what became known as Little Africa, located in the **Mangue**, a red-light district inland from the port. Tia Ciata's home is hailed as the birthplace of samba and provided a refuge for Afro-Brazilian religious and musical gatherings that were outlawed at the time (Roberto Moura, *Tia Ciata e a Pequena África no Rio de Janeiro*, 1983).

Andrade got a firsthand account of Tia Ciata's gatherings from Pixinguinha (Alfredo da Rocha Vianna Filho, 1897–1973), a flautist and saxophonist who is among the most prominent composers of choro and samba. The Black bandleader appears here as **Olelê Rui Barbosa**, which combines a Congolese salutation with the name of a white Rio de Janeiro statesman known for his erudition (see chapter 9 notes). The author also links him to **fado**, a musical genre associated with Portugal, though Andrade claimed it originated in Afro-Brazilian forms.

Candomblé priests and priestesses are called "mothers" and "fathers" of the saints or of the temple (**mãe/pai-de-santo or mãe/pai-de-terreiro**), and worshippers are initiated as "sons" and "daughters" devoted to particular orixás. Tia Ciata and her young helper are children of **Oxum**, goddess of fertility, and the Pixinguinha character is a son of **Ogum**, god of fire and war. An **ogã** is a man who plays the **atabaque**, an African drum, in Candomblé ceremonies.

Macunaíma's talisman in this chapter is an Afro-Brazilian **milonga**.

The **sairê to hail the saints** corresponds to the *xirê* salutation that opens Afro-Brazilian religious ceremonies. Its spelling also suggests *sairé*, an Amazonian song-and-dance ritual that merges Indigenous and Catholic traditions. The refrain **"Saravá!"** is a variation on *"Salve!,"* similar to "Hail!"

The first "saint" that Tia Ciata invokes is **Olorung** (also Olorum or Olodumarê), the God-like Supreme Being who reigns over the orixás. The **Dolphin-Tucuxi** (*Boto-Tucuxi*) is a gray river dolphin and benevolent *encantado* from Amazonian mythology. **Mothers-of-Water** refer here to orixás: **Iemanjá** (or Janaína) is the mother of all the orixás and rules the ocean; **Anamburucu** (also Nanamburucu or Nanā Buruku), the oldest water goddess, reigns over deep waters; **Oxum** rules waterfalls, rivers, and lakes.

King Nagô, who appears in chapter 1, is **Xangô** (or Shango). He was a legendary Yoruba king of the Oyo Empire who became deified as the god of thunder and lightning; *nagô* designates Brazilians of Yoruba descent. **Baru** is an obscure orixá who appears in a list by the writer João do Rio in *As religiões do Rio* (1906). **Oxalá** (or **Obatalá**) is the father of all the orixás, and was ordered by Olodumarê to make people out of clay; he corresponds to Jesus.

The **White River Dolphin** (*Boto Branco*), also known as the pink river dolphin (*boto cor-de-rosa*), is one of the best-known Amazonian *encantados*, said to transform into a man who impregnates young women. **Omulu** (or Omolu) is the orixá of epidemics and diseases. **Iroco** is an orixá who inhabits a sacred tree. **Oxosse** (or Oxossi) is the orixá of the forest. See chapter 4 notes for **Boiuna**.

The invocation that begins **"Bamba querê"** (something like "I want a powerhouse") mixes Bantu and Yoruba words, whose staccato rhythms and rhymes I wanted to maintain. **Aruê** is a salutation for **Exu**. None of my sources identify **"Mongi gongô,"** though it may refer to *gongá*, an altar in Umbanda. **Orobô** is a West African kola nut with ceremonial functions. **Mungunzá** is hominy porridge, and **acaçá** is corn mush wrapped in a banana leaf, a main offering in Candomblé. **Nhamanja** is Iemanjá. None of my sources identify **Pai Guenguê**, possibly a *pai-de-santo* priest.

In the next stage of the ceremony, a chosen worshipper enters a trance to channel a spirit—here, a Polish woman becomes a medium known as the **saint's horse** in Umbanda; she's also called a **babalaô**, usually a male priest or seer. Andrade uses the term *polaca* (**Polack tart**), a pejorative term for Polish women that also became a euphemism for prostitute—many Eastern European women who immigrated to Brazil in the World War I era became sex workers in the Mangue district. This character also suggests the *pombagira*, a woman-of-the-night figure who is Exu's female counterpart in Umbanda. The **jet ring** that she expels after the devil leaves her body is based on Brazilian missionary Frei Jaboatão's 1761 account of an exorcism from "the time of the Dutch" one century earlier.

After receiving a new stool from a **mazomba** (a pejorative term from Kimbundu for children of immigrants to Brazil, especially the Portuguese), Tia Ciata anoints the chosen medium with **efém** (or *efúm*), a chalky colored paste used to mark female initiates. The **jongo** is a call-and-response song and circle dance with soloists, a precursor to samba. **Urari** (or *curare*) is a Carib name for a poisonous powder used by Indigenous people for hunting.

The **giant's song**, which begins, **"Go slow when you whack me!,"** is based on what the captured monkey sings in the folktale "The Monkey and the Granny," the source of the black wax doll episode in chapter 6.

The **Our Father Exu** prayer combines a satanic twist on the Lord's Prayer and the Gloria Patri (Glory Be to the Father) with references to Afro-Brazilian culture. A **sanzala** is a traditional Angolan village and the origin of the Brazilian word *senzala*, meaning slave quarters. **"Chico-t was a Jeje prince"** (*Chico-t era um príncipe jeje*) is a pun on the first line of the Latin Gloria Patri prayer: "Sicut erat in principio." The name Chico-t resembles *chicote* (whip) and is a euphemism for the Devil—but also evokes Chico Rei, a legendary eighteenth-century Congolese king brought to Brazil enslaved but who bought his freedom and is commemorated in Brazilian *congado* parades. **Jeje** refers to people from the Kingdom of Dahomey (present-day Nigeria, Benin, and Togo).

Macunaíma leaves the ceremony with Mário de Andrade's carousing buddies in Rio de Janeiro: composer **Jayme Ovalle** (1894–1955); the wealthy bon vivant **Geraldo "Dodô" Barroso do Amaral** (circa 1882–1934); **Manuel Bandeira** (1886–1968), one of Brazil's most celebrated poets and Andrade's close confidant; Swiss-French poet **Blaise Cendrars** (1887–1961); modernist poets **Ascenso Ferreira** (1895–1965) and **Raul Bopp** (1898–1984); and art critic **Antônio Bento de Araújo Lima** (1902–1988), who introduced the author to Pixinguinha.

Notes to chapter 8. Vei, the Sun (pp. 63–69)

Most of this chapter is adapted from the Pemon tale "Akalapi-jéima and the Sun" (saga 13), about an ancestral hero who tries to catch a magic toad named Walo'ma and ends up on an island where vultures defecate on his head. The sun rescues him, and the hero is meant to marry one of the sun's daughters but fools around with the vulture's daughters instead.

In Andrade's version, Walo'ma the toad becomes **Volomã** the tree, whose fantastical abundance recalls the **Dzalaúra-Iegue tree** in chapter 5. The phrase **"Boiôiô, boiôiô! quizama quizu!"** comes from a Brazilian Indigenous folktale, "The Turtle and the Fruit," as transcribed by Sílvio Romero in *Contos Populares do Brasil* (1883). It's unclear what language this is, but the words are the tree's secret true name, which enacts a spell that makes it give up its fruit.

Alamoa is a wicked blonde fairy in Brazilian folklore who guards Dutch treasure on Fernando de Noronha, an island off Brazil's northeast coast that was controlled by the Netherlands from 1629 to 1654. Her name comes from "German woman" in Portuguese (*alemã*).

Vei the Sun and **Capei the Moon** (see chapters 4 and 15) appear as male characters in the Pemon myth, but here Andrade makes them female. He turns the masculine Portuguese word for sun (*o sol*) into a feminine noun (*a sol*); the moon (*a lua*) is already feminine. **Caiuanogue, the morning star** (Venus), is also male in Pemon mythology but here takes the feminine pronoun for star in Portuguese (*a estrela*).

The scene in which **flames puff out from Vei's bottom** comes from a Pemon myth on the origins of fire (saga 23), in which people tie up an old woman and squeeze her to make fire come out her rear; she "defecates" the flint stones called **Vató**, which Vei gives to Macunaíma in this chapter.

One of Vei's daughters plays an **urucungo** (berimbau), an African percussion instrument made from a gourd and a bow, used in capoeira, the Brazilian martial art and dance.

Andrade calls Vei's daughters *chinoca* (**little China girl**), a southern Brazilian word for young Indigenous women,which can also mean prostitute. It is a diminutive of *china*, a largely (though not always) pejorative term that carries the same meanings as above but can also refer to people of Chinese descent. Most Brazilians unfamiliar with *chinoca* would assume the latter association, though *china* also derives from the Quechua word, *tchina*, for a female animal.

Macunaíma's ballad incorporates lyrics from different Amazonian songs in Nheengatu (modern Tupi). One of the verses goes: "When I die / put me in the woods / with the **giant armadillo / as my grave-digger**." The refrain, **"Mandu sarará,"** combines a nickname for Manuel with *sarará*, which refers to people of African descent with reddish or light hair (from the Tupi word for a red ant in chapter 5). In Andrade's notations of folk songs, an em dash seems to denote a second voice coming in.

The phrase **Yerup France 'n Bahia** (*Oropa, França e Bahia*) comes from a colloquial expression meaning "the whole world," which appears in an old Brazilian country song.

Macunaíma's declaration **"Burn it all down!"** is based on a Tupi saying, which a tortoise shouts before attacking a dangerous tapir in the legend "The Tortoise and the Tapir."

The **hero's dictum, "Ants aplenty and nobody's healthy, so go the ills of Brazil!"** (*Pouca saúde e muita saúva, os males do Brasil são!*), evokes critical views of Brazil. French botanist Augustin Saint-Hilaire (1779–1853) is credited with saying, "Either Brazil must bring an end to the ants, or the ants will be the end of Brazil," referring to the **saúva** leafcutter ants that devastate crops. "Brazil is a vast hospital," declared Brazilian doctor Miguel Pereira (1871–1918). The dictum's second part recasts the refrain of the seventeenth-century satirical poem, "Milagres do Brasil são" ("So Go the Miracles of Brazil") by Brazilian baroque poet Gregório de Matos. It also echoes a popular rhyme that lists laziness and ants among Brazil's misfortunes, quoted in *Retrato do Brasil* (*Portrait of Brazil*, 1928), by Paulo Prado.

The **statue of Saint Anthony of Pádua** at a Franciscan monastery devoted to the saint was credited for saving Rio de Janeiro from a 1710 French invasion and rewarded with a salary and the rank of infantry captain.

"Compadre Chegadinho" is a Portuguese song that was popular in Rio de Janeiro in the late nineteenth-century.

Mianiquê-Teibê is a warrior prince from an Amazonian Tupi legend who lost his head after putting on the cursed headdress of an enemy chieftain.

SELECTED FLORA, FAUNA, AND FOOD
Various Brazilian popular names for the **pitiguari bird** (rufous-browed peppershrike) translate its insistent, melodious whistle into some version of: **"Look who's a-coming down the road!"**

Notes to chapter 9. Letter to the Icamiabas (pp. 71–84)

Macunaíma's letter back home describing his encounter with the **marvels and customs of a new civilization** is a parody of the founding document of Brazilian history—scribe Pêro Vaz de Caminha's 1500 letter to Portugal's King Manuel I recounting the "discovery" of Brazil by the Pedro Álvarez Cabral expedition. The hero's elaboration on the attributes of the **"French" and "Polish" ladies** (Brazilian euphemisms for prostitutes) echoes Caminha's excessive attention to the native women's bodies. Macunaíma's praise for São Paulo rewrites rapturous descriptions of Brazil's lush natural setting by Caminha and other **"early chroniclers"** of colonial Brazil, such as Pero de Magalhães Gândavo, author of a 1576 tract promoting Portuguese emigration to the colony, and Baroque poet Manuel Botelho de Oliveira, whose 1705 poem "À ilha de Maré" is a paean to Brazilian abundance—the **"three A's"** here (aqueous bodies, air, and area) are inspired by his four ideal A's: *arvoredos, açucar, águas, ares* (trees, sugar, waters, airs).

The hero shows off his newfound erudition using belletristic language and classical citations in the style of Brazilian scholars like **Rui Barbosa** (1849–1923), an influential statesman, jurist, and writer, and **Friar Luís de Sousa** (1555–1632), a Portuguese monk and historian whose writing is considered a model of classical Portuguese. He also cites Portugal's revered national poet **Luís de Camões**; the line introducing the loss of the muiraquitã—**"Not five suns had come and gone since we took leave of you . . ."**—echoes the part of Camões's epic poem *The Lusiads* (*Os Lusíadas*, 1572) in which the hero encounters a giant named Adamastor (Canto V, stanza 37).

His discussion of the Asian origins and orthography of the **muiraquitã** parodies *O muryakytã* (1889), João Barbosa Rodrigues's study of the Amazonian artifact, including a passage in which the folklorist enumerates the word's various written forms: **muyrakitan**, **muraqé-itã**, buraquitã, puuraquitan, uaraquitan, and more.

Embracing European influences, Macunaíma prefers to identify the **Icamiabas** with their classical Greek namesakes, the **Amazons** (see chapter 3 notes). He compares the muiraquitã to the **golden fleece** that Jason and the Argonauts set out to steal and references the opening of Virgil's first *Eclogue*—**"sub tegmine fagi"** (in the shade of a beech tree)—as well as the *Aeneid*: **"horresco referens"** (I shudder to relate, 2.204) and **"per amica silentia lunae"** (through the friendly silence of the moon, 2.255). Macunaíma quotes Horace's *Satires* to propose a **"modus in rebus"** or "middle ground" between his newly adopted Brazilian city customs and the Icamiaba way of life (1.1.106). He also draws parallels between São Paulo and ancient Rome, using the Roman term for city officials, **aediles**, and signing off as **Imperator**, Latin for Emperor.

Macunaíma sometimes lapses into ungrammatical Brazilianisms, misspellings, and malapropisms, which I've rendered as **platina** for patina, **macrobes** for microbes, **Orpheus** instead of Morpheus, the god of sleep, and **texticles of the Bible** (*testículos* for *versículos*). He confuses *eugenia*, the Portuguese term for eugenics—which influenced early twentieth-century Brazilian immigration and public hygiene policies—with a woman named **Eugenia**. He misspells *urbi et orbi*—the Latin name for a papal address, meaning "to the city (of Rome) and the world"—as **"urbi et orbe."** And he writes the Latin *Odor di femina* (scent of a woman) as *Odor di Fêmia*, a phrase made famous by Mozart's opera *Don Giovanni*.

The hero also picks up words in French, English, and Italian used in the cosmopolitan metropolis. The English word **Bond** refers to the origin of the Brazilian word for tram, *bonde*: "bond" was printed on tickets for Rio de Janeiro's earliest trams in the 1860s, run by the American-owned Botanical Garden Rail Road Company. Macunaíma notes the Paulistanos' fluency in Italian—Italians made up thirteen percent of São Paulo's population in 1886 and thirty-seven percent by 1916—though he misspells the Italian *chi lo sá* (who knows) as *qui lo sá*.

Andrade refers to one of São Paulo's founding fathers, **Father José de Anchieta** (1534–1597), a Spanish missionary who established the Jesuit education system in Brazil, wrote an influential Tupi grammar, and is considered a forefather of Brazilian literature. Andrade also calls São Paulo the **"land of the bandeirante frontiersmen"**; *bandeirantes* were colonial-era adventurers who explored and settled regions beyond the city, looking for gold, establishing trade, and capturing Indigenous people to sell into slavery.

The chapter also alludes to the politics of the time, in which coffee and cattle oligarchs in São Paulo and **Minas Gerais** colluded to **control national elections**, with tactics like **inflating voter rolls**. The list of warriors includes **legalists**, members of the military who supported the government during a series of lieutenant uprisings, including the short-lived 1924 Paulista Revolt. The **"rogue bands of cannibal giants"** that **"topple honest Governments"** may refer to the development of this movement into the Prestes Column, a group of rebels who roamed the country from 1925–1927 and eventually helped President Getúlio Vargas seize power in the 1930 revolution. **Big Daddy** (*Papai Grande*) was the nickname for the country's last monarch, Pedro II, and for subsequent presidents, among Indigenous Brazilians.

Notes to chapter 10. Pauí-Pódole (pp. 85–92)

Antônio the Indian was a Tupi prophet who led a late-sixteenth-century religious uprising in the **backlands of Bahia** with his wife, Santa Maria, also known as **Mother of God**. Their millenarian movement blended Catholicism with Indigenous rites and was called Santidade (Sanctity)—**Caraimonhaga** in Tupi. The prophets challenged the dominance of Jesuits, Portuguese slaveholders, sugar-mill owners, and colonial authorities, and encouraged migration in search of the **Land Without Ills** (*Terra Sem Mal*), the Tupi-Guarani concept of paradise.

Flower Day alludes to young women in 1920s São Paulo who sold flowers to raise money for charity.

Master Cosme is a reference to **Mestre Cosme Fernandes**, who some historians believe was the colonial-era **Bachelor of Cananéia** (see chapter 4 notes).

The word **puíto** comes from a Pemon origin myth (saga 25) in which Pu'yito was the name of an anus that would sneak around farting in everyone's faces until two parrots caught him, divvied him up, and passed out the pieces to every animal; and that's how we all got our anuses.

Fräulein is a German governess hired by a wealthy São Paulo business man to seduce his son in Andrade's 1927 novel *Amar, verbo intransitivo* (titled *Fräulein* in the 1933 translation).

The phrase **a most mulatto of all mulattos** (*um mulato da maior mulataria*) is a corruption of the line "a most leprous of all lepers" (*um malato, da maior malataria*) from a Portuguese medieval chivalric romance in which a maiden wards off a knight's potential sexual advances by claiming to be the contagious daughter of a leper. The word *malato* became *mulato* in a nineteenth-century Azores version of this romance called "O caçador" ("The Hunter"), as noted in Sílvio Romero's study of Brazilian popular ballads (*Cantos Populares do Brasil*, 1897).

The Southern Cross constellation is the **Cruzeiro do Sul** in Brazil, where it is a national symbol. Macunaíma tells the origin story of Pauí-Pódole, the Pemon version of this constellation (saga 20), in which a man tries to hunt three different ancestral fathers: Mauaí-Pódole, Father of the Crab; **E'Moron-Pódole, Father of Sleep** (see chapter 14); and **Pauí-Pódole, Father of the Mutum** (*mutum* is the Tupi word for the turkey-like curassow). The hunter's shaman brother-in-law tries to help by transforming into **three different ants**—Andrade uses the word **tacuri** as if it were an ant, though it's a Tupi word for a large anthill or termite nest. He takes the shaman's name, **Camã-Pabinque** (dog-ear mushroom), from a Kaxinawa origin myth about mushrooms.

Notes to chapter 11. Old Ceiuci (pp. 93–109)

Macunaíma's lies about **hunting deer and finding tapir tracks** come from the Pemon story cycle "Kaláwunség the Liar" (saga 50). The phrase **"Tetápe dzónanei pemonéite hêhê zeténe netaíte"** is an amalgam of Pemon words that Koch-Grünberg left in the original and can be paraphrased as: "The tapir hid its tracks under the people's tracks, I found them right here."

A **ganzá** is a cylindrical shaker of African origin used in Brazilian folk music.

The **"land of the English"** in the Pemon tales refers to Guyana, a British colony until 1966 (also in chapter 17).

The **Matarazzos** were a prominent São Paulo family, like the Rockefellers, whose patriarch immigrated from Italy and grew rich by selling canned pork fat.

The **competition between Macunaíma and Drizzle** to see who can scare Piaimã's family is based on the Pemon tale "Jaguar and Rain" (saga 44).

The list of **fishing implements** includes both Indigenous and obscure regional Brazilian fishing methods. The scheme to steal a fishing hook comes from the Pemon tale "Makunaíma's Other Feats" (saga 5). The Pemon word **aimará** (wolf fish, *Hoplias malabaricus*) comes from this story and is more commonly known in Brazil by its Tupi name, *traíra* (see **Father of the Traíra** in chapter 14). **Tapuitinga** (white man) is an amalgam of two words from Tupi: *tapuia*, which refers to non-Tupi speaking Natives, as well as people of Indigenous descent who have assimilated into Brazilian society; and *tinga*, meaning "white."

Ceiuci is the Tupi name for the Pleiades constellation; she was originally the virgin mother of legendary Tupi patriarch Jurupari. She was adapted into Brazilian folklore as a voracious old woman cursed with eternal hunger in stories like **"Legend of the Greedy Old Crone,"** which forms the basis of the episodes from the fishing scene through the chase scenes that end the chapter. Andrade merges this character with the **Caapora**, a Tupi forest protector who appears as both male and female figures in Brazilian folklore (see chapter 5 notes). Andrade updates Ceiuci's bird call, **"Awooga!,"** into the onomatopoeia for the klaxon, used for automobile horns.

The daughter's **three riddles** are based on Brazilian popular rhymes.

The **horse rhymes** come from a Brazilian folk ballad, "The Devil's Horses," in which a young man gallops off with the Devil's daughter, while Satan tries to catch them on various horses.

The **galley slave from French Guiana** alludes to the Devil's Island penal colony where France sent its worst criminals from 1852–1953; the convicts were still called *galerien*, even after they were no longer used as galley slaves.

Araripe de Alencar refers to Tristão de Alencar Araripe, a judge and writer whose 1887 article about archaeological evidence of advanced pre-Columbian civilizations in Brazil cites various locations mentioned in this chapter. Araripe recounts how a farmhand duped the ***Comércio do Amazonas*** newspaper into reporting the discovery of a **buried Greek sculpture**. He also notes enigmatic inscriptions on huge boulders at **Poço do Umbu**, in the backlands of Paraíba state, which French scholar Ernest Renan identified as **Phoenician**.

The **Hole of Maria Pereira** (*Buraco de Maria Pereira*) is a depression along the São Francisco River in Alagoas state, named for a legendary Portuguese settler said to have hidden there during the seventeenth-century Dutch invasion.

Bartolomeu Lourenço de Gusmão (1685–1724) was a Brazilian priest who was ridiculed and investigated by the Inquisition after presenting the designs for an airship resembling a huge bird to Portugal's King João V.

SELECTED FLORA, FAUNA, AND FOOD

Paricá beans produce a hallicinogenic snuff used in Amerindian healing rituals. **Maquiras** are either hammocks (*maqueira*) made from tucum palm fiber, or trees in the fig family (*Moracea*). **Mumbucas** are not an ant but a stingless bee. Andrade defines **caxipara** as the male saúva leafcutter ant (*sabitu*), but none of my sources identify this word. Macunaíma rides on the back of the **tuiuiú**

stork (*jabiru*) in an **aturiá** (or aturá), a large cylindrical basket, which shares a name with the shrub or bird in chapter 4.

Notes to chapter 12. The Perky Peddler, Shiny Cowbird, and the Injustice of Men (pp. 111–119)

Bento Milagroso was an early-twentieth-century miracle healer who cured people with water from the **Beberibe River** in the northeastern city of Recife.

The **leper colony in Guapira** operated from 1904–1930 in what is now the northern São Paulo neighborhood of Jaçanã.

Having a **magic little woodpecker leaf** is a northeastern Brazilian idiom for being lucky, based on an Indigenous belief in a miracle plant that only woodpeckers can find.

The **fast-talking peddler and the monkey who fool Macunaíma** are inspired by the Pemon trickster Kone'wó, who gets a man to exchange his hammock for an opossum that supposedly poops silver coins; the trickster also leads a jaguar to smash his own testicles and die (saga 49). None of my sources identify **toaliquiçus**, but it follows the novel's pattern of using Indigenous names for genitals (it likely goes with **toaquiçu** in chapter 15).

Zé Prequeté is the object of a taunting children's rhyme popular in 1920s São Paulo.

Butecaiana is a neologism for rabies that poet Ascenso Ferreira mentioned to Andrade in a 1927 letter.

See chapter 10 notes on the Pemon word **puíto** (anus).

A Brazilian folk belief claims that **beating a cadaver will make it lighter**, and thus easier to transport through the countryside.

SELECTED FLORA, FAUNA, AND FOOD

Andrade uses two words for opossum: **micura** (or *mucura*) from Tupi, and the Portuguese *gambá*, which can also mean skunk. **Tapipitinga** is an unspecified kind of ant. **Guaju-guaju** and

murupeteca are Amazonian names for army ants. The **sapupira** is a Brazilian alcornoque, trees thought to resemble cork oaks. The **guaruba** (or *guarajuba*) is a timber tree (*Terminalia acuminata*) native to the Atlantic rainforest. **Parinari** refers to trees in the Rosaceae family. **Baguaçu** nuts come from the babassu palm. Andrade calls the monkey *macaco mono*, an ambiguous term for a large monkey that can refer to the **muriqui** (woolly spider monkey), the largest primate in the Americas. The monkey's gloves are made from latex extracted from **balata trees** in the Amazon.

Notes to chapter 13. Jiguê's Lousy Lady (pp. 121–128)

St. Anthony's fire—named for the third-century Egyptian saint whose bones reportedly cured ergotism—is an inflammatory fungal disease, but the name can also refer to **erysipelas**, a bacterial skin infection that causes a burning rash.

Antônio Carlos Gomes (1839–1896) was Brazil's first internationally recognized composer, whose opera *Il Guarany*, based on Brazilian Romantic novelist José de Alencar's fictional Indigenous hero, debuted at La Scala in 1870; his statue sits across from the São Paulo Municipal Theater, near stairs leading down to a monument modeled after Rome's Trevi Fountain, in **Anhangabaú Park** (now called *Vale do Anhangabaú*).

Mother-of-Water in this chapter refers to the mythical **Boiuna water snake** (see chapter 4 notes), who is said to take the illusory form of various boats in order to lure men to their deaths.

Lloyd Brasileiro, founded in 1890, was one of the largest ship companies in Brazil, and operated the steamship that Andrade took from Rio de Janeiro to the Amazon in 1927. The **Hamburg line** refers to the German ship company founded in 1871, which operated routes between Brazil, Lisbon, and New York. The **SS Conte Verde** was an Italian transatlantic liner named for the 14th-century Count of Savoy, nicknamed the

"Green Count" (*il piróscafo* is Italian for "steamship"). The passengers dance the **cururu**, a folkloric dance from rural São Paulo and the Central-West region that mixes Catholic and Indigenous religious rituals.

The **love triangle between Jiguê, Suzi, and Macunaíma** is based on two Kaxinawa tales. In the story, "The Brave Young Man," a woman uses a flute (not the **foxtrot**) to signal her secret lover; her husband finds out and kills them with a spear; Jiguê beats the lovers with a **mirassanga** club, a word of seemingly Indigenous but obscure origin. The **final episode** comes from "One Brother Tricks the Other," in which a young man tricks his brother into searching for a fruit tree that attracts all the animals while the man stays home to fool around with his brother's wife. The husband discovers them and beats them; the beaten brother tries to get sympathy from other family members, who realize he's a no-good liar.

Macunaíma casts a **mandinga** spell, magic associated with the West African Mandinka people. None of my sources identify the **Lords of Water** that he invokes.

Maissó comes from the word for vagina among the Amazonian Miranha people, as it appears in Martius's glossary. It is also the name of the first woman, who puts a piece of wood into her vagina and births the rivers, land, and people—in a legend from the Paresi in central Brazil. **Maanape's refusal to eat Suzi's cassava** echoes a Pemon tale in which a shaman refuses the catfish that his mother-in-law secretly procures from her womb (saga 19A). Maanape mutters a São Paulo popular rhyme that ends in a Latin prayer, **"Libera nos, Domine"** (Deliver us, O Lord). He chews **ipadu** (coca leaves) to anesthetize his stomach.

The episode with **Suzi and the lice** comes from the Kaxinawa tale "The Lice-Ridden Woman," which tells of the first man and woman; she secretly removes her scalp to pick out her lice. Andrade also adapts a Brazilian folktale, "Why Women Pick Fleas," in which Our Lord Jesus Christ saves an idle old woman from boredom by teaching her how to pick fleas; Andrade replaces Jesus with the sixteenth-century Jesuit missionary **José de Anchieta** (see chapter 9 notes).

Geracina from Ponta do Mangue was a renowned lacemaker from the northeastern state of Rio Grande do Norte.

Notes to chapter 14. Muiraquitã (pp. 129–139)

"Did you see a little green birdie?" is a Brazilian expression for when someone seems happy out of the blue, said to originate in an old practice of using parakeets to send love letters.

The story of the **tick selling on credit** comes from a Brazilian folktale called "The Tick."

Emoron-Pódole, Father of Sleep, appears in the same Pemon myth as **Pauí-Pódole, Father of the Mutum** (saga 20, see chapter 10 notes). In the Tupi fable, "The Fox and the Jaguar," a jaguar plays dead to catch a fox, who **tricks it into burping**. The idea that people used to **sleep standing up** comes from the Bakairi people in central-western Brazil.

Macunaíma's **exchange with the fallen tree** about looking up the girl's dress is based on an Amazonian Tupi folktale, in which the tree tells a whippoorwill (whose Tupi name, *jurutahy*, means "mouth wide open") that it saw, "A big mouth like yours!" (*Poranduba amazonense*, Barbosa Rodrigues).

"Go on, let it flip!" comes from a popular Brazilian nursery rhyme in which a canoe flips over. Andrade uses the Tupi word **igarité**, for a large canoe.

The verses that Macunaíma sings to **bum a cigarette, and the chauffeur's reply**, come from a rural genre of singing a request for handouts called "Beggar Songs" (*Canto de pedinte*). Andrade bought custom tortoiseshell objects from Belém artisan **Antônio do Rosário** while traveling in the Amazon.

The story about **Palauá the puma and the black tiger**, an archaic name for jaguar, is based on the Pemon myth "Game of

Eyes" (saga 46), in which a shrimp sends its eyes out to Palauá, the Pemon word for the sea, then gets chased by a jaguar whose eyes get eaten by **Aimalá-Pódole, Father of the Traíra** (wolf fish, *Hoplias malabaricus*). Andrade winks at the arbitrary grammatical genders of relatively new car brands; São Paulo was Brazil's motor city, where the **Ford** factory opened in 1919, and General Motors, manufacturer of **Chevrolet**, arrived in 1925.

Afonso Sardinha was a colonial *bandeirante* adventurer who became one of the richest men in colonial Brazil after discovering gold. He built the country's first **iron foundry** in 1597 on the Araçoiaba (or **Ibiraçoiaba**) ridge west of São Paulo city.

The end of the chapter is based on the Pemon tale **"Death of Piai'mã"** (saga 26): after the giant and his wife lure a young man to his death, the man's younger brother tricks the giant into falling off his own vine swing to his death. In a Kaxinawa legend, **Icá** the devil plays the same swinging vine trick to kill and eat people (he's associated with Exu in chapter 7). **Macunaíma's ploy** also resembles the children's trick at the end of "João e Maria," the Brazilian "Hansel and Gretel." The hero literalizes the Brazilian expression **"eating snakes,"** which means someone is furious.

The chauffer's lament that begins **"If only Mama and Papa were here godwillin' "** is what a wife sings loudly while hoping to be rescued from her murderous husband in the Brazilian folktale "The Bad Husband."

Macunaíma's **song about the captain** comes from a Brazilian nursery rhyme that children sing while swinging their playmates.

The giant's lines, **". . . if I get outta this thing"** and **"Outta the way or else . . ."** come from the Brazilian Indigenous folktale, "The Turtle and the Party in the Sky," in which a heron drops a turtle while giving him a ride to a three-day party in the sky. While falling, the turtle shouts, "If I make it out of this, no more parties in the sky ever again!" and, "Get out of the way, rocks and trees, or else I'll crush you!" (Couto de Magalhães, *O selvagem*).

Macunaíma's lament, **"Muiraquitã, muiraquitã of my lovely . . ."** echoes an encantation that turns three young men into swans in the Brazilian fairy tale, "The Three Swans."

SELECTED FLORA, FAUNA, AND FOOD
Lambari (or **piaba**) is a small freshwater fish with serrated teeth in the Characidae family. A **tambiú** is a large lambari with a yellow tail. Cigarettes rolled with **tauari** tree bark (*Couratari tauari*) are used in Amazonian Indigenous healing rituals. The **taxi** is a wasp-like arborial ant with a venomous sting. The **titica** vine (*Heteropsis flexuosa*) is one of the most common Indigenous weaving materials in the Amazon.

Notes to chapter 15. Oibê's Innards (pp. 141–152)

Macunaíma casts a **caborje**, an incantation of Yoruba origin, to transform São Paulo into a **stone sloth**.

The hero's interest in **the people of Goiás** is a nod to Andrade's maternal grandfather, Joaquim de Almeida Leite Moraes (1834–1895), president of the Province of Goiás from 1880–1881. Moraes's 1882 travelogue, *Apontamentos de viagem*, details a trip on the **Araguaia River**, which includes an anecdote about his aide and future son-in-law, Carlos Augusto de Andrade (Mário's father), falling asleep in a **cockroach-covered room** like the one in Oibê's shanty.

Macunaíma's **three homecoming songs** mix Amazonian lullabies with the style of folk ballads improvised by rural northeastern bards. In the Tupi lyrics: **antianti** is a gull, **tapejara** is a guide, **pirá** means fish, **ariramba** is a green kingfisher, **taperá** is a swallow, **tapera** with no accent is an abandoned home, **caboré** is a ferruginous pygmy owl, **arapaçu** is a woodpecker, **paçoca** is a peanut candy, **panapaná** is a cloud of migrating butterflies, and **panema** means cursed.

Macunaíma's exclamation, **"Eropita boiamorebo!"** (Make your companions linger over us), is based on a Tupi phrase by which sixteenth-century missionary **José de Anchieta** was said to have miraculously summoned a flock of scarlet ibises to form a canopy over his canoe, according to his biographer Jesuit Simão de Vasconcelos in *Vida do venerável padre José de Anchieta* (1672).

The transformation of the hero's spit into **matamatá turtles** is based on an Amazonian Tupi tale in which a chieftain named Buopé spits in the water, and the gobs transform into his people.

"When far and away true loves must part, long is the labor for the suffering heart" comes from a traditional love song (*modinha*) called "Little Sister" (*Maninha*). See chapter 4 notes on the **love god Rudá**.

Pondê is a monster from a Brazilian folktale who tries to eat a little girl; Andrade merges him with a child-eating giant named Yacurutu who transforms into an evil owl in a legend from the Amazonian Mura people—the **jurucutu** horned owl is the same as **jucurutu** (chapter 3) and **murucututu** (chapter 4).

Natives along the Japurá River in the Upper Amazon region would place an ant called **curupê** in Tupi on their arrow tips to keep their aim true.

The **Mapinguari Monster monkey-man** is a monster from Brazilian folklore that eats people. None of my sources identify **toaquiçu**, but it most likely refers to the male member (paired with the **toaliquiçus** from chapter 12).

None of my sources identify **Oibê**, though his epithet, *minhocão* (**great big worm**), refers to a mythological snake that lives in the São Francisco River, a version of the Amazonian **Boiuna** or **Great Snake** (*Cobra Grande*).

Francisco de Mendonça Mar (1657–1722) was a Portuguese goldsmith and painter who was jailed after demanding payment for his work decorating the Governor General of Brazil's palace in Salvador da Bahia, the colonial capital at the time. Upon release, he left for the **sertão** backlands and eventually built the **Bom Jesus da Lapa** shrine—one of Brazil's most popular Catholic pilgrimage sites—in a grotto near the São Francisco River. In 1706, he was ordained as a priest and took the name **Francisco da Soledade**.

Hércules Florence, or Antoine Hercule Romuald Florence (1804–1879), was born in Monaco and went to Brazil as an illustrator and draftsman on the Langsdorff expedition in the Amazon. Seeking a way to print his **musical notation for birdsong** and other sounds, he developed a photographic process he called *la photographie* (light writing) in 1833—six years before Sir John Herschel coined *photography* in English and Louis Daguerre debuted his daguerreotype. Florence tells Macunaíma in French, **"Mark this date: 1927! I've just invented photography!"**

The **starfruit tree's lament** comes from a Luso-Brazilian fairytale, in which a wicked stepmother buries her two stepdaughters alive after they fail to shoo birds away from her fig tree. Brazilian modernist composer Heitor Villa-Lobos wrote a 1926 piano composition based on this song, "Xô, xô, passarinho," at Andrade's suggestion.

Macunaíma's ploy to escape Oibê is based on two Brazilian folktales in which a jaguar gets outsmarted, first by a tortoise, then by a rabbit. In another folktale in the same series, a jaguar tricks a deer into **eating the green bananas and tossing him the yellow ones** (Couto de Magalhães, *O selvagem*).

In a Kaxinawa myth about a great flood that destroys the world, a snake gives birth to a **blue butterfly** (likely the morpho butterfly) as life renews on Earth. Piai'mã also **transforms into a butterfly** after his death in the Pemon myth (saga 26).

The **Carrapatu** is a bogeyman from a children's lullaby.

Iriqui and the six blue-and-gold macaws become the **Seven Sisters constellation** (the Pleiades), which marks the start of the planting and rainy season in South America.

Macunaíma's retinue is comprised mainly of parrots and macaws, with the exception of the **camiranga** yellow-headed turkey vulture and the **xarã**, which none of my sources identify. The list includes different Tupi names for the same parrot species (**ajuru** is "parrot" and **arara** is "macaw"); most of them, from **ajuru-curau to anaca**, appear in a section of Martius's 1863 glossary of Tupi animal names. Iriqui sits on a **samaúma** (kapok tree), scratching her **mucuim** (spider mite) bites.

Notes to chapter 16. Uraricoera (pp. 153–165)

Fort São Joaquim was built on the Uraricoera River in the 1770s to defend the Portuguese Amazon against Spanish infringement on the orders of the Governor of Pará, Francisco Xavier de Mendonça Furtado, whose brother, the **Marquis of Pombal**, was the most powerful statesman in the Portuguese empire.

João Ramalho (1493–1582), known as "the patriarch of the *bandeirantes*," was a Portuguese castaway in southeastern Brazil around 1512, who helped found São Paulo. He lived among the native Tupiniquim, married their leader's daughter, and had many children with her and other Indigenous women.

The rest of the chapter—from the **magic gourd** to the **vulture's two heads**—is based on the Pemon myths "Etetó: How Kasána-Pódole, the King-Vulture, Got His Second Head" and "Wewé and His Brothers-in-Law" (sagas 28 and 29). The fish that eats the gourd is a **pirandira**, which Koch-Grünberg defines as a batfish; it doesn't appear in Brazilian dictionaries, but contemporary sources point to the *payara*, a sabre-toothed dogfish (*Hydrolycus scomberoides*). The main character's brother-in-law dies and becomes a ghostly **shadow**, then transforms into Wewepódole, Father of Gluttons, who gobbles up everything in sight, including his wife, mother-in-law, and another man, as they bring him fire. The wraith perches on a tapir's back until the animal starves to death, and the shadow then becomes the second head of the **Father of Vultures**.

The episode in which **Macunaíma naps while the others work** comes from the Amazonian tale "The Vulture and Her Married Daughters," in which two of the vulture's sons-in-law, the lizard and owl, sleep all day but make their hardworking brothers-in-law, the duck and the pigeon, seem like the lazy ones. Macunaíma's **lie about hunting a deer** comes from the same Pemon myth, "Kaláwunség the Liar" (saga 50), as when he fibs in São Paulo (chapter 11).

The **birigui** (phlebotomine sand fly, *Lutzomyia longipalpis*) transmits leishmaniasis—a parasitic disease that causes **skin sores** known as **Bauru ulcer**, named for the São Paulo town where the Leishmania protozoa was first discovered in 1909. The **princess suffers from zamparina**, an 1870 Rio de Janeiro influenza that was named for Italian opera singer Anna Zamperini (who caused such a "fever" among aristocratic young men that the Marquis of Pombal kicked her out of Portugal). Maanape contracts Chagas disease from the bite of the **kissing bug** (barber or triatomine bug), which transmits the parasite *Trypanosoma cruzi*. Before Brazilian doctor Carlos Chagas discovered the condition in 1909, in Minas Gerais, locals mistook it for **hookworm** (an intestinal parasite).

The legendary **White-Armadillo Indians** come from a Brazilian folktale about a group of *bandeirantes* captured in the northern backlands of Minas Gerais state by this tribe of cave-dwelling, pale-skinned cannibal pygmies who hunt at night. **Domingos Jorge Velho** (1641–1705) led a troop of São Paulo *bandeirantes* to the northeastern state of Alagoas, as part of a 1694 government-sponsored attack on Palmares, Brazil's largest and most famous quilombo, an autonomous community of mainly Afro-Brazilians who had escaped slavery. **Zumbi dos Palmares** (1655–1695), the quilombo's leader, initially escaped but was later killed and is now celebrated as one of Brazil's national heroes.

The episode in which the hero **taunts workers** comes from a Tupi tale in which a jaguar goads a deer into mocking farmhands clearing a field.

The final section combines the Pemon myth of the two-headed vulture with a song cycle from **Bumba Meu Boi** (Beat My Ox)—**Boi-Bumbá** in the Amazon—an annual ritual pageant that Andrade called "the strangest, most original, and most complex of our dramatic dances" and whose popular medleys often get grafted onto the ends of other folk ballads and religious pageants. Andrade incorporates verses from different sections of the Bumba-Meu-Boi plot, in which a Black ranch hand named Pai Francisco (or Nego Chico) kills a white rancher's prized ox to satisfy the cravings of his pregnant wife **Mãe Caterina** (or **Catirina**), for its tongue. After discovering the theft, the rancher sends a band of Indigenous trackers to capture the fugitive Francisco. An Indigenous healer resurrects the animal, and the drama ends with Francisco's confession and redemption, followed by a celebratory dance with the ox. Andrade incorporates Bumba-Meu-Boi verses—including one about a **giant** and a **vulture tap dance**—that he collected from 1928–1929 at a sugar mill called **Bom Jardim** in the northeastern state of Rio Grande do Norte, though here he relocates it to **Rio Grande do Sul**, Brazil's southernmost state. A **Malabar bull** comes from an Indian zebu bred with Brazilian cattle; some verses name the ox **Espácio**, after *boi-espácio*—a regional term for wide-horned steer.

SELECTED FLORA, FAUNA, AND FOOD

Puraquê (or *poraquê*) is an electric eel, and **pitiú** is a small Amazonian river turtle. None of my sources identify **arezi**, though *arebé* is a cockroach in Martius's 1863 glossary of Tupi animal names. The **catalog of fish** includes various catfish, **aviú** shrimp, and big game fish, including the **guarijuba** (or *guarajuba*), or horse-eye jack. The **sabatira tapir** is a version of a Brazilian variant for tapir (*anta-sapateira*). Colonial chronicles of Brazil describe the **"belly button"** (a dorsal scent gland) on the back of the **peccary**, a New World pig whose genus name, **Tayassu**, comes from Tupi. The head spike of the **anhuma** (horned screamer) was used to treat snake bites. This chapter lists various leafcutter ants: **tanajura** (the female leafcutter), **saúva**, **tracuá**, and **guiquém** (from *guikem* in Martius's glossary, likely the same as **quenquém**). None of my sources identify the **jaguataci** or **aqueque** ants. **Mumbuca** is a black stingless bee (*Melipona capitata*). The **"forest fruits and roots"** include **biribá** and **guacá**, in the same Sapotaceae family as sweetsop; **cajuí**, a wild cashew fruit; and **uxi** (*Endopleura uchi*), which has a yellow pulp and medicinal properties. **Tamorita** is a spicy Pemon broth, according to Koch-Grünberg. The tuberous roots of the **umbu** hold substantial water, making it "the sacred tree" of Brazil's arid **sertão** backlands. The hero hides under a **mucumuco**, a Pemon word for an arum with arrow-shaped leaves (*Montrichardia linifera*), which the mythical Makunaíma transforms into a stingray (saga 7). The list of **vultures** includes the **camiranga** from chapter 15; none of my sources identify **ruxama**, though its usage implies the king vulture (*Sarcoramphus papa*).

Notes to chapter 17. Ursa Major (pp. 167–177)

Venus appears in three incarnations: **Papaceia**, the northeastern Brazilian **evening star** (see chapter 1); **Taína-Cã**, from the Karajá people of central Brazil; and **Caiuanogue**, the Pemon **morning star** (see chapter 8). All take feminine pronouns when referred to as stars (*estrela* is a feminine noun in Portuguese), though both Caiuanogue and Taína-Cã are male characters. Andrade follows the Karajá myth of Taína-Cã but adds the Pemon **Emoron-Pódole, Father of Sleep** (see chapter 14), changing the father's name to **Zozoiaça**, from the Pareci people, and calling him **morubixaba**, a Tupi word for leader.

The **lagoon's gold-and-silver face** alludes to a popular Brazilian nursery rhyme based on a Portuguese ballad, which opens: "Senhora Dona Sancha, / Covered in gold and silver / Reveal to us your visage / We wish to see your face." This Dona Sancha comes from the late 1570s, a century prior to Dona Sancha of the jasmine-mangoes in chapter 6.

Uiara is the same as **Iara** (see chapter 5 notes).

None of my sources identify **nuqiiris** (likely the same as **Bahian-coconuts**).

The **Ururau Gator Monster** comes from southern Brazilian folklore; the **ururau** is a broad-snouted caiman.

The hero's lament that begins with **"My memento!"** echoes a line from the Brazilian fairytale "The Three Swans" (see chapter 14 notes).

The **blue forget-me-nots** come from a Brazilian folktale in which the blue-eyed Virgin Mary's tears stain a field of white flowers.

Macunaíma contemplates going to live on the **Isle of Marajó** (*Ilha do Marajó*) in the Amazon River—"the only place in Brazil where traces of a superior civilization remain," Andrade once said, referring to the pre-Columbian Marajoara culture—or joining **Delmiro Gouveia** (1863–1917), an industrialist who brought hydroelectric power and running water to the town of Pedra (Stone), a stop on the British Great Western railroad line in Alagoas state. In a newspaper column, Andrade called him "a genius of discipline," who achieved "an urban mechanical perfection" in Pedra "that remains unparalleled in our land" ("O Grande Cearense," 1928).

"I didn't come into this world to be a stone." Macunaíma writes this Tupi saying for throwing caution to the wind with an **itá** (stone); it's what the **jabuti** tortoise shouts before seeking revenge on a tapir in the Amazonian tale "The Tortoise and the Tapir."

Macunaíma's farewell verse is based on an Amazonian song that mixes Tupi and Portuguese; its original refrain, **"Mandu**

sararã" (see chapter 8) is replaced here by **"Taperá"** (a swallow, see chapter 15).

Andrade changed the name of this chapter from "Eiffel Tower" to **Ursa Major** (the Big Dipper) sometime after he saw the constellation in the Amazonian night sky in 1927 and wrote: "Equatorial Sky, dominion of Ursa Major, the great Saci..." (*The Apprentice Tourist*). Macunaíma is once again mistaken for the **one-legged Saci** (see chapter 4 notes). The Saci can also transform into the **tincuã** (squirrel cuckoo), a harbinger of death or misfortune. The **German professor** who claimed that **Ursa Major was the Saci** was anthropologist Robert Lehmann-Nitsche (1872–1938). The Pemon have a myth about a one-legged man, Jilijoaíbu, who goes up to the sky to become Tamikan, the Pleiades (saga 18). In another myth collection, *Indianermärchen aus Südamerika* (*Tales of the South American Indians*, 1927), Koch-Grünberg recounts the story of "Makunaíma and Piá," in which Makunaíma loses his leg in a snare and becomes the Pleiades; his leg is Orion's belt.

SELECTED FLORA, FAUNA, AND FOOD
Ajuru-catinga means "stinky parrot" in Tupi. The **aruaí** is a white-eyed parakeet (the same as **araguaí** and **maracanã** in chapter 15). The **araponga** (bare-throated bellbird) is known for its loud call; it disrupts the **quiriri**, an obscure Tupi word for the never-absolute "silence" of the nocturnal forest (though here it's the diurnal forest). **Matamatá** is a vine (the same Tupi word refers to a turtle in chapter 15).

Notes to Epilogue (pp. 179–180)

The **guanumbi** (Tupi for hummingbird) is a messenger from the dead in Brazilian Indigenous myth and another bird associated with the **Saci** (see chapters 4 and 17 notes).

The **parrot who preserves the Tapanhumas language** is

based on an anecdote from German naturalist Alexander von Humboldt: on the Orinoco River in Venezuela, he encountered a parrot that none of the local Maypuras could understand because it spoke the language of the extinct Atures people (*Views of Nature*, 1807).

The **parrot flying to Lisbon** recalls how the colonial Portuguese would teach the birds to say "Royal parrot, for Portugal," claiming them as property of the crown (Vicente do Salvador, *História do Brasil*, 1627).

The story-ending refrain, **"And that's all,"** which closes the novel, comes from the Kaxinawa tales collected by Capistrano de Abreu (see also chapters 10, 14, and 17).

ACKNOWLEDGMENTS

This version of *Macunaíma* is dedicated to Macuxi artist Jaider Esbell, who left us too soon, and to all the heirs of Makunaima. Jaider and others expanded my thinking about this book at the 2019 Amazonian Poetics conference hosted by the Brazil LAB at Princeton University, including Maria Virgínia Ramos Amaral, Denilson Baniwa, João Biehl, Jamille Pinheiro Dias, Carlos Fausto, Marília Librandi, Pedro Meira Monteiro, and Lilia M. Schwarcz.

My translation is the fruit of conversations across North and South America and the support of various institutions. I am indebted to: the National Endowment for the Arts; the Brazilian National Library Translation Residency and participants in my workshops at the Biblioteca Nacional and the Casa Guilherme de Almeida; colleagues at the Banff International Literary Translation Centre and MacDowell; and students and faculty at universities where I spoke, hosted by César Braga-Pinto, Christopher Dunn, Patrícia Lino, Marcelo Lotufo, Alfredo Cesar Barbosa de Melo, Ramona Naddaff, José Luiz Passos, Luiz Fernando Valente, and Nelson Vieira. Thank you to Eduardo Navarro for Tupi instruction (USP), Marco Antonio Gonçalves for your 2020 anthropology seminar (UERJ), and Júlio Diniz for my introduction to *Macunaíma* in your 2004 Brazilian literature course (PUC-Rio).

The team at the Mário de Andrade archive at the Instituto dos Estudos Brasileiros (IEB-USP) was central to my research, including Marcos Antonio de Moraes. Former archive director Telê Ancona Lopez and her co-editor Tatiana Longo Figueiredo helped inform where my version would diverge from the text they established for the 2016 edition of *Macunaíma* (Companhia das

Letras). Other interlocutors in Brazil were: Cristhiano Aguiar, Beatriz Bastos, Paula Berbert, Milena Brito, André "KIDIDS" Czarnobai, Alison Entrekin, Emilio Fraia, Angélica Freitas, Marília Garcia, Noemi Jaffe, Bia Lessa, Denise Milfont, Antonio Prata, Iara Rennó, Tiganá Santana, Eduardo Sterzi, Verónica Stigger, and José Miguel Wisnik.

I am indebted to the ideas and support of: Rafaela Bassili, Eric Becker, Sam Bett, Krista Brune, Kathryn Crim, Corrine Fitzpatrick, Isabel Gomez, Tiffany Higgins, K. David Jackson, Madhu Kaza, Erin Klenow, Ananda Lima, Bruna Dantas Lobato, Simeon Marsalis, Erín Moure, Lúcia Sá, Julia Sanches, Kit Schluter, Shook, David Simon, Renata Wasserman, and Tristram Wolff, as well as my MFA students at the University of Iowa and Columbia University. Brenno Kenji Kaneyasu Maranhão was my secret weapon for going over the Brazilian text.

Thank you to *Triple Canopy*, especially editors Alexander Provan and Matthew Shen Goodman, for publishing the excerpt "Piaimã the Giant" and the essay "Impure Speech," the basis for my afterword; and for partnering with the Brooklyn Academy of Music to let me program the "Brazilian Modernism at 100" film series, which began a dialogue with Rodrigo Séllos, director of *Searching For Makunaíma*.

I am grateful to New Directions for taking on this strange book, especially publisher Barbara Epler and my editor Declan Spring, as well as Tynan Kogane and Brittany Dennison; and to John Keene for your wisdom and generosity.

For your loving support, thank you to the Sharnoff family and to the Dodsons: my parents Thao and Jerry, siblings Tran, Minh, and Stephen, and their families. And infinite love to Dan Sharnoff, who has nourished me in countless ways.